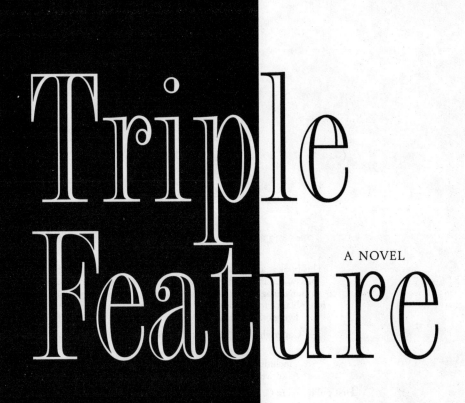

Triple Feature

A NOVEL

Louise Bagshawe

Simon & Schuster

SIMON & SCHUSTER
Rockefeller Center
1230 Avenue of the Americas
New York, NY 10020

First published in Great Britain in 1996 as *The Movie* by Orion

SIMON & SCHUSTER and colophon are registered trademarks
of Simon & Schuster Inc.

Designed by Elina D. Nudelman

Manufactured in the United States of America

1 3 5 7 9 10 8 6 4 2

Library of Congress Cataloging-in-Publication Data

Bagshawe, Louise.
[Movie]
Triple feature : a novel / Louise Bagshawe.
p.   cm.
"First published in Great Britain in 1996 as The movie by Orion"—T.p. verso.
I. Title.
PR6052.A317M68   1997
823'.914—dc21   96-44059
CIP

ISBN 0-684-83069-8

*This book is dedicated to
My mate Brian Celler, the most stand-up
guy in New York. You and I are gonna live forever. . . .*

Acknowledgments

I would like to thank my family for their constant support: Tilly, James, Alice, Seffi, and all my aunts, uncles, and cousins, but most especially my wonderful mother and father, who have given me their unconditional love all my life, and who always told me that I could do whatever I wanted to. I owe anything I've ever achieved entirely to them.

I also want to thank my friends for alternately holding my hand or kicking my butt, as called for: Peter, Nigel, John, Gina, Lizzie, Ion, Fred, and the whole gang. And without Barbara Kennedy-Brown, my best friend, all my major female life-support systems would close down.

Most writers are so insecure they make Woody Allen look like Donald Trump, and since I am no exception I'm extremely fortunate to have the world's best and most level-headed agents looking after me. I would especially like to thank David Black for managing to be a great agent and a great guy at the same time, and most of all for speaking my language. I'm also very grateful to Greg and everybody at Black Inc. for taking such good care of me.

Triple Feature could truly never have happened without my wonderful, patient, and inspirational editor Laurie Bernstein, who often seemed to understand my characters better than I did myself. She was such fun to talk to she made the editing process actually enjoyable. And I also thank Annie Hughes in particular for being there when I needed her and saving my bacon on more than one occasion. Finally, thanks to whichever bright spark at Simon & Schuster came up with the great title!

Seven A.M., and the morning sun was already blazing down on the LA Freeway. Driving a traffic-free path to work—there had to be *some* advantages to getting up this early—Eleanor Marshall opened the sun roof of her dark green Lotus in order to get the full benefit. Her neat bob of platinum-blond hair was still damp from the shower, and she needed it to be dry and impeccable before she reached the wrought-iron gates of Artemis Studios. Everything about her had to look immaculate. Of course, elegance had always been a priority, but since last month it had become an immutable law. Now Eleanor *had* to be perfect at all times.

Now she was president of the studio.

"The Boys of Summer" by Don Henley flooded the car's luxurious interior with soothing, mellow sounds, and Eleanor let the music wash over her, finding a small haven of relaxation in the blend of speed and melody. God only knew that once she stepped inside the lot she wouldn't have a chance to breathe all day. And when she got home . . .

Eleanor shrugged, feeling guilty. She knew she ought to look forward to going home. She pictured Paul Halfin, her partner. Forty-five years old, aristocratic, thick gray hair and intelligent, cold blue eyes. Very sober, very suitable, Paul was a pinup boy for the new, eco-conscious decade; he worked out, shunned red meat, always stood in the presence of a lady, and was utterly faithful. He preferred opera and fine art to watching a baseball game, was well-read and highly polished, and had been at home in the finest country clubs since birth. His career as a respected investment banker neither overpowered, nor was overpowered by, hers. Paul had no problem with Eleanor's promotion, the day it finally came. Why should he? His own firm, Albert, Halfin, Weissman, had completed another successful takeover that very week. On the contrary, Paul took Eleanor to Ma Maison for champagne and celebration, and basked in all the little tributes she'd received as Hollywood queued at their table to kiss the hand of the new queen in town.

He was a perfect escort. Everybody said so. And in the nineties, that was what it was all about. The days of cocaine and musical beds were long over. Now, if you weren't half of a loving, devoted couple, or at least a couple which *appeared* loving and devoted, you were nobody. And a Hollywood woman's top accessory of choice had shifted from a diamond necklace to a diapered baby.

The CD skipped to a sexy James Brown track, and the president of Artemis Studios pushed her foot almost to the floor, picking up a burst of speed, trying to drive through the sudden stab of pain, blinking rapidly to get rid of the instant film of tears that had settled across her eyes. She couldn't afford this weakness. She couldn't afford to surrender to the permanent ache, the feeling of emptiness and pressure, the terror that she'd left it too late. Not now. She couldn't think about a baby now.

By the time her gleaming car swung into the executive parking lot, past the saluting guards, Eleanor Marshall, the most powerful woman in Hollywood, looked like somebody who was always, always, always in control.

·:·:·

"Hey, good-looking."

Tom Goldman, chairman and chief executive of Artemis for the past ten years, stuck his head around the door of Eleanor's office. "Thought I heard you coming in."

"I know you're a sucker for my light, tripping footsteps, boss."

They smiled at one another, coconspirators at the top. Eleanor felt the inevitable small shock of pleasure at seeing him for the first time that day. Goldman was her closest friend and best ally. He'd been her mentor at Artemis since when she was a rare female staffer, albeit just a lowly reader, and he'd been number two in the merchandising division. Their paths up the greasy pole had run pretty much together, although Eleanor had taken far longer to make that final push into the Artemis inner circle, the tiny little group of people who, despite all the fancy titles and vice presidential perks of the common or garden management, were the only ones with any real power to get anything done. For five long years Eleanor had done time in marketing, making bucketloads of money for the head honchos in New York, all the time trying to prove that she had what it took for a creative position. Tom had always pushed for her in the mild way senior Hollywood people push for favored juniors. After all, no one can afford to be *too* closely linked to an untried exec. They might screw up and make you look bad. But finally, last month, Goldman had really come through for her. After Martin Webber, the last president, was fired for a hit-free year, Tom gave a slick presentation in the boardroom of the parent corporation, and Eleanor Marshall was the newest recruit to the world's most exclusive sorority. Female players. Girls with the clout to cut it with the boys.

She was thirty-eight years old.

Goldman looked his new second-in-command over. This morning, she reminded him more than ever of Grace Kelly; a soft de la Renta suit in buttery silk setting off her flawless blond bob and impeccable complexion, and low heels from Chloe elongating her already endless, slender legs. No jewelry except a subtle Patek Philippe watch on her right wrist. No makeup except a light base, maybe a tiny dash of blusher across those high cheekbones. Elegant Eleanor. He smiled, thinking how well she dressed for the part, how perfectly she matched up to all those insulting nicknames that the male VPs threw around. The Ice Princess. The Blessed Virgin. Killer Queen.

"Always."

It was true; nobody made him laugh like she did, nobody understood him better. Tom wondered for the millionth time if there'd been a chance for him with Eleanor once, but they had both been so wary playing the studio game, making sure the correct amount of distance was always between them . . .

Eleanor tapped a heel on the soft carpet.

"Better watch out for these footsteps, Tom. A woman's shoes can be a deadly weapon."

"Yeah?"

"Sure. Didn't you see *Single White Female?*"

He laughed.

"You coming after me in a wig? That scene doesn't play."

"You never know."

They smiled at each other, but there was an edge to it. Since last month, all the rules had changed. If Eleanor screwed up, Tom would be the one who'd have to fire her. And if she did great . . . maybe he would look good to his bosses on the East Coast, or maybe they would replace him with her.

They had been friends for fifteen years, but now, at the top, it was harder.

"We have a meeting with Sam Kendrick this morning," Goldman told her, throwing himself into a leather armchair opposite her and resting his shoes on top of her desk.

"General or specific?" Her brittle professionalism always took him aback.

"General, as far as we're concerned. I wanted to brief him on what we might be interested in this season."

Standard practice. Talk to the big agents, let them know roughly what you needed right now. It was a time-saving device; that way they weren't pitched with a billion *Pretty Woman* clones when they were looking for *Terminator XV.* She nodded.

"OK, that's useful. But your tone would seem to imply that this isn't routine for Sam."

Goldman shrugged.

"I got the feeling he had something in mind. I pressed him a little, but he didn't let on."

She felt her second small thrill of the day. A deal . . . maybe. Sam Kendrick didn't usually drop false hints. She wanted to do a deal, she'd already been here a month. Not that anybody expected her to prove that she was Jeff Katzenberg in a little over four weeks, but the pressure was still there. Martin had finally got fired, but the internal whispers about him, the nasty little rumors, the lack of respect at certain key restaurants in town—that had started earlier, *much* earlier. Like about three months into his presidency, when no major deals had been signed . . . Of course, Martin's reaction had been to green-light that terrible soft-porn flick that made the grosses on *Body of Evidence* look like *Jurassic Park,* and the other dog about the handicapped cop. She wasn't about to make the same mistake, please God, but she could understand now how Martin had felt. The pressure to do a deal, to make a movie, to have a hit, mounted from the second they put your name on the stationery. And with her being a woman, not having come from the creative side of the business, and following Martin and his equally disastrous predecessor, the pressure was now up to steel-crushing levels. Artemis was desperate for a hit. Eleanor was desperate to find them one, desperate for the right deal.

Sam probably knew that. Well, she wouldn't bite unless it was good.

She hoped it was.

"We'll see in Sam's own sweet time," she said casually.

Goldman nodded and stood up. She admired the way he moved. She had a brief flash of fantasy, of Tom inside her, stroking her with his cock, teasing her over the edge. He would be wild in bed, he would fuck like a savage. Not perfunctorily, like Paul, ticking off another goal for the day.

"Are you guys free for lunch next Saturday, by the way?" Tom asked, already on his way out. "Jordan and I are having a small party on the yacht."

"Surely," said Eleanor. They would just have to cancel on the Wintertons; Paul owed her one anyway. She liked spending free time with Tom, away from the relentless pressures of work. Even if it did mean socializing with that jailbait Barbie doll he'd married; Jordan Cabot Goldman, twenty-four years old, with hair down to her ass and tits out to the horizon and baby-soft skin that always made Eleanor feel like a wizened old crone. A self-styled feminist with no career and an IQ smaller than her bust measurement, but an unerring knack for giving the right parties and supporting the charity de jour. Eleanor was sure her picture was in every dictionary right next to "trophy wife."

One look at Jordan in her skintight wedding dress, slender young arm possessively wrapped round a besotted Tom, and Eleanor had smiled gently at Paul and felt hope shrivel and die inside her.

"How sweet of Jordan to think of us. We'd be delighted," she said brightly, smiling back at him.

The phone shrilled on her desk.

"No rest for the wicked," Tom told her, grinning and walking out.

chapter 1

MEgan Silver woke up with a million-dollar story.

Not that she realized it. The adrenaline rush sweeping through her was just a sudden panic to jot something down, to capture the dream before it faded. Groaning, Megan reached blindly for the cheap notebook she kept hopefully by her bed, in case something like this ever happened. It never had before.

Her pen had rolled onto the floor. Megan patted the dusty wasteland under her bed feebly, not wanting to get up to look for it. A brutal hangover throbbed under her temples, but she didn't care, *couldn't* care. She had to get the dream down right now.

Thank God, Megan thought, her fingers closing around the Biro.

She grabbed her notebook and began to scribble, long, flowing sentences, spidery handwriting streaking across the page. Outside her tiny bedroom window, the first red streaks of dawn appeared over the San Francisco skyline.

❖

"He left me," Declan announced an hour later, marching into her bedroom without knocking. "Do you hear me? He *left* me." He struck a pose of exaggerated grief, looking across at his roommate to check she was suitably shocked.

"Who left you?" Megan murmured, barely looking up from her story. Ripped-up sheets of paper littered the bed, covering the old copies of *Spin* magazine and British music papers she'd been reading last night. She'd been jotting down ideas since she woke up, not stopping to use the bathroom or make a coffee. Like she had time for Dec's crash-and-burn dramatics right now! This story was different from all the others. She was sure about that. She didn't know why, but she was sure.

"Jason," Declan said, in tones of utter despair. "We were at The Box last night and he left with somebody else. Some *asshole*," he added viciously. "The guy had a crew cut and a signet ring. A real yuppie."

Megan smiled despite herself.

"Dec, you've been on exactly three dates with the guy."

"But I thought he was—"

"The One? You think every guy's The One," Megan said, putting the notebook down. She'd just about got it, and when Declan wanted to talk, he wanted to talk. "Come on, you don't even care. You just want me to tell you how attractive you are and how you can have anyone you want."

"That's not true," Declan said, giving himself a smoldering glance in the mirror. "Although I have put on weight lately. Does it show?"

Megan sighed, turning her full attention to the sculpture of masculine beauty that was Declan Heath. Wiry, muscular torso, thin and fit from dancing all night on Ecstasy. Eyes the color of Irish mist with silver-gray lashes to match. Black hair curling loose round the nape of the neck in accepted Gen X style. Totally gorgeous, totally unavailable. Like just about everything she wanted in life.

"No," she said. "But you look great anyway."

"Why don't you get dressed," Dec suggested. "We could go down to Ground Zero and get coffee . . . Don't look at me like that, I got paid yesterday. I'll buy. OK?"

He sauntered out of her bedroom, and seconds later *Wonderwall* by Oasis flooded the tiny apartment.

Megan got dressed, not wanting to face the day. She felt like shit after last night and she dreaded whatever the mail was about to bring—another bill, another sheaf of rejection letters from New York agents. Or worse, the printed rejection slips from publishers, attached to the top of her thick manuscripts by a single paper clip, her only acknowledgment for eight solid months of work. Sometimes it was so tough to be hopeful. Megan had worked so hard on that novel—nights, weekends, whatever time she could sneak out of her dismal, ten-dollar-an-hour job at the library—and it seemed like it was being turned down by more people than she'd even sent it to.

In a way, it was uncool to care. The slacker generation wasn't supposed to give a damn about material success. You needed some kind of job to get by, just enough money to pay for the essentials, like coffee and music and clubs and speed, but that was about it. Megan and Declan could cover a tiny rent between them, afford minimal amounts of food, and dress at the hippest thrift stores in San Francisco—Wasteland and AAadvark's on Haight, Hunter's Moon on Valencia in the Mission district. They got into most clubs for free and went to every chic gig in the city. Declan was a failed artist and part-time comics store sales assistant, and Megan was a failed writer and part-time filing clerk at the public library. They *defined* style.

Except that Megan Silver was getting sick of style. She wanted someone besides Dec to read her book.

She dressed in seconds, snatching her oversize Levi's from the floor where she'd left them last night, belting them over a Metallica shirt, and pulling on large, clumpy biker boots. No makeup, but she finished the effect with two armfuls of jangling copper bracelets and a heavy crystal ring. Megan didn't have that many clothes, so choosing an outfit never took long. Whatever she had that was clean lay strewn casually about the bomb site that was her room, over the bed and the tatty Indian rug, under her beloved posters of Oasis and Veruca Salt and Dark Angel. Dark Angel was her favorite band; their huge, bleak soundscapes had been the backdrop to her college years, the hammerhead rhythms and black harmonies firing her up when she worked, lamenting with her when depression bit, slipping under her skin when she made love. A superband for the late nineties, the sound track of the generation.

They'd split up last week, and Megan felt ridiculously upset about it. Not that she'd been the only one—Sasha Stone, a friend of Declan's, had sat in front of them in the Horseshoe Café and sobbed her heart out, mascara running down her cheeks in grimy black rivulets.

"Come on, this is embarrassing," Megan had said, trying to get Sasha to accept a tissue. "They're just one band."

"Don't be bourgeois," Declan snapped, flinging a velvet-covered arm round her shaking shoulders. "It's serious. All art is serious."

"Zach!" sobbed Sasha wildly. "Zach Mason totally betrayed everybody who believed in him!"

"He was a singer, not the Messiah," Megan said rather coldly. "And you wouldn't be so upset if you didn't want to screw him so badly. He'll make some solo records, I guess."

"Do you think so?" Sasha gulped hopefully.

"Jesus Christ, how *old* are you?"

"Megan!" said Declan. "Sasha is hurting here! Show a little compassion!"

"Nobody died," Megan muttered rebelliously.

How old was Sasha? Wasn't the real question, how old was *she?* Twenty-four, and not a damn thing to show for it, except an English degree from Berkeley. And here she was, sitting in a café, with an adult woman who was cracking up because a rock group disbanded.

That was the day when the restlessness had started to creep back in.

Now Megan twisted in front of the mirror, semisatisfied. She looked good. Nothing special, but pretty good. She had soft chestnut hair curling gently down to the nape of the neck, clever brown eyes, a clear skin rendered somewhat pallid from too much partying all night and sleeping all day. Underneath the funky, shapeless uniform she'd pulled together, her body was nicely curved in an unfashionable way: swelling breasts, feminine calves, maybe a little chunky round the thighs, weight she had never been able to shake. Megan was glad of the hip-hop culture and its outsize style. She hated her body. Most days she hated her looks; OK, so she wasn't exactly ugly, but among all the golden California butterflies she was a death's-head moth. Invisible.

It had been like that since the day she was born, youngest of six in a Catholic household in Sacramento, one more mouth to feed for an overworked electrician and a harassed mother who found it hard to cope. Not that she'd been abused or neglected, but they just didn't have much time or attention for her. Megan was no beauty, like her twin sisters, Jane and Lucy, slim and lithe as gazelles, nor a strapping sporty guy like her three elder brothers, Martin, Peter, and Eli. Not ugly enough to inspire pity, not smart enough to inspire concern, Megan grew up dating the OK guys Jane and Lucy didn't want, and making average grades, and resenting the hell out of everybody, all the time. When she did scrape into Berkeley, Megan Silver suspected that the congratulations of her family had been mingled with relief that she was leaving Sacramento.

Well, that's mutual, Megan thought angrily, tugging the Metallica shirt more loosely over her waist. If I never see that dump again, it'll be too soon. Why should I stay there and rot in Sacramento?

When you could come here and rot in San Francisco? finished the snide, carping little voice in her brain.

"Are you ready?" Declan yelled. "We'll be late."

She took one last look at herself, shrugged, and went to join him.

"We already are," she murmured.

⋰⋱

Everybody struggled out of bed at eleven, the days they didn't have to work, and sometimes on days they did; Jesus, if you believed all the excuses and hacking coughs that went singing down the phone wires to employers every morning, you'd think a serious epidemic had afflicted San Francisco's twenty-something population. Mostly, the bosses rarely complained. What they were offering was dead-end jobs paying little more than minimum wage, hardly worth coming off welfare for; what they were getting was sullen, unproductive employees who knew their worth and thus sold themselves cheap. Everybody's just marking time, Megan thought, as they strolled up Haight toward Ground Zero. Like time will last forever.

It was quarter of twelve, and the cold mist was just beginning to clear, melting away in the thin sun. Declan strutted down the street, waving and smiling at all their friends hanging out; Haight truly was the center of his universe, Megan thought, smiling affectionately at her friend. *He* never feels hemmed in. Why should he? This is more than enough for Dec . . . Why can't it be enough for me?

"Hey, Megan! Hey, Dec! What's up?"

Trey, Declan's best friend and ex-lover, waved at them from an inside table, and they threaded their way through the usual crowd to join him; beat poets, bikers, art students, potheads, and the occasional brave tourist from Europe. Megan had once seen Ground Zero listed in a student guidebook as "the official café of the Apocalypse," a description that always made her laugh.

"Not much," Megan said. Declan ordered them espressos and a decaf for Megan. She felt too down for caffeine jitters right now.

"Jason walked out with some rich boy last night," Declan told him. "I should never have trusted him. He's a tramp."

"I heard that." Trey nodded amiably. "What about you, Megan? How's the Great American Novel? I missed you and Rory around town this week."

"Rory and me are history," Megan said curtly. "And I got two more rejections yesterday. Which makes a list of thirty-five so far."

"You should be *glad* the big corporations haven't signed away your soul," Dec said loftily.

"You left Rory?" Trey, the gossip hound, leaned forward eagerly. "I don't believe it. You guys have been dating so long you're like part of the furniture."

"Exactly." Megan took a sip of her coffee.

"But there's nothing wrong with Rory Harris."

"Sure. But there's nothing *right* with him either." Megan drummed her fingers on the tabletop. "He was just OK . . . Don't you ever look around and wonder where your life is going? Where's the passion, where's the dreams? I want more than this! I want . . ."

"Hearts and flowers? True love? Fame and fortune?" Trey teased.

"For a start," she agreed, pushing soft candied-chestnut curls away from her face. "Is that so crazy? I'm twenty-four years old. I haven't done anything with my life."

"But it just doesn't happen to people like us," Trey said.

"It *will* happen, darling. You're a novelist," Dec protested. "You're supposed to suffer. For your *art*. It's what writers do."

"I'm not a writer, I'm a filing clerk," Megan said coldly.

"They'll discover your talent," Trey predicted serenely. "*Qué será será.*"

"That's the problem. We're sitting around, waiting to be discovered," Megan said. "And they're not gonna find anything in my novel. They rejected it because it sucked."

The second she said it, she knew it was true. Her mannered, poetic study of teenage ennui was in fact stunningly boring.

"So, what are you going to do about it?" Dec demanded. "Talk's cheap, sugar. You know that."

Megan curled her fingers around her mug. Outside the café windows young, hip San Francisco kids drifted past in the sunshine, smiling and laughing. But that's all they were doing. Drifting.

She remembered the hot, brilliant story she'd dreamed up last night. The reams of notes lying scattered across her bed.

The answer hit her like a lightning bolt.

"I'm going to LA," Megan said. "I'm gonna write a movie."

chapter 2

The excitement was so strong you could almost taste it.

In 1996, Alessandro Eco *ruled* fashion. Where he led, the press followed panting. He was this year's brilliant new discovery, the darling of the demimonde, the first real superdesigner to shoot to fame since the meteoric rise of Donna Karan. *Vogue, Harper's, Elle, Style with Elsa Klensch*—you name it, they all swooned over his tight bodices, sculptured heels, clever little bias-cut skirts, the *dramatic* choice of fabrics, the way he *owned* color, darling, it was simply too wonderful . . .

Real women loved Alessandro too. His clothes—and the cheaper knockoffs of them that reached Main Street two seasons late—flattered curves, rejoiced in breasts, and forgave a multitude of sins around the thigh area. Last year every working woman had saved for that one Alessandro suit, every socialite had themed her wardrobe around him, and every teenager had bought her copy of *Vogue* and fantasized. It was fashion's version of the American Dream—that one collection by an unknown that takes the world by storm.

That was the first reason everybody was here. In *Chicago*, for God's sake. Paris, New York, Milan, even London at a pinch, but Chicago? Surely only Alessandro would dare. It was a power trip, pure and simple, for Alessandro Eco to show his summer collection—just one designer, mind you—in Chicago and expect the entire aristocracy of style to rearrange their travel itineraries just around him.

Which was where the second reason kicked in.

Fashion editors and photographers milled around, mingling with famous Hollywood actors, minor European royalty, rock stars escorting their model girlfriends. Leeward Hall was packed to the gills, bubbling with excited talk and reeking of perfume, spotlights, and money. Behind the front-row seats reserved for the serious players, anorexic-looking wives of Wall Street tycoons fought bitterly over the exact positions of their little gold-backed chairs. It was important to be noticed, vital to be seen. Because it wasn't merely Alessandro's new collection that was being offered here. Millions of dollars had gone into ensuring that this collection would have the eyes of the entire world trained upon it. And in the 1990s, there was only one way to do that.

Supermodels. *All* of them. It was a coup unparalleled in the history of fashion, and God alone knew what it had cost, but Eco's people had done the impossible, obtaining every single one for the same show. Security was tight enough for the President of the United States. If this hall was bombed tonight, the most beautiful flowers that the Western world had discovered would all be crushed together.

Cindy. Linda. Naomi. Eva. Saffron. Nadja. Shalom. It was a pantheon of goddesses, beauty in its most ideal form—all age groups, all body types. (Jerry was returning to do this one show, that was the rumor, and there was Mick in the center front row, sitting right next to Oprah, so it must be true!) Helena, Christy, Claudia, Isabella, Yasmin. The list went on forever! Paulina, Shiraz, Lauren, Tatijana, Kate . . . If she had graced the cover of a major magazine, she would be there, a blossoming supernova, when the moment came, among the lesser stars that would glitter, only fractionally less beautiful, up and down the runway in a constant, seamless slipstream of perfection.

It was even being hinted that *she* might appear.

A fresh wave of suspense swept the room. The big chandelier lights faded to black, leaving the stage darkened apart from a single beige spotlight selected from the hundreds rigged at the top of the ceiling, filtered with all the different colors of the rainbow. The only sound was the heavy, excited breathing of the spectators and the hushed whir of TV cameras, positioned around the runway and suspended from the walls. The vast screens erected at either side of the catwalk were dull and dead.

They waited.

And then, with the perfect synchronicity of a ballet, Aretha Franklin blasted from the Siemens speakers lining every wall, the stage erupted in an explosion of colored lights, rose petals fluttered down from the ceiling, and the first figure strutted, alone, onto the catwalk—

Naomi! It was Naomi! Opening the show in a long, white dress, a formal evening gown, the last thing anybody had expected from Alessandro, but too perfect, backless and gathered, an exquisite contrast against the rich chocolate of her skin . . .

Pent-up anticipation was released in an orgasmic frenzy of applause, popping flashbulbs, scribbling pens. They were in seventh heaven! And now Tatijana, in a black leather jacket and shining blue pants—what were they made of? Vinyl? Spandex? The fashion editors gave a single sigh of satisfaction. So it *had* been worth cutting Paris short. This season at least, the king would not be dethroned.

❖

"She won't do it, she say she won' do it!" Alessandro moaned, his words a wail of despair. He could hardly be heard in the commotion that was backstage, the supermodel sisterhood greeting each other raucously, the less famous models panicking about their hairpieces and bitching because a favored stylist had hung a jacket wrong—the blare of the music, the din of joy and hysteria, and at least two hairdressers in tears, and Michael Winter, Alessandro's PA, had to strain to catch him. "I cannot believe it! She is promised me, now for two months! She will be the finale, she will make the show live forever! But now she will not come out! She will not do it! She has ruin everything, everything I work for for so long!"

"The show will live forever anyway," Michael soothed him loudly, shouting above the noise. "They love you, Alessandro! They are going crazy for the girls and crazy for your clothes. Like we planned. It is *perfetto*."

He kissed his fingertips in an extravagant gesture of reassurance.

The designer grabbed his lapels.

"*Non è perfetto*," he yelled. "It is good! OK, this I understand! But it is not *perfect*! *It has to be perfect!*" He took a breath, and Michael winced; the veins on his boss's neck were standing out like whipcords.

"*Michaele*, they are vultures! They expect only the best, and if they do not get it, they will turn on me! Don't you understand? Now, yes, now they clap, now they are happy to see all the girls . . . but if she does not appear, later, after the show, that is when the doubts come in. That we are *nearly* good enough, but not quite . . . not good enough for *her*."

Michael paused, unwilling to accept that possibly, just possibly, Eco was right. He had always admired Alessandro for his street smarts, and above all, for realizing that great clothes—even inspired clothes—were just half the battle. Fashion was just that. Fashion. Style. *Show business*. And by promising to deliver all the world's most beautiful women, all wearing Alessandro, they'd taken a huge PR gamble. If it worked, the company name could be shot to a level where it would sit alongside, not Katherine Hamnett or Ralph Lauren, but Chanel, Gucci, and Christian Dior. That was the Holy Grail; to be so big no fashion ed could shoot you down.

But maybe they wouldn't get there. A show this expensive was one hell of a PR stunt, and it had better work. And if the focus was not on the girls who were there, but on the one girl who *wasn't* . . .

Winter shuddered.

"Why won't she do it?"

"She is lock herself in her dressing room, she is refusing to come out," snarled Alessandro. "She not tell me why. I hate her. She is a grade A bitch."

"You got that right."

"*Michaele*, I want you to find her agent," snapped Alessandro, his English miraculously improving under pressure. "Promise him anything he wants. Anything at all. We need her for the finale, and we must have her."

⋅⋖⋗⋅

"Babe, please."

Robert Alton knelt in front of the bare door, models tripping over his calves as they rushed to the stage, and the eyes of several amused cameramen boring into the back of his head. Sweat trickled down his pudgy neck and ran in nasty little rivulets under his collar. His career was flashing in front of his eyes.

"Sweetheart?" he tried again, yelling, his plump little chin pressed close to the keyhole.

"Get lost, Robert," snapped the voice inside. "I have no desire to talk to you whatsoever."

A couple of the cameramen sniggered, and Robert felt the familiar well of hatred and humiliation boil up inside him.

"Honey, I know you like to be private, but we really have to do this show."

"*We* don't have to do anything."

It was a sweet voice, the tones low and dulcet, but packed with such venom that even her agent, used to it, took a step back.

"We're committed. We took a million dollars in fee."

"You mean *you're* committed. You put the dress on, Bob. You'll probably really enjoy it."

Bitch! Bitch! Bitch! God, how he loathed her!

"Alessandro is tearing his hair out, babe. You know that the whole deal will be nothing without you. Please, angel, everybody's counting on you."

"We all have our problems." A beat. "And he has enough stars out there. He doesn't need me. There are a million girls. Tell him to use Cindy for the finale."

Was that it? Alton felt a surge of hope at the faint chink in her armor. A drowning man, grateful for a straw to clutch at, he thought bitterly.

"Stars? Those are *ornaments!*" he yelled contemptuously, praying to Christ that nobody heard him. Elite and Models One would put a contract out on him if they did. "There's only *one* star here, sugar, and she won't come out of her dressing room. Cindy won't do, you know that. Christy,

Claudia? Phhh!" He made what he hoped was a suitably dismissive noise.

"It won't work, Bob. I don't do cattle calls. Not even with a superior grade of cattle," she shouted, ice dripping from every melodious syllable.

Cattle calls! Alton thought, picturing the cream of the world's superstar beauties pirouetting on the catwalk behind him. But he was encouraged. Half the battle was always finding out exactly what type of reassurance she needed that day, what precise homage she wanted to extract.

"Sweetie, think of it this way. You aren't working the main show, you're only coming on for the finale. You'll be right in the center front of all the girls. Everybody out there is waiting, hoping, *praying* that you'll appear"— *me especially, since I'm finished if you don't,* he added silently—"and they'll go just *crazy* when you do. Just for that one time."

"They always go crazy," came the bored reply, but he thought he detected an infinitesimal softening. ·

"Of *course* they go crazy. Who *wouldn't* go crazy for you, babe, if you showed up wearing a sack." *Or a body bag, preferably.* "But the point is that you'll be leading them all out. Just *once.* In *front.* For the *finale.*" Robert took a deep breath, and played his ace.

"It'll make it official, as if the world didn't already know, that you rule them *all.* It will be"—he paused dramatically—"your *coronation.*"

Silence.

What was she thinking? Alton loosened his collar, nervous tension eating away at his stomach like corrosive acid. He could almost see his ulcer expanding under the pressure. Did she like that idea? Did she *agree* with it?

As much as he hated this woman—and oh boy, did he ever hate her— Robert had come to understand that there was a fierce intelligence burning under that lovely cranium. You could slip nothing past her, *nothing.* If she did something he suggested, it was because she'd already decided it was a good idea. Independent. Astute. Determined. And if she wanted something badly enough, he'd learned, there was no point standing in her way. You'd be better off arguing with a ten-ton truck.

"OK, I'll do it," she shouted.

The agent practically sobbed with relief.

"On one condition. I don't lead out the finale, I *am* the finale. Just me, by myself. None of the other girls."

Robert wanted to throw up. "But sugar, that's impossible! Everything's already rehearsed! You can't expect Naomi and Kate to sit still for that—"

"Kate? Why are you mentioning her name to me, Bob? I thought I told you never to discuss that anorexic washboard in front of me again."

Mistake. Mistake. His circuits were flashing red alert.

"Honey, I'm sorry, but—"

"No, Bob. No buts. And let me tell you what's impossible. What's *impossible* is that I appear in this show unless it's for the *finale* and by *myself.*

OK? Am I being clear enough? Now you run along to Alessandro and tell him what I said. And if he doesn't like it, call my driver, because I'm going home."

The silken voice was threaded with absolute steel.

"Do you understand?" she demanded.

Robert Alton fumbled with his collar again, but nothing could ease this choking panic. He knew that tone. It was the end of the line.

"Sure, sweetheart," he shouted through the keyhole. "I understand."

⬦

"Is this a joke?" inquired Michael Winter, glancing at his watch. The show was running on perfect time, down to the split second. They had ten minutes to the finale, and she wasn't even in makeup yet.

Robert spread his fat hands in a well-worn gesture of helplessness.

"No. She doesn't joke, as I'm sure you're aware," he said.

"Unique took a million-dollar appearance fee on her behalf."

"And we'll refund it if she doesn't appear," Alton said with a sigh.

Winter glared at him. The fee wasn't an issue, and both men knew it. A million dollars was pocket change, compared to what might happen to Alessandro Eco's company if this show crashed and burned.

"Can't you guys control your clients? For the biggest show of the god-damn decade?"

Robert Alton looked him straight in the eye.

"Michael. Please," he said. "Nobody, and I do mean *nobody*, can control *her*."

Nine minutes and counting.

"So you're telling me that I have to personally insult—to *demote*—eighteen of the most famous models in the world, in front of the entire fashion media, just so Her Majesty will walk down that catwalk for *thirty seconds?*"

A fresh burst of perspiration beaded Alton's neck. Winter was quite correct, of course. These backstage shenanigans would leak down to the hawks sitting out front at light speed. She was demanding that Alessandro snub every supermodel alive, in public, in her favor.

"That's what I'm telling you," he said firmly.

Eight minutes and thirty seconds.

Michael Winter glanced at his watch. Either way, they would only just make it. The pressure of the decision beat down on the back of his shoulders like a lead weight.

"OK," he said. "Tell Her Highness she's got a deal."

⬦

Rapt, the audience, the cream of the glitterati, stared hopefully at the empty stage. Notebooks were covered in scrawls thick with underlinings and multiple exclamation marks. The T-shirt dresses, sculptured bodices, and flowing coats in waterproof silk had all been sensations. The swimwear line added a whole new dimension to thigh lines, and he'd come up with some amazing bias-cutting in the evening gowns that turned the demurest walk into a lilting dance, the tiniest movement setting off a tide of motion in the skirts. But that was hardly the point . . .

It was the reams of film their photographers had shot that sent moist twitches in between the fashion editors' legs. That was what would sell magazines; the show as *event*, Alessandro as king of babe city. Kate in a strawberry satin dress that was really a T-shirt with pretensions. Goddesslike Cindy in a simple black swimsuit that would make every woman who saw it join a gym the next day. Jerry's blond cascade tumbling around a severe tailored pantsuit. Yasmin, regal and aloof in a full evening gown with a crinoline skirt. Awesome! No other word for it!

And now the finale . . .

The room was thick with the sound of held breath, the photographers nervously jockeying for position. Every supermodel in the world had graced this show—with one exception. As each song shifted pace, as each new set of outfits debuted on the catwalk, they had expected to see her. But nothing.

Surely now would be the moment. With mounting excitement, the eagle eyes of the journos were trained on the black-curtained entrance to the runway, their talons scenting blood. She had triumphed yet again. God knew how, but somehow Unique had swung it. Their megaclient would appear only in the grand finale, setting herself, by definition, in a class of her own, outranking every supermodel in the world. Perhaps she would lead all the models out, or was that expecting too much? When all that female loveliness poured out together onto Alessandro Eco's catwalk, would she slip in with the others? Or would she try some new trick, some little fillip, that would "spontaneously" catch the eye of every camera in the place?

Leeward Hall shivered in anticipation.

There was a slight rustle of velvet at the side of the stage and Alessandro Eco, his aristocratic face reflecting nothing but the profoundest calm, stepped forward to a microphone, holding up one imperious hand in silence before the room could explode into applause.

"Ladies and gentlemen, it has been great honor for the House of Alessandro Eco to present our collection for you tonight. For your attendance and patience, I thank you." He gave a courtly bow. "As you may know, I have, since I was a boy, cherished the dream of one day being like the great masters—Balenciaga, Dior, Chanel—who in our modern age paid the beauty of woman the homage it deserves, a homage I attempt, all my life, to pay. The moment of greatest loveliness for woman is surely the day of her wedding, and traditionally, the couturiers present last the wedding dress, a tradition I am proud to continue."

The spotlight on the designer faded gently away, and one by one the other lights in the hall were shut down and dimmed until the stage was plunged into darkness. A haunting line of Mozart spun into the still air.

And then the curtains drew back, a web of brilliant lights lit up the platform—but instead of thirty models exploding onstage, a single figure appeared from the darkness, stepping demurely into the spotlight. A simple shift of cream silk clung to her perfect body like a second skin, a bouquet of pure ivory lilies was clasped in her delicate hands, and a single white rose threaded through her long, dark hair, as she proceeded slowly, gracefully, down the front of the stage onto the catwalk.

For a second there was complete silence, as the crowd was struck dumb by her sheer beauty, by the fragile, nervous, virginal quality of her walk, the way she seemed to glance shyly out at them from under those doelike chocolate eyes, as though completely overwhelmed by the attention. Then, as the fashion world realized what they were witnessing, the hall erupted in an orgasmic frenzy of cheering and applause. The fashion editors were shooting to their feet in a standing ovation, the photographers snapping and snapping, flashbulbs exploding around her for the one picture that would make the front page of just about every tabloid in the Western world the next day—the magnificent, minimalist finale of Alessandro Eco, now without the shadow of a doubt Designer of the Year, and the best PR coup for any mannequin this decade: to oust eighteen other supermodels, to appear for just these few moments, to close the show herself, as though it was she, and only she, that they had all been waiting for . . .

As she walked gracefully out toward the frenzy in front of her, Roxana Felix permitted herself a tiny smile.

⋯⦂⋯

"Roxana!"

"Rox! Rox!"

"Roxana, *please!* Just for one second!"

They were everywhere, clamoring for her attention, begging for the tiniest hint of a smile or a glance—reporters from the favored shows and magazines, trade photographers, the normal fashion camp followers. Backstage was a battleground as people scrambled for a word from Christy, a comment from Naomi, a precious shot of any supermodel in glorious *déshabillé*. But by far the largest cluster of drones hovered around Roxana Felix, undisputed queen bee. Disgusted, numbers of the other girls were leaving, with a curt "No comment" and frantic agents trailing in their wake.

"Never again will she work for me," hissed a distraught Alessandro to

Michael Winter as another beauty swept past him, tiny button nose in the air. "*Michaele*, that bitch spill blood over all my collection . . . Never another cover girl weel wear my clothes. All I hear, all I see is controversy!"

"Yeah? All *I* hear is cash tills," replied Winter, a wide grin plastered across his tanned face. "Controversy and coverage are synonymous in *Webster's*, amigo. Didn't you know that?"

"Roxana, did you know in advance that Alessandro would cancel the other girls for the finale?" somebody asked.

Pushing a lock of glossy raven hair out of her brown eyes, the young woman laughed softly.

"He did *what*? Damian, you've got it wrong. It must have been planned that way."

"No, everybody was pulled in your favor," another hack told her eagerly.

Roxana's sculptured cheekbones and smooth pale skin registered nothing but confusion for a few moments, while the pack bayed its assurances that she had been honored above the rest. Then a delightful girlish blush spread across her face, and she dropped those infamous lashes, murmuring helplessly, "Look, I don't know, you guys. Robert handles business," and every man in the room was in love again.

"Robert Alton, was it your idea to insist on the change in choreography?"

"Absolutely," Alton said easily. He was almost enjoying himself. In her eagerness to pass the buck, his vicious little cash cow was turning him into a powerful Svengali of the beau monde. Surely other stars would flock to him now, he thought, and then recalled with another pang that Roxana didn't allow him to rep any other big stars.

"Why? Didn't you realize that you would be upsetting some of the most powerful women in fashion?"

Alton placed a fatherly hand on Roxana's alabaster shoulder, felt her stiffen under his touch, and instantly withdrew it.

"It wasn't about egos," he said shamelessly, "it was about the clothes. I felt that no one but the most beautiful girl in the world should close the best show in the world."

"Oh, Bob, really," Roxana reproved him, in low tones of molten honey.

"Were you trying to say that Roxana is in a class of her own, like Alessandro is in a class of his own?" suggested a girl from English *Vogue* hopefully.

"No comment," said Robert sternly, treating them all to a flamboyant wink.

"Enough, enough, please, *signore, signori*," Alessandro insisted, knowing a good exit line when he heard one. "My little *bambina* is exhausted. You know how she hate publicity. Please, this way, we have much champagne . . ."

Roxana Felix exchanged little kisses, pressures, and hugs with the favored few as they trooped dutifully off in search of liquid and more basic refreshments, confusion and embarrassment at causing such a fuss written all over her face. As soon as the door to her dressing room closed she pulled out a small bag of white powder from her blusher box and licked a minute pile off the back of her tiny wrist, perfect bones almost translucent under the skin. Alton eyed it hungrily: the new form of ground Ecstasy that was all the rage at the shows this summer. She made no move to offer him any.

"A triumph, if I say so myself," he announced.

"You had nothing to do with it, Bob. Play the big guy with the schmucks out there, but never try and scam *me* for credit. OK? 'Cause you'll be fired faster than an AK-47."

"OK, OK," Alton said, forcing a grin through the shame. Long ago, she had cut off his balls to play marbles with. "You're right, sweetie, of course you are. You just added another thirty thou to every single shoot."

"Fifty."

"Fifty, right," Alton concurred, wondering if Madonna's manager took as much shit as he did.

"I'm not interested in that. You know what I'm interested in," Roxana said, slowly and with menace, turning those limpid chocolate eyes at him as though they were bayonet blades. "Have you found me a suitable vehicle yet?"

Alton twisted helplessly.

"Didn't you get *Beach Party Two?* I had it messengered over."

She gave a delicate little cough.

"Let me see. *Beach Party Two.* The part was for the stupid bimbo who dates the lifeguard. Yeah, I remember that one. It came right after *Living Doll* and *Sweet Sixteen*, the ones Unique sent me last week."

Her agent swallowed hard.

"Don't bother to send me any more scripts, Bob."

"Honey, I knew you'd see reason. Those parts aren't worthy of you, I know that, but it's all we could come up with—lots of the girls have dabbled in acting, but the studios just aren't interested . . ."

Seeing her expression, his voice trailed away.

"You're fired," Roxana Felix said calmly.

Alton almost choked in surprise and dismay. He had discovered Roxana and repped her for the last five years.

"What?"

"Lost your hearing, Bob? I said you're *fired*. As my personal agent and personal manager."

Robert Alton's pudgy face had gone ash-gray. Over the years, Roxana had demanded the removal of every other star model the Unique agency represented, for the privilege of controlling all aspects of her own career—

the lucrative T-shirts, the calendars, the straight campaigns, the catwalk appearances, the perfume franchise . . . It had been done so slowly and subtly that none of his colleagues had really noticed, but the Unique agency *was* Roxana, Inc. Without her they were nothing. A handful of bread-and-butter girls with no star potential in sight.

"I told you two months ago I wanted to act. And I do mean *act*, Bobby, not drape myself over some moron in a teen beach flick."

"But the other girls—"

Roxana sighed, a deep, whistling sigh drawn in through her perfectly applied soft berry lipstick.

"How many times, Bob? I am not 'the other girls.' Something that SKI never failed to realize."

SKI? She was going to Sam Kendrick? Bob felt a fresh burst of sweat erupt down his collar. He could not believe this was happening.

"I've been talking to a guy called David Tauber over there. He's young, he's lean, and he's hungry. My plane leaves for LA at ten tomorrow."

"Please," Bob managed. "Roxana, just give us one more chance."

Laughing at him, Roxana Felix shook her lovely head.

"No way, Bobby boy. There are no second chances with me. You think that you can treat me like a piece of pretty meat, just because I'm a woman? You have another think coming."

"Roxana, *please*," Bob repeated desperately. He was begging her now, and they both knew it.

"Relax. You can still book my modeling activities."

Alton almost wept with relief.

"For the moment," she added icily. A pleasant feeling began to contract in her upper arms, the first sign of the drug kicking in. She wanted to be alone to enjoy it. "Get out, Bob. And tell the driver to make sure my car is ready at eight."

"Yes, sweetheart," Alton said meekly, the useless sack of lard. Jesus Christ, what she had to put up with. Roxana stared coldly at him until the door to her dressing room closed and she was finally alone.

Her painted nail tapped gently on the first-class ticket to Los Angeles pinned up on the mirror in front of her.

This was going to be fun.

She was Roxana Felix, and she always got what she wanted.

chapter 3

Eleanor Marshall was the most powerful woman in LA.

That was the thought that kept drumming away at the back of Sam Kendrick's mind as he turned his steel-blue Maserati into the agency parking lot, the velvet-smooth handling of the big machine slipping him into his acre-wide parking space with its usual grace. Nearly every other space in the lot was already full, but that fact scarcely registered on Sam. It was seven-thirty in the morning, and he expected his damn offices to be full. Never mind that the contracts stated nine to six. If you wanted to work for Sam Kendrick International, the third most powerful agency in Hollywood, you'd better be there by seven and you'd better not leave till ten.

Out of the corner of his eye Sam recognized David Tauber's neat little Lamborghini parked in the space directly opposite his. It was the best unreserved space in the lot, which meant that David Tauber had got here first. Probably around five-thirty A.M. He smiled briefly; Tauber had wanted him to notice that, and he had. Of course. After twenty-five years as an agent, Samuel J. Kendrick II had acquired the habit of noticing pretty much everything. So Tauber—young, hungry, ambitious—was already fluent in Hollywood's secret code. *Look, boss, I was in first.* Well, OK, kid, Sam thought, dismissing it. David Tauber wasn't important right now. Eleanor Marshall was.

Don't sweat the small stuff, and remember, it's all small stuff. The nineties stress-relief phrase of choice. Sam snorted; they were wrong on two counts. One, "Don't sweat the small stuff" wasn't a pressure valve, it was a commandment. If you sweated the small stuff, you were dead. You'd drown. Two, it wasn't all small stuff.

Some of it was very big stuff indeed, and if you planned on being a player, it was highly advisable to know the difference.

Focus, focus, focus. Something else he'd learned. In this town, where everybody had a million projects a day, focus was absolutely key. If you had a big star, satisfy that star first. If there was a bidding war for some hot property—be that a script, an actor, or a director—aim your fire at that until the opposition was blown away. Maybe he didn't return a couple calls he should have for a couple days. So? That's what kids like Tauber were for. And if you had a major problem, you thought about nothing else and concentrated on nothing else until that problem was solved.

Sam Kendrick International had a major problem. But after five days of brainstorming ways to get around it, his reliable subconscious had started coming up with suggestions. And the first suggestion was Eleanor Marshall.

"Mr. Kendrick, Mrs. Kendrick called from the country club about catering for your party next week. Mr. Ovitz's office called ten minutes ago. Fred Florescu rang at seven-fifteen," said Karen, his assistant, briskly. She had learned long ago not to waste Sam's time with "Good morning" or other pleasantries of that sort. "Plus thirty or so more which I've prioritized on your desk. Debbie has clipped the trades and the papers for you. Joanie has stacked most of the mail, there's just the Zach Mason contract and the coverage on *Hell's Daughter* that you might want to check out yourself. And everyone's ready for the meeting at eight."

Kendrick nodded absently. "Fred called, huh? That's good. I'll get back to him and CAA now. You can call my wife and tell her that whatever she wants is fine by me."

He tried not to show his annoyance. How many times did he have to tell Isabelle not to bother him at the office with this dumb domestic trivia? As if he had *ever* given two pins for what interior designer they used, which benefit they attended, or whatever idiotic food fad was being served up on smart LA tables that week. Of course, Isabelle lived for that stuff. No, the calls were a power play, pure and simple. She liked asserting her position, knowing that no matter what superstar or studio head was trying to reach him, she would always be put through first, her call would always be on top of the pile.

Kendrick strode down the soft gray carpeting of the corridor toward his offices. You had to pass through three outer rooms, each with its own secretary *and* personal assistant, before you gained entrance to the inner sanctum. Standard superagent fare, but also, these days, pretty necessary. It was barely half past seven, and he'd already had thirty calls.

"Good morning, Mr. Kendrick."

"Morning, Sam. Looking good."

"Great to see you, boss."

Agents and assistants passed him, smiling, waving, kissing ass. Only to be expected. At SKI, Sam Kendrick was king. He'd ceased to be tickled by the routine morning contest to catch his eye.

Reaching his office, Kendrick slipped into his black leather Eames chair and reached for the phone without looking at it, a reflex movement. He left a message for Mike Ovitz—Christ knew when the two of them would ever get five minutes free at the same time—and tried Fred Florescu at home. The hottest young director in Hollywood and a new SKI client; signing Fred had been one of the few bright spots in a bleak fall.

He picked up on the third ring.

"Fred Florescu."

"Hi, Fred, it's Sam."

A pleased chuckle. "That was quick."

"You're the first call." Sam lied easily. He was a master of the art of flattery, among other things. He knew how to make people feel good without sliming up to them. In the movie business, that made a nice change.

"Why? Because art comes first?"

Kendrick snorted rudely. "You're the artist, buddy. I'm the businessman. The only art I care about is the little ink sketch they do on the hundred-dollar bill."

Florescu laughed, delighted.

"Sam, you have no shame."

"Did you hire me to be a blushing violet?"

More flattery. The superagent humbles himself before the talent. *I work for you. You're the boss.* Well, unless you're Julia Roberts or John Grisham, talent reports to its agent most of the time. Talent that forgets this simple rule tends to have a short-lived career.

"You're the only guy I know who watches *Wall Street* as a motivational tool, instead of a warning tale."

Now Kendrick was laughing. "You're calling me about . . ."

"You hinted you had a line on a certain ex–rock star. Is it true? I'd like to work with him, if it is."

The first real satisfaction of the week flooded through Kendrick's lean torso. He had the system down so well, now his stars were starting to package themselves!

Packaging. What an eighties concept. What a beautiful concept. Everybody claimed to have invented it, CAA, ICM, William Morris, you name it. The truth was that it had just evolved, like Venus rising from the waters, like Pallas Athena springing fully formed from the head of Zeus. "Packaging" was the name given to the process whereby an agency took one of its star actors or actresses, or preferably both, hooked them up with a director it represented and a script whose writer was being repped by their literary department, and sold the whole project to a studio as a package deal. This ensured that agency commission was maximized, all the credit went to your own firm, and maybe some client whom you wanted to break got their first big credit on the back of one of your major stars. Of course, it was your own big-name clients that you had to sell it to, but a package deal was worth any amount of bowing, scraping, and downright begging. The studios hated it, because they had to pay through the nose—always cheaper to make a movie à la carte—and because every big package deal further increased the power of the agency shopping it. On the other hand, it minimized risk—all that talent, washed and ready to serve right on the table. Not that even incredibly large amounts of talent could guarantee filled movie theaters. Look at Steven Spielberg, Julia Roberts, Bob Hoskins, and Robin Williams in *Hook*. Kendrick winced at the memory. Can you say "over budget"? At least that turkey hadn't been his film.

No, Sam never bothered to claim that he'd fathered the packaging idea. He hadn't, and he didn't care about being first. He only cared about being best. Fifteen years ago, he'd spotted the brilliance of the idea early on and had started tying his small, classy roster of talent together for deals. Within ten months the Sam Kendrick Agency had shifted from being a Tiffany boutique to a medium-size comer with an unparalleled fee rate for its clients. In another ten, it was Sam Kendrick International, with as many cheesy superstars on its books as critically acclaimed Oscar winners, and offices in Rome and London. Sam loved it. He'd never looked back.

Packaging had made him a star; not the kind of star he bought and sold, whose box office dwindled as their looks failed, but the real kind, the type trade magazines referred to using their first names alone. The kind that pinned up the firmament, not merely glittered within it. It had made Sam his first million, and then his first ten million. But right now it was the cause of his problems.

Times were lean, margins were small, and the major film studios had become far less accommodating than most of the big players were used to. Since the recession of '90 to '93, the leisure dollar had shrunk considerably; everybody who used to cackle about the entertainment industry being depression-proof had proved horribly wrong. The record, TV, magazine, and film industries had all suffered; Kendrick could still remember the wave after wave of redundancies and big-budget movies that stiffed all summer long in those two terrible years, '91 and '92. At the same time, star power, and price, had increased to ridiculous proportions as studios searched desperately for ways to *ensure* recouping their investment. Of course, there's no such thing, and gradually it became clear that even the biggest star and the most well-worn formula could not guarantee a hit. File that under *Last Action Hero*. Anyway, they became even more terrified of green-lighting anything; money committed is money risked, right? And when Demi Moore demanded seven million dollars for the third Batman movie, they told her to take a hike.

It had been a lean few years for SKI. Nobody was starving—they repped too many big names for that to happen—but the studios had turned aside all their package deals, permitting only named stars to sign up for fees which were high but, despite the best efforts of Sam and his minions to the contrary, still well within the accepted ballpark. But no packages. No blockbusting movies stamped "Property of Samuel Jacob Kendrick" on them with big gold letters. Not that the other agencies hadn't had problems, but at least they'd seen one or two fat deals come together. SKI had been coasting. And you know the old story about the LA agencies being like sharks? If they don't move forward, they die. As far as Sam Kendrick was concerned, a truer word was never spoken.

He needed to get a package deal on screen, a major movie that would grab all the headlines in *Variety* and blow away his critics. And he needed it fast. Only last week, James Falcon, the forty-something superstar who'd been with Sam for ten years, had had his lawyers call to say he was now represented by Jeff Berg at ICM.

That was when the situation had shifted out of yellow alert. It couldn't be more than a week before *that* little snippet leaked to the papers, and then everybody else would be considering their position . . . and the shark-infested waters would be alive with movement, circling, circling, as the other firms scented blood and moved in for the kill.

Sam knew the score. He'd done it often enough himself.

Hence the full staff meeting at eight o'clock this morning.

Hence his delight that Fred Florescu wanted to work with David Tauber's new client.

Hence the reason that he'd woken up this morning with *Eleanor Marshall* branded into his brain.

"I shouldn't tell you that, man. Confidentiality," he replied, carefully keeping the elation out of his voice.

"Bullshit, Sam. Anyway, that's a yes."

"How do you figure that out, Fred?"

"You can't have confidentiality with someone you don't represent."

Sam chuckled darkly. "Wait a second." He scribbled his name on the bottom of Zach Mason's contract, holding the receiver over the pen. "Hear that sound? Know what that is?"

"No. What is it?"

"That's the sound of ink drying. On our deal with Zach Mason," Sam confirmed, feeling the satisfaction return.

Fred Florescu's voice was a hiss of drawn-in breath. "Think you can get us together?"

"Think, nothing. I know you're the only director for him, Fred."

"I'd appreciate it. *West of the Moon* was a really vital record in my life."

That took Kendrick aback for a second. Christ, he'd forgotten Florescu was only twenty-nine. He was a *fan* of Mason's band! He was just a kid himself! Lord, that he should live to see the day when a red-hot director was panting to work with a rock star because of the guy's *music*! Slackers my sweet ass, he thought silently. They're the pushiest little bastards since the fifties. And they gaze so hard at their own navels it's a miracle they don't walk around cross-eyed.

"You know what I'm saying? Zach Mason is, like, a prophet of his generation. Really on the level. The shit he was singing about was important, Sam. Dark Angel is a major loss to us. I want to put him in a movie very badly. I hope I can help him share some of that vision."

Kendrick was staggered. Not only was Florescu coming out with all this garbage, was that *humility* he heard in his tone? Fred Florescu, the director who famously told the studio head on his last picture to go fuck himself, was speaking about some two-bit singer as if he was his personal god. He wondered how Florescu would feel if he knew what David Tauber had told him—that Dark Angel had split up over a petty squabble about T-shirt royalties, and Zach Mason himself was a spoiled brat who threw a tantrum if the mineral water in his dressing room was the wrong brand. A real prima donna whose only concern was the megabuck career of one Zachary Mason. David was a smart kid; he could see that right off. Yolanda Henry, the band's manager from the beginning, hadn't wanted to kiss Mason's ass in the way that twelve million records had led him to expect, plus she thought it was a dumb idea for him to dabble in movies. The woman was another of these music junkies, reckoned that time spent away from the studio or the sage was time wasted. No wonder her little canary was ready to sing a new tune. David Tauber was to be commended for checking out the opportunity; he'd kissed up to Zach like he was Roxana Felix herself, and promised him the sun, moon, and stars, yesterday. It had taken the "prophet of his generation" exactly ten days to split his band, dump the woman who'd discovered him sleeping rough and playing for money in the streets of Miami, and ship out to LA from New York, bringing with him only the second ray of sunshine SKI had seen that lean summer. And according to Tauber, he'd picked Florescu's last smash, *Light Falling*, to watch on the private jet on the way down.

Sam leaned back against the supple leather. *He* had his mind on music too. The sweet sound of cash tills chiming.

"I understand completely, Fred. You might not believe this, but I was young once! I think you guys can make something really magical on screen together. Forget *Reality Bites*—"

"That fakola bullshit."

"—and just start thinking about what kind of a dream you might create with Zach. I think your generation deserves a spokesman."

"Spokesmen," said Florescu reverently.

Kendrick's eyes rolled in his head. "Absolutely." He glanced at his watch; five to eight. "Hey, I have to split. Let me talk to Zach, set a meeting up. OK?"

"You got it," the director said, hanging up happy.

⋯⋰⋱⋯

The SKI conference room was packed and nervous. Stress hung in the air like humidity, an almost palpable feeling of tension rising from the hunched necks and taut postures of the agents seated around the table and standing lining the walls. Nobody knew what to expect; Kendrick had called this meeting personally, the word of God descending from on high, summoning the miserable sinners to account for themselves in his presence. Everybody knew that Sam was unhappy, despite the decent business SKI was doing in commissions. They were fading from the limelight, and that wasn't a good position to be in in Tinseltown. Plus, James Falcon had walked last Friday. Kendrick's Commandos, as they were popularly known, had good cause to be anxious—when Sam was unhappy, that emotion seemed to have a magical way of transferring itself to his employees.

The rookies stood against the wall; they'd been there for a couple of hours, most of them, but nobody would have dreamed of taking a chair. Those were strictly left for the head honchos, whenever they should choose to appear. No, the new kids stood up with their well-thumbed copies of *Variety* and the *Hollywood Reporter* and tried to memorize weekend grosses, commission records for the SKI stars repped by their departments, whatever significant sand shifting had taken place in the business that week, and the current dollar exchange rate to the pound, mark, yen, and Swiss franc. You never knew. It was pure torture, all the mindless cramming, but that was part of the deal. They were rookie agents. They existed to be tortured by their betters. And heaven help you if Sam Kendrick, or even your department chief, decided to call on you for a question and you couldn't answer it. They were worker ants, but they were worker ants in Hugo Boss or Donna Karan, and to a man and woman they looked forward to the time when they would be able to torment their own rookies.

The wall also gave the grunts a chance to observe those mighty merchant princes, the department chiefs and senior agents who rated the thirty or so hard chairs ranged round the long mahogany table. Lisa Køepke, the elegant head of TV, responsible for dreaming up *Beechwood Halls, American Hospital,* and *Joe's Princess* among other hit shows. TV was like Lisa, a solid performer with occasional flashes of brilliance, but nothing much to write home about. Phil Robbins and Michael Campbell, the heads of the international and domestic film divisions, respectively. Phil, a slim, good-looking blonde in his mid-thirties and rumored karate expert, had less to worry about; his boys and girls had been energetic in the sale of foreign rights over the past quarter and SKI commissions in Southeast Asia had never been higher. Plus, went the whisper around the back wall, that David Puttnam/Hugh Grant Brit flick looked as if it might be gonna happen. Now *that* would surely give Mr. Kendrick something to smile about. Mike, a cropped brunette in custom-made Ray-Ban shades and a dark Savile Row suit, obviously had more problems—after all, why were they here? And finally, among department helmers, there was Kevin Scott, the fifty-something Boston Brahmin who'd been in charge of the literary department for fifteen years. It was he who had brokered the four-million-dollar *Sweet Fire* deal in '89, an industry record at the time, and he who'd discovered eight novelists who'd gone on to top the *New York Times* best-seller list.

But that, as they say, was then, and this is now. Kevin Scott was in over his head. The world of literary rights had changed a little from the courteous, handshake business he was used to, where a gentleman's word was his bond. Deals were now done in unseemly haste, prices seemingly bearing an inverse ratio to critical merit. The leisurely, well-lubricated publishing lunch was a thing of the past in New York. And the old school of donnish, intelligent literary agents with English degrees and a passion for the written word were being replaced everywhere Kevin looked by hyenas in designer jeans, twenty- and thirty-something puppies with mobile phones glued to their ears and Sonic Youth blaring from their in-car CDs. He shuddered to think about it. Most of them probably read five books a year, and all of those courtroom thrillers. And yet, despite his stern protests, Sam and Mike had insisted he fill his department with these obnoxious creatures.

Somebody had turned up the volume on his world, and Kevin Scott was not happy.

Nor was his division selling any scripts.

But most rookie eyes glanced lightly over the four principals today. It wasn't the division heads that they were really interested in; it was the senior agents, the comers, the two-year veterans seething for position under their bosses. Joanne Delphi and Sue Sussman in foreign rights. Peter Murphy in TV International, and John Carter in TV East Coast. And particularly, David Tauber, the shooting comet blazing across Domestic Movies, the most vital division they had.

Tauber lounged slightly in his chair, sitting in pride of place at Phil's right-hand side. If he was aware of all the hungry eyes crawling across his muscled torso, he gave no sign of it. At twenty-six, David Tauber was a gorgeous creature, and sexual charisma radiated from every inch of him. Thick hazel hair, cut into an almost military crop, complemented his tanned skin, hazel eyes, and a body that paid tribute to his nutritionist and personal trainer. Nice toys if you could afford them, and Tauber could afford them easily. He'd pulled three times the commission of the other agents of his rank last year and earned double the salary. He drove a cherry-red Lamborghini and already rated a good table at Spago's.

Hollywood prides itself on scenting out the Next Big Thing, and right now David Tauber was smelling of roses. Last week had seen the biggest coup of his young but glittering career so far; the defection of Zach Mason, ex–lead singer of Dark Angel, from the stable of Yolanda Henry to the mahogany doors of SKI.

His colleagues hated him.

"Ladies, gentlemen, good morning," Sam Kendrick barked, striding into the meeting room and pulling up the chair at the head of the table.

Everybody stood.

"Sit down," Kendrick said sourly.

Everybody sat.

"OK, here it is," Sam continued briskly. Just because he was in a better mood didn't mean he was gonna cut these sniveling layabouts one inch of slack. "This year, the agency has seen its worst billings since I founded it. We've stuck a couple of our big names in movies, but that's about it. We're trailing the fucking pack and I don't think it's the luck of the draw. I want, one, a convincing explanation of everybody's performance over the last quarter; two, a list from every person in this room of who they represent, what they're doing with them, and who they're gonna bring into this agency in the next month."

Several faces round the room paled.

"That's the warm-up. Later we're gonna discuss the studios—and I expect everyone to have some new knowledge to share with us—and how we fix this problem. I want this agency to *package a deal*. Now. If not sooner. Are we clear on that?"

Frantic nods. They were clear on that.

Out of the corner of his eye, Sam noticed that useless old lush, Kevin Scott, surreptitiously pop a Valium into his mouth. Christ, he was pathetic. He should fire him, but the guy had once been so good. And they had once been friends. He also noticed the Tauber kid, slouching in an Italian suit, looking confident. He hadn't nodded with the rest of them.

Kendrick had a good feeling about Tauber.

"OK, people. Let's go," he ordered, sitting back to watch the dogfight start.

⁘

"David, I don't think you understand."

Kevin Scott was getting redder and redder in the face.

"With respect, I think I do, Kevin. Jason wrote a script for that TV movie—"

"*Beyond Loving*," someone supplied.

"*Beyond Loving*, right. Sold very nicely. Seventy thousand for, what, two weeks work? I think he'd be perfect for this project."

Scott almost choked on his outrage. This damn junior agent from the *movie* division, who'd been butting into everybody's reports all meeting long, was now trying to tell him how to run *his* literary department? Some boy who'd just started shaving?

"Jason felt he had to take the *Beyond Loving* script on to pay his rent. He is a Serious Novelist," he managed, hoping to shame Tauber into shutting up.

An elegant shrug.

"So explain that if he writes this movie he won't have to worry about rent. He can buy his own condo." Tauber glanced up at Sam Kendrick. "This is the nineties, Kevin. Starving in garrets is right out of style."

Scott glared at him bleakly. "Thank you for your advice, David."

"My pleasure."

"But the literary division need not be your concern."

A direct rebuke! Now every agent in the room was on the edge of their seat, holding their breath, waiting for Kendrick to step in and intervene.

David Tauber sighed.

"I wish that were true, Kevin. But unfortunately, it's not. I represent some interesting new clients in the movie division, and we would like to be able to package them"—the magic word—"with a script from SKI. But everything that comes down to me from you guys is an art movie."

"We have one of the best records for Academy Awards of any screenplay department in Hollywood," Scott wheezed. The tiny broken red veins on his nose were glowing like Rudolph.

"We're still interested in quality, here, David," Mike Campbell said brusquely. His protégé was going too far. It was bad policy to let a two-year guy bad-mouth a division chief.

"Indeed we are," added Sam Kendrick loudly.

Tauber was unfazed by the general wince that rippled through the spectators. He stared arrogantly back at Scott.

"Anyway, what do you mean, *clients?*" Kevin demanded, his gentlemanly sangfroid deserting him. "You got one new guy. Mason."

David Tauber stretched his legs under the table, catlike, before replying, and when he did, he looked directly at Sam.

"Well now, Kevin, that was yesterday," he said softly. "I had a new client sign with me this morning."

"And who was that?" the older man inquired with acid skepticism.

Tauber studied his nails.

"A model who'd like to be an actress."

The room groaned.

"Ten for two cents," snapped Kevin, delighted.

David shrugged. "Maybe. But I don't *think* you'd get Roxana Felix at that price."

Instant pandemonium. Kevin Scott went purple with confused rage. Mike Campbell spun on his chair to look at his lieutenant, Lisa Køepke laughed quietly, and the rookies lost their composure, some clapping, some whistling. Tauber ducked his head minutely, acknowledging the triumph.

From his throne at the top of the table, Sam Kendrick had been watching the duel closely. He hadn't known about the supermodel, but it didn't surprise him. So, the Tauber kid was a real hustler.

Time to show him who was king of this jungle.

"That's great, David," he began, to the immediate cessation of all other noise. "When do we start booking her modeling?"

Tauber looked wary.

"I've only signed her to us for performance, Sam. Unique in New York is still her booker."

Kendrick shrugged. "Too bad. Still, I guess she must have a hot show reel."

"Uh, no . . . she hasn't acted before now."

"Then maybe she *can't act.*" Kendrick's voice was a whiplash. "What are you going to tell me? She looks hot, so she'll be huge box office? Did it work out like that for Isabella Rossellini? For Paulina what's her name? For *Madonna?*"

The room was stunned. Tauber shifted a little on his chair, creditably hiding most of his embarrassment, and Kevin Scott suddenly had a nasty smile fixed on his puffy face.

"We'll have to see. It's still good that you signed her, though, David," Kendrick continued, his tone more soothing now. "But let's not jump any guns. It's your other client I really want to build a package around. We've seen Zach Mason test, and he's hot enough to fry breakfast on."

The room had turned from the battle between the old and new guards now. Every eye was trained on the boss. When Sam spoke like this, he sounded like the Oracle at Delphi. They waited, eager for guidance. For whatever brilliant idea Kendrick had that would add luster to the tarnished SKI star, and therefore glitter on all their résumés.

"In fact, I think it *is* a woman who'll provide the solution to our problems," Kendrick went on. "But her name isn't Roxana Felix."

He waited, letting them hang in the air, dependent on him, for a few seconds.

"It's Eleanor Marshall," he said.

chapter 4

Eighty-nine . . . ninety . . . ninety-one . . .

David Tauber raised his torso up from the polished hardwood floor of his home gym, arms locked together over his head, bronzed legs stretched out straight in front of him, using only the well-developed muscles of his stomach. Heavy rock music thudded around him, but the melody was just so much background noise. Tauber's handsome face was set in a grim expression of pain and determination as he brought his trapped elbows down to his knees, right, left, then lowered himself back down to the floor and started again. *Ninety-three . . . ninety-four . . .* The agony was visible in the sweat that was beading all over the tanned, toned body that stared back at him from his mirrored walls, but then that was the prize. Two hundred and fifty pounds of solid muscle, with body-fat composition a mere thirteen percent. *Ninety-eight . . . ninety-nine . . .* David Tauber never gave up, no matter what torment his muscles were suffering. *One hundred.* There. Done. Tomorrow he might go for one-thirty.

Tauber stood up painfully and switched off the music, an incomprehensible rant about alienation and heartbreak by Dark Angel. Definitely not his normal thing. He preferred Gershwin and Cole Porter, but if Zach Mason was going to be his client, then David Tauber was the world's biggest Dark Angel fan, as of the second Zach's inky scrawl had dried on his deal. He was going to learn to like industrial metal. If it killed him.

"I guess I'll see you later, then."

A tanned, stacked blonde hovered in the doorway, hesitantly. Tauber's eyes flicked over the tight T-shirt pulled across jiggling breasts, real ones, which had made a nice change for him, the equally tight jeans stretched across a butt that was fractionally too wide, the long, soft hair, and the dumb hazel eyes. He was pleased to feel a twinge of desire, which was amazing really, considering that he had come in her mouth so recently.

What was she waiting for? Did she expect to be invited for breakfast?

"Sure. I'll call you."

"OK," said the girl, disappointed but having the good sense to pick up her purse and leave. David glanced back into the bedroom, saw that she had left a neat pile of glossy eight-by-tens on his bedside table. He smiled. Some things never change. Maybe he *would* call her . . . she had just the right looks for a small walk-on in *Baywatch* he'd heard was coming up, if she lost ten pounds. That should be no problem, it was just puppy fat she was carrying around. Only sixteen. And on the upside, you got great skin at that age. Plus, he thought he might want seconds. She'd been supple and compliant, she'd shaved herself between the legs, and she knew how to suck. And she'd left in good time, too.

Tauber flashed onto a mental picture of her soft lips sliding up and down his cock, reddened with lipstick in the way he'd told her to do it, so he could get more pleasure out of watching her. He sensed himself get hard again, remembering her perfect sense of pace, the warm juices of her mouth closing round him, that tricky little thing she'd done with her tongue. Yeah, he would definitely call her.

He flicked on the percolator and went to take a cold shower. All his energies had to be directed just one way this morning. Toward the meeting at Artemis. This was exactly what he'd been waiting for and hustling for ever since he arrived at SKI two years ago, a green kid fresh from Yale with little more than a small trust fund, an OK grade-point average, and limitless ambition. He'd hustled his way into a secretary's job right off—no messing around with the mailroom for David Tauber—and he'd hustled his way right back out again, making junior agent within two months. After that it had been a little tougher. No talent wants to risk association with some greenhorn kid playing agent, but no greenhorn kid gets up to agent status without a talent. Catch-22. *Your problem. You figure it out.*

But he had. And how.

David twisted under his power jets, letting the icy blasts instantly eradicate his moment of lust. He wanted to raise the temperature, but resisted the temptation. Two more minutes. His trainer insisted cold water did wonders for the circulation.

The first signature had been hard. Colleen McCallum, a fat, fading Irish actress with a great career as a sex bomb ten years back, now reduced to putting out decent-selling schlock-folk albums and doing guest spots on summer specials. ICM had basically given up on her, but that didn't mean

Colleen was ready to chance it with a new face. Jesus, how he'd had to chase the bitch. A twenty to the local florist had revealed a taste for orchids, and sure, they had to be the most expensive ones, and David had sent huge bunches morning, lunchtime, and night for three weeks. Cost a fortune. He called six times a day. He put clippings together of all the shows he thought she'd be right for. That was when she'd permitted him more than a few seconds on the phone when he called. He remembered now that he'd thought about taking her out and sleeping with her—that was what she'd really wanted, wearing those see-through pink chiffon robes over her chunky body when he went to see her. David shivered at that memory, shutting the water off. Hell, he should just think of that whenever he wanted to cool down. More effective than cold water any day. Thank God he'd realized just in time that if he faked a relationship with Colleen he'd be stuck with it. You could pack cuties like Dara off in the morning, but not so a client. Your gig was to make them big, and if they got big they could make big trouble. Tauber shuddered at the thought of Colleen complaining about him to Mike Campbell, or worse still, to Sam Kendrick. Because he *had* made her big, and now his job was to keep her both big and happy.

It had been the research that had done it. Finding out exactly where she'd come from, a little Irish village called Dunkenny, and then arranging to have the local paper flown in for a week. Other guys would have ordered a Chanel suit or bought her a little sports car. But David Tauber was more imaginative than that. He'd worked on the rule he applied to everyone and everything—find out what they want, then give it to them.

It worked with Colleen McCallum. She'd signed up with SKI the day the third paper arrived, put herself in Tauber's hands, and the rest was a breeze. He'd put her on a strict vegetarian diet, sent her to a trainer and a very expert, very discreet New York plastic surgeon, and fired her old record producer. They got a stylist to eliminate the faded prettiness and pink chiffon numbers, and Tauber began the rebirth. First, they stiffed MCA for a huge budget increase and hired the best country-and-western producer in the business, and the new, mature, elegant, slender Colleen had come out with a middle-of-the road hybrid they called "Celtic country." It sold across the Midwest like it was going out of style. Then, by dint of months of old-fashioned groveling, he got Colleen onto an *Oprah* special on comebacks, where midshow she broke down in tears, confessing a past addiction to drugs and alcohol and her rebirth in Christ Jesus. Sales in the Midwest soared, the press got involved, Tauber found her a support slot in a Fred Florescu remake of one of her old movies, playing the mother of her original character, and one season later she had an Oscar nomination and a big-rated chat show on one of the Christian networks.

Colleen McCallum had been David Tauber's shot, and one had been all he needed. Weird that it was someone like Colleen that had brought him Zach Mason. But that producer knew everybody, and the music business, as Tauber had discovered, was a very small place indeed. . . .

He dried himself briskly and slipped into his Joseph Abboud suit. Milk chocolate cashmere, the perfect weight and cut and color for a midmorning pitch. Set off his hazel hair and gleaming tan, too. Sam had made such a big deal about Eleanor Marshall chairing the meeting, and Marshall was a woman, after all. A woman with the power to green-light his project. A woman with the power to make his career.

Then he could really tell Kevin Scott to go fuck himself. He wanted that loser out of the agency. He wanted to break Roxana and Zach *together.*

He checked himself out in the mirror. Armani shoes, leather briefcase, classic Wayfarer shades, and a movie package that Sam Kendrick had OK'd himself.

David Tauber was ready to go to work.

⋯⋰⋯

Sam Kendrick strode into the Artemis lobby like a pro football player or a running politician. He always moved that way when he was under stress; kind of a natural defense mechanism. Nobody would ever guess it, the way he beamed at the receptionist and headed down the right corridor to Eleanor Marshall's office without being asked. The secretaries and a few low-level female execs sighed slightly as he passed. Kendrick had that rolling confidence, that animal gait to his body that spoke of money, power, and excess testosterone. Such was the force of Kendrick's personality that they almost missed the incredibly cute young guy dogging his left heel. The blonde that looked like a refugee from Muscle Beach . . . kind of young to be turning up to a meeting like this. Which meant he was a new kid on the block, one of the handful that get straight on the fast track every year . . . more female sighing. Studio work didn't give a young woman a lot of time for socializing. David Tauber smiled at each one of them, right into the eyes.

"OK, guys, are we ready?" Sam asked his team as they stepped out into the back lot, standing in front of the small, exclusive building where Tom, Eleanor, and a few of the most senior VPs had their offices. "Are we all clear on everything?"

They nodded; Tauber, who was repping Zach and Roxana; Mike Campbell, head of his domestic movie division, who was repping Fred Florescu; and Kevin Scott, because he needed a script guy to be in on this. Kendrick winced again at the sight of Kevin's crumpled tweeds. Couldn't the guy get some style lessons from his movie boys? Mike, in his regular black Armani, and the Tauber kid in that chichi little brown deal? Personally, Kendrick didn't like a man who so obviously took trouble over his appearance. Seemed a little faggoty. But shit, the girls in the office seemed to melt into a pool of seething hormones all over Tauber's feet. And it was his first big meeting as an equal with agency hotshots, so Sam guessed he could dress how he liked. Maybe Eleanor Marshall would go for it too, but Sam knew Eleanor and he doubted it. The Ice Queen was all business, always had been.

"We should be clear, after that briefing you just gave us," Campbell replied.

Sam grinned. He'd had them all meet at SKI an hour earlier, just so he could hone this pitch to perfection.

"You got that right. Eleanor Marshall is our best shot. She's new, she came from marketing, she badly wants to do a deal and we badly want to help her. And if any of you assholes screws it up for me, I'm gonna give you a new one."

Kevin Scott frowned at his boss's language, but said nothing.

"We won't screw it up," David Tauber said soothingly.

"Not if you want to stay working for me," Kendrick confirmed grimly, unimpressed.

The SKI group walked inside the dark glass doors and Sam announced them to another receptionist, who rose in a graceful slither of Donna Karan and conducted them across acres of original-weave Persian carpet to Tom Goldman's office.

"That's OK, hon, we can take it from here," Sam said.

"Welcome, gentlemen, come in," Eleanor Marshall said, standing to greet them.

Tauber noticed that Kendrick, Campbell, and Scott almost involuntarily straightened themselves. Christ, he was doing it too! How did she do that? Maybe it was the buttermilk suit, maybe it was the sleek hair, maybe just the intelligent, modulated tones . . . Everything about Eleanor Marshall said *lady*. It wasn't a first impression he'd had of any other woman since he'd arrived in this city.

He flashed her his deepest, sexiest smile, the one he reserved for babes already hooked up with other guys. Women had told him it made them think of his lips on theirs. And he didn't mean the pair located under the nose.

Ms. Marshall returned him a steady gaze.

David snapped the smile off.

"Tom, Eleanor, you already know my guys, Mike from Domestic and Kevin from our script department." He ignored Kevin Scott's imperceptible shiver of distaste. He loathed his precious literary division being called the "script department." As far as Kevin was concerned, Kendrick knew, scripts were a necessary evil. But they were having a meeting with Goldman and Marshall, for God's sake. Maybe little David was right about

Kevin . . . "And let me introduce you to David Tauber, a very bright young man, who represents two of our new clients."

"Mike, Kevin, David." Tom Goldman nodded at the three of them, polite but reserved, like a king holding court. "Have a seat. Sam, you know we convened this meeting so Eleanor could discuss with SKI a broad framework of what we might be looking for this season . . ."

". . . but I take it that you already have something to pitch to us," Eleanor continued, gesturing at David. "Since you've brought along a specific agent."

Sam noted the way they seemed totally at ease with each other, finishing off each other's sentences, sharing that chintz couch together. Not often you saw a studio chairman and president so well attuned. He didn't like it; strong studios, weak agents.

"Let's hear it," Goldman was saying.

"You're right, of course." Kendrick shrugged charmingly, like a little boy caught stealing apples.

"We should know you by now, Sam," Eleanor Marshall said, smiling at him. They had been old sparring partners from her marketing days; Sam had always wanted huge promotion guarantees for his stars, and Eleanor had always fought to keep the spend down. Eleanor had usually won.

"Well, Sam Kendrick now represents two new stars and we want to build a film around them," Sam said.

"We have a number of very established actors that would be perfect in support roles. We think this could be huge," Mike Campbell chimed in. "We're looking at a motion picture that will appeal to kids *and* their parents."

"Who?" asked Eleanor Marshall bluntly.

"David signed them, so I think he should do the honors," Sam said expansively. "You guys are absolutely the first to hear about this. The deal was only finalized yesterday."

David Tauber turned his dark gaze toward Eleanor.

"Zach Mason and Roxana Felix," he said.

Tom Goldman breathed in sharply.

"We have a screen test for Zach," Sam added, patting his briefcase. "He can really act. I'll run the tape for you." He leaned forward, looking at Eleanor, the new kid on the block. This would be the coup de grâce. "And we have also signed a new director—Fred Florescu."

"Does Fred want to work with Mason?" Eleanor demanded, trying not to show how excited she was.

"He *asked* Sam to hook him up with Zach," Mike Campbell said.

Eleanor shifted on her seat. She could feel the waves coming right out of Tom's eyes and boring into the back of her neck—*Do a deal! Now! Quick! Before they show this package to anyone else!*

But although he was straining at the leash, she knew he wouldn't override her. Not in her first meeting. Tom had appointed her president, and he'd let her make her own decisions. It was one of the reasons she liked him so much. . . . Was that the right word?

"Sam, we'll need to see that test. But Zach Mason with Fred Florescu sounds very strong." She didn't care about the supermodel. Not unless she could act. Most of those clotheshorses had no idea what to do once they had to open their mouths. "And I think we can offer you a deal. But there is one condition."

"Name it." Kendrick was still leaning toward her.

"Zach Mason's a superstar . . . *in rock 'n' roll*. But there's nothing to say his appeal will hold for moviegoers. It didn't even work for Madonna. Now I know you guys have got a lot of established talent for support, but this project needs one more element. It's crucial. And we won't green-light anything without it."

Eleanor nodded at Kevin Scott, completely certain of what she was saying.

"We need a dynamite script. Get me that, and we're in business."

chapter 5

"**H**oney, over here!"

Megan paused for a second, just a second, to catch her breath. She'd managed to get the order of three plates heaped with fried chicken and slaw and two pitchers of beer over to table six and set down without spilling it, even when the fat slob with acne had made a grab for her ass, cackling, and she'd had to swerve away. How could they eat mounds of fried chicken in the LA summer? Sweat beaded her forehead, making her fringe cling damply to her skin. Her thighs felt heavy and sticky, gross in the too-short skirt. She'd put on twelve pounds since she started working here; at the end of the shift she was always too hungry and too exhausted to resist her free Mr. Chicken employee meal. Even though the mere thought of all that stale batter frying up in pools of grease made her nauseous. Jesus, she thought, when I get out of here I'm never going within ten miles of a piece of fried chicken for the rest of my life. *If* I ever get out of here.

"Honey, we need some service."

"I'll be right there, guys," Megan called out, threading her way past the other waitresses toward table four. Nearest the bar. Oh God, it was them again. The drivers. Worked for some Hollywood chauffeuring service and turned up here once a week with their seersucker suits and attitude, boasting to the other girls about what they'd said to Demi Moore last Tuesday or Tom Hanks on Friday.

"OK, fellas, what'll it be?" she asked nervously.

"Two buckets, four slaws, and a pitcher," the scrawny one gabbled. Megan wrote furiously, trying to ignore the geek with the sideburns who was staring right up her skirt. She longed to slap him, but what could you do? It had taken her three weeks to find any kind of a gig. Even the waitressing slots were hotly contested in this town, and by wannabe actresses too, 115-pound babes with legs that went on forever and eyelashes so long you could braid them. Overweight and over twenty-one usually meant over and out. She had no savings. She needed this job.

"Great. Like a piece of corn with that?"

"No, but I'd sure like a piece of your sweet ass," cracked Oscar Wilde with the facial hair. His companions roared with laughter.

Megan felt the anger bubble up inside her throat, but forced it back down.

"Not on the menu today. Sorry."

"Mebbe tomorrow." Oscar wasn't giving up when he was on a roll. He leaned forward and jabbed a grimy finger into the cellulite on Megan's upper thigh. "Mebbe you'd like to drop a couple pounds. I could help ya with that. Sweat it off. Get it?"

Jesus. She felt even hotter, her clammy skin prickling with rage and humiliation. Had it come to this? Being propositioned by a bunch of slobs who were telling her she was fat?

"I'll get the order," she mumbled, and broke away from the table, her face the color of the ketchup bottles.

"Don't mind them." Stacey, one of the other waitresses, put a soothing hand on her arm. Stacey was a petite redhead from Indiana who'd started two weeks before Megan, and the only girl in the place who'd give her the time of day. "They're just assholes. Standard-issue."

"Stacey, am I fat?" She was transfixed by the sight of her friend's slender legs, looking so cute in the itsy-bitsy yellow frilled uniform. And her clear skin, with no gathering pudginess under the chin. Green eyes and neat red hair. Stacey could even look good in canary, a color Mr. Chicken might have chosen on purpose to make its waitresses look sallow.

"No way." Stacey wasn't looking at her. "This society's all hung up on weight, anyway. It's natural for a woman to have curves."

"I *am* fat," Megan said, horrified.

"No you're not. You might think about losing just a touch. But only if you wanted to," Stacey added hastily.

Both of them glanced involuntarily down at Megan's soft thighs spreading out under the ruffled hem, orange-peel dimples just beginning to form across them.

"How's the script going?" Stacey asked hastily, changing the subject. "Got an agent yet?"

Megan laughed bitterly. "Of course. Jeff Berg rang yesterday. Which is why I'm still here, schlepping for standard-issue assholes." She broke off at the sight of Stacey's hurt face. The younger girl wasn't exactly Simone de

Beauvoir, and she wounded easily. "Oh, Stace, I'm sorry," she sighed. "I didn't mean it like that. I guess it's just getting to me today. I got rejections from William Morris and Sam Kendrick this morning."

"Oh, Megan, I'm real sorry. That's too bad."

"Yeah," Megan said curtly. She glanced at her watch. Half past ten. Thank God. "At least I get off in fifteen minutes."

"You go on home. I'll cover for you," Stacey offered, thinking how low Megan looked this evening, like a puppy with all the fight kicked out of it.

"Would you? Oh God, thanks, Stacey. I'll come in early tomorrow," Megan promised, rushing through the dirty double doors of the kitchen to get changed. She knew she should't have accepted, shouldn't have taken advantage of Stacey's soft heart. It only meant Stacey would be stuck with the jerks on table four instead of her. But God help me, she thought, tonight I just can't make it through another minute. She felt so exhausted she could lie down here and just sleep through all the racket and shouting without any problem at all. At least, she told herself grimly as she struggled out of the horrible uniform and pulled on her loose jeans, I could if the floor were cleaner.

"See you tomorrow, Megan. Quarter of nine. Sharp," Mr. Jenkins, the supervisor, said pointedly to her, nodding at the clock on the wall. "You don't keeping mucking around with your shift times like this. OK? Shifts are set for a reason."

Megan mumbled something placatory, hating herself.

"Want your Mr. Crispy Special?" Jenkins demanded, proffering her a small tub of fried chicken wings packaged with a tub of barbecue sauce and a microscopic corn on the cob.

"Not tonight." She was totally starving, but the humiliation had been too recent. Even her loose jeans had gotten snug round the waistband.

"Sure?" He was surprised.

She ignored the growling in her stomach. "Yeah. Thanks."

On the long drive back to Venice, Megan checked herself out in the rearview mirror of her beat-up Fiat. It was practically a felony to drive a car this old in the city of gleaming Mercedeses and personalized Rolls-Royces, but at least it was night. And there were some advantages to having lousy wheels. Like nobody would bother carjacking someone who so obviously had nothing worth stealing, and the drive-by shooters wouldn't waste a bullet. Megan smiled to herself, with grim humor. She better find *something* to laugh about. Because her reflection wasn't funny.

The weight was the first thing; OK, so she wasn't *fat* fat, not obese. Roseanne was fat fat. Oprah before the diet. No, Megan was just—what? Plump? Fleshy? Twelve pounds heavier, and she'd been no Kate Moss before she left San Francisco. Now it showed on her face, as well as her ever-thickening thighs. An unsightly bulge under the chin. A rounding of her features, enough to give her a moon-faced expression. And a stomach that was nudging at the waistband of her baggy jeans. Megan knew that when she sat down in the bathtub, a small roll of flesh would crease over her midriff. She'd started to use bubble bath regularly, and now she guessed it was so she wouldn't have to look at what was happening to her. At those little dimpled cushions developing at the tops of her knees.

Tears started to film across her tired eyes. Oh, God. She didn't want to see this, didn't want to take a good look at herself. What would Rory say if he could see her like this? Rory, her last boyfriend up in Frisco, the one that she'd dated for nearly a year and then dumped, three months ago now. He'd been as comfortable to Megan as her favorite old sweater. But still, nothing special. Rory never got passionate about anything except sex. He was happy with their little world exactly the way it was.

Though Megan had liked going back to Rory at nights, she never got worked up about it. The thought of Rory waiting for her never gave her that wet, pressing feeling in her pussy she got when she was fantasizing about Harrison Ford or Keanu Reeves in the library. And Rory only gave her quick little orgasms, not the more satisfying, deeper spasms she got when she shut her eyes and guiltily imagined it was Zach Mason she was fucking. So eventually, Megan got around to chucking him, because she couldn't shake the feeling that she was missing something. Something *special*, something *different*. Passion. Infatuation. Her heart speeding up, that faint sickness . . . the stuff she saw in the movies, the stuff she read about. *Sleepless in Seattle, Romeo and Juliet,* Scarlett O'Hara melting for Rhett Butler. God, listen to me, Megan thought, pressing her foot on the gas, picking up speed. Even thinking about it, it sounds ridiculous. When does it ever happen to anyone? How many Richard Geres are out there waiting for your average streetwalker? And dumping Rory, for that. What a joke. If he had seen her like this, he wouldn't have stayed with her for ten minutes. Even Dec would have been embarrassed by the total mess she was sliding into.

It wasn't just the pudginess. The whole thing was a disaster. Poor diet and no exercise and lack of sleep had shot her skin to hell. Her face was gray-complexioned, pallid and dull. On top of that, she had breakouts, nasty little whiteheads peppering her forehead. The lank hair was probably making that worse. She washed it every morning, but cheap shampoo was no match for the spitting oil and rank steam of the Mr. Chicken kitchen. And she noticed that the real beauty, the red zit on the end of her nose, had triumphed over the six layers of cover-up she'd plastered on it this morning, and was now throbbing dully and noticeably at her in the rearview mirror.

Well, Megan thought, if the car breaks down, at least I'll be able to light my way home. And then she was really crying, big, salty tears that spilled out of the corners of her eyes and tickled as they ran down her plump cheeks.

She slowed down, sniffing and reaching up with one hand to dash the water away. She didn't want a car wreck. Wouldn't that be the perfect end to the perfect day.

It had started off on the wrong foot this morning, not that there was anything new about that. Her alarm shrilling at eight; waking up with a headache, stumbling into the shower to wash it all away. That had been OK; the hot kiss of the water, the soft bubbles of her shower, her fingers slipping between her legs for a little relief, and a shockingly good orgasm five minutes later, leaning back against the thin plastic shower rack, warm rivulets of water flowing across her fingers, mingling with her own juices, letting her come, knowing that her ragged gasps would be hidden from the others by the noise of the shower. Toweling off quickly, she'd almost felt good; relaxed and unstressed, like some soothing hand had temporarily untied all the knots in her muscles. But it hadn't lasted.

"What's up?" she greeted Jeanne and Tina, her roommates, who'd already had breakfast and were sitting at their small table in the cramped kitchenette, drinking instant coffee. The apartment was grimy and too small, the showerhead needed jiggling every other day and the paint was peeling in most of the rooms, but it was also incredibly cheap. And thus in demand. She'd been really lucky to have the other two pick her out of a long list the day she answered the apartment-to-share ad; maybe it was because she was so much plainer than all the other girls who'd applied, and they hadn't wanted any competition. Whatever, neither of them had gone out of their way to make her feel at home once she'd moved her single suitcase in. At least they weren't overtly hostile. Maybe that was what passed for friendship in this town. And they hadn't objected when she'd tried to make the dump seem a little more like home, hanging a surrealist print over the stain in the hallway, putting her faded afghan down in the kitchen, and tacking her Dark Angel and Oasis posters up in the front room.

"Hi," said Jeanne, a French girl with a chic brown bob and impeccable skin. Jeanne sold insurance over the phone, downtown, and wanted to be an actress. Central Casting sometimes called her in to do extra work, and she'd once had a speaking line in a dog food commercial.

"Declan called to say hi. And you got mail," Tina added, not without sympathy. Tina was dyed-blond and silicone-breasted and checked coats at a not-so-exclusive nightclub. She always had more money than her salary would explain, and Megan never asked how she got it.

Megan had walked forward to the table, her mouth suddenly cottony-dry. No mistaking it. Two fat envelopes, addressed to her in her own handwriting. Fat, about eighty pages fat. Her script. Returned to her again, rejected again. Dismayed, she looked at the franking on the top. Sam Kendrick. Oh *no*. William Morris.

She sank into the vacant chair, feeling despair envelop her in its familiar thick fog.

"It isn't that bad," Jeanne said, offering some uncharacteristic sympathy. "No one gets accepted right off."

"You have to know someone," Tina confirmed. "Do you want some coffee? I'm gonna get some more."

Megan didn't want coffee or anything else unless it was laced with strychnine, but she also didn't want to offend Tina. "Thanks." She ripped open the envelopes, saw those death kisses, the stapled sheets marked "RETURNED UNREAD," with a form letter saying that the agency was not accepting unsolicited scripts at this time.

"That's so you can't sue them," Jeanne told her, wisely. Jeanne considered herself a veteran, a pro. She knew all about "the Business."

"I don't understand," Megan said faintly. At least in San Francisco her novel had been rejected. Here she couldn't persuade one agency to even read her screenplay. "Unread." "Unread." "Unread." They'd all said the same thing, and they'd all sent it back by return mail. Megan couldn't afford to make huge numbers of copies, so she'd sent out two manuscripts, sending the same copies out again when they came back. Which they always did, like the world's most accurate boomerangs. Megan had started with the small agents, where she felt she had the best chance, and worked her way up. Not that it mattered; she'd struck out all the way up the pond, from the minnows to the whales. And now that William Morris and SKI had told her to get lost, she was about through her entire list, with only ICM and CAA remaining. *Yeah, right!* Like either of *them* were gonna give her the time of day.

"It's so you can't sue them if they rip off your idea," Jeanne explained. "So if a studio makes a movie, and it's kind of like your script, you can't sue them and say they used your idea and ripped you off without paying for it."

"Really?" Megan asked. She felt so helpless. "But then how does anybody ever get a script read?"

"Beats me," Tina said, putting a mug of coffee down in front of her. Megan knew Tina looked down on her, compared to Jeanne. Not only did Jeanne have looks and style, at least she was failing to be an actress. Megan was only failing to be a writer. How low could you get?

"You have to know somebody. Tina's right," Jeanne said.

"But I don't know anybody." Not in show business, and not in this whole fucking city, Megan thought. She picked up her copies of the script, ready to slot them into new envelopes for CAA and ICM. They felt like lead in her hand, heavy with the weight of foolish ambition and frustrated dreams.

"So what are you going to do?" asked Jeanne.

Megan shrugged. "Right now I guess I'm going to work." And she'd gone back into her bedroom to pick up the Mr. Chicken uniform, all ready for another fun-packed day in Tinseltown.

⋄⋄⋄

She turned down Carillo, nearly home now. Pretty quiet out there tonight; only a few bodies huddled in doorways, the normal nighttime groupings you didn't look too hard at, kids selling skin or crack, more likely the latter. More money in it. The tears had stopped now; she was too tired to cry. She just wanted to get inside, get something in her stomach so she could sleep. There would be a little less time tomorrow morning, too, because she'd have to get in fifteen minutes earlier. Although there'd doubtless still be time to get back both copies of *Triple Feature*, her script, from CAA and ICM. And Megan wondered for a second what she'd do then. When she had literally run out of chances.

⋄⋄⋄

"Hey, Megan," Tina yelled out as she walked through the door. "Come and have a beer."

"What is this?" she asked, hanging up her uniform on the back of her bedroom door and wandering into the kitchen. "Are we celebrating?"

"We are." Jeanne had picked up two six-packs of Bud and some grass. The heady, bittersweet scent of marijuana smoke hung in the tiny room, and Megan was assaulted with a sudden rush of homesickness. "Want some of this?" Jeanne proffered an expertly rolled joint, and Megan accepted it, taking a deep drag, right into her lungs. Maybe a little dope would relax her.

"Beer?"

"Yeah. No," Megan said, thinking of the calories. "I'm gonna try and lose some weight."

"Jeanne got a part," Tina told her smugly.

"You did?" Megan asked. "Truly?"

Jeanne nodded her sleek head proudly. "Second lead in an art film by Ray Tyson. I'm getting twelve hundred dollars."

Twelve hundred dollars! Megan was appalled to find herself swamped by a wave of envy and resentment. What had Jeanne ever done that was worth so much? Jeanne was stupid, a bimbo with an accent. But she was slim, she was chic. Things Megan would never be. It was so unfair.

A quotation from the Bible floated into her mind: *To him that hath, more shall be given; and to him that hath not, even the little he hath shall be taken from him.*

"Congratulations," she said, as brightly as she could. "Who's going to be your agent?"

"Oh, I'm not gonna bother with an agent," Jeanne said loftily. "Why should some jerk take twenty percent of what I make? I got this part myself, I guess I can get other ones, too."

Megan was too weary to argue with her.

"OK," she said.

"Hey, Megan, maybe you should send your script back to SKI," Jeanne said, with the generosity of the fortunate.

Megan shrugged. "Thanks, Jeanne, but I don't see the point. If they wouldn't read it the first time, I don't see why they'd change their minds just because I repeated the process."

"Jeanne heard some girl at the casting saying that SKI is suddenly desperate for scripts," Tina butted in.

"It's a real hot rumor," Jeanne confirmed. "That Artemis is looking for a vehicle for this new star they've signed."

Megan laughed. "But that would only work if my script was suitable for this star." She thought about her screenplay, the labor of love that took her less than two weeks to finish off. God, the way the words had just tumbled out of her head, so quickly she'd been scared she might not be able to type fast enough to get them down. The movie had written itself, playing in her head as clearly as if she was sitting in some darkened theater with a bucket of popcorn. The bittersweet story of a young musician and how he is warped by fame on his way to the top, only to be rescued in the third act by the girl he'd previously cast aside. It had sex, drugs, and rock 'n' roll and mad passionate love, too. She'd been so proud of it, so filled with certainty that it was her ticket out of nowheresville.

Certain enough to draw out her entire meager savings account from Wells Fargo and get on a Greyhound bus. Certain enough to risk everything she had. And, it seemed, to lose it.

"But it's totally suitable," Jeanne said. "I guess, anyway. If he doesn't mind being typecast."

"Who is this guy they've signed?" asked Megan, only slightly interested. Like it should affect her if Tom Cruise or whoever switched agents.

"Zach Mason," Tina informed her.

"Say that again?" Megan stammered.

"Zach Mason. You know, he used to be a rock star. Sang in that band you like," Tina said. She added grudgingly, "I guess he *would* be right for your script. But I'd forget about it. If Jeanne heard, every real writer in town knows about it too, and they're all connected. You'll never get them to read your script."

Megan hardly looked at her. Suddenly she knew it was going to be OK. This movie had her name on it. All she had to do was get her script read by the right person at SKI.

"Oh yes I will," she said.

"And how are you gonna do that?" demanded Tina nastily.

"I don't know," Megan told her. "But I will."

chapter 6

His cock felt like it was going to explode. It was huge, desperately thickened, throbbing with need. When he glanced quickly down, gasping with almost unbearable lust and pleasure, Howard Thorn could see the long blue vein that ran down the side of it swollen fat as an earthworm. He could dimly register that his cock seemed to have grown to twice its usual size when he had a hard-on. That had everything to do with the slender, perfect fingers wrapped round its stem, opening and closing in a tiny butterfly movement, then pinching him very faintly around the bucking velvet tip, just enough to stop the violent orgasm he was sure would burst out of him any second. He pushed helplessly, mindlessly, guided by instinct, rubbing his dick, wet with the juices of her million-dollar mouth, against her baby-soft skin. Not that Howard was thinking about her skin. He could hardly think about anything at all. His company, his jealous wife, his power, his receding hair, had all evaporated into the mist. The universe had shrunk and contracted, until the only things that Howard Thorn were aware of were his cock and her hands and his acute need to come, to end this exquisite torture she was inflicting on him. Right now, the entire cosmos was wrapped up in the nine inches of his erect, straining, pulsing dick. And the only lucid thought in his head was, *Roxana Felix is the fuck of the century.*

"Now?" Roxana asked him, her gentle voice low and teasing, laced with a breathy sensuality that sent another sharp stab of pleasure right through his balls, hardened and shrunk and totally ready. Howard stared glassily at the cloud of her ultraglossy, jet-black hair, hair he could practically see his face in. He managed to choke out the words. "Yes. Please, yes."

"Are you sure? I could last another ten minutes."

She could last forever, with Rudolph Valentino here. Jesus. She couldn't come for him if he was the last man on earth and masturbation was banned.

"Please. Please." He was begging, his cock leaping at her touch, beading at the head with his liquids. He wasn't going to last ten more seconds, let alone ten minutes. "I have to come. I'm gonna die," Howard choked.

Maddeningly slowly, she lifted herself forward over his supine body, positioning herself directly above him, sliding her pussy right down the length of his shaft with immaculate timing, so that the movement from her hands to her crotch was seamless.

Howard Thorn cried out from sheer pleasure.

"You're not going to die, baby. But you *are* going to heaven," Roxana Felix whispered, and then, to his utter astonishment and bliss, Howard found his cock being caressed by the inner walls of her pussy, the tight, controlled muscles of her vagina milking him out like a second set of hands, and he saw her rocking above him, her small pert breasts bouncing, her flat stomach pearled with sweat, her exquisite face contorted with the violence of her orgasm, and he erupted inside her, his come ripping out of him in great spasms of ecstasy that shook his entire body, the most incredible, intense climax he had ever experienced in his entire life.

"My Christ," he said weakly.

She was smiling at him, a languorous, sated smile, like a pedigree kitten that had just been fed, and Howard Thorn, billionaire financier and Wall Street raider, felt his heart flip over like a lovesick teenager.

"You're so good, baby. What you do to me," Roxana Felix murmured faintly.

Thorn felt his pride swell up nearly as much as his dick had been swollen a moment ago. He felt a wash of sheer machismo roll over him, as though he were a caveman who'd dragged the world's most famous supermodel back to his den by her long black hair, and then shown her what good loving was all about. The possibility that Roxana might have faked it never entered Howard's typically male head. The idea that one of the most breathtaking women he'd ever seen might *not* go gaga for his middle-aged spread, beady eyes, and encroaching baldness simply did not occur to him.

"Honey, you inspire a man," Howard said, smiling fatly at her. The little rolls of flesh on his cheeks twitched upward in a smirk.

"If only you were free." She gave a delicate sigh, glancing sadly at his wedding ring.

"Roxie, Roxie," Howard said, patting her knee as though she were a favorite schoolchild. Damn, he was sorely tempted to promise to give Bunny up, the dry, frigid bitch, and take this hot tamale back to Dallas with him. But he'd married in the fifties, without a prenup, and Bunny had raised three kids with him and been there the entire time he'd worked to make Condor Oil a reality, including the last five years, when he'd expanded into broadcasting and real estate. Condor Industries. An American colossus, and a company that Bunny might be able to claim fifty percent of, or so his lawyers had told him. Goddamn women's movement with its goddamn communal-property laws.

There was only one thing Howard Thorn loved more than sex, and that was money. He patted Roxana Felix's slim leg again. "You know I'd love to, but I just can't do it to Bunny. We were not meant to be."

Obviously disappointed, she turned away from him and started to dress.

"But I got you those other things you wanted," Thorn said quickly. "All of them. I called Tom Goldman last night about screening your tests. And my guys have talked to the trades and the press. Even the *New York Times*. It'll be pandemonium when you get there."

Completely covered up in her opaque Mark Eisen scarlet shift, Roxana turned back to him, her chocolate eyes shining with pleasure. She took his breath away.

"Really? You called Tom Goldman?"

"Yes ma'am," Thorn confirmed. "Told him he better make sure everybody watched your tests and that he'd better be positive about it." He hoped he sounded suitably menacing. "Jeez, I *told* him to cast you, but he said it don't work like that."

Roxana beat down a scathing retort. Howard Thorn was not Bob Alton. He had to be played carefully.

"Why not?" she asked, disappointed, pouting, little-girl lost.

Howard looked at her and felt his anger at that little kike come rushing back.

"Christ, honey, I know what you're thinking. He runs the damn studio. But there's a new president appointed, a woman"—and one who sat on a few charity committees with Bunny, he couldn't push Roxy to *her*—"name of Eleanor Marshall. Seems like it's her first project, and he can't override her 'creative control.' " He put quotes around the phrase. The only creative control worth a damn to Howard Thorn was the kind his accountants practiced on the company books.

"Oh, Howard. I want it so much. I just don't know what to do," said Roxana helplessly, her long lashes beading with tears.

Thorn looked at her, furious with Tom Goldman. If Roxana Felix wanted something, by God she was going to have it. Fuck Eleanor Marshall. Fuck anything that stood in his way.

"You just go to LA and do your thing, honey. I'll get you that movie."

"Promise, Howard?"

Roxana stood in front of him, looking up at him like a little girl looking at Santa Claus. A little girl whose gorgeous raisin nipples were winking at him through the cherry satin of her dress.

For a second, Howard Thorn thought of the risks involved in messing around with the casting of a movie. A financier like him with a large stake in Artemis Studios really shouldn't be concerning himself with petty little things like that. And when Roxana Felix was the girl he was hawking, the situation more or less invited attention. *Begged* for suspicion.

But then he thought of her fingers tickling the stem of his cock, the clutching, intimate caress of her pussy, that superman-size hard-on she'd given him. Roxana Felix had shown him things no hooker he'd ever had could even dream of. But she was no hooker, she was a world-famous supermodel. The classiest piece of ass on the planet.

For fat, plain Howard Thorn, she was a wet dream come true.

"I promise," he said.

⁘

In the relaxed comfort of the first-class cabin, Roxana Felix was doing a lot of thinking.

This wasn't behavior she normally indulged in. Thinking was for when you were traveling by private jet, when you had time for it. When she was slumming first-class, Roxana treated it like a show. Every move worked out with precision; the dramatic entrance, just a fraction late, but never late enough to delay the plane—she'd decided the superbitch, prima donna image was passé these days—and the sexy, stylish, never overpowering outfits she picked to travel in. Her small, dark green cases, made to order on Bond Street and *so* much more chic than boring old Gucci or Louis Vuitton. The gentle politeness to flight attendants. The sweet but firm requests for privacy if some odious businessman wanted an autograph, and the equally sweet acquiescence if his four-year-old kid asked for one. After all, she had a duty to her public. She was more than a model. She was Roxana Felix, a lady, a role model, America's sweetheart. And you never knew who the first-class crowd actually were—heaven forbid she should lose face, when a *Vanity Fair* reporter might be taking notes in the row behind her. You might even snub that reporter himself without realizing it.

Roxana frowned. Reporters took themselves so seriously. Stupid writers mistaking themselves for people other people might be interested in. Look at that Norman Mailer interview with Madonna a few years back—more about Mailer than the lady he was supposed to be talking to, and all he could ask her about was why she hadn't done beaver shots for *Sex*. Christ. As if anyone in the whole world gave a shit about Norman Mailer, that pretentious fat fuck.

Anyway, today she just couldn't be bothered with reporters or kids or anyone else. She'd had her travel agent arrange for her to be seated at the end of an empty row, and the stewardesses were under strict instructions to keep the great unwashed away from her.

Incredibly, things were not going according to plan.

It had started with that call from David Tauber last week. Two days after her Chicago triumph, with the entire fashion business falling over itself to be the first to fling itself at her Salvatore Ferragamo heels. Bob Alton had melted into a seething pool of adoration and dollars as the phone at Unique rang off the hook. Guess Jeans. Chanel. The new Calvin Klein perfume. And best of all, Revlon's offer to feature her, alone, in a one-off lipstick campaign—"The most beautiful *woman* in the world wears Revlon."

When she read that, she'd practically come. What was it Bob said? Her coronation. Right. Sometimes he was nearly worth tolerating. The Alessandro show *had* been her coronation, the apex, the zenith of the beauty tree. She, Roxana, had finally been crowned queen, succeeded to the throne she'd always known she was born to occupy. When she strutted into the Limelight, her favorite club in New York, the DJ had put on RuPaul's "Supermodel of the World" in tribute, and the kids all applauded when she'd glided onto the dance floor.

How Cindy must be seething. How Linda must be livid.

As if she gave a damn!

It was all she'd ever dreamed about. As far as she was concerned, all that kissy-kissy, babe-can-I-borrow-your-blusher, Naomi-loves-Christy crap was the purest bullshit. And she was sure all the other girls secretly felt the same. This wasn't about there being enough work for everyone, this was about supremacy. About who was top. Who could beat off the new girls— Brandi, Amber, Meghan, Shalom et al.—the longest.

And at Alessandro's little shebang, she, Roxana Felix, had simply walked over the pack of them in her made-to-measure sandals.

So why wasn't that enough? She couldn't figure it out, truly. She just couldn't see why the sweet sense of victory had lasted such a very short time, such a mere heartbeat of space before all the demons had come back, all those ugly, nagging black feelings she had to work so hard to bury . . .

Roxana shook her head, hard. No. She wouldn't think about that now.

Just take it as a given that although the new contracts she'd signed since the Alessandro sensation would keep her in first-class seats for the rest of her life, that simply wasn't enough. As she'd found out when David Tauber called her from LA to tell her of her problem.

Sam Kendrick International had put her forward as a contender for female lead in the Zach Mason vehicle, to be directed by Fred Florescu.

Merely the sound of his voice, hearing him *say* "Zach Mason" and "Fred Florescu" and her in the same sentence had sent shivers down her perfect, jaded little spine. Zach Mason! She loathed that dreadful music Dark Angel spewed out, she'd had to endure it screaming from the speakers at enough of the ultrahip shows. In fact, music in general left her cold. Most things left her cold. But Zach Mason was a god to billions of kids around the globe, a sex god and soothsayer rolled into one. People she *knew* had reacted to Dark Angel splitting up as though it was John F. Kennedy getting shot in Dallas all over again. He defined his generation. And Fred Florescu was not only the hottest, most commercial director around after Spielberg, he was by far the most credible, the only Generation X–er to really make a mark on the American consciousness.

To play opposite Zach Mason in a Fred Florescu film . . .

She would no longer be a clotheshorse. She would be more, even, than the biggest celebrity in the world. Yeah, Roxana thought, maybe that was what she had realized—that as a model, it was her perfect face and her perfect body that were famous, not *her. She* was nobody. Nobody cared what her opinions were on anything, what she planned to do after she'd finished modeling. My God, she thought, I might as well be *unknown*.

To be a movie star would give her more than celebrity.

It would give her *fame*.

And as soon as she realized this, she'd realized that she must have it. The demons had swarmed up in a black cloud like bats. Any lingering pleasure over the Alessandro triumph had become so many ashes in her mouth. And it was just at that moment when Tauber had informed her that Artemis had said they weren't interested, but he'd try to get them to look at some tests.

"I guess I didn't hear you right," she'd said, her heart hammering with blind panic. "I thought you said you were going to *try* to get them to *look at my tests?*"

Her voice had been colder than liquid nitrogen.

Tauber sounded placatory, but he'd stood his ground. Bob Alton fainted dead away when she used a tone like that.

"Yeah, I did. And I will try my absolute hardest, Roxana, but I can't guarantee they will see your tests."

"You're telling me that *I* have to take a screen test? Do you know how many commercials I've done? And you're telling me that even if I *accept* this insanity, Artemis may not even *look* at them? Does this Eleanor Marshall have me mixed up with somebody else?"

Tauber hadn't flinched.

"I'm—*we're*—incredibly thrilled to be representing you, Roxana. You're the most beautiful woman alive, and *I* know you're one of the most talented." The implication was not lost on her. "But unfortunately, the motion picture industry needs a whole new set of skills. We're gonna have to persuade them that you have what it takes." His tone was as warm as his words were chilling.

"You're saying I can't go in at the top." Her words were a flat monotone. Disbelieving.

Tauber had changed tack, gone for intelligent candor.

"Roxana, I told you I would never bullshit you"—she rolled her eyes—"and I won't. This is the truth. The talent I see in you, talking to you, other people out here don't. We have to prove it to them and that's gonna take a little work." And then he'd added the magic phrase: "But I know you love a challenge."

Oh yes, Roxana thought, yes, indeed I do. And this will be as nothing compared to the real challenges I've already faced. Challenges that you can't even begin to dream about, California boy, not in your worst nightmares.

"I'll do those tests, David," she said calmly. "You just hustle them at Artemis. They'll get seen."

Already she had flashed onto Howard Thorn, one of the many hugely powerful, hugely stupid, hugely married names in her little black book. Men she threw a mercy fuck at now and then, who provided her with favors as needed. Howard Thorn was one of the most useful. Chained to his wife by billion-dollar handcuffs, he was guaranteed not to give her any trouble or bother her overmuch, and his massive holding conglomerate, Condor Industries, had helped her up the ladder with magazines, cosmetics contracts, and many kind little whispers in smoky clubs. Naturally, Howard was besotted with her, and every time she screwed him she made sure it was better than the last. And like all her other sugar daddies, Howard thought he was the only one.

Thank God, Roxana thought contemptuously, for the fact that a girl can rely on *some* things in this life. The vanity of men was one world resource that would never run out.

Howard Thorn had bought fifteen percent of Artemis Studios only last year.

"They'll get seen?" Tauber repeated, questioningly.

"Yes, they will."

"OK," Tauber answered, not pushing it.

She was glad they understood each other. Because she found herself in a position that she hadn't known for years—helplessness. She couldn't threaten David Tauber with firing him, because unlike at Unique, she wasn't Sam Kendrick International's only client. Jesus, from the sound of it she wasn't even an important client. And anyway, Sam Kendrick had Zach

Mason and Fred Florescu, and that was the *perfect* movie, the one she wanted to be in. Already she knew that much. *A* movie would be no problem. But it was this movie she wanted. *The* movie.

That was why she'd taken time out last week to do the test, and showed that jerk banker a little bit of nirvana this morning. She was already working for it, struggling for it. Roxana needed this film, and if laying Howard Thorn was what it took, laying Howard Thorn was what she would do. She loathed him, but this morning she'd fucked him like she was Scheherazade and her life depended on it.

The plane banked and dipped, preparing for the descent into LAX. Roxana Felix gazed out at the glittering grid of the city, laid out before her in a jeweled web of light, sparkling against the darkness.

It was a strange thing.

She was frightened.

chapter 7

Jordan Cabot Goldman was in an agony of indecision.

She twirled in front of her floor-to-ceiling mirrors, ignoring the reflection of the palatial bedroom behind her—the king-size four-poster, an Elizabethan original imported from England; the carpet of delicate Chinese silk; and the sunken Jacuzzi she'd had installed at the foot of the bed. Silver vases were scattered in a careful way about the room, crammed to overflowing with white and yellow roses, flowers that, as usual, had been changed that morning. The huge bay windows had a polished mahogany window seat, laid out invitingly with soft downy cushions, embroidered in Scotland. The whole effect was an absolute triumph of wealth over taste, in the grand tradition of the Duchess of Windsor's jewels, and Jordan was very proud of it, just as proud as she was of their ultraneat gardens, which she'd had equipped with the very latest in both sprinkler and security systems. Tom Goldman had taken a while to get married, but Jordan Cabot Goldman was here to see that he never regretted that decision. Not for an instant. Hence the Jacuzzi in the bedroom and the cupboard full of erotic parapher-nalia hidden behind a bookshelf. And hence Jordan's own slender, toned, worked-on young body that was bouncing so gratifyingly as she twisted about, pretending not to watch herself, holding up first the pink Chanel suit and then the navy Bill Blass dress. Both such *grown-up* designers. But Jordan knew it was her duty to re-flect the status of her husband in the outfits she wore. She no longer owned a pair of jeans, even designer ones. It was so annoy-ing that she couldn't get Tom to do the same thing. Hugo Boss chinos. That was what he should be wearing when he needed to go casual.

The pink was more attractive—it set off her tan and her blond hair and her dazzlingly white teeth—but the navy had more gravitas, made her look older. She could be twenty-eight in that navy.

Isabelle wouldn't hesitate for a moment, Jordan thought jealously. She'd know exactly what to wear. She'd know before she even got to the closet.

Isabelle Kendrick was Jordan's lunch date. Sam Kendrick's wife had been a social powerhouse in the city for fifteen years, and Jordan was in awe of her. She didn't like her, of course, but that didn't matter. The fact was that Isabelle sat on every important charity committee in LA, gave the definitive Oscar night party since Swifty Lazar passed away, and somehow, invisibly, imperceptibly, marked out every new girl on the scene and ranked her desirability. It drove Jordan crazy; after all, wasn't *she* the wife of a studio head? And Isabelle only the wife of an agent, even if he was a fairly heavyweight agent? But there was no getting away from reality, and in LA, the reality was that Isabelle ruled. From Cedars-Sinai to the San Francisco Opera House, she sat on every important board. Her little soirees were the most sought-after, reported-on dinner parties in the city. And at her big spectaculars once a season—there was the ball coming up at the end of this month—more business got done than at Cannes. If President Clinton came to town and wanted to eat with somebody besides David Geffen, Mrs. Samuel Kendrick was the second name on his list. With her own ears Jordan had heard Isabelle chatting to the First Lady on the telephone as though she were an intimate friend. "Yes, Hillary, Irish salmon." "No, Hillary, I promise I'll keep the cholesterol down."

It was all fantastic, and Jordan wanted it for herself. *She* was Tom's wife and *she* should get that respect. Well, she knew how jealous they all were of her, even the ones that were nearly as young and nearly as attractive as she was. And the older women were just *green*. Too bad, Jordan thought maliciously, surveying her large, firm breasts and slim thighs. You had your chance once, and now it's my turn.

After all, nobody had dared to actually *snub* her, much though they might have liked to. It was Los Angeles, and when all was said and done, she *was* the wife of a studio chairman, and thus unsnubbable. Plus, Jordan had a certain survivor's instinct that had served her very well all her life. She knew better than to try and compete with Isabelle Kendrick. No, she had to carve out a new place for herself, a complementary place, as the queen of the new generation. Jordan had started to support the more modern charities, giving nice little dances for AIDS research, sponsoring walks for the war against drugs, and throwing well-attended dinners at five thousand bucks a plate for whatever issue was in the news. Her last one had been a minor victory: An Evening to Stop the Killing, raising money for the struggle against gang warfare in South Central LA. They'd played hard-core rap music very quietly over the speakers while entertainment industry big shots sipped Dom Perignon and toyed with their caviar and blinis. It was too bad that she hadn't been able to get Spike Lee to attend—or indeed, even *answer* her gilt-edged invitation—but then everybody knew how difficult *he* could be. Her Serene Highness Princess Caroline of Monaco had been guest of honor. Such a step up from that little tramp Stephanie. Yes, it had been quite a triumph, and Jordan had been able to seat Isabelle next to her and bask in her approval.

There was only one aspect of that evening to mar her enjoyment of it, the reason she'd pleaded with Isabelle for some time today. By deftly positioning herself alongside, and not against, Isabelle Kendrick on the LA circuit, Jordan Cabot Goldman had acquired a major advantage. Isabelle was becoming her mentor.

With a flounce of her nicely tanned ass, cheeks high and tight in the mirror as she turned round, Jordan tossed the navy dress over a Regency armchair and selected the Chanel. Just the thing for lunch. Surely you could not go wrong with Chanel.

❖

"Mrs. Kendrick, how good to see you. Won't you step this way," gushed the maitre d', leading Isabelle deftly into the main restaurant and up to the second-best table. Normally, she might have protested; Isabelle had huge clout at Morton's, but her practiced eye settled almost instantly on Madonna and Abel Ferrara sitting at the place she normally occupied.

Oh well, thought Isabelle. *C'est la vie.*

She smoothed down the featherweight cashmere of her Ralph Lauren jacket, supremely confident in the elegance of her look. At thirty-seven, Isabelle graced every best-dressed list in the country; her hair was a smooth, beautifully permed cap of chestnut brown, with the tiny gray streaks in it marvelously covered over every month by Dino Castoni, this year's favored Beverly Hills stylist. Her dermatologist ensured that her skin had excellent elasticity for its age, and while Isabelle would have died at the vulgarity of a public gymnasium, Liz Xanthia, her fanatically discreet private trainer, and Margot Guise, the Kendricks' vegetarian chef, between the two of them kept her in wonderfully svelte form.

Isabelle's green eyes, so perfectly matched to her emerald earrings, latched onto Jordan Goldman immediately.

Dear Jordan, she thought. Tries so hard. But pink Chanel for a blonde! So *obvious*, so lacking in imagination . . .

The younger woman stood up to greet her and the two women leaned forward, planting loud kisses on the air next to their respective cheeks.

"Isabelle, how kind of you to come," Jordan gushed, hoping for exactly the right mix of gratitude and graciousness. "I know how busy you must be, with the party in two weeks."

"A nightmare," Isabelle agreed. "The flowers are giving me all kinds of headaches. You must let me have the name of that man you used at your last dinner."

Glowing, Jordan promised to look it up for her, while Isabelle ordered a Caesar salad and mineral water.

"I'll have the same. Thank you."

"What would we do if they ever ran out of Caesar salads?" Isabelle joked.

Jordan laughed, too brightly.

There was an awkward silence.

Isabelle looked at Jordan sharply, feeling her curiosity begin to pique. Good Lord, something was wrong! She'd assumed this lunch was just par for the course, a further sign of Jordan's respect, possibly a bid to get closer to her now that Sam was cooking up some deal with Artemis. Not for one second had she thought Jordan would actually have something to discuss. But there was no mistaking it, that hesitation, the reluctant blush, the way her irritatingly lovely blue eyes kept dropping to the table. And it wasn't as if Jordan had a job, which meant . . . *trouble with Tom.* They had only been married a year.

Isabelle felt the unfamiliar sensation of excitement. What problem was the little *shiksa* about to blurt out? How did she expect Isabelle to help? And would she, should she help? Did she want Jordan Cabot to stay married to Tom?

With the lightning speed at which she made every major decision, Isabelle decided that yes, she probably did. Jordan might be annoyingly young and stupid and disturbingly sexual, but she had paid Isabelle proper tribute. She represented no threat. Who knew what another Mrs. Goldman might be like, how far Jordan's successor might try to push it?

Better the devil you know.

"My dear, I can see that you've something you want to tell me," Isabelle said gently, ignoring Jordan's look of surprise. *Oy,* she really had no idea how obvious she was. "Don't be embarrassed. I only hope I can help you. What are friends for, after all?"

"It's Tom," Jordan said, carefully hiding her delight at being asked what friends were for by Isabelle Kendrick.

"Is it really? I had no idea. I thought things were wonderful between you two."

"It's Eleanor Marshall," Jordan said bitterly.

There. It was out. The thing she'd been carrying around for months,

wondering what to do about it, if anything, wondering if she was imagining things. She'd thought about asking Isabelle for some advice ages ago,
but had resisted the impulse until the last possible moment. After all, not
only was there the danger in confiding worries about your relationship to
anybody, there was the sheer embarrassment. After all, how could *she*, Jordan Cabot, twenty-four and the youngest wife in Hollywood, with her
long blond hair and *Baywatch*-approved figure, she who had introduced
Tom Goldman to such excesses of sexual pleasure that he'd proposed
within three months—how could she admit that she was concerned about
her husband's feelings for some flat-chested bitch more than *ten years*
older than she was?

At first, she hadn't even recognized the danger, because she just couldn't
conceive of it. Tom and she were so great in bed together, or at least she
was great for him. She'd worked hard on that. And he'd been working
with the Marshall woman all his single life and yet they'd never dated.
Plus, Eleanor Marshall was *thirty-eight*. Practically forty. What man in his
right mind would find that attractive? Jordan wondered, as she checked
out her own, supremely youthful body in the mirror every night, rubbing
Donna Karan body lotion into every inch of it, the musky, sensual fra-
grance that drove Tom so wild. Would Eleanor Marshall know how to do
that trick in the hot tub, the one where she lifted herself slightly out of the
water and pressed her wet, warm pussy against the center of his spine, rubbing herself up and down him until he turned round with a growl and
screwed her on the spot? No, she would not. The woman didn't even wear
figure-hugging clothes when she came to dinner, although her figure
wasn't bad. She didn't even *flirt* with Tom when they came to the house.
This Jordan was quite sure of; after all, she never took her eyes off the
bitch for a second.

But there *was* a problem, all the same. It was there in Tom's eyes, following her round the dinner table, watching her when she got up to refill
her plate from a buffet. The way he always seemed to be so damn interested in what she was saying, like business was all that mattered. He
laughed at all her jokes, as if somehow they were really amusing. OK, it
wasn't a crisis or anything. She knew she could still get him hard for her,
even at a table Eleanor was sitting at, by lowering her hand under the
tablecloth or flashing him a quick sight of her pantyless crotch, crossing
and uncrossing her legs in a way that revealed her to his eyes only. He
needed her sexually. She made him feel like a man—he said so often
enough.

So why was Tom so negative to Paul Halfin?

He was never rude. Quite the opposite, in fact; always pressing Paul to
refill his glass, or asking him boring questions about investment banking. It

was uncomfortably like watching a man who had something to prove. But she, Jordan, she noticed the way his body tensed, his eyes narrowed, and he kept glancing back at Eleanor.

So he had a little crush. She could have lived with that.

Only lately, they'd started to fight. Tom was being so crass it was as though he didn't care about the house or their parties or *anything*. Except sex. Sex was the only way he communicated with her now. He'd even been refusing to stay on the Pritikin diet she'd put him on! And he was being such a boor. Like that night with the De Veers last week. She'd finished off her cream silk gown with her little AIDS brooch, the one all studded with rubies in the shape of a ribbon, and he'd actually got all angry with her and asked her when was the last time she'd visited an AIDS ward or volunteered at a counseling center . . .

Jordan had sobbed that she guessed he wanted her to get a job, that she wasn't as good as the women he worked with, just because she wanted to be a homemaker and raise a family.

Tom had melted, all contrite. He wanted a family too. He knew how disappointed she was not to be pregnant yet, why didn't they practice . . . ?

She shivered in her pink Chanel. Thank God Tom had never even guessed at the little white pills she hid in the kitchen cupboards.

So that quarrel had been made up.

But she couldn't help but wonder why he was getting so grouchy. And he was asking Eleanor and Paul over all the time!

Oh, Jordan Cabot Goldman was very worried indeed. And she'd never tell Isabelle or anyone else about the final straw, last Wednesday, when she'd been woken by him muttering in his slumber, and had twisted in their black silk Pratesi sheets to see his massive hard-on stiffening from the dream, ready to take him in her mouth, to wake him up in the way he most adored and make that dream a reality, when he'd jerked in his sleep, his back arching a little, and murmured: "*Eleanor.*"

Jordan had been frozen to the spot. He was lying next to her, twenty-four, a world-class babe, every man's fantasy wife, and he was having a wet dream about some middle-aged career spinster with gray streaks in her hair?

She had called Isabelle Kendrick first thing the next day.

"Eleanor Marshall?" Isabelle said, leaning forward, shocked.

"Oh, he hasn't said anything. They haven't done anything," said Jordan delicately.

"But you see signs. You're worried. Oh, my dear, you were so right to come to me," Isabelle breathed, reaching across the table and patting Jordan's hand.

Eleanor! Ridiculous. Just look at Jordan . . . but of course, as soon as she'd said it, it made all kinds of sense, Isabelle Kendrick thought, her heart speeding up. She'd started recalling all kinds of functions where she'd seen them together. Was it possible they had been at the same studio all this time, and not . . . But of course it was *possible* . . . what an appalling thought. Eleanor Goldman. Oh, dear Lord, but that would be just too much.

"I know I must be putting you in a terrible position, Isabelle," Jordan was breathing, "knowing her for as long as you have . . . ?"

The question mark hung in the air, but Isabelle, for once, was not inclined to keep her supplicant on tenterhooks.

"Well, that's true. But it's a moral question, isn't it? After all, you are his wife." Jordan nodded her coiffed blond head eagerly, and Isabelle added, "And dear Eleanor . . . she *works* so hard. I'm sure she would not wish any unpleasantness."

Jordan breathed out as the Caesar salads were set before them, almost overwhelmed with relief. There could be no mistaking Isabelle's tone. She *hated* Eleanor Marshall, hated her even worse than maybe she did herself. Now she came to think of it, hadn't she heard stories from some of the other girls? About how Eleanor was always turning down Isabelle's invitations to sit on committees, because she was "too busy"? As if *she* was the only busy one, Jordan thought with disdain. They all had things to do. Dressing properly required an investment of your time, and of course, they were all so active in charity work, and charity work was very important . . .

Isabelle hadn't taken kindly to being blown off. And as Jordan stared at her across the table, she noticed something else. Weren't Isabelle and Eleanor about the same age? That meant, she realized, that Isabelle resented Eleanor, more than just for her superior attitude, for the fact that she had no hold over Eleanor because Eleanor simply *did not care* about the social world. Isabelle resented Eleanor for working, being a working woman, one who now wielded power, real power, in Hollywood.

Eleanor was a queen regnant, not a queen consort, and Isabelle Kendrick simply hated her for it.

There was no way she was going to allow her to marry Tom as well. It would be the cherry on the cake, a final triumph Isabelle, resentful and furious, would simply not allow her to have.

The two women gazed at each other with perfect understanding.

"Will you forgive me if I speak frankly?" Isabelle said. "Jordan, you must understand that men are . . . *sexual* creatures." Her tone held up the word to the light as though it were something disgusting she'd discovered on the sole of her shoe. "No matter what they have, they always want something else. No matter how ridiculous."

Both women thought of Eleanor Marshall and compared her to Jordan. Unfavorably.

"The thing is—and I know this will be a difficult thing for you to accept, darling, such a newlywed as you are—you must learn to turn a blind eye to their little peccadilloes. Men are such simple creatures, they really can't help themselves."

Isabelle dismissed unfaithfulness and betrayal with a light laugh, aware that Jordan was hanging on her every word. Good. At least the child was going to see sense; it was never those irritating little diversions their husbands found that were a problem, it was the state of the marriage. After all, everything was founded on, centered on the marriage. A divorced queen was a dethroned queen, something she had realized about ten years ago, coldly, precisely, about the same time that she'd seen the love draining out of her relationship. That was when her ascent to superhostess had begun; recognizing that Sam no longer felt for her as a woman, Isabelle had identified a different desire in him, the beating, rampant, killer ambition that was driving him forward day by day. She had set out to help him satisfy *that* need, to become such a social lioness that Sam Kendrick could never divorce her, never leave her, because his business would be hurt by letting her go. Sam continued to screw around discreetly and she continued to throw exquisite parties.

Love and hope had died in Isabelle Kendrick a long time ago, but she was still rich, still stylish, and still accorded respect in this town.

She was still married.

"What shall I do?" Jordan asked her.

"In cases like this, there's only one answer, dear. Give him what every wife should. What she can't."

"You mean—"

"Yes, I do. Give him a baby."

chapter 8

Kevin Scott was having a bad day. Another one. In fact, it was shaping up to be a very bad week. Ever since that blasted meeting at Artemis Studios on Thursday, his department had been in complete chaos.

"Ten more Elsie thinks you should take a look at," panted Katherine, his English assistant, waddling into his office. She was waddling because she was weighed down by a pile of scripts, the paper stacking up against her bony torso, her normally pallid face bright red with physical effort.

Kevin gestured wearily to the free corner of his desk not already covered with manuscripts. That made thirty-five he had to wade through by the weekend, and there would be more in by then. Many more. The ones that had made it to his desk were typical of the hundreds that had only got as far as his subordinates in their variety—dog-eared, pristine, typed on vellum, covered in clear plastic or leather-bound. Some leather-bound *and* embossed. Some with spurious gifts attached to them, like little packets of Cuban cigars or a pair of solid gold cuff links.

Those were the ones he was always tempted to bin first, but alas, that wasn't how it worked. Suppose he were to throw away the specimen written on pink parchment, with the Mont Blanc fountain pen attached to it by orange velvet ribbon. With his luck it would turn out to be another *Ghost* or *Jurassic Park*. Just because the writer was a vulgar oaf didn't mean his script was necessarily unusable. After all, Kevin reflected, all screenwriters were vulgar oafs by definition. And in this crass and vulgar world, many of them were very highly paid.

He took a slice of that high pay, which normally consoled him for having to put up with hawking their trash for a living. Today, it didn't even come close. What had happened, Kevin wondered, to the appreciation of Literature? To delicate sensitivity and fine writing? Oh, for a Proust or Joyce that he might represent, selling exquisite penmanship for large amounts of money. Or at least a Norman Mailer.

Kevin Scott was fifty-five, and a long time ago he had been educated in England. How his old masters at Eton would cringe for him now. How his Oxford dons would wince. He considered himself a gentleman in a world overrun by ruffians, subliterate, ill-educated ruffians who wanted Judith Krantz, John Grisham, and *Forrest Gump*. Even the President of the United States had had a "popular music" group playing at his inaugural ball. There was simply no end to it. And now, he himself was embroiled in the indignity. For a while, at least he had been able to carve a small oasis of sanity in the Hollywood madness—while the unpleasantness of working with scripts could not be avoided entirely, his literary division had managed to work almost wholly with quality films, producing a run of Original Screenplay and Adaptation Oscars that was the envy of all the other big agencies. Although the division hadn't turned out all that much profit in and of itself, the Oscars and Golden Globes had attracted acting and directing talent Sam's way, and once in a while one of the obnoxious kids that reported to him—all hired by Sam or Mike Campbell direct—shopped some piece of violent or pornographic trash to Columbia or Paramount, and they cleaned up. Thus Kevin had been tolerated, allowed to go about the more serious business of selling novels in New York.

Lately, that had all gone to the wind. As the packaged movies dried up, Sam had been putting more and more pressure on him to come up with commercial scripts. The pushy little Tauber brat hadn't helped that situation much, either. But after the Artemis meeting, forget about it. Word from the top was loud and clear. They wanted a script for the rock star and they wanted one yesterday.

Outside the air-conditioned, sound-proofed sanctum of Kevin's office, he could see hordes of people milling about, many carrying bound manuscripts or parcels, their noiseless mouths opening and closing furiously as they argued with the harassed assistants and a couple of the junior agents. They'd been arriving all morning—the scumbags, the bottom of the pile, low-life writers with no contacts and no reputations and not so much as an article in the Nowheresville, Alabama, *Gazette* on their résumés, and yet every one of the losers thinking that SKI would be impressed with their bravado if they crashed the doors in person.

They'd been watching too many movies, Kevin thought, pleasing himself with the ironic conceit. Turning up as singing telegrams. With huge bou-

quets of flowers. Holding massive bunches of balloons. One, heaven pre-
serve him, had even sent a stripper. He recalled seeing her shaking her tassels in poor Katherine's astounded face, thrusting a script forward between
two sets of blood-red talons, before the grinning SKI security arrived to
throw her out on the sidewalk. There was, as he had discovered, absolutely
no limit to how deeply embarrassing this business could be.

And yet the sheer volume of these wretched scripts was taking him
aback somewhat. The meeting with Artemis had obviously been leaked
minutes after it had finished, because by the time their limo had returned
him to the SKI offices, there were already ten calls on his sheet about "the
Mason/Florescu project," and the first manuscript, about a rock star who
lives a double life as a sexual serial killer, arrived an hour later. They might
as well have put up a billboard on Sunset and an ad in *Daily Variety*. Forget the information superhighway. Show business gossip was the universe's
most efficient communication mechanism, because by the end of that day,
every two-bit hack in LA knew all about it. And by Monday, six hundred
of them had written instant movies over the weekend.

And yet not one of them was any good.

"Mr. Scott." Katherine was buzzing him.

"What is it?" Kevin snapped, chucking another pile of neatly typed pages
onto the floor. The trash basket had given up the unequal struggle this
morning, so now he was just throwing them on the floor for the janitors to
deal with. "I thought I told you no calls."

"But it's Mr. Tauber again, sir. He insists on being put through," said
Katherine weakly, sounding distraught.

"No! Goddamnit, Katherine!"

Scott felt, rather than saw, his blood pressure rise. Two calls per hour
from Sam and one from Mike and now that—that *odious* little toad Tauber
thought he had the right to bother a department head? "Especially not
Tauber! Not under any circumstances! Do I make myself clear?"

"Yes sir," said Katherine meekly.

He slammed down the receiver and tried to concentrate on the next
script, *Hot Rockin'*.

> *FADE-IN*
> *INT. BACKSTAGE—A SEEDY CLUB*
> *A SERIES OF ANGLES*

> A naked WOMAN is tied down with scarlet rope across two
> Marshall amps. ZEKE and BERTIE stand to one side, watching
> the DOBERMAN PINSCHER that is licking her between the
> legs.

Sighing heavily, Kevin Scott lifted the manuscript and threw it behind him without another glance.

⁘

"You OK, hon?"

The waitress looked Megan over with genuine concern. Most of the time, she was too busy or too hardened to worry herself with the customers' problems—bleak-eyed hookers that might stumble in with bruised faces and call for coffee, or the shabby-dressed unemployment types that turned up for the cheap burgers and beer. Don't talk, don't get involved. Too much heartache that way, not to mention that you wanted them out so you could serve someone else. In cafés as cheap as this one, volume was where it was at. Pack 'em and rack 'em. Shit, this wasn't The Ivy. But something about this girl was touching; a little fat and plain maybe, but she'd ordered a full meal and then hardly touched it, just drinking pot after pot of coffee and sitting there shaking. She looked real innocent, in a way. Soft and lost. Must be new in town.

"What? Oh, thanks. I'm fine," Megan said, giving her a little smile to back up the lie.

The waitress hesitated, hovering, but what could she do? If they don't want to talk—

"OK. Well, if you're sure," she said, moving off.

God, how obvious I must be, Megan thought miserably. She'd arrived there half an hour ago and ordered lunch, all keyed up, excited, nervous, but a little thrilled in a way. After all, this was it. She'd taken the day off work, as little as she could afford to piss Mr. Jenkins off, and she'd taken the original copy of *Triple Feature* out of its special hiding place in the back of her cramped closet, and she was going to come out here to storm right through the hallowed doors of Sam Kendrick International, script in hand, to make their deal come off and her dream come true.

Dec thought it was a great idea.

"Megan, that's so *cool*. When you're, like, the new Joe Eszterhas, can I come down to LA and do your costume design?"

Ha, ha, ha. Nice joke, God.

Pete's Café had been her choice for a good reason—despite being crowded, noisy, dirty, and full of scumbags, it was situated just off Sunset, and through its grimy windows she could watch the immaculately clean black marble fronting of the SKI offices, check out the agents coming and going, psych herself up. Megan recalled what a good idea she thought that would be; she could get all inspired, get up the courage to just burst in there and blow them away.

It hadn't exactly worked out like that. From the moment she sat down at eleven-thirty, Megan had watched with growing horror as a stream of people—men, women, and your guess is as good as mine—all clutching scripts, or parcels that looked like scripts, or briefcases that must contain scripts, had filed steadily through the doors. Some of them in the most outlandish setups, including some raddled hag in an overcoat and stilettos. Megan had watched with a kind of sick fascination when she landed on the sidewalk, nude except for tassels and a gold G-string—and still clutching a script. In they poured and right back out they poured, cursing, shaking themselves down, and *still clutching their scripts.* She saw some of them trying to warn off the others coming in, who merely cursed them and tried their luck anyway.

The plan that she'd thought was so unique was being tried by every schmuck writer in LA, right in front of her eyes. And it was failing.

"Jerks, huh?" the waiter had asked, refilling her coffee cup. "Some people."

"Some people," Megan agreed.

She wondered if she'd been this dumb growing up, or if it was a talent she'd only recently perfected. What was she going to do now? Sitting here with her script, opposite SKI, with her perfect story for their perfect deal and not a damn way she could get them to read it.

❖

Above him, David Tauber could see the craggy side of the cliff, with a smattering of green scrub vegetation clinging gamely to the rock face, determined to survive and grow, no matter how hostile the conditions. He focused on it for a second. He empathized with it. It could have been an agent.

But there wasn't much time to start meditating on the Malibu vegetation. His dick wouldn't allow it. There wasn't much space for concentration on anything except the obvious—Gloria's heavy, sculpted silicone tits bouncing nicely in front of him, her curvy ass grinding from side to side as she danced for him, crooking her long, tapering legs as she twirled, letting him get a good look at the silky brown hair on her pussy, damp with her arousal. Jesus, this was turning him on. A little strip on the sand, a little head in his Lamborghini at the side of the road while he talked to Sam Kendrick, making his point about Kevin Scott. His cock pulsed a little harder at the thought of it, Gloria making those little sucking noises he loved to hear while he was being fellated, his hand covering the car phone so Sam wouldn't hear, while he slid the knife deeper and deeper into Kevin Scott's useless fat belly. The old guy had snubbed him one too many times and now he was going to pay. The image warmed David's already hot blood, adding to the hot sensations of desire and languorous lust that were pooling in his cock. God, look at Gloria. She was totally wet for him now, her pussy flexing closer and closer toward his face, golden-brown haunches shuddering forward. That was what got him going, the way she wanted him, just for him. Sure, David enjoyed the power trip fucking, the little starlets, the Hollywood wannabes who'd do anything you cared to suggest, whether it involved bringing their friends round for a floor show or going down on one of your buddies in front of you. That had a thrill all its own which had nothing to do with desire. But this was different; this was a woman who desired him for himself, for the muscled body and deep tan, the hazel hair, and his big, thick, beloved cock. Gloria was a corporate attorney and one of the best lays he'd ever known. Her desire, the way she chocked out his name when she came, the way she'd start breathing raggedly if he talked dirty to her down the phone—all of it tickled his vanity.

Shit, they had a mutual fan club. He loved her large, berry-brown nipples and the way they jumped in his mouth, the tips of them hard as sundried raisins. He admired her large, toned butt and the way it tapered into a minute waist. The original hourglass figure. Jesus, that butt was something else, the way she'd grind and swing it. David grunted, his cock aching now. Enough. He reached up to grab her, tripped her over on the sand, and felt her crotch. Ohhhh, man . . . slippery-wet like somebody poured a bottle of baby oil all over her.

"Want it?"

His question was a tease, asking her like that while his fingers were busy stroking her labia, making her moan and twist into him.

"Yes. Now," she gasped. He could sense that he'd better be quick if he didn't want her to come right there. He could see her lower belly tightening up, flattening. Swiftly, he took his hand away and twisted her over, placing her on her hands and knees. Gloria groaned. He put his hand under her, giving her a quick, almost patronizing caress between the legs. She knew better than to break position, just lifted her head, shuddering with arousal. His hand slipped to her midriff, lifting her up, arranging her for his entrance. David felt her respond all over her body as he touched her, the nipples on her delicious pendant breasts stiffening even more, shrinking tiny and tight like his balls. The skin of her belly was incredibly hot, warm with her blood pooling in desire. He fluttered his fingers across it and heard her gasp. That was so horny, *feeling* her lust literally burning at his touch. He saw a drop of moisture pearl on the end of his cock. Time to go for the main event.

David walked round behind her, crouching in front of him like some wild beast, the smoky scent of her arousal distinct even through that designer perfume she was wearing. He put his two hands on the soft curves of her hips, allowing himself a little leverage. Then he was leaning forward, over her back, his dick finding the entrance to her like some military fucking torpedo guided by radar, and inserted just the tip, going maybe a quarter of an inch inside her, forcing himself to resist the temptation to shove it right in and just nail her fabulous fucking ass until he boiled over, emptying himself inside her. Time for that later. Control, control.

"*Madre de Dios!*" Gloria sobbed. "More! David, Jesus Christ!"

"More?" he asked softly, sinking in another inch.

She was so aroused now, she was desperate. She was sobbing openly from wanting it.

He slid in another inch, smiling despite the fury of his own lust.

"Hey, take it slowly, baby. Don't get greedy."

"David!"

She'd come any second. So would he. David Tauber pulled out, slowly, until he was almost completely withdrawn from her, and then thrust savagely, quickly, back inside her, all the way in, right up to the hilt, hearing her ecstatic scream only dimly because of the burning blood pounding in his own ears, finding his rhythm immediately, thrusting, thrusting, feeling her spasms start up, and then there it was, that great white fucking wall, Oh JesusJesusJesus, oh, yes . . .

❖

Gloria moved first, shifting forward and easing him out of her, and just as quickly Tauber tucked himself away and started buttoning his fly. DKNY Men pants in the lightest cream wool, and he didn't want to be getting sand in them. The Rolex said it was five after four. Time to be heading back; a few more instances of that old faggot Scott refusing to take his calls, and he was gonna bust into his office in person. David knew Sam would back him this time. They had a window of opportunity for this deal, and he wasn't about to let that fake-ass would-be Limey jerk him around because he couldn't pick one good script out of, what, eight hundred? How many had they seen this week? And he called himself a literary agent.

Writers were scum, but even writers deserved better than Kevin Scott in their corner.

Gloria Ramirez handed him his copy of the latest Colleen McCallum contract when they got back to their respective cars, and Tauber put it carefully in his briefcase.

They shook hands briskly. He could see her mind was already somewhere else, at her next appointment, on the next deal.

"Nice doing business with you," David said, flashing her a warm smile. She'd be back for more, he knew it. He was good, really good.

"Sure," she said absently, adding, "You know, David? If that Kevin guy is really so bad, maybe *you* should take a writer on. Show Sam Kendrick how bad he is by doing better."

"But I'm a movie agent," David said, slowly.

"So?"

He blew her a kiss as he slid into the low-slung leather of the Lamborghini. Not only was Gloria a great lay, she was a smart bitch, too. So, indeed. Just because it hadn't been done before didn't mean he couldn't do it.

All the way down the Santa Monica Freeway the idea blossomed in his head, exciting him so much he didn't even bother to put on his meditation tape.

If he could find a writer for this movie, he could get Kevin Scott fired.

He could put a part in it so perfect for Roxana Felix, they'd have to cast her.

He would represent the lead male, lead female, and the writer.

Fuck the literary division.

Jesus.

David Tauber pressed his foot on the gas.

⋅⁙⋅

Quarter of five, and the asshole supply had finally dried up. Maybe it was because everybody knew that Kevin's department shut its doors at five on the dot, but the singing telegrams and balloon ladies had given up the game about twenty minutes ago. The phone was still ringing off the hook, but his assistant was dealing with it. Kevin stared morosely at the huge pile of paper on his desk, waiting for somebody to take it out to his Rolls. He would have to try and look at about twenty of these tonight, but he was almost past caring. Rarely had he been so glad to get to the end of a working day.

"No. There's no way."

Katherine's voice, louder and shriller than normal, floated toward him from the department lobby. He could see the tight silhouette of her back blocking the entrance to his office. "You cannot come in. We only accept scripts referred to us by known sources."

Somebody was arguing quietly, a young woman. Enraged, Kevin thrust back his chair and lumbered to his feet. This was the last straw! These people had no manners, just wouldn't take no for an answer. Well, he would give this one something to think about before she next barged in to somebody's private offices.

"Katherine, what is the matter here?" he demanded portentously, flinging open the door. Yes, he'd been right. Some plump, mousy girl stood all alone in his reception, a final, forlorn figure standing on crushed flower heads and bits of popped balloons and wrapping paper. Dear God, it looked like some child had thrown a birthday party out here. It had better, he thought ominously, be all cleaned away by the time he got in tomorrow.

"It's this young lady, Mr. Scott. I was trying to explain to her that we do not accept unrecommended scripts," Katherine said thinly.

"What in God's name do you think you're playing at, miss?" Scott roared. The girl shrank, clutching her script to her chest. "We have a policy in this agency, you know! Didn't you understand my assistant? We do not accept unrecommended material!"

"But I'm newly arrived here," the mouse said. She appeared to be on the verge of tears. "How can I get something recommended when I—"

All he registered was that she had made no move to leave.

"*We do not accept*—" Kevin practically screamed.

"What's going on?"

Apoplectic with rage at being interrupted, Scott whipped round to face the intruder and promptly found his blood pressure rising even further.

It was David Tauber.

Instantly, the girl was forgotten.

"Do you have an appointment?" Scott spat, his face mottled puce with hatred.

"No sir," Katherine said quickly.

Tauber shrugged. "You wouldn't take any of my calls, Kevin. So I thought I'd come to see you, see how you're getting along with a script for Zach."

Megan, watching silently from beside the desk, felt rather than saw her own face blush. The stranger who had so suddenly diverted all Kevin Scott's rage toward himself was the picture of nonchalant calm and composure. The nuclear blast of Scott's wrath that had threatened to break her down right there in his lobby merely washed over this guy like a gentle summer breeze. He was so masculine, so self-assured. Scott did not frighten him.

And he was so *handsome*. Movie star–handsome, male model–handsome, with thick hazel hair and an exquisitely muscled body. She could see his biceps outlined through the sleeves of his gorgeous cream wool suit, which contrasted so beautifully with his golden-brown tan. Her heart sped up, she felt a small wash of warm desire seep through her lower belly. It wasn't just his good looks and confidence; there was something else . . . masculinity, sexuality. The way he moved, he just gave it off. If it hadn't been five in the afternoon, Megan would have sworn this man had just had sex.

Her mouth went dry.

Tauber turned round to the girl Scott had been yelling at, knowing she was staring at him. He could feel her eyes on the back of his neck. An unprepossessing kid, shy, needed to lose weight, but she had a pretty face—pale skin and dark hair wound up in an unflattering bun. She was looking at him with a mixture of awe and admiration, maybe lust, too. No, definitely lust.

Megan dropped her gaze, flushing red with embarrassment.

"*When* I have something I think is suitable," Kevin was sputtering, "I'll show it to Sam." He rounded on Megan. "Get *out*."

"Hey, don't be so hasty," Tauber said. He didn't give a damn about the girl, but she was bugging Kevin. Plus, she'd looked at him in a way that he liked. "Maybe the little lady wants to submit a script."

"Her and a million others," Kevin Scott hissed, hardly able to credit that Tauber would countermand him. "This division does not accept unrecommended material."

Megan was gazing at David Tauber, holding her breath.

He looked her over, a slow, assessing look.

It felt like a caress, like feathery hands feeling up and down her body. Her nipples hardened.

"I'll bet you waited all day to come in here. I'll bet you waited until all the others had gone," Tauber said to her, guessing shrewdly. She looked desperate, determined. He knew the type.

She nodded.

"I'm not looking at that script!" Scott bellowed.

Tauber held out his hand and took the script from Megan.

"Your name and number on this?" he inquired.

She nodded.

"Tauber, what the hell are you doing?" Kevin Scott shrieked.

David turned to him with an insolent smile. "I'm accepting submission of this manuscript." Not a hope in hell it'd be any good, but that wasn't the point. The point was a declaration of war, and this script would be as good as any for that. "Since your department has its policy, I'm going to look at it myself. We don't demand recommendations in the movie division, and Kevin, I *do* need a script."

"But you don't represent writers!"

Tauber shrugged.

"As of now, I do." Ignoring the older man's incensed look, he turned to the little mousy girl and gave her a friendly smile. "You can run along, honey. I'll take a look and be in touch if it's suitable."

With one final glance at Kevin Scott's maroon complexion and Katherine's expression of mortal outrage, Megan turned on her heels and fled.

chapter 9

Flashbulbs exploded around her like firecrackers, microphones from local TV stations were thrust forward in a little forest under her nose, and a crowd of print reporters jostled around the airport security guards, tape recorders shoved wildly in her general direction. Behind her, Roxana could see the other passengers swamped as a pack of fans broke through the yellow security ribbons, many of them screaming her name. With a practiced eye she assessed the situation; no, there were too many guards here for them to get anywhere near her.

Inwardly she smiled. Howard Thorn had done a good job.

"My God, am I safe?" she whispered loudly to her nearest body-guard.

A hundred mikes picked up the comment. She watched the TV hacks dutifully train their cameras on the melee of fans behind her. That turned the story from "Supermodel Arrives in LA" to "Roxana Causes Riots at Airport."

"Roxana, does it bother you to get mobbed everywhere you go?"

She bent her gorgeous head toward the electronic thicket in front of her, replying bravely, "No, I love to see my fans. But it's a little scary when I haven't made enough security arrangements." An elegant shrug. "It was supposed to be a secret that I was coming to LA."

Good-natured laughter. "Are you here to meet with producers?" "Are you planning on acting?"

"I'd rather not comment right now." She smiled dazzlingly at them all, angling her head for the best pictures.

"But isn't it true that you've signed up with the Sam Kendrick agency for an acting career?" somebody yelled.

Score two for Howard.

Roxana turned in the voice's direction, surprise written bright across her face.

"How did you know about that?" she gasped, and then covered her mouth with her hands, as though caught out. More flashbulbs. All the other reporters babbling at once, firing off questions.

"When did you decide to start acting?"

"What's your first project? Why SKI?"

"Is this the end of your modeling career?"

"OK, people, that's enough. Let the lady through, she has no further comment at this time," snarled the bodyguard, hustling her with admirable slowness through the journalists toward her waiting limo, giving everybody enough time to get a snap of Roxana in "casual" clothes—cut-off denim shorts that came right up to her ass, hugging her rock-hard, slightly curved butt and displaying slender, supple thighs that tapered down to endless calves and slim ankles. This had been teamed with a Richard Tyler T-shirt in caramel silk that set off her glossy black hair and million-dollar face to perfection, clinging to her heavenly breasts that were lifted even further skyward by a satin WonderBra. The whole effect was calculatedly casual, displaying her breathtaking body in the best possible light. It had cost her over three thousand dollars—the shorts were Chanel originals—but Joe Public would think that she'd picked it up in JC Penney, and she looked stunning anyway.

Roxana smiled gently, apologetically, at the crowds of press and fans that crammed their noses and lenses against the tinted windows of her limo, maintaining her expression until the car had rolled forward onto the tarmac and the last one had slipped away.

"The Beverly Hills Hotel," she ordered the driver sharply.

She'd be staying at the best bungalow in the grounds, the absolute height of luxury in a city where luxury was second nature. Not that she'd be footing the bill. Unique, her modeling agents in New York, were paying; she'd thought about asking SKI to pick up the tab, but the bald fact was that she wasn't sure that they would. To Unique, she was invaluable. To SKI, she was disposable.

Roxana frowned. By this time next week, that attitude would have changed.

She flicked open her Filofax, looking for the list of numbers she'd jotted down in the plane. Around thirty calls to make before they got into the city, and her little campaign would be all set.

The first name on the list was one of the most useful; an old school friend, a girl she hadn't seen since they were at the Sacred Heart, San

Francisco, together. But that wouldn't matter. She wanted to be a hostess, and she, Roxana, was the biggest supermodel in the world right now.

Deliberately, she punched the number into her car phone.

Jordan Cabot Goldman.

❖

"Hey Megan! Over here!"

Moving up in the world, Megan thought, as she dumped two trays of dirty dishes on the sideboard. They know my name now.

Bob Jenkins shoved a dishcloth at her. "The machine's full and we need more plates. Wash these."

Disbelievingly, Megan stared at the sink. It was piled high with greasy plates, some of which hadn't been properly scraped off, so that rank gobbets of undercooked chicken and oily skin swam around in the water. The whole sink was vibrating from the rattle of the huge antique dishwasher stacked next to it, filled to capacity and struggling to cope with the load. The movement was making the filthy water eddy about in murky rivulets.

"What are you waiting for?" Jenkins was watching her like a hawk. "Got some problem with that? They're only plates, for Chrissake. All the other girls are busy."

That was a blatant lie, Megan thought, looking round at Sandra leaning against the wall with a cigarette, and Lisa, who was hanging on to the pay phone like it was her personal life-support system. She'd been on the damn thing all day. Maybe it *was* her life-support system. But she didn't dare object. Lisa and Sandra kissed up to Jenkins and they hadn't taken Tuesday off.

"No, it's fine," she said, taking the dishcloth from him.

Jenkins grunted. "Yeah, well, you better make it snappy. We got another six in five minutes ago."

"OK." She'd be Zen about this, take the path of least resistance, Megan told herself as she sank her arms in the water, right up to the elbows. It was lukewarm and viscous, almost made her want to gag. That was the way the guys handled things in Frisco.

"Are you all right?" Stacey said. "You look real upset."

"I'm fine," Megan said, but she couldn't keep it up, and the tears started to roll down her cheeks, big, splashy tears that pooled at the end of her nose and dripped into the slimy water.

"Hey, don't let it get to you," Stacey whispered, squeezing her arm. "It's the weekend tomorrow."

Which meant it had been three whole days since the gorgeous SKI agent had taken her screenplay. Which meant he hadn't liked it. And God, that story could have been written with Zach Mason specifically in mind. If it wasn't good enough for his project at Artemis, it certainly wasn't good enough for anyone else. She was also absolutely sure that *Triple Feature* was the best she could do.

Time to face reality. She wasn't good enough.

"Yeah, I know," Megan sobbed, not wanting to discuss it. She searched for a reason Stacey would understand. "I was thinking about my ex-boyfriend."

"I understand," Stacey said gravely, patting her sympathetically.

Miserably, she started to wash up the dirty dishes as fast as she could, grateful to have some work to do, but it just couldn't keep her mind off it. It was so viciously heartbreaking to want something so hard, wait for it so long, and then fail so completely. And what made it even worse was that finally, she had had that shred of hope. The way the young agent had taken her screenplay—the older guy, the literary guy who should have been in charge, he was ready to hit him, but that hadn't stopped him from taking her script. It was as though she'd finally stumbled across an ally. And he was so hot-looking, and he'd given her that sexy once-over that made her feel so wet and squirmy, so that when she pulled up outside their apartment, she'd felt more alive, more bright with hope than she'd done in years. Like she was on a threshold. And that night, a hot, sticky night, she hadn't been able to sleep, had just lain on her bed with her eyes open, listening to the cars and the gangbangers streaming past in the street, until finally, she started to touch herself, thinking about that agent—somebody Tauber, the other guy had called him—thinking about his muscles and his eyes and his tan and his walk, what that silky hazel hair would feel like brushing between her thighs, until she'd had a gentle climax, orgasm running sweetly over her like ripples across a pool, and finally slept.

The phone had rung on and off all that week, sometimes for her. Calls from the café, one call from Dec up in Frisco. But as Wednesday became Thursday, and Thursday became Friday, the trilling of the phone turned from hopeful music into sadistic mockery. There were a lot of calls for Megan, but not one of them from SKI. Today was Friday, Friday afternoon to be exact, and Megan Silver had learned enough about the movie business to know that if they don't call you quickly, they don't call at all.

She shook her head, aware that Stacey was still gazing at her sympathetically.

"You must miss him like crazy, Megan. I've never seen you this upset."

"I'll get over it."

Stacey wasn't convinced. "If you want to go home, you can always just go, honey. You don't have to stay here. I know you wanted to try out with your script, but . . ." Her southern twang trailed off, embarrassed. "Well, you know how you hate the place . . ."

Megan glanced down at the greasy washing up. "It's not exactly Shangri-la."

"Kids come here all the time and try out. Mostly it doesn't work, an' I seen a bunch of them slip into really bad stuff. You might be better off going home. You worked for the library, right? Maybe you could get a mortgage, get a house." She shrugged. "Gotta be better than this."

Somehow, Megan just didn't want to hear it from somebody else, especially somebody as pretty and as stupid as Stacey. It sounded so true. Jesus, it *was* true. But is that all there is to life for me, truly? she wondered. A detached bungalow, a mortgage, a comfortable, passionless marriage? Was that, in real life, the highest goal, was that as high as she should set her sights? And just pray God that at least she'd feel something when the kids came along?

"It worked for Jeanne," Megan said defiantly. "She got a part just last week. Second lead in an art movie by a guy called Ray Tyson."

For a second Stacey just gaped at her, and then looked swiftly down, obviously trying to stifle a laugh.

"Christ, honey, you have to be kidding. Everyone knows Ray Tyson around here. He bugged me for weeks when I first started this job. The guy shoots, you know, *dirty movies*. Sells videotapes direct to the sex stores, gets a flick screened in a porno house from time to time."

"Everybody knows this?" Megan repeated weakly, feeling sick. "Jeanne knew?"

"Sure. She must have. He's a dirty old man, sixty maybe. Not even in the Guild. He pays a good rate, that's what they told me before." Stacey wrinkled her perfect little nose. "I'd never be *that* desperate. And I know you never would either, but this place ain't good for you. You got a college degree, you need a real job."

"You work here," said Megan stubbornly.

Stacey gave her a long, cool stare, and then said, not unkindly, "But honey, you're twenty-four. I'm still in high school."

"What are you two gabbing about?" Mr. Jenkins snarled, passing them. "Stacey, they need two pitchers on seven. Megan, Jesus. Get a move on, willya? I told you we need this done, and that means now, not sometime before you die." He jabbed her back with a bony elbow, watching until she picked up the scourer and began to attack the plates, the slimy water splashing across her bare forearms. Mr. Chicken didn't bother with mundane luxuries like washing-up gloves.

Two more hours, Megan thought, bowing her head so Jenkins wouldn't see her reddened eyes. Two more hours before I get paid for the week. And that's it. It'll be enough for a bus ticket back to Frisco, and I'm gonna be on the first one tomorrow morning.

She was ashamed at how swiftly she'd given in, turned into the quitter she swore she'd never become. She'd been so certain that she was destined for a real adventure in life, something better than Dec and Trey and Francine. So sure that there had to be something out there for her, something bigger and better than listing textbooks at the San Francisco Public Library and talking about beat poets over coffee.

Well, how wrong she'd been.

⋯⋯⋯

"Take a look at this."

Sam Kendrick flung the paper across to Mike Campbell with a snort. It landed on the polished marble coffee table with a heap of other papers and magazines, all of them adorned with pictures of Roxana Felix. Smiling, pouting, winking. Standing up, sitting regally on a chair in the Polo Lounge, walking into Le Dome, lying curled on the beach like the proverbial sex kitten. In each and every shot she looked utterly stunning, endless legs stretching on forever, raven hair glistening halfway down her back, pale skin freshened with luminous blusher. The clothes were always impeccable, from the silk T-shirt she'd worn at the airport to the black cashmere blazer that had starred at her dinner at Morton's, the first evening in town. Looking at the mountain of press, you'd imagine that Roxana was on some mission to check out, and be snapped at, every star hangout in LA, from Twin Palms to the Viper Room, the Roxbury to House of Blues.

"Yeah," Mike said, attempting to frown but unable to drag his gaze from one shot of Roxana in a copper silk dress which showed her full nipples clearly outlined under the delicate fabric. "I gotta say I've never seen anything like it."

"Three days! That's all she's been here, three days. She's trying to snow me."

Sam was seriously pissed off.

"It's not just the papers, either. She's on every radio show, every local TV station, *Entertainment Tonight*, did a guest slot on *MTV at the Movies* just yesterday," Campbell agreed hastily. If Sam was pissed with Roxana, then so was he, no matter how much of a world-class babe she was. "I guess she's trying to force us into pushing her, going flat out for her. If we don't get her something good after all this . . ." He gestured at the copy of *LA Weekly* Sam had thrown him, which had "PUTTING HER FAITH IN SKI" written in large black type under Roxana's picture.

"Yeah. Thanks, Sherlock," Sam said sourly.

MTV at the Movies? Damn, the woman was better than he thought. She was running this campaign more precisely than most politicians. Of course, most politicians had a harder time getting coverage than Roxana Felix. But still! This was crazy. Surely the media would have tired of her by now, or at least kept her off the cover pages and the prime gossip slots.

Her arrival in town was news, but after that? You'd think this broad was the Queen of England, the way they were fawning over her every move. They put her on the cover when she blew her little retroussé nose.

Sam Kendrick had been around the block a few times, and something about this frenzy smelled odd. To be exact, it smelled of friends in high places. Very high places. And Sam hated the idea of any shadowy puppet master trying to yank *his* strings.

Still, he had to hand it to her. She was pretty fucking determined. My God, the first night she'd arrived, Sam came back home to find his wife out at an impromptu dinner with Jordan Goldman and Roxana Felix! Apparently Roxana and Jordan had been Catholic schoolgirls together in San Francisco and now just couldn't wait to celebrate their joint elevation to the Baby Millionairess Club. Obvious what Roxana wanted, and right on cue, according to Isabelle, Jordan had spilled her bimboid guts about the Zach Mason project at Artemis, *including* the news about the script. Jordan, meanwhile, gets a new member of the board for her chichi little dinners against gang violence and AIDS, and a new star at the dinner table. And Isabelle, who for some reason had lately adopted Jordan Goldman as her protégé on the social scene, just sat there and invited the bitch to their next frigging party.

Normally, both Jordan and Isabelle would have cut somebody like Roxana dead. He knew that. Roxana was far too beautiful. Too much competition. But by marking herself out as an actress, she had, in that single move, eliminated herself as a danger. She would need both Tom and Sam in her attempt to get this deal, and that meant she needed their wives.

And if Jordan was pushing Tom for Roxana the way Isabelle was pushing him, she'd succeeded.

"Did you check out her tests yet? David Tauber got the film through this morning, sent a tape to both of us."

"He did, didn't he?"

David Tauber. His instincts had been right, yet again. That kid was a comer; the way things were going, he'd have his fingerprints on three out of the four deal principals. Only Fred Florescu, the director and therefore the most important guy in the package, was repped by somebody else— namely Sam himself.

Kendrick admired Tauber, pleased with himself as he undoubtedly was. He just hoped the kid knew his place.

He better, Sam thought grimly.

"Not yet. I've been on the phone to Eleanor Marshall about the script all morning."

"They're OK."

"OK, they suck, or OK, they rule?"

"Just OK. Not too bad, not too good. Like Madonna in *Desperately Seeking Susan*."

"As opposed to *Body of Evidence*."

"You got it. She's better than Isabella Rossellini, but not so good as Andie MacDowell. She's—"

"All right, all right." Sam held up a gnarled hand. "I get the picture. Why don't you shove the tape in the machine, let's see what the little *chiquita* can actually do."

Mike reached forward and slid the video into the recorder, artfully concealed under an original Matisse. Across the other side of Sam's office, computerized dimmer switches automatically darkened the lights and a wall slid noiselessly back to reveal a huge digital television the size of a cinema screen. As the two powerful agents settled back into the Eames leather sofa, Roxana Felix's stunning face, her pores flawless and tiny even at ten times life size, swam into view.

Sam Kendrick watched with something like real curiosity. Interesting. So this was the woman who'd been turning the media heat on him like it was her personal flamethrower. Even though they hadn't bent over for her right away, and she must have been used to that as a model, it hadn't stopped her or even slowed her down. As much as he would have liked to chuck her tests in the can and send her gift-wrapped over to ICM—Sam *hated* clients that tried to push him around—he knew that Roxana Felix had, in three days, just about removed his power to do that. The entire LA wolf pack were now watching him with their little yellow eyes, checking out what he was going to do with his pretty new toy.

And holy shit, was she ever pretty.

Maybe it didn't all come across in still photos.

Would you look at that!

Mesmerized now, Sam Kendrick stared at the screen. The supermodel was reciting some Shakespeare with bare competence, but he wasn't listening to the dialogue. He couldn't lift his eyes from the way her skimpy little costume swung on her slender hips, the tiny flashes of brown thigh she kept turning to the camera, the way she would pause every couple of minutes and run the barest tip of her tongue over her lower lip. Her bra was definitely not underwired, the way those titties were swinging. If she was wearing a bra. Shit, maybe if she moved a bit faster he'd be able to tell for sure. And how she walked. And how she walked. Demurely from the outside, a woman might say demurely, but with just that suggestion of a sway, no, more than that, of a *grind* that put you in mind of the better strip bars, up in Canada maybe. She was batting her eyes down now, playing it vulnerable, but somehow managing to suggest with her whole body that she'd be a tigress in bed, as soon scratch your eyes out as look at you.

Her dialogue was wooden, but her body language was eloquent.

"I am asham'd, that women are so simple
To offer war when they should kneel for peace;
Or seek for rule, supremacy, and sway,
When they are bound to serve, love and obey."

Unbelievable. Sam felt himself getting hard. Beautiful women were usually cold narcissists, one more LA cliché that was totally true. But Roxana
Felix was obviously nothing like that.

He wondered if she'd ever been fucked the way she deserved. He
doubted it. Most guys would be utterly terrified by a woman as gorgeous
as Roxana, would just thrust in and out a few times before they came. Performance anxiety. Yeah, well, not him. He'd show her exactly what that
flat little stomach could give her as well as him, how much he could get
those perfect thighs to tremble, what happened to those plump, pointy
nipples when they were sucked and stroked properly. Yeah, he'd like to
have her underneath him, thrashing about in orgasm, all ready to fake it
again and then suddenly realizing what was happening, tensing underneath
him as her pussy started to get tight, but he wouldn't stop, he wouldn't
break pace, he'd ride her like a thoroughbred filly, until she was incoher-
ent, all scratching at him and biting his shoulder, wet with her own sweat,
and just at that moment he'd slip his right hand in between her legs, just
above where his cock was, and rub her lightly so he'd be pressing on the
clitoris above and below. He'd show her that he was a powerful man and
powerful men had beautiful women all the time, that they were just a
perk of his job like any other, and he wasn't afraid of her, he was going to
enjoy her, in fact, he was going to fuck her ambitious little brains out.

And she'd love it. And she'd come for him, she'd come screaming.

As the tape ran to an end, Sam moved a copy of *Variety* onto his lap to
hide his arousal. No need to get locker-room with Mike at a time like this.

On screen, Roxana's jet-black eyes, frozen in digital perfection, seemed
to look right through him, as though the woman herself was up there,
mocking, teasing him, calling to a part of himself that had seemed long
dead, laid out cold in the headlong rush for glory.

For a second, Samuel Kendrick wondered uneasily if he had finally met
his match.

⋯⋯

David Tauber punched the redial button on his mobile phone, the other
hand resting lightly on the wheel as he bombed down Sunset. Engaged
again. Shit, he was making a habit of this—first Kevin Scott, and now some
five-and-dime restaurant. What was the point of living in the age of technology, of being a surfer on the information superhighway, if you could
never get through because people were always using the goddamn phone?

Well, if you need something done, do it yourself. As he'd snidely said to Kevin Scott when Artemis finally came through with their draft-screenplay approval.

He, David Ariel Tauber, the next Mike Ovitz, was *pleased* with little Megan Silver. Pleased with her for turning up in Kevin's office, pleased with her for writing such a kick-ass first-draft script, not that it wouldn't need a load of work, and pleased with her for obviously not knowing the first thing about the movie business. And being violently attracted to him. She was nothing to look at herself, but at least she had taste. And it was kind of sweet, watching her blush when he caught her staring at him. "Sweet" was not an adjective often applied to LA screenwriters; it might be fun, working with Megan, showing her a thing or two. She was close to his perfect client; talented, naive, and desperate. Which was why, having failed all day to get through to the two-bit joint she was working in, David was doing her the honor of turning up to tell her the good news in person.

And shit, the girl must have been psychic. Not only was her little movie absolutely tailor-made for Zach Mason—the guy would practically be playing himself—but she'd also written in a hefty female lead for the musician's girlfriend, who was, check it out, a *supermodel*. If Roxana had looked dicey for a female lead before—and he didn't know what Sam's reactions had been to her test—surely this part would at least double her chances. The PR blitz would help as well. In fact, sometimes he got the feeling that Roxana didn't even need his help. This, he didn't like. Who needed to feel like an accessory? Who needed a client who knew what they were doing, and worse still, knew what *he* should be doing? Roxana Felix kept track. She was on his case, really on his case. Six times a day. But now, finally, David Tauber reckoned he had something for her.

Yeah. Megan Silver didn't look like a sorceress, but maybe that's just what she was—waved her magic wand, and made all David's problems go away. Which is why he was running red lights on the Boulevard at ten to nine, going to pick her up himself.

She *deserved* it.

⋅⋅⋅

Fifteen minutes. That was all she had to keep telling herself. Fifteen minutes, and then she could get out of here.

Megan kept busy. Wasn't difficult, what with the men all screaming for beer, and new heaps of greasy chicken and gray frozen fries being shoveled into pans a foot deep in spitting oil, and buckets of indifferent-looking slaw hefted round the kitchen, she barely had time to glance at the clock. She tried not to. If Jenkins saw her, he'd say she was slacking and dock her pay.

"Five minutes, sugar," Stacey muttered in her ear, sweeping past with a basket of corn. She dumped it unceremoniously on the front of table twelve and came back into the kitchen, her pretty face alive with excitement. "Look at this, Meg! The most incredible car just pulled into the parking lot."

Megan, like most of the other waitresses, craned her neck for a quick look.

"Man or woman?"

"It's a man," Megan said, watching a figure in an expensive-looking gray suit step out of a stunning cherry-red sports car. "Maybe you'll get lucky, Stacey." She dusted her hands on her canary Mr. Chicken frilly skirt. Nine P.M. exactly. *Well, thank you, God.* "I'm going to get paid."

Utterly exhausted, she walked over to the little cash counter where Jenkins was sitting.

"So we'll see you Monday," he said sourly.

Megan didn't have a decision to make. She'd been thinking about what Stacey had said all night and she knew she was right. It was OK to be a waitress at seventeen; twenty-four, and you had serious problems.

Dec would have her back. He probably wouldn't even laugh that much.

"No, I don't think so. I quit." She tried to give him a smile. *That's it, Megan, kiss ass like the corporate little chicky you are.* "Thanks for the try-out, Bob, but I just don't think it's worked out."

His eyes had a mean glint to them. She could see it even through the clouds of steam fogging up the kitchen.

"You can't do that."

Megan shrugged. "I gotta go home."

"Shoulda checked your contract."

"My *contract?*" Megan asked, mystified.

"You signed it when you got hired."

That little scrap of paper? That was a contract?

She tried humility. "Look, I'm really sorry if this is any bother for you, but—"

"You need to give me a month's notice. If you ain't giving notice, you ain't getting paid for the week."

Despite the heat, Megan went pale.

"You must be kidding, Bob. You can hire anybody, you don't want to make me stay a month. I'm a lousy waitress. You said so yourself."

"You're not that bad." He was eyeing her speculatively, greedily.

My God, Megan thought, suddenly realizing what this little charade was all about. He doesn't want me to stay, he wants me to get so mad I'll just storm out and he won't have to pay me for the week. Guess he doesn't realize how badly I need that check.

"OK." She stared back. "If it's what you want. Consider this a month's notice. I'll put it in writing, if you like."

"You sure?"

She was right. Now he was mad. God, he must have been sure she'd burst into tears and run off.

"Yeah, Bob, I'm totally sure. You owe me a week's pay and I'm not leaving without it."

"Why, you—"

"Megan." Stacey, blushing red to her roots, had come over to interrupt them. "Bob, I'm sorry, but we need Megan right now. There's a guy out here asking for her personally. Won't talk to anyone else."

Dec? thought Megan wildly.

"You know the rules, Megan. No personal visitors," Jenkins said nastily. "I'm coming with you."

"Jesus, Bob. I finished my shift. I can see a visitor."

He rounded on her. "Not on Mr. Chicken premises you don't. This is where you work, not where you get to hang with your friends. Assuming you *want* to stay working here."

"Megan?"

The three of them spun round at the strange voice to see a tall, blond man in a Yohji Yamamoto black wool suit standing at the entrance to the kitchen. He had a gold watch on his right wrist and was carrying a briefcase in soft pigskin leather. He reeked of money and confidence, absolutely aware of the sensation he was causing in a dump like this. Enjoying it too. Stacey could hardly take her eyes off him.

Megan couldn't breathe.

"Who the fuck is this?" Jenkins demanded, recovering himself. "Look, mister, she isn't allowed visitors here. Not if she wants to keep the job."

"She doesn't."

"And who says so?"

"My name is David Tauber, Sam Kendrick International," David said, giving Megan his most brilliant, luminous smile. "I'm Ms. Silver's agent. Isn't that right, Megan?"

Megan felt faint, almost dizzy with joy. Eventually, realizing that Jenkins was staring at her with a glare that could strip paint, she found her voice.

"That's right, David," she said. She turned round to Jenkins, suddenly unable to keep a huge grin off her face. "Hey, Bob. You know what, you're absolutely right. You can keep that paycheck, because I quit. Right now. And I'll tell you something else."

She leaned forward, right in his acne-pitted face.

"It's worth every cent, just to see the look on your face."

"Ms. Silver, shall we go? I've got the Lamborghini waiting outside for you."

David Tauber stood there in the doorframe, handsome as Adonis, offering her his arm. And Mr. Chicken frilly uniform and all, Megan took it like a queen.

"Why not?" she said.

chapter 10

The script felt good in her hands. That was a strange thing to notice, but Eleanor couldn't help thinking about it as she walked into her office and hefted it out of her briefcase. The physical weight of the paper, the neatness of the edges, all the telltale signs that let her know that it had been handled by so few people. She had a tiny thrill of electricity just picking it up.

That same electricity had been with her ever since she pulled out of the garage this morning, sending the blood tingling round her veins, giving her the feeling of wanting to get into the office, to start the day, to make this deal work. One of those mornings that reminded her why she'd longed to work in this business in the first place.

Excitement.

Triple Feature was good, she could feel it, she could sense it in her bones. From the moment that slimy little jerk Tauber over at SKI had messengered it across with that pretentious message about "the next *Close Encounters*" and "*Pretty Woman* meets *The Doors*," she'd been convinced. And God knew she hadn't picked it up with any expectations—after all, nobody had heard of Megan Silver, whoever she was, and it hadn't even come from Sam's script department. If she hadn't wanted the deal to work so badly, she might have refused to look at it, might have passed it down the food chain to one of Artemis's "readers," the amoebae at the bottom who normally accepted screenplay submissions. She'd have liked nothing better than to snub David Tauber. He was a two-bit hustler barely out of diapers, the type who expected all women to fall at his feet with their legs open just because he had a cute smile and a tan. She was used to guys like Tauber. Probably worked out in a gym with mirrored walls.

Still, there was no way she could have refused to look at the script. Jerk though Tauber was, he was also the classic model of the Hollywood comer. Breaking on the scene from nowhere with Colleen McCallum, and now Zach Mason as well as the model. Heavy-duty clients eventually turn the most featherweight agent into Mike Tyson. So she'd started reading it at nine last night, intending to skim it in ten minutes.

She'd finished it at quarter of ten and called Sam Kendrick immediately.

Triple Feature. An incredible love story. An action-thriller plot. A backdrop of sex and drugs and rock 'n' roll.

It was going to make her name, and she'd come into Artemis this morning with the intention—oh God, God, this was so great, and so terrifying—of green-lighting her first movie.

"You look happy."

"Hi, Tom," Eleanor said, looking up to see her boss standing in the doorway of her office. He was wearing some nondescript black suit that made his brown hair look darker, but did nothing for the slight jowliness of middle age that had settled around his chin. He moved like a man long accustomed to power.

She felt a familiar longing twitch between her thighs.

"I brought breakfast," Tom said, striding across the room and dumping a grease-spotted paper bag down on her desk. He took out a jelly-filled doughnut and a paper cup of coffee and offered them to her with a grin. "Caffeine. Refined sugar. Saturated fat. Eat."

"I can't eat that!" Eleanor protested, laughing. "It'll head straight to my thighs. Paul wants us to go on the Pritikin diet, that one where you eat no fat at all. He says we should hire a vegetarian low-fat cook."

Goldman shook his head. "So? Jordan wants me to become a goddamned vegan." He leaned toward her. "This is why people have jobs."

"So they can secretly eat doughnuts?"

"Absolutely. Now eat it. That's an order."

Smiling, she took a large bite. It was sweet and oily and delicious.

Tom watched her with immense satisfaction, then reached into the bag for his own doughnut, polishing it off in three bites.

"My God, it's Captain Caveman," Eleanor said. "And I bet you ate at home, too."

Tom shrugged defensively, grinning. "I work out. Sometimes." He reached forward and wiped gently across her cheek, removing a small oozing trickle of jelly that was slowly running down her chin, licking his thumb clean. "President of a movie studio, and she has no doughnut-eating technique at all. I find that very sad."

"Talking of which—" Eleanor put down the rest of it and patted her script. "I've got something you should see."

"We can talk business later. It's only eight o'clock, you'll have all day for that," Goldman said impatiently. "When do we ever get a chance to talk? Tell me how you are."

Eleanor shifted on her seat. She was almost embarrassed. Her feelings for Tom were long recognized and admitted, filed neatly away under "might have been." But that didn't stop the private joy that ran through her during their early-morning moments together, when she was alone with him before any of the assistants arrived. And, she was dismayed to find, it didn't stop the wild arousal that had swum hot and squirming into her belly when his hand touched her cheek. She'd wanted to press it into his palm, to turn her lips to his wrist and cover it with hot kisses, to take that thumb into her own mouth and lick and suck it clean. From that one faintly erotic touch she was wet. There was more sensuality in Tom brushing jelly from her cheek than there was in the whole of the sexual act that she'd performed with Paul this morning.

The morning session with Tom was enjoyable and innocent precisely because they never did or said anything of consequence, unless it was business. But now he was looking her straight in the eyes and asking her how she was!

"Fine," she said. "I'm fine."

"Are you?" Tom asked softly. "How's life at home? How are you getting on with Paul?"

Words trembled on her lips. "Just great." "Terrific, thank you." "Oh, he's incredible." All the safe, stock answers she came out with every day. They were the solid couple. Rock-steady, the way LA royalty should be; the studio head and the investment banker; William III and Mary II, joint sovereigns. Monogamous and neatly paired off. Very nineties.

But somehow, sitting here looking at Tom Goldman, she found it hard to say. She flashed back to the scene today. The first light of dawn creeping through the fragrant darkness of their garden, the scent of hibiscus and jasmine in the cold morning air, the way it always was when they woke, at five A.M., to the strains of whatever soft classical music he'd programmed into the CD the night before—Bach or Mozart. And then Paul would reach for her. No preliminaries, he would just reach for her, as much a part of his early-morning routine as the jog at half past five, or the orange juice and mineral water at six.

Only this morning she'd turned away.

"Come on, what's the matter?" he'd asked sleepily, nuzzling against her shoulder. "Don't want to?"

"I'm just tired."

But the truth was she *didn't* want to. Not right now. Not after going to sleep on *Triple Feature*, with all that raw passion and obsessive love. She'd dreamed about Tom, and just for today, just for this morning in the gentle half-light, something in her skin rebelled at the thought of Paul touching her.

"You're never tired."

She hated that tone—it was accusatory, whining.

"You just forgot to put your diaphragm in last night."

Eleanor started to deny it. "No I didn't, Paul, I—"

"I don't see why I can't make love to you without it. I don't see why you always have to insist on using that damn thing." He was angry and cold now. Thankfully, she felt his erection shriveling against her thigh. "You say you want kids, but you know it's getting later and later. I don't see why we can't get married."

"We've had this discussion before," Eleanor said, feeling her defenses fly up. She hated, utterly hated, to talk about this. She didn't want to acknowledge it or see it, didn't want to confront it. "This just isn't the right time."

"When *will* it be the right time? When you're fifty, and we have to adopt?"

Paul threw back the covers and stood up to dress, his long, lean body blackly silhouetted against the weak dawn light from the sash windows. Eleanor could see anger in the whole way he carried himself, in the set of his muscles.

"Will you marry me?"

It was a demand, not a request.

She tensed.

"Not yet."

"I won't wait forever, Eleanor," he warned her as he walked toward the bathroom. "*I* want kids."

Oh, so do I, she'd thought as she lay there, Irish cotton sheets clutched protectively around her. *So do I*.

Children. A baby, maybe two or three, little infants with their wide eyes and tiny hands and all the love and fears that they couldn't even articulate. She had always wanted children, in that confident way that young beautiful women have, sure that life will send them the husband they desire and deserve, happy to trust in their wombs, unhurried and unpressured. "Kids someday."

She couldn't now mark out, couldn't recall, the exact moment that the first flush of youth had left her, the precise period of months when she'd started to get concerned and anxious. Maybe it combined with the period when it had dawned on her that Tom Goldman was never going to take his flirtation any further, when one girlfriend replaced another, and suddenly all the girlfriends were five, seven, ten years younger than her. Teenagers and twenty-two-year-olds.

That was when she'd accepted the best, most eligible of the bachelors that swarmed round her, fetched her drinks at charity balls, and monopolized her at Isabelle Kendrick dinners. Paul Halfin had then been handsome, rich, educated, charming. He was fun to talk to, if you didn't want anything too wild. Knew everything there was to know about Shakespeare and Vivaldi, and his firm was pretty hot, had been involved in a couple of high-profile entertainment deals just that year. Eleanor was thirty-two. They were two "beautiful people." They would be a power couple, Bill and Hillary on their way up their separate ladders.

Eleanor thought Paul was cute. She moved in with him.

The relief had been amazing, so much so that it revealed to her as though for the first time how pressured she'd felt being single. For the first time, in social situations she had nothing to prove. Executive wives thawed perceptibly to her. She always had someone to take her to Artemis premieres, and a wonderful, enviable escort for firm dinners. For the first few months together, they had teetered on the brink of marriage, which, inevitably, would have led to children. An ideal Beverly Hills family.

She couldn't do it.

That was what stopped her. Children, the thing she'd dreamed of since she was a child herself, tucking her doll into its cot, nursing teddies through their various exotic ailments. She'd been an only child of elder parents, and she'd always imagined herself as a beautiful young mother with a gaggle of babies. When she got older and started to dwell on it, the precious wonder of human life, she simply couldn't understand how so many people treated their children so lightly, divorcing without the slightest effort at patching it up for the kids' sake, or starving them of affection. She couldn't believe all those deadbeat fathers that snuck away from mothers they no longer desired, frightened of responsibility or scared of another mouth to feed. God, surely they were curious? A baby was such a miracle, it was their descendant, their link to the future, their line spanning down the generations. Did they never see it like that, those men? Eleanor wondered. Did they never look at their babies and see their own eyes staring up at them, the future small and soft in their arms when they laid it in the crib at night? To *create life*, together—was that not the ultimate bond two people could have?

And in her own mind, when she thought of her child, flesh of her flesh and blood of her blood, she could not see it with Paul's eyes, his nose, his chin.

When she saw the features of the father of her child, she imagined Tom Goldman's eyes staring back at her.

Of course that was quite ridiculous. Tom felt nothing for her. He had this string of interchangeable nubile babes, he was her boss and her friend. So she'd had a crush on him once, so what?

It was the advent of Jordan Cabot that finally drove Eleanor to admit what she was feeling. Jordan, who'd arrived in LA a year ago from San Francisco, the blond scion of a rich, gentile family, just another stupid bimbo looking to hook a Hollywood executive. By this time, of course, Tom was chairman of Artemis and the biggest catch in town. Jordan, possibly, had simply lucked out by being the right girl at the right time, coming along when Tom was so newly promoted and pleased with himself and his life. And let's face it, in a town full of pneumatic flaxen-haired cuties, Jordan Cabot was something else. A perfect hourglass figure combined with a truly pretty face of the all-American type. Great skin, white teeth, athletic muscle tone, and a mere twenty-three years old. But even that might not have been enough to get a ring on Tom's finger, as chary of tying himself down as Eleanor knew he was. What had finally swung it for Jordan was her ability in bed. Whatever skills she'd perfected, Tom was addicted to them. This Eleanor knew because he'd told her, buddy to buddy. He wasn't coarse about it; he would just come into her office and marvel at how incredible, how alive, how *young* Jordan made him feel. Said he could never get enough. Could never get tired of it. Soon, Eleanor had to knock on his office door instead of just walking in like she used to, for fear of interrupting one of his heavy phone-sex sessions.

Tom became obsessed. He said Jordan made him feel like a teenager again.

Eleanor began to have nightmares, dreaming of Jordan, young, flawless, perfect, contorting her body in wild ways which she, Eleanor, could not even begin to imagine.

Six months after he'd met her they were engaged. A month later they were married. And when Tom, two months into their marriage, confided in Eleanor that he wished Jordan would get pregnant, that children were the one remaining consuming desire of his life, she was forced into recognizing the great tragedy of her own life.

She loved Tom Goldman, loved him desperately. It was the only explanation for the searing, ravaging pain that swept through her as she listened to him. And she wanted no man but Tom to be the father of her children.

It was never going to be. She knew that, accepted it as the clear truth. If she, Eleanor Marshall, wanted to be a mother, she was going to have to find a different set of genes to mix with. Moreover, she was going to have to find them pretty soon. She was thirty-eight. And if not Paul, who else? If she left Paul, would that do her any good? Whoever else she hooked up with, they wouldn't be Tom either. So shouldn't she avoid making the perfect the enemy of the good? When there was no guarantee that she was ever going to find anything better? And the feeling of desperation, of end-less longing for that child waiting so impatiently to be born, was beginning to swamp her. Sometimes seeing little children with their mothers in the mall would make her cry. She'd started to dream about babies, torturingly realistic dreams, where she could smell the milky, sleepy smell of their vel-vety skin, see every tiny finger curl with its miniature fingernail, notice how their fragile lashes seemed too long for those minute eyelids.

And Paul was pressing her to marry him, to conceive.

So far, for three months she'd been stalling.

This morning, Eleanor had felt all the walls starting to close in. She'd have to decide. And she had no idea what to do.

Eleanor gazed up at Tom, leaning over her, staring at her with his odd intensity.

"You want the truth? Things aren't so hot."

"Work pressure?"

He was probing her now. For a moment Eleanor sensed he didn't want her to answer yes, that he wanted to hear something more personal.

She thought about saying that Paul was swamped over at Albert, Halfin, Weissman.

"Paul wants me to marry him. I guess I'm not sure if I'm ready," she said. "And you? How are things with Jordan?"

"Not so hot."

Tom smiled ruefully at her, but then looked away. "I probably didn't re-alize what the age difference would mean."

"Nothing serious, though." God, look at me, Eleanor thought, mad at herself. All I do is reach out to comfort him. Why don't I *do* something about it.

"No. I'm sure it'll all work itself out. Especially when we get pregnant."

She nodded, trying to stifle her disappointment. Not to mention that horrible ironic stab—"when we get pregnant." Tom was burning to be a fa-ther, then. He longed to beget children. But not with her.

"But I gotta tell you, sometimes it's really hard. Talking to her, I mean. It's not"—she could see him struggle with his words, wanting to tell her his problem, trying to avoid criticizing his wife—"not like it is with you. She's not interested in . . ."

She's not interested in anything. Except social climbing, designer dresses, and making the gossip columns, Tom thought. He'd thought that he could never get tired of sex with Jordan. And he wasn't. But he was wondering if he'd tired of everything else.

He heard his own voice trailing away. He couldn't admit it, not even to Eleanor, as well as they knew each other. In fact, especially not to Eleanor. Not as she sat there in that deep blue suit, radiating intelligence and sensu-ality. Flirting with her had been a constant as long as he'd known her, but lately every flirtation seemed to have taken on a new edge. He had always desired her, but his respect for their friendship, his wariness of professional misconduct, and his terror of—what? Of being tied down? Of sex that wasn't the type you could walk away from? Well, his terror of that nameless connection, all those things, had kept him from making his move. Desire was joyous and clean. Desire you could control. And he had, in the end, married a girl who could satisfy his desire with the skill of a virtuoso.

Jordan. She was far more attractive than Eleanor, surely. And fourteen years younger.

So why was lust curling around his crotch? Why had he felt his sex get warmer and harder the instant his thumb touched Eleanor's cheek?

"I think I'm just too old and too square," Goldman finished.

Eleanor looked across her desk at him, the coffee in its Styrofoam cup cooling in front of her.

"No you're not, Tom," she said.

The silence between them hung in the air.

Then Goldman reached forward, his large right hand closing over her small left one, his grip solid, even tight, and said, "Eleanor—"

"Hey, my two favorite people."

Without so much as a glance at her, Tom Goldman snatched his hand away as though her skin had suddenly become corrosive acid. Past his back, Eleanor could see the dapper figure of Jake Keller, her most senior vice president of production. Her deputy at the department, Jake had been the man passed over for the presidency when Eleanor got the job. He'd always been totally friendly and polite to her since, but Jake was an enemy and Eleanor knew it. He was bitter. The sight of him interrupting them sent shivers down her spine. Unpleasant ones.

He hadn't seen anything.

She hoped.

"Eleanor, do you have a second? I wanted to discuss that script you sent me yesterday. *Triple Feature.*"

"Sure, Jake. Of course."

Eleanor picked up the copy lying on her desk and passed it to Tom, briskly. "Tom, you might as well take this away too. It's the script for the Zach Mason/Fred Florescu project, which is a go."

"You're green-lighting this?" Keller asked. His tone was heavy with disapproval.

"I am." She refused to be rattled, or to respond to the insult. Jake Keller was not to approve or disapprove of her decisions. She was his boss.

Tom Goldman looked swiftly from one to the other, all business now.

"Jake, maybe you should bring it up in the production meeting at ten."

He was backing up her authority, Eleanor knew. She also knew that Tom would listen carefully to whatever criticisms Jake had. He wouldn't prevent her from green-lighting this project—after all, being president was all about making those decisions—but Jake would get to register his protest. And if this movie screwed up, Jake Keller would get credit for his warnings.

"Sure," Keller said easily. "See you later."

He turned to leave, and Tom followed him.

"See you later, Eleanor."

"Of course." All traces of their earlier intimacy were wiped away, but she had expected that. He was probably regretting it right this minute. "Tom, try and skim through that script before the meeting if you get a chance. It's really hot. David Tauber at SKI is representing the writer."

"I thought Kevin Scott had all their writers."

"All except this. Tauber found her himself."

"He did?" Tom grinned, amused. "That kid's in a hurry. OK, I'll check it out now."

Eleanor watched his retreating back, realizing with a slight misgiving that already David Tauber's name carried some weight. Tom was more inclined to read it quickly because Tauber had found it. Well, that made sense—it was David Tauber who had brought in Zach Mason, and this was his movie. Fred Florescu was the *most* important element of the deal, and Fred was Sam's personal client, but still . . . if Hollywood was a jungle, in the nineties it belonged to jackals like David. And she noticed that Tom hadn't responded to her assurance that this screenplay was terrific. She knew him well enough by now to see when he was reserving judgment.

Eleanor glanced at the clock on her computer. Quarter of nine. The big Artemis production meeting was in just over an hour.

Damn, she hoped Tom liked it. But even if he didn't, in this meeting she was going to back her own judgment. She had found the right script for Mason and Florescu, and when they had cast the female lead—Julia Roberts, Jennifer Jason Leigh?—they were going to have a smash.

Despite her ragged emotions, Eleanor Marshall felt a small thrill. She was going to exercise her new power for the first time. This was scary. This was exhilarating. This was the *movie business*.

It was everything she had always wanted.

Well, almost everything.

chapter 11

As she threw open the last window, the scent hit her. First thing in the morning, and the air in the Hollywood Hills was fragrant with jasmine, hibiscus, she didn't know what else. Up here she was above the smog line, and the sky was humid, not exactly threatening to rain but allowing myriads of minute water droplets to hang shimmering in the air in a transparent, warm mist. Birds were singing, a sound so unfamiliar to Roxana—Ms. City Girl numero uno—that for a second she hadn't known what it was. Standing there, looking out at LA, a peaceful grid laid out below her, silent from this height, she felt a strange sensation. Happiness.

Roxana shook her lovely head in a movement so graceful it was a shame she had no audience for it, her long black hair swinging behind her in a pigtail, her normally pale cheeks flushed from her morning workout. Her first morning in LA out of a hotel, and already she was getting weak and stupid.

David had found her this place and she had to admit he'd done a good job. The house was perched on a nearly secret ledge high in the hills above Sunset, protected by cleverly grown hedges from any long-range lenses or curious fans with binoculars. It had been designed by an unknown but very talented architect, probably back in the thirties, and reequipped several times since. Now she had a Moroccan villa on the outside, all coffee-colored plaster and Hispanic white details, with a marble fountain playing day and night in the courtyard, and a New York penthouse on the inside, with a private gym, a home office complete with several phone lines, faxes, and a PowerMacintosh, the ultimate in electronic-sensor security systems, and plenty of natural light. Not to mention mirrors. The swimming pool was sunk in the middle of the central reception room, another detail she had approved of. Roxana didn't like outdoor pools. Any schmuck with a helicopter could gawk at you.

The rent was astronomical, but so what? She was astronomically rich. And very soon she'd be astronomically famous, too. When the call had come from Tauber last night it hadn't surprised her in the least. Everybody else, perhaps, but not her. This was what she'd come out to LA to do, and she was going to succeed, of course. She always did.

She was Roxana Felix, and she always got what she wanted.

⬥

"And what did you tell her?"

Sam Kendrick tensed, not liking Eleanor's tone. Fifteen years as one of the best agents in Hollywood had given him near-psychic powers in reading people's moods. And Eleanor was pissed off. He scrambled to recover his ground.

"Actually, Eleanor, David called her. He told her she'd been short-listed for the part of Morgan. Which you told us. Nothing more, nothing less."

"Uh-huh." The president of Artemis tapped one manicured nail on the papers in front of her. They all bore inset stories on the front page with headlines like "Roxana Starts Acting Career," "Silver Screen Supermodel," and the worst, the *New York Times*, ran "Roxana beats out Julia, Winona, et al."

Sam stifled his own fury. God, how he agreed with Eleanor. It was the most unprofessional thing he had ever seen. But he simply could not show his feelings to his old friend. The bitch was, after all, his client.

"Eleanor, I swear, we had nothing to do with this."

"It puts me in an extremely difficult position, Sam. As you know, we're still considering casting. We haven't got back to Bridget's people, or Jennifer's people, or Julia's people *or* Winona's people. And they read this in the fucking press."

Sam was on red alert. Eleanor never swore, she was more decorous than a whore at a christening.

"I'll speak to her, Eleanor, I promise."

"You do that." She was still angry. "I swear, I should just issue a release saying the whole thing is a fabrication by your client. But just in case we *do* cast her, I'll have to keep quiet about it. For now."

"OK." Kendrick nodded his head, accepting blame.

"You'd better go, Sam. I have to make my apologies to Mike Ovitz and Jeff Berg and every other major player Roxana Felix just spat on." Eleanor took a deep breath, composing herself. "And Sam—make sure you see her yourself. Don't send that little jerk Tauber in to do it. I want someone who's gonna give Ms. Felix a lesson in how we do business in the movie industry, not crawl up her ass instead of kicking it."

Despite himself, Sam grinned.

"OK, Eleanor, I'll see to it personally. It won't happen again."

"It had better not."

She was the Ice Queen again, cool and menacing. Kendrick almost regretted the reversion to type as he shook her hand and left. It was kind of interesting to see Eleanor Marshall steamed up, even if he was on the receiving end. He'd always imagined Paul Halfin shoved her in the deep freeze when she got home nights, to warm her up a little bit.

Eleanor dismissed Sam from her thoughts almost before he had left, dialing CAA and ICM and everybody else to offer her apologies, smooth practiced words disassociating Artemis from any involvement with these stories. They couldn't afford to offend any of the big female stars—no studio could. Female actors were still paid far less than their male counterparts, but their cents on the male dollar crawled up every year. Something she, Eleanor, welcomed, although she'd never paid a woman star a cent more than she had to. If equality happened for actresses, it would happen naturally, when market forces dictated. You couldn't bring feminism or any other agenda into it. Business was business. It was that attitude that had ensured, at long last, that she got to sit in the president's office. And it was that attitude that now forced her to look at the Roxana situation with as much detachment as she could bring to it.

God, it made her mad, the way the woman obviously thought she could just walk all over Artemis and SKI. She was incredibly beautiful and incredibly arrogant. And no Meryl Streep, either. She thought that lovely face was her passport through life, and Eleanor dearly longed to show her otherwise, to rule her out for this part and show her up in every major paper that was fawning over her today.

But she couldn't do it.

Roxana, Roxana, Roxana. That was all she'd heard for a week. As soon as the project had been green-lighted, David Tauber was calling her twenty times a day, local press and TV shows had asked for her response to the rumor, and Tom Goldman was suddenly insisting that she test with Zach for the part. Eleanor had shrugged her shoulders and agreed. After all, the original tests of Roxana that Sam had sent over weren't *dreadful*, even if they also weren't good enough. With the male star making his acting debut, *plus* a first-time screenwriter, she'd wanted to play it safe with the female lead. After all, they had a lot of money riding on this production. As it was, Sam Kendrick International was looking at a fat package deal for the director, star, and scriptwriter. And Jake Keller had raised objections at literally every stage of the process, from the first production meeting to the marketing budget. Eleanor had overruled him, but effectively Jake had forced her to put her ass on the line. She'd had to sit there and watch Tom Goldman, magisterial chairman and CEO, observing the polite duels of his two most senior execs as though from the heights of Mount Olympus, not taking sides, just taking notes. Standard Hollywood-mogul practice; Tom neither blamed nor praised *Triple Feature*, and that way he could take all the credit if the movie was a smash, and disassociate himself if it bombed. Every senior guy played it that way, and she had tried not to take it personally. But it still hurt. *Triple Feature* was her first project, she could tell he loved the script as much as she did, and she longed for Tom to back her. Maybe because there would have been something deeply sexual in the idea of him throwing caution to the winds for her sake.

But that was dreaming.

At any rate, it had amazed her to see Tom getting involved in casting matters; he was far too busy for that. The creative side wasn't the realm of the chairman; he was the one who concentrated on making them look good to their shadowy lords and masters on Wall Street. Still, if he wanted Roxana Felix to test, so be it. He was her boss. And he had been quite insistent on the matter; why, she couldn't figure out.

"Eleanor, you must be insane. All these no-name people—"

"I wouldn't call Zach Mason a no-name." she'd said at the casting meeting, her light tone covering a steel reproof. Who the hell did Jake Keller think he was? She hid her satisfaction at the thought that Keller was criticizing Tom's suggestion in front of him, and not her own, as he imagined. Tom had spoken to her privately, so she gave out that the decision to test Roxana had come from her.

Jake therefore attacked it, right on cue.

"*Movie* no-name. OK, so he's a rock star. Like Mick Jagger and Sting and Madonna. *Great* box office."

"That's true. But we've seen Zach's tests as an actor, and we're all agreed he has an amazing talent."

"OK, maybe." Keller couldn't deny it; Mason had tested like God's gift, he acted as good as Olivier and he looked as good as Keanu Reeves. "But it's still a risk. And we didn't like Roxana's tests."

"That was before we had decided on *Triple Feature* as the script. The male lead is a rock star, the female lead a supermodel. They'd both be playing themselves. I think that's a strong angle."

"You can't seriously want to cast this on the basis of *publicity*," Jake sneered.

Eleanor remembered staring at his upper-class Waspy suit, his red hair combed in a neat center parting, and feeling a dislike of the intensity she normally reserved for Isabelle Kendrick and her coven of Beverly Hills ladies who lunch. She'd smoothed her Georges Rech pink silk skirt across her legs before answering him, a feminine, appealing gesture calculated to contrast with her next words.

"We're testing Roxana Felix tomorrow." She paused, to let that sink in. They should all take note, all those baby vice presidents eagerly watching the grown-ups fight. She was the president and she intended them to have no doubt about that. Jake Keller had ten years as a creative type and she'd come from marketing, and he intended to show up her creative "weakness" wherever and whenever he could. And if she showed any weakness whatsoever, he'd exploit it like a germ warfare expert faced with an open wound.

"Tomorrow morning. Jake, tests fall within your jurisdiction, so you can arrange it. I'll come to a screening in the afternoon; we can review everyone's tests together. Tom, will that be good for you?"

"That'll be fine. I don't have anything then I can't shift."

Tom had looked at her with just the faintest gleam of amusement and approval in his brown eyes, nodding his head slowly, in a way that made her heart skip over, and Jake Keller had gone the color of a beet.

"You OK with that, Jake?" she'd pressed him coolly.

"Sure. Fine."

He had to agree. He knew it, she knew it, everyone in the room knew it. And damn, maybe this was her nasty, male, aggressive streak, but—admit it—she'd really enjoyed rubbing his nose in it.

Walking into the darkened screening room had felt strange. All of a sudden Eleanor had a personal stake in Roxana Felix, a woman she hadn't particularly even wanted to test. It was a big deal, too; her first movie, a rock musician starring, an unknown screenwriter, and a huge budget. That much she would have to give Keller, the female lead was important. And they had looked at some of the biggest females in the industry. Competition to work with Zach and Fred was intense among a whole generation of actresses, Jordan Goldman's generation, the X-ers, to whom both director and star were pop-culture gods. The reaction had made Eleanor feel old and out of touch; she'd known Mason was a huge star, seen his sales figures and the rest of it, but she somehow had had no idea of the quasi-religious feeling the guy could inspire. For the twenty-somethings he was a prophet, their Bob Dylan. Weird. It was why people like Fred and Julia and Winona, all Hollywood royalty and way higher up the movie-business tree than Zach, were scrambling to work with him, even before they'd seen him act.

But as the various lovely faces replaced each other on screen, testing with Mason, she'd had a sinking feeling in the pit of her stomach. It didn't *work*. Not with any of them. Oh, they were all great actresses and they all looked fine, even believable in the role of a supermodel. But the magic, the chemistry with Mason—that wasn't there. *Triple Feature* had to crackle with sexual energy. That was why only guys normally attended these tests for female leads in blockbuster movies—a woman had to chart high, not just on her acting ability, but on what was known on the lot as the "peter meter." Vulgar but effective, and for years Eleanor Marshall had not been required to attend. Well, they couldn't stop her now. Now she was president. So now she got to sit in this dark baby cinema with the boys, watching unhappily as actress after actress triggered off little more than polite murmurs. Great skill, no sizzle. For *Triple Feature*, that wasn't gonna work.

And then, last, they'd shown Roxana's test.

Instant reaction.

As the camera panned onto Morgan, the girlfriend, making her way backstage, every man in the room shifted on his chair. Roxana was wearing jeans and a T-shirt, but as she strutted into the center of the screen, emanating arrogance and boredom, she was as graceful and deadly as a lioness. A lioness in heat. Mason's response to her was something else, his eyes raking over her chest and crotch as they started to run the fight scene, stripping her with his eyes so blatantly that Eleanor, to her astonishment, found herself getting aroused, a silken line of sexual heat trailing down her belly. Now Roxana made to slap him round the face and Mason caught her arm viciously, pinning her up against a crate. She twisted free, defying him, the look upon her face so feral that any minute you expected her to draw back her lips and snarl at him. The excited babble of the male executives stilled, the sound of their breathing heavy in the room. Zach and Roxana went through their lines on screen, but Eleanor could see that nobody was listening to anything but the body language. Desire seemed to rise so strongly between the two of them that she almost felt as if she'd walked into somebody's bedroom. You expected to see them abandon their lines any second and just go to it, right there. Involuntarily, Eleanor found herself looking round for Tom Goldman, wanting to see his reaction, wanting to be near him while she felt like this. Warm, slow feelings trawled across her crotch, as though a feather-light hand were stroking her there, as though Tom were breathing softly on the nape of her neck. She was actually wet. The sexual energy on screen was so strong she felt like holding up a match, to see if it would ignite. Was she imagining things, or had the crotch on Zach Mason's pants got tighter? And were Roxana Felix's high, tight nipples contracting under that cotton T-shirt?

As the test faded to darkness, Eleanor Marshall listened to her male colleagues consciously control their breathing, and smiled to herself.

Fuck you, Jake Keller. This movie's gonna work.

They'd announced no decision then and there, of course. Too much of an insult to all the other candidates. Eleanor had merely remarked that it seemed an interesting performance, and Tom had agreed with her, and then everybody had gone back to work. But privately, the casting of Morgan was a given.

Which was why, even though there had been no announcement of casting and her behavior was unforgivable, Eleanor Marshall knew that she wasn't going to slap Roxana down.

Roxana Felix was their new star.

Eleanor finished up her call to Mike Ovitz, groveling abjectly in apology, and quickly pressed the red light on her phone. Tom Goldman buzzing her.

"Have you seen Sam?"

"Yeah. He's going to talk to her. I told him to do it himself."

Goldman grunted. "Good. Well, I think we better confirm it as soon as possible. If we keep them hanging on for another two days and then announce Roxana, it'll look like we're dicking them around."

"Language," said Eleanor automatically. "OK, Tom. I've just got off the phone with CAA, so let me leave it an hour and I'll put out an announcement. Yes?"

He laughed, a low, warm sound.

"Sure, I'll leave it to your impeccable judgment."

There was a moment's silence.

"Are you coming to Isabelle Kendrick's party tomorrow?" Tom asked casually.

"Only for ten minutes. We're just going to show up and leave." Eleanor smiled into the receiver. "If I cut the whole thing, Isabelle and—" She nearly said, "And Jordan," but stopped herself just in time. "And the rest of them will stick all their little voodoo pins into me."

"Oh." He sounded disappointed, hesitant. "I was hoping you'd stay longer. We might get a chance to talk."

Eleanor felt herself tense up, that same sick-excitement feeling she'd had with Tom yesterday morning.

She had to test it.

"But we talk all the time."

"Not about business."

"We get to see each other socially, though. We all played tennis together only last weekend."

A pause.

"I meant on our own."

A jolt of electricity surged through her.

She tried to control it. As casually as she could manage, she said, "Do you mean that at a big party we'd be able to slip away and talk?"

"Yeah. Exactly." He was grunting again, obviously embarrassed.

Eleanor thought the sound of her own heart beating in her ears might deafen her. She couldn't speak.

"Whatever," Tom said. "I was just hoping you would stay."

"I'll stay," Eleanor said.

He hung up.

For a full minute, Eleanor Marshall gazed at the phone, attempting to still the wild, strange pulse racing through her blood.

❖

David Tauber had taken over her life. Megan didn't know which part was the most wonderful—how he turned up in his red charger and whisked her away from her shitty little job; the champagne and pink roses that he sent her the next morning; or actually signing the contract in the marbled offices of SKI, under the impassive gaze of Sam Kendrick himself and the baleful stare of Kevin Scott—a contract which, David had taken great pleasure in telling her, was for $250,000. *A quarter of a million dollars!* Tina and Jeanne had been utterly blown away, unable to stifle their jealousy even for the sake of sucking up to her, which was what she'd expected. Maybe it was un-nineties, but Megan had enjoyed it when she saw their mouths drop open. Although it was nothing compared to the pleasure she had in driving down to Mr. Chicken in her newly leased BMW to pick Stacey up on her lunch break. Bob Jenkins had tried to slime his way back into her good graces, apologizing for "being a little short with you" and attempting to kiss her butt—"We all knew you would make it, Megan. We could tell the second you walked in the door, *you* were gonna be someone special." At which she'd turned round, in the middle of the hushed diner, and said loudly and sweetly, "Unlike you, Bob, you pimply little fuck."

Well, it was true what they said.

Revenge is sweet.

❖

"Tell me you're kidding." Dec's soft voice crackled with excitement. "Smile, you're on *Candid Camera*. Right?"

"No." She was still almost hyperventilating. "Oh, Dec, it feels like I'm dreaming."

"He's sold your script? Not optioned it?"

"No! It has a green light! They're actually gonna make the movie!"

Megan hugged herself as she babbled into the receiver. She was holding her contract in her hand while she talked to him, clutching it to her. In case it turned back into a pumpkin at the stroke of midnight.

"Your agent did *that?*" Dec asked with deep respect. "I thought it took years to happen."

"Normally it does." She sighed happily. "Oh, God, he's so wonderful. He's changing my life."

"What does he look like?" Dec asked curiously. "Some ugly, money-grabbing troll with a cocaine sniff and melanoma, I'll bet."

"You lose." Megan grinned as Tauber's perfect body, golden skin, and chiseled face flashed in front of her eyes. "I wouldn't let you within a million miles of him."

"That good, huh?"

"Better," Megan said.

Megan could hardly believe it was true. She had to pinch herself every time she got up in the morning, look around her, and wonder if this could actually be happening. It still took her a second or two to figure out where she was; the new apartment was so clean and spacious compared to what she was used to, and it was as silent as the grave. Apart from the traffic rushing by, of course, but you tuned that out in a city. No, what she meant was she didn't have to hear Jeanne and Tina bickering anymore, didn't have to wake up to find all the hot water gone and some unshaven jerk that Tina had brought home with her sitting in their kitchenette drinking coffee out of her mug. This place was all hers; it had a fully equipped kitchen, soft carpets in every room, and even a little home office for her to write in. David had found it for her, and when he'd shown her through the door she had to fight back the impulse to tears.

"It's beautiful, David! But I can't afford it."

"Sure you can." He'd been so certain, so confident, Megan looked at his immaculately tailored suit and platinum Rolex and felt like an idiot for even suggesting it. Of *course* she could afford it, or David wouldn't have leased it for her.

"We're paying rent and amenities directly out of your account. You don't have to worry about it. You don't have to worry about anything."

"Out of my account?"

"We set up a facility with Norman Drew for you. They'll be your accountants now. You'll get on great with them, I always use them for my new clients."

Her accountants! She hadn't known whether to laugh or cry. What would Mom say if she could see her now? Plump, plain Megan, the perennial loser, always the last one that the family thought about, installed in a chic little apartment of her own in the heart of Century City, LA. Megan knew she should have called back to tell them the news, but somehow she'd been putting it off. Her family were normally so discouraging, deep down inside she was afraid that they might snipe at her, and worse, that she might care. She didn't want any of the bloom taken off this particular rose just yet.

"*All* your new clients?" she couldn't help asking. "Does that include Zach Mason?"

David laughed at her indulgently. Damn, what a sexy laugh, Megan thought. Sated, as if he just had sex. But then everything about David Tauber made her think of sex.

"It does." He craned his head around to look inside her bedroom, noticing her Dark Angel and Oasis posters tacked up on the wall. Megan always stuck those posters up first, wherever she was—they helped keep her rooted. But for the first time she felt ashamed. He would think she was too old for posters. "I see you're a fan."

She nodded, blushing.

"So now you share accountants. It'll give you something else to talk about besides music when I introduce you."

"When you introduce us?" Megan repeated, holding her breath.

"Sure. At Isabelle Kendrick's party tomorrow night. I asked Sam if I could bring you along. Everybody will be there—Zach Mason, Fred Florescu, Sam, the Artemis execs in charge of your project."

Her project!

"And me." David gave her that special, lazy smile, his polished white teeth dazzling against his tanned skin. In that Gucci suit that pulled taut across his impressive chest, he reminded Megan of every college football hope she'd ever seen, or of some gorgeous male model right out of an Armani campaign. She couldn't dwell on her own bad skin or her plumpness when she was with him. There was no chance to consider anything physical except David. He was so perfect she found it tough to look away from him.

As though aware of her thoughts, Tauber winked at her.

"I'm no Zach Mason, I know. But you'll let me be your escort to this party, won't you, Megan? I can't wait to show off my latest client."

He wants to show me off? Megan thought, wanting to hug herself.

"I'd love to go with you, David," she said shyly.

"Great." Another dazzling smile, and he was turning to go. "Oh, and Megan—" He handed her an American Express gold card, made out in her name. "You should go buy a new dress. No offense, but this is a serious party and I don't think what you have there will cut it." He glanced neutrally at her plain black dress, her one "good" outfit that was hanging by itself in an open closet.

"No. Sure. Of course," Megan said hastily, burning with embarrassment.

"Terrific." He raised her hand to his mouth and kissed it, and the slight pressure of his lips burned on her skin. "I'll see you tomorrow."

And he'd gone, leaving Megan alone with a fifteen-thousand-dollar line of credit, one day to get ready for her entree into her new life, and not a soul in the world she could talk to.

chapter 12

The Kendrick mansion was in complete chaos. Only two hours to go to the party, and a horde of immaculately groomed waiters were swarming over the grounds like black-and-white bees, radios crackling like the Secret Service as the party director relayed his orders to various parts of the ground.

Standing on the terrace, Sam Kendrick sighed inwardly. He didn't understand the subtleties of party giving and he never would. The whole place looked fine to him: mini-orchestra set up in the ballroom, chamber quartet out by the pool, which was covered in a thousand minute sandalwood candles, floating across it like perfumed fireflies, not to mention the food and different types of champagne set up all over the house and grounds. His wife had never done things by halves. There would be caviar in ice sculptures laid out all over the place, together with real truffles, plates of oysters, dim sum, and Belgian chocolates, all the normal Hollywood tidbits; but Isabelle eschewed the trend toward poolside buffets in favor of a formal sit-down dinner, with the seating arrangements worked out more carefully than most of his contracts. The pillars out front of the house were all wreathed with pink roses, solid columns of color, and the rest of the flowers appeared to be a kind of weird mix of roses, orchids, violets, and mistletoe, imported from northern Europe and flown in specially by the florist.

The effect was certainly magnificent, Sam thought wryly. Jeez, they had probably scented the air above the whole of Beverly Hills this evening. *And* provided it with a free New Age sound track—talk about stress reduction, Isabelle had wreathed their entire garden with miles upon miles of the most delicate Japanese bells, strung on invisible silk threads, so that the slightest breeze provoked a gorgeous whispering music. He knew Isabelle would have liked to hire a few peacocks to strut around the grounds, but Elizabeth Martin had done that for one of her bashes in New York a few years back, and Isabelle would as soon call in McDonald's for her catering as imitate Elizabeth.

Sam grimaced. Maybe it was his biggest failing in their marriage, that he would never make as much as Alex Martin, the oil billionaire, and thus never enable Isabelle to throw the kind of party she would really enjoy. His budget didn't stretch to flying their guests to a tropical island for some end-of-hop beachcombing. Nonetheless, Isabelle considered Elizabeth her only rival, so peacocks were out. Instead she had, despite his misgivings, brought in sixteen tiger cubs which were tethered to different pillars and sculptures on very short leashes, their collars studded with diamonds. Insurance was costing him a fortune, and although the little bastards were semisedated, Sam didn't trust beasts that grew up to prey on human flesh. He had enough of those at work.

"Excuse me, sir," gasped a waiter, staggering past him with a bowl of beluga so heavy it made Sam's wallet ache just thinking about it.

These parties were important to his position in town, vitally important. Every year he added another stack of favors in his credit ledger by granting invites to actors and directors whose wives were desperate to attend. Isabelle had worked hard at making herself a social force in the city, whatever the hell that meant. It gave him a nice feeling of male superiority not to know exactly. All these charity committees and thousand-dollar-a-plate dinners. Hospital boards and museum-benefactor lists. All total bullshit, but that was the way things worked. The wives wanted to join the right committee, they had to be on the right side of Isabelle. And that gave him more pull with their husbands, it let SKI punch above its weight. You never knew when that might be important. In their recent lean patch, Sam was uncomfortably aware, it had been vital.

Well, that was all over now.

Sam fiddled with his tux in the scented air. Maybe it *was* a good thing that Isabelle was so obsessive about this party. Everybody would be here to congratulate him on his latest big score—Artemis Studios presenting *Triple Feature*, a Fred Florescu production, starring Zach Mason and Roxana Felix. Screenplay by Megan What's Her Name. A great, big, fat Sam Kendrick International *package deal*.

Kendrick smiled to himself. He was back in the game.

❖

Megan twisted in front of her new mirror. Was this OK? She couldn't *believe* she'd spent this much money on *one dress*. Four hundred dollars!

More than a month's rent back at the Venice apartment. And she still wasn't sure it looked right.

It was another long number in black. When you weren't sure, black was the only choice, but this was a bit more formal than her old "good" gown that David had heaped such scorn on. It came right down to the floor for a start, hiding her still-plump legs, and then gathering in gently at the waist before flaring up with a built-in push-up bra to give her some semblance of a decent cleavage. In San Francisco, Megan had always been faintly proud of her breasts; a good 34C cup, and Rory or whoever had always seemed impressed. Here in Los Angeles, home of Woman as Art Form, Megan felt flat-chested as well as dumpy.

Still, this dress went some way to remedying that. It was exquisite— she'd nearly passed out when she learned the price, but it was worth it. Made of gorgeous silk, it was bias-cut and it moved with a swing. Megan had purchased a pair of silk heels to match it, trying not to glance down at the amount she was signing for. They had made her feet look so hot, slimming her ankles and throwing a whole new gait into the way she walked.

Good enough to meet Zach Mason?

Megan flushed from sheer excitement. She had no idea how she'd react. Zach Mason, long black hair, predator eyes. Genius.

There was an involuntary twitch between her legs just at the thought of it. Megan had managed to catch Dark Angel live sixteen times. Scrimped and saved for the tickets. Turned up with friends and a six-pack, caught the magic in the scented, pumping darkness of the clubs and amphitheaters.

But Megan was alone when Zach started singing. A face in the crowd, staring up at him. Adoring. Believing.

Once—at the Stone?—Megan thought he'd looked her way. Just for a second. But she'd never forgotten the burning in her heart as his wolf eyes locked on hers.

It felt like destiny.

I was just a kid.

Megan shrugged and returned to her mirror.

She'd put on new L'Oréal makeup, sweeping blusher under the chin and cheekbones to give her face more definition and dabbing white eyeshadow underneath the brow as Declan had taught her. It was supposed to make you look more alive. There was no jewelry, of course, but perhaps they'd all assume she was aiming for the simple, sophisticated look, Megan thought hopefully.

Her reflection stared back at her from the mahogany frame. Not bad. No true Angeleno beauty of course, but not bad all the same. She'd lost six pounds since leaving Mr. Chicken, and though she was still overweight, most of the excess fat was hidden under the forgiving sweep of her skirt. The heels almost made her look tall, and her hair, which had been set at a beauty parlor earlier in the day, fell in loose, soft curls to her shoulders. She looked young and pretty. Feminine.

If Dec and Trey and the others could see me now, she thought, they'd all howl with laughter and then they'd say I sold out. Swapped my soul for a quarter of a million. Look at me! Back home, would I ever have given a damn what a bunch of suits thought of how I looked?

The door buzzer shrilled.

David!

Suddenly as nervous as a virgin, Megan went to open the door.

·:::·

Roxana Felix took all of five minutes to prepare for Isabelle Kendrick's party. She had selected her look the day she arrived: strappy silver Manolo Blahnik heels, bright red lipstick, to contrast perfectly with her pale skin and raven hair, and the simple cream shift dress that Alessandro Eco had used for the wedding gown in his Chicago collection. No jewels. No makeup, either; that was a particular arrogance, to show that she had skin so flawless she didn't even need foundation. Down her back, her long, jet-black hair flowed freely, shining and full of body like some ad for the world's most expensive shampoo.

She was traveling to the party in Jordan Goldman's limousine and she had no doubt that even sexy little Jordan would be sick with envy when she caught sight of her. She looked even more breathtaking than usual. If that was possible.

·:::·

"You look great," Paul said automatically, coming out of the bathroom with one hand on his bow tie.

"Do I?" Eleanor asked. "Do I really?"

Her partner turned, surprised by the nervous tension in her voice. Her normal response was "So do you." Which was fine by him; why waste time on flowery compliments and checking each other out? They already lived together.

Eleanor was pirouetting in front of the mirror like a nervous teenager. Actually, she *did* look great. It was a new dress, a floating, romantic number in dusty pink chiffon, with a scoop-collar neckline dusted over with tiny rosebuds in scarlet satin. Her icy-blond hair was swept upward in some elegant French style, and drop diamond earrings glittered at her cheek, a matching necklace sparkling exquisitely against her delicate collarbone. Pink satin shoes he could only just see peeped out from under the hem of her gown, and her makeup was subtle and understated.

"Yes. You look . . ." He searched rustily for some poetic word. "Ravishing."

"You don't think I look too young? Mutton dressed as lamb?" Eleanor asked, anxiously.

Paul Halfin glanced at her. What was getting into her tonight? This was his wife-to-be, the queenly president of Artemis. Not to mention one of the most impeccable dressers in the city. Jumpy nerves were simply not her style.

"You're only thirty-eight, for God's sake, Eleanor. You're a young woman."

Not as young as Jordan Goldman, Eleanor thought.

"You look lovely, dear. Really."

"Thanks, Paul," said Eleanor, and she wondered why his compliments made her feel so guilty.

·:⬦:·

Tom Goldman shifted on his bed to get a better look at what his wife was doing. Her tongue had ceased licking his balls for a second, but he didn't care. One pleasure was replaced by another as he watched her, eyes shut tight kneeling in front of him, slip her right hand across the downy mass of curls in between her supple thighs, rubbing her fingers backward and forward over herself, the knuckles suddenly glistening in their soft bedroom light, slick with her own moisture. His cock throbbed in response. Jordan always knew how to do such hidden, wicked things, it made him harder than a baseball bat. Opening one eye to check his reaction, Jordan grabbed his dick in her free left hand and started to tease him, opening and closing her fingers in a fluttering movement, then sliding up and down him with perfect rhythm, playing with herself, knowing he was watching her, mesmerized. A bead of pearly liquid dewed the tip of Tom's straining cock and he moaned, the normal signal, so she finished herself off in front of him with two deep circular thrusts, knelt forward, and took him in her mouth, as deeply as she could, sucking him hard, strongly, not allowing the pace of pressure to slip. Tom's last conscious thought was to thank God for one woman who understood that if he'd reached a certain point he wanted to come, not be taken back down and then brought up again or whatever . . . It was never as strong if you did it like that . . . *Oh, God* . . .

His back arching as though in agony, Tom Goldman lifted himself half off the bed, thrust into his wife's throat, and came.

Jordan waited barely a second and then spat him out, turning her face aside. She reached fastidiously for a box of tissues she kept next to the bed and wiped her mouth, grimacing with distaste. Goldman watched as she went to the bathroom, reaching for the mouthwash, his hard-on shrinking almost as quickly as it had arrived. Somehow, after sex, he always felt older. More disgusting. As though she was a hooker, or he was a dirty old man, not her lawfully wedded husband.

Mentally, Goldman chided himself as he reached for his shirt and pants. He should say *making love*, not *having sex*. After all, their child might be conceived on any one of these encounters.

He tried to ignore the fact that at the moment of climax, it had been Eleanor Marshall's face he had imagined. And not that of his gorgeous wife.

Jordan emerged from the bathroom, dressed and ready to go in a tailored Yves Saint Laurent pantsuit, a neat Chanel purse swinging from her left shoulder.

"Come on honey, let's go. I promised Roxana we'd pick her up at half past eight."

"So we'll be ten minutes late." She looked cute in those silk pants; they hugged her ass. Tom reached for her. "Once more, for luck."

She swatted his hand away as though it were an irritating fly.

"Tom! We can't be late. You know Roxana, she won't wait, she'll just call a limo service. And I *want* to arrive with her. It will be *such* a coup. You know? Because she promised to get me some sponsorship from *Vogue* for the next gun control party! Isn't that wonderful? And we did go to school together . . ."

Goldman listened to her chatter on, his mind already elsewhere, desire totally evaporated.

"Tom, are you listening to me?"

"Sure, honey, sure." This was an important party; they had a movie at SKI now. And Isabelle's parties were always important. He didn't want to argue with his wife tonight.

Besides which, if he was lucky, he'd get to talk to Eleanor alone.

Suddenly, Tom Goldman couldn't wait.

"Let's go," he said, smoothing his jacket down.

⋯⋰⋯

Eight P.M. exactly and everything was in place. Not a servant, not a leaf out of place, not a ripple on any one of their four hundred Irish linen tablecloths could be seen to mark the cyclone of activity Sam had witnessed just half an hour before. My God, it *is* like a military operation, Sam thought. In fact, scrap that. No military operation was ever that efficient these days, not with that asshole Clinton in charge. At any rate, their house had been transformed in just a few hours into Isabelle's personal Arabian Nights fantasy. It was perfumed, it was belled, and it was wreathed in flowers and glittering with gems, like some doe-eyed houri in a pasha's harem. For a second, Kendrick imagined Roxana Felix like that, robed in see-through silk, her long black hair caught in a diaphanous veil, chained to a jeweled collar at the foot of his couch. He felt his groin grow warm and heavy with blood at the thought, desire tugging at his crotch with sharp little fingers. Yeah, on another planet that would be nice, he thought. A doubly pleasant way to take his revenge. Jesus, that bitch was running rings around him! First the little game with the PR. Then she has Isabelle nagging at him on her behalf, and Isabelle was not an easy woman to ignore. Then somehow, and he was still trying to figure out exactly how, she gets Tom Goldman to push her at Artemis. Topping it off, she issues a bullshit release to the press before she's been cast, and Eleanor Marshall is eating him, Samuel Jacob Kendrick, for her low-fat lunch. Then somehow, despite all the above, she manages to get herself cast! The woman was un-believable. And he had sworn blind to Eleanor that he was personally gonna put a rocket up her ass.

What a joke. He'd called every half hour yesterday, and she'd simply re-fused to take his calls. "Sam, I'm so sorry, I'm busy right now." "I'm just in the shower." "I'll call you right back." Then she'd switched on the machine.

Even now, a whole day later, his blood was still boiling.

Well, he knew she was coming tonight. With his wife's latest protégé, Jordan Goldman. And that would mean she couldn't run from him for-ever.

Right on cue, Isabelle appeared beside him at the top of the steps in a Balenciaga original as the first headlights appeared at the end of their drive.

Banishing all thoughts of anger and lust, Sam composed his face into a rare smile.

Showtime!

❖

Megan Silver clutched onto her agent's arm like it was a voodoo talis-man. David Tauber—she'd only known him for four days, but that was four days longer than anyone else she could see.

A sense of complete unreality had descended on her. She couldn't stop looking around, her head turning constantly, as though she expected the whole place to shimmer and disappear like a desert mirage. Back in San Francisco she'd always been the clever one, intellectually self-assured, cyni-cal, worldly. A perfect nineties twenty-something, a girl who'd been raised on grunge and political apathy. She might not have made any money, but she was cool. She wore Caterpillar sneakers and Veruca Salt T-shirts and nobody fucked with her. She was in with the in crowd.

But here Megan felt totally lost. Hundreds of people thronged past her: big, powerful men who walked nowhere and strode everywhere; shorter, meaner-looking ones whom everybody else seemed to be afraid of; and women, crowds of women, practically every one of them sporting gemstones the size of small birds' eggs, floating past her, pushing past her, in clouds of taffeta and chiffon and the finest moiré silk, in designer outfits so signature that even she could not fail to recognize a few—sparkling Versace designed for a wearer thirty years younger, immaculately fitted Chanel, impossible for anyone to mistake, Gucci with its signature buttons. Every one of them had tight, clear skin that she imagined would crack if they laughed, And every one of them moved with utter self-possession, accepting a crystal flute filled with pink champagne from a waiter like she might reach for a cold Bud, or turning down caviar or truffles as though they were M&M's. Megan guessed they might add an ounce or two to all those 110-pound frames.

From the second David had helped her out of their hired limo Megan had ceased to feel successful. Looking around at her fellow guests, she knew what she was. The smallest of the small fry. Unsophisticated. Fat. And poor.

"You're doing fine. Relax," David whispered in her ear, steering her toward the buffet.

"Oh, David, I can't eat anything," Megan said miserably. She was twenty-four, and she felt heavy and unattractive, as though her youth was a cruel joke. What good did it do her to be twenty-four when there were women here with thighs barely bigger than her upper arms?

"Sure you can," David told her, a brilliant smile permanently fixed on his face, adding, "Best go for the caviar and the fruit. No fat that way. And skip the breads. You don't need complex carbohydrates right now."

"OK," she said, feeling fatter than ever. But *grateful*, of course. David had been so good to her, and now he was going to help her with her diet . . . and David should know. He was a prime physical specimen, Megan thought, as she snuck a glance in at her companion, waving and nodding at four different players a minute. He'd told her his tux was from Ralph Lauren's latest collection, and it certainly looked stunning on him—the wool was the darkest, deepest blue, practically black, but with just enough color to set off his hazel eyes and blond hair, and it was flawlessly cut, fitting his large, athletic frame to perfection.

Being with David was the only thing that gave her any reassurance, Megan thought. At least she didn't have to be ashamed of her escort. The dress she'd been so proud of earlier now looked as though it had walked right out of a Frisco thrift store, but nobody would notice the dress while she was with David. Moguls and movie stars swarmed all around her, but she knew she was with the best-looking guy in the room.

"Here." He handed her a small plate heaped with glistening fish eggs, a slice of lemon, and a minute silver dish of sliced strawberries and goose-berries. There were two delicate silver spoons on the side. "And take a glass of champagne, too."

"Can I?" Megan asked doubtfully.

"This is a celebration," David said generously. She felt his strong hand take her elbow, leading her deftly through the crowd to one of the rose-strewn tables on the terrace, the area nearby flickering and dancing with shadows thrown up from the hundreds of little candles drifting across the darkened surface of the pool.

He picked up the lemon and squeezed it deftly over the caviar, a thin trail of juice trickling over his palm and wrist. Megan felt need stir in her groin. She hadn't been touched since she left Rory, not that any man would want her. Still, she had a strong urge to bend her head toward him and lick him clean.

To her complete embarrassment, David looked up and caught her star-ing at him.

Megan blushed bright red.

He gave her a soft smile, and dug one of the silver spoons into the mound of caviar, scooping up a wet, shining pile of miniature black pearls, and held it out toward her.

"Try some of this."

Dutifully, Megan swallowed the caviar, taking it in her mouth as deli-cately as she could. Essence of salt fish and slime. Ugh.

"You like?" Tauber was asking her.

"Delicious," Megan said.

"It's an acquired taste." He can see right through me, Megan thought, sensing her blush deepen, but David was already on his feet. "And you'll get used to it. All my clients do. Within six months you'll be able to tell a good champagne vintage with your eyes shut. Come on, I have to intro-duce you to your new colleagues."

With a regretful glance at her untouched champagne, Megan followed him, unsteadily. Jesus Christ. She would never get used to high heels.

⋄⋄⋄

Jordan was burning up. She couldn't help it. They hadn't even gone into dinner yet and already she was being thoroughly upstaged! Every society wife she'd ever met was pressing Roxana to attend this dinner or that party; the news of her casting had gone round the room in twenty seconds, and all Jordan could hear was "the next Julia Roberts." As if the bimbo had one ounce of Julia's talent. And worse still was the way their husbands had started to jostle the Goldman party as if Roxana were some incredibly rare wild animal in danger of extinction before they'd had a chance to gawk.

They stared, they ogled, they paid her inane compliments on her dress, they asked about her new career. All the attentions that *she*, Jordan Cabot, was used to receiving—for the last eighteen months, she'd been the youngest woman at any high-powered party by a good ten years. And now she might as well be invisible.

Furiously, Jordan flashed Barry Diller a beaming smile and took a deep sip of her Roederer Cristal champagne. She noticed that Roxana, next to her, had not so much as glanced in the TV mogul's direction. But of *course* not, Jordan thought bitchily. Roxana waits for the Barry Dillers of this world to come to her.

She began flashing back to unpleasant memories of their shared school days at the Sacred Heart. Even there, she'd always been the prettiest girl at the convent—bar one, of course. Was she destined always to take the silver medal?

In the scented, darkened air, Jordan slipped her perfectly toned arm through her husband's. At least *Tom* wasn't fawning over Roxana, and she should know, because she'd watched him like a hawk from the moment the bitch had stepped gracefully into their limo. He had given her a once-over, of course, but in a cold, detached way. Jordan had seen him give other movie stars the same clinical look. He was checking her out for her box office potential, nothing more. In fact, while she'd been explaining all about the gun control dinner, Tom had interrupted them just once, asking her if she'd spoken to Sam Kendrick recently. And Roxana had smiled coolly and replied that no, she'd been too busy to speak to Sam, and after all, David Tauber was her agent.

Jordan had no idea what all that was about. But she was glad her husband didn't seem to care for the supermodel. That would have been all she needed.

"Sweetie."

Tom was bending down to her, whispering in her ear.

"Do you need me? I have to go and talk to Jake Keller about something."

He was amazed at the easy smoothness of the lie. Why didn't he just say Eleanor? Eleanor was his president of production. He talked with Eleanor all the time.

"Oh." Jordan gave him her best little-girl pout. "You know how I hate all your silly business talk. Well, don't be long."

"I won't."

Why did she have to act like that? It was stupid, Tom thought, almost angrily. Since when was she six years old?

"Come back soon. Me miss oo." She blew him a kiss from her full, perfectly lined lips.

Oy vey. Goldman turned away, sighing.

-:::-

Sam Kendrick moved fluidly around the room, working the groups Isabelle wasn't covering. Over the years they had this down to a fine art; Isabelle chatted with the players and female stars, he attended to the male stars and wives. It was exactly the opposite of what everybody expected, but it worked perfectly; the men gave him beaucoup Brownie points for being able to lay off business for one night—how many of them would be capable of the same thing?—and their wives, normally expected to just show up, shut up, and smile, were insanely flattered to have a heavy hitter, especially one as sexy as Sam Kendrick, ask their opinions as though he were actually interested. It bought him a lot of extra influence, and it was another social trick Isabelle had wised him up to. *Take care of the wives.* They won't forget it. And they'll push their husbands for you all year long.

The second trick was timing. You said as little as possible to as many people as possible; that way you could make an impression on everyone.

Sam glanced at the time on his subtly lit Cartier watch. He was making good progress.

Then, out of the corner of one eye, he saw Tom Goldman break away from the little throng of people crowding Roxana.

His blood pumped a little faster. Now was his chance. With a murmured excuse to the wife of some TV producer, Sam crossed the terrace.

"Ladies, gentlemen, would you excuse me?" he said loudly. "I have to monopolize this beautiful lady for a few seconds."

"Your latest client, right, Sam?" one of the suits inquired.

"She is indeed." He smiled proudly.

"Lucky dog," somebody else said, and there was general laughter as his guests moved away.

Roxana Felix leaned back a little against the marble pillar she was standing in front of, and regarded the head of her agency with a cold stare.

Sam looked. Then he looked again. And again.

In the soft light from the Japanese lanterns, her face and hair framed by a wreath of pale pink roses, Roxana Felix reminded him of a picture by those British painters—what were they called?—the Pre-Raphaelites. All pure white skin and silken, perfect black hair, her full mouth red as blood, her eyes dark as sin, and her slender, perfect figure, simultaneously hidden and revealed by the cream shift dress, the most tempting thing since Eve introduced Adam to harvesting. But no, maybe not. The way those Victorians had painted, their ladies seemed pure, ethereal, and ghostly. Roxana Felix was none of those things. She was everything he had seen on screen, everything that he'd been fantasizing about. Sex projected and oozed out of every tiny pore of her perfect skin. She was no cold, narcissistic mannequin. She was a flesh-and-blood woman and she conjured up images of the hottest fuck you would ever have in your life. Even the way she was standing right now, defiant and outraged, regarding him with such hostility. Her body seemed poised to strike, as graceful and deadly as a panther.

She was the most attractive woman he had ever seen in his life, and Sam Kendrick had seen a *lot* of attractive women.

Desire hit him like a lightning bolt. Savage. Intense. Astonishing.

"Are you done?"

She had a low, sensual voice, but the tone was absolute steel.

"Are you done, Mr. Kendrick? Do you think you could pick me out of the police lineup now?"

"We have to talk," Kendrick said firmly. He dragged his gaze back up to meet her eyes. Jesus Christ! Just because she'd been around the block in the fashion business didn't mean that some twenty-four-year-old baby was going to chew him, Sam Kendrick, out at his own party. He recognized that note in her voice. It was the same one he used to demolish his various underlings, or to poleaxe studio execs that were screwing with his clients. That was the tone of command, of a person used to authority. OK, so Roxana Felix had been boss in her world up to now. But this was a different universe and he was its resident god. This, she had to learn. This, he was going to make her learn. Sam Kendrick had not reached the summit of the game to surrender his authority to some sassy piece of ass.

"I *was* talking. To those gentlemen, whom you so rudely interrupted."

"Listen, Princess." He saw her eyes narrow in shock and anger, and felt adrenaline start to knot in his stomach. This was the tough bit; blasting the client without getting fired. You had to bluff, and you had to gamble on how badly they wanted whatever part. Poker with people. He'd always been an expert.

"You can hold court with the boys some other time."

"Who the hell do you think you are?" Roxana demanded, scarcely able to believe her ears. Sam Kendrick was just another salt-and-pepper suit. A looker, but so what? Did he think she was going to cut him any slack because he'd retained a little masculinity? Nobody, but *nobody*, spoke to her like that. Not anymore.

"I'm the head of SKI, Roxana. And if you want to stay represented by us, you'll shut the fuck up and listen to me."

She gave a disbelieving laugh. "My God. Do you think you're the only *agency* in this *city*?"

Kendrick looked her over, slowly.

"No. But we're the only agency with *Triple Feature*."

There was a long pause.

"I've been cast," she said finally. Defiantly.

Sam leaned toward her, a pleasant, businesslike smile on his face, so that anyone watching would think nothing of it. When he got close enough to smell the faint tang of cinnamon on her breath, he said softly, "And I can have you *un*cast. In ten seconds. With five words to Tom Goldman."

"You wouldn't do that," Roxana said, staring right back at him.

Doesn't give an inch, Sam thought admiringly. Very good.

A player less skilled than he was might even have been fooled. But Sam had been in the game too long not to notice the tiny tremor, the inability to control the breath, that gave away her horror at that idea.

Still speaking softly, he said, "Try me."

She didn't reply.

"The stunts you've been pulling with the press," Sam said. "I didn't like them, but I didn't care. When you know me a little better, you'll realize that nothing you can do will pressure me into anything." She looked sharply at him, and he gave her a knowing, indulgent smile. "You thought I didn't realize? Come on, baby. I'm forty-four. I've been doing this stuff since before you were born. But your cute little games aren't the point here. What *is* is that you put out a release to the press about getting cast before you were. Now, that embarrasses Artemis and it embarrasses me. And if you ever, *ever* do anything like that again, this will be the last big movie you ever make. Understand?"

Roxana felt humiliation crash over her like a tidal wave. She couldn't even look at Sam Kendrick as she nodded her head.

"OK. Good."

This was turning him on, Kendrick realized. She was too gorgeous to spar with like this and not want to fuck. Despite himself, his cock was hardening where he stood. He had to get away from her, or he'd be the chief talking point at his own goddamn party.

"I'm sure you're going to do us all proud in this picture, Roxana. See you later," he said in more normal tones, and strode off toward the dining room.

Momentarily alone—she could see all the tame suits waiting to swarm back in on her—Roxana Felix watched Sam Kendrick go.

Jesus, how ridiculous. She sensed something stir in her that she hadn't felt in years. Lust. Why? Just because Kendrick hadn't crumpled in front of her like every other guy? Or because he had that strong, wild look about him, that maleness, a sense of raw power, the real kind? Sam was a lion, whereas David was just a peacock. Roxana had been around the block enough times to know the difference. And it wasn't just money. She could wrap Howard Thorn round her manicured finger, but this one was the real deal. The dominant male.

As the fawning crowd engulfed her again, Roxana seethed under her designer silk, almost paralyzed with mortification. She could not and would not feel like that. Sam Kendrick had just insulted her. And Sam Kendrick would pay.

⸱⸱⸱❖⸱⸱⸱

Ten minutes to go, ten minutes till dinner. Tom Goldman thrust his way through the crowd, feeling the pressure pulse against his skin with every tick of his platinum Patek Philippe. Isabelle always held dinner bang on time, and he wanted to speak to Eleanor alone. Before they sat down. He knew that afterwards, he wouldn't get a chance; Isabelle had arranged for everybody working on the Mason/Florescu project to be seated at one table, and he, Tom, as studio head, would be expected to make all the introductions and steer the fucking boring small-talk conversation.

Guests rustled past him in designer tuxes, velvet gowns, tailored suits in silk jersey. Producers, agents, actors. Blondes, redheads, blue rinses, brunettes. Long hair, short hair, balding. And just about every one of them appeared to want to talk to him. Goldman smiled and muttered incoherently, said, "Great to see you," and, "Call the office tomorrow," at least twenty times, kept himself moving, his sharp eyes scanning the crowd for Eleanor. He had to speak to her; he didn't know why, he just had to. About Jordan. About the way he'd been thinking of her lately. Or whatever. Maybe that was too indiscreet. And yet he knew he had to talk to her, even if he had no idea what the hell he was going to say . . .

"Tom."

"Look, I can't talk right now," Goldman snapped, turning to see who was plucking at his sleeve. He stopped walking, half jumping out of his skin. "Eleanor!"

"Hey, it wasn't important. I'll catch up with you later."

"No, no, wait." He was nervous. Forty-five years old, with a woman he'd worked with for the last fifteen years, and he was nervous. Jesus. He passed a hand self-consciously across his thinning hair. "I was looking for you."

"You wanted to talk, right?" Eleanor said, feeling her heart speed up. "I thought we might take a walk into the grounds."

Away from the party. Away from all these people. OK, Goldman thought. You did deals totaling a hundred and ten million dollars last week. You can handle this.

"Sure. Let's go."

As he followed her down the Kendricks' alabaster steps, Tom flashed for a second onto the irony of this. He, Tom Goldman, the playboy, the man of a million women, each of them as pretty and forgettable as the next. Except Jordan, who was prettier than the rest and thus his wife. He'd never had a second's trouble with girls since he joined Artemis at twenty-five, straight out of Yale. Making forty-seven grand a year, and *that* was in the seventies. If he hadn't left a trail of broken hearts, exactly, he'd certainly left a trail of disappointed starlets, students, debs. Women got nervous around him, not the other way round.

They walked together along the raked gravel path that led to the nearest sculptured grotto, silently, in the aromatic darkness, the hubbub and laughter of the gala behind them. Goldman realized that Eleanor was the only woman he knew who wouldn't have to ask where they were going. She knew the Kendricks' gardens as well as he did; she'd been a senior movie executive for more than a decade.

Just as they turned off the path into the little marble sanctuary, with its polished oak bench and statue of a rearing unicorn, he heard Jordan calling his name.

"Tom! Tom?"

Her voice carried clearly enough; she was shouting. Goldman realized with acute discomfort that Eleanor could hear her. It was unmistakable. Eleanor could hear his wife shouting for him, and they both knew that he could too.

He should excuse himself. Go find Jordan. Bring her to join them.

"Eleanor, we need to talk."

"So you said." But she wasn't mocking him, Goldman realized, with a quick flush of gratitude. He looked at her, the first real chance he'd had to see her since he arrived. Jesus, she looked stunning. Elegant and classy as ever, but somehow—softer, more appealing. Those tiny rosebuds. She looked like Cinderella at the ball, her intelligent sapphire eyes glinting even in this darkness, her creamy white breasts pushed high up, spilling over the boned bodice of her gown, the minute lines around her mouth welcoming. Her hair was swept up, and even though she'd never made any attempt to cover the few gray strands weaving through the blond he didn't care. It looked beautiful, like gold shot with silver thread. It suited her. *She* was beautiful.

Eleanor tried to look away. She knew she should break the moment. It was dangerous . . . Paul, Jordan . . .

But Tom Goldman was standing there, eating her with his eyes, looking as though he wanted to kiss her, and . . .

"Tom," she said gently. "You're staring at me."

"You're so lovely," Goldman said, without thinking.

Eleanor turned her head aside, not wanting to let him see her eyes fill with tears. At this moment, in this spot, she felt lovely. Not middle-aged, unwed, overpromoted, or barren; just beautiful. For one blessed second, she had seen herself in the mirror of his eyes, and she felt beautiful.

"Thank you," she said.

"I'm lonely," Goldman said, and felt a huge release, as though a physical weight had been lifted from his shoulders. The words had come by themselves, and the second he said them, he knew they were true. "I'm so lonely, Eleanor. I can't talk to her."

Eleanor Marshall felt time freeze around her, her own pulse thudding out of rhythm, out of control. She tried to breathe normally. Did he say that? Had he really said that? A million obvious responses presented themselves. "Is this your version of 'My wife doesn't understand me,' Tom?" "Shouldn't you be discussing this with a shrink?" "Try getting in touch with your feminine side." But she refused to trot one of them out. Tom Goldman did not play games. Not with her.

And besides, she wasn't sure if he *had* a feminine side, she thought, smiling a little in the shadows.

"It's hard, to be with someone," she said.

The effort to keep a check on herself was overwhelming. Why do humans do this to themselves? Eleanor thought, agonized. Why have we erected these huge, sacred walls? What she longed to say was, *Tom, I love you. Get a divorce and marry me and we'll have children and we'll be happy.*

But she just couldn't. Tom was a married man and her oldest friend. For all she knew, this was a passing phase, and next month he'd be as wrapped up in his kid bride as he had been at first . . and then where would she be? And she, Eleanor, she was still with Paul Halfin . . . Could she cold-bloodedly betray him, here, now, for the sake of a sweet look and a little perfume in the air? Expose him to knowing glances from Tom for the rest of his life? Because she was kidding herself if she thought Tom actually meant it. There was no way he was going to divorce that young, stacked, tanned sex goddess he'd married, the one who was the new social force with all the hot LA charities, for her, Eleanor Marshall, a career woman with gray streaks in her hair and the odd line on her skin. She had to get real. This was life, and not the movies.

"Are you going to marry Paul?" Tom asked her, urgently.

She shivered at the force behind his question.

"I don't know."

"But it's not certain."

She said as lightly as she could, "Nothing's certain, Tom . . ."

"Eleonor . . ." he murmured, and then he was leaning closer to her, his stocky body closing on hers, his head dipping toward her . . .

"Tom Goldman and Eleanor Marshall. I'm so glad I found you."

Eleanor spun around to see Isabelle Kendrick standing in front of them, her emerald-green Balenciaga trailing in the nighttime dew. Her expression was one of the purest delight at having stumbled across them, but Eleanor wasn't fooled. Not for a second. She wondered how long Isabelle had been watching them, and she didn't even have to glance at Tom to tell that he was thinking the same thing.

"Hello, Isabelle! It's a wonderful party," Eleanor greeted her. "You must excuse Tom and me for sneaking away. We were talking shop—about your husband's latest project, actually."

Eleanor knew the tight-assed cow would hate that—*I'm* talking business with the boys, dear, so stuff your stupid canapés.

"But how marvelous." Isabelle's professionally made-up face was totally inscrutable, her smile fixed and gleaming. "That's exactly what I came to find you for. We're starting dinner in a moment, and Sam simply *insisted* that all the people on this *Triple Exposure* film—"

"*Triple Feature*," Goldman muttered.

"—sit together. So I've put Roxana Felix, the model, next to you and Paul, Eleanor; and the screenwriter next to you, Tom. Jordan will be sitting with the rock star."

Her face contracted tautly with disapproval, and despite her bitter frustration, Eleanor felt a flicker of amusement. So Zach Mason had done something to piss the old witch off, had he? Maybe he hadn't pressed his tux correctly? She was pleased. When she'd been into rock 'n' roll, musicians existed for the sole purpose of pissing off people like Isabelle Kendrick.

"That sounds great, Isabelle." For the second time in two days, Eleanor had seen Tom Goldman snap straight back into character. Now he was all the relaxed mogul at play, being gracious to his hostess. "Let's go."

⋯⋯

Megan's head was spinning. Partly from the exhaustion of following David around as he constantly introduced her to people as his new client, the "first-time screenwriter—she wrote the Mason/Florescu thing over at Artemis," and partly from lack of food. She was dying to take one of the little dim sum or handcrafted chocolates that the waiters kept thrusting under her nose, but David kept giving her friendly little warning looks. It was humiliating, but, she reminded herself, it just showed that David cared about her. He obviously knew how to look after his own body. If she hadn't been such a pig, such a slob, beforehand, she wouldn't feel her thighs grazing each other under her skirt now. And her feet were in agony. The homegirls back on Haight didn't even own a pair of heels between them. Jesus, did women wear these things voluntarily? It was a new world for her now, she'd have to tear up her old rule book. *We're not in Kansas anymore, Toto.*

Still she couldn't get enough of the party. Pure luxury everywhere you looked . . . on the walls, in the food, in the dresses of the women . . . baby tigers! In diamond collars! And no one remotely surprised! And the stars . . . she'd seen Michelle and Winona and Julia, Richard and Cindy, Arnold and Maria . . .

Megan squeezed David's arm tighter than ever. She gave him a look of pure adoration. One week ago she'd been shoveling fries in some rathole. Now she was mixing with the A-list.

David Tauber had believed in her. He'd given her this. He made the dream come true. And just as a bonus, he was the best-looking guy in LA.

Megan felt like a jerk for staring. Nobody else gave the stars a second glance. They were all too busy with their double-Dutch movie conversations—"Did you hear what the rolling breakeven on that thing was?" "Five points off the top. *And* ten percent of the merchandising." "Fifteen million, and that's just for above-the-line." None of it fazed David, of course, but why would it? That was his business. So Megan Silver stood, suffered, and smiled.

But now they'd called dinner. Thank God. And David, handsome and confident as ever, was steering her through the marble lobby, past the huge crystal vases heaped with orchids, and through the vast ballroom, with its sea of opulent tables, to one particular table at the head of the room, right under two of the largest cut-glass chandeliers she'd ever seen. Most of the chairs were filled already. Sam Kendrick and his wife she'd met; the middle-aged man and elegant lady in the pink ball gown David had told her were chairman and president of the movie studio; an incredible-looking blond girl; another middle-aged man—and Roxana Felix! And who was that in the corner, and what the hell was he wearing?

Roxana looked at Megan with contempt and indifference as David introduced her.

"Everybody, this is our screenwriter, Megan Silver. Megan, this is Roxana Felix, Paul Halfin, Jordan Cabot Goldman . . . Sam and Isabelle and Tom and Eleanor you've met . . ." He coughed, insistently, and Megan felt her heart lurch as the figure at the end of the table turned around. He was wearing a crumpled black jacket, thrown casually over a Metallica shirt, and his eyes narrowed, cold and hostile, as he looked at Megan standing there with David Tauber's arm around her waist.

"Zach, say hello to Megan," David said. "She wrote *Triple Feature.*"

Faced with her all-time hero, Megan suddenly clammed up. He was glaring at her. He seemed in a really, *really* bad mood.

She just nodded at him.

Utterly unperturbed, David pulled out a chair for Megan, and the two of them sat down.

"And that makes everybody."

Isabelle Kendrick looked around at her table with satisfaction, as though she'd personally created each one of them. "We must have a toast. What shall we toast to?"

"Isn't that obvious, Mrs. Kendrick?" David Tauber asked respectfully. He took the bottle of pink champagne nearest him and filled Megan's glass, then raised his own. "To *Triple Feature.* One thing everyone here has in common; the movie."

"The movie," everybody said.

Megan lifted her glass to her lips, terrified, but she managed to smile.

"The movie," she repeated, and drank.

chapter 13

David Tauber rolled the film; it was live footage of a Dark Angel concert from three years ago. The screen showed teenagers and twenty-somethings in black jeans, plaid shirts, combat boots. Longhairs, skinheads, glamorous babes in bright red lipstick and Anarchy T-shirts, they formed one seething mass of rebellion, Generation X in full cry. They crammed the stadium, heads banging, bodies flying, arms outstretched toward the stage, their expressions ranging from adulation to fury.

The crowd barrier down front was ten rows deep in human bodies. Security guards stood to one side shaking their heads, useless and helpless.

Dark Angel came onstage, followed by lead singer Zach Mason, prince of the counterculture. Never gave interviews. Endorsed no politician. Spoke to the fans only live or through lyrics. And at moments like this, when you saw eighty thousand kids utterly mesmerized, you knew that if Mason but said the word, they would riot. They would rise up and follow him. The camera panned from left to right, across the throng of heaving, chanting kids, their aggression focused in the music with laserlike precision.

Dark Angel was the first band in years to scare parents. They were angry. They had something to say. And looking at this wild, incensed, unified crowd, it was obvious American youth was listening.

Zach Mason shifted uncomfortably on the soft leather sofa.

"Turn it off," he said.

"But Zach, I thought—"

"Turn it *off.*" Mason's voice was a low growl.

David Tauber turned it off.

"I don't want to watch that," Zach almost snarled. "That was three years ago. I'm not interested in the past."

His gaze swept the Artemis conference room, challenging any one of the suits to disagree. Jake Keller, the vice president of production, looked away, unable or unwilling to meet his glare. Sam Kendrick, the head of his agency and a man whom Mason had got to know a little, nodded sagely. Good. At least one of these fuckers understood where he was coming from. And Eleanor Marshall, the stern-looking lady in the dark green suit, was completely impassive. Only the dumpy little kid sitting next to David Tauber, the screenwriter, looked anguished. She was staring at the now-blank screen with a mixture of wonder and regret. And he'd seen the way she looked across at him while the tape was playing—almost accusingly. Did he need this? He didn't need this. Not from some kid who was younger than he was. Not from some kid who looked like one of his fans, reminded him of things he preferred to forget.

Megan Silver. That was her name. He'd asked Tauber about her; she was twenty-four years old, she'd gone to college at Berkeley, and she'd written an awesome screenplay.

He hadn't said two words to her, but she still made him nervous.

"Sure. I understand," David Tauber said smoothly. "I just thought it might be a good idea for us all to get a *feel* for the backdrop of this movie. Fred Florescu messengered over the tapes, and I know Roxana's studying them, but since this is our first script meeting together . . ."

"I don't *need* to get a feel for what it's like to be around a band." Mason nodded insultingly at Megan. "Maybe she does."

The girl started to say something, but Tauber's hand descended on her shoulder, and she relapsed into silence.

"Of course, Zach. This was more for Sam and Jake and Eleanor," David said. "We've all been examining the script, and I know they have some suggestions. I thought it might be beneficial if everybody knew what they were dealing with here."

Yeah, right. Like any one of those forty-something corporate assholes would suddenly "get" rock 'n' roll from watching a half-hour video.

"You have script suggestions? Let's hear them," Zach said, his brown eyes narrowing. Personally, he'd thought the script was just fine as it was. But David had told him scripts could always be improved. And he wanted this movie to be the best it could be. Let's face it, for him, now, to reinvent himself, the movie *had* to be superb. Millions of dollars were at stake. His career. His future. His *life*.

It was the only reason he'd come to this meeting in the first place—artistic control, creative control. He'd had it with his record company and now he'd have it with his film studio. So what if the director was usually the only guy involved in the rewrite process? He was Zach Mason. Rules that applied to other actors didn't apply to him. *No* rules applied to him.

"OK, Zach." Jake Keller was falling over himself trying to kiss his ass. "Let's look at the opening scenes first . . . I had some ideas for beefing up your entrance . . ."

As the agents and executives began to rip her opening sequence into tiny pieces, Megan Silver lowered her head, scratching the odd word on the notepad in front of her. She didn't want to have to look at any of them. It was great being at Artemis, great that she was having her movie made, but . . . she just wasn't prepared for *this*. The way they were all talking at once, discussing her story like she wasn't even there. Movie business terms flew around the room—"plot points," "the inciting incident," "counterpointing with the Morgan strand," "the action sequence, eight through ten," "pushing up the CIA payoff." And they thought she understood?

God, it was such irony. When she'd finally had the guts to call the others back in Frisco, they'd reacted with stunned silence, stammered congratulations, and utter jealousy. Only Dec had the generosity of spirit to really be happy for her. He'd enthused about how glamorous her life would be now—her own office on the lot, working with big shot studio executives, hanging out with Roxana Felix, and best of all, getting to know Zach Mason.

"You're actually gonna talk to Zach Mason! On a regular basis?" Dec gasped. "My God, how great is that? First David gets you this movie, then he sits you next to *Zach Mason*. You must be having trouble breathing straight. You're the envy of millions, you bitch!"

And he'd been right.

And he'd been wrong.

Megan had got her own office on the set—a windowless cubicle in the main building, with an assistant who resented her. She'd got to meet Eleanor Marshall, who seemed a nice woman but who'd explained that her script would need "a little work." By the time David explained to her what "a little work" meant, Megan was more upset than she would have believed possible. Artemis had paid $250,000 for her script, but she wondered why they'd paid anything at all—since it was patently useless and would have to be written again. More or less from scratch. Probably five or six times.

"Megan, sugar. It's all in the rewrites," David had told her patiently. "It never works any other way. You gave them a great first draft, but obviously, the *movie* will end up nothing like that at all."

Obviously. And she'd looked at her handsome agent, smiling benignly at her like she was a beloved but rather slow infant, and felt like a moron for ever thinking otherwise.

Her first day at the studios, a vice president named Jake Keller had come round and made it very clear that if she was bothered about rewriting, she could just quit and they'd hire someone else to do it. Oh, and give them back $100,000, since that was the part of her deal allocated to rewriting.

Megan smiled sweetly at him and said she wasn't bothered.

As for hanging out with Roxana Felix—well, she'd met the lady at Isabelle Kendrick's party and been thoroughly snubbed. She'd met her a second time at Artemis and been told "You're the writer? Morgan needs more lines. I think that's obvious. We need at *least* fifty percent more lines for Morgan"—and here she'd been flashed a smile as cold and deadly as liquid nitrogen—"or I'll have to find a writer who understands this movie better. Character dynamics, Megan."

And Roxana had swept out, with a contemptuous glance at her still-too-thick thighs.

For a week she'd practically starved herself. Roxana was so exquisite and so cruel she made Megan feel like the ugliest woman on earth. And she had power—she was threatening to have Megan replaced. *A writer who understands this movie better?* She'd written the damn thing!

But, as Megan was finding out, that counted for very little.

A writer is disposable.

A star is not.

In the world of *Triple Feature,* her movie, Megan Silver had the least money, the least looks, the least knowledge, and the least style, and no power whatsoever.

She was the low girl on the totem pole.

She didn't like it.

And as for talking to Zach Mason . . . she didn't dare. He'd refused to speak to her at the Kendricks' party, and he was scowling at her every time she caught his eye. The video of Dark Angel moved Megan almost to tears, but Zach Mason, sitting there, more physically attractive, dark and brooding, than she'd ever imagined even in her fantasies, hadn't even been able to watch it. Jesus, was he saying that none of it ever mattered to him?

Right now, Megan felt deeply unhappy, foolish, and naive. The young man opposite her had been her idol since she was fifteen years old. A *star* first and foremost. And music was apparently just not part of his game plan anymore.

Megan glanced across at David Tauber and felt her heart melt a little more. If Zach Mason was a fraud, there was nothing much left to believe in. Roxana Felix was a bitch, Keller was a bully, and her script sucked.

Without David she'd be lost.

Roxana was crossing and uncrossing long, nut-brown legs, flicking her glossy, jet-black hair over her perfect shoulders. To think, David represented Zach *and* Roxana and he still bothered with her.

Maybe it was shallow, but Megan suddenly longed for supermodel beauty and rock-star cool. What would it be like, to be one of the chosen?

Would a prince like David Tauber look at her then?

She remembered Dec's words of warning when he had warned her off.

"Baby, he sounds too perfect. There's no way he's not taken . . . Watch your back, it's dangerous," he sympathized. "Guys like Tauber hook you like heroin."

She flashed guiltily onto the warmth blooming under her groin as she looked his way. Megan thought about David all the time. It gave new meaning to the phrase "hopeless romantic."

"Honey, you get all that?" David asked.

Megan blushed, startled. "Yeah. Thanks." She patted her notepad. "I'll get right on it."

"Well, make it snappy," Jake Keller said coldly. "We only have a month allocated to preproduction."

Hating herself, Megan nodded brightly. "Sure."

"Thank you, Megan," Eleanor Marshall said, more kindly. She and Jake gathered their papers together and stood up to leave. "We have another meeting we've got to get to, but I know Zach wants to talk to you about his part."

Oh great, Megan thought. He probably wants me to up his lines by fifty percent as well . . . This should be good!

"Zach," Sam Kendrick prompted, "you were telling us earlier about touring, some of the script ideas that maybe couldn't really work . . . "

Zach Mason looked across at Megan Silver, his tongue suddenly stuck in lockjaw. It was easy enough to tell the suits where they got off—he'd been doing that all his life. It was easy enough to order SKI about, too. David Tauber was a good agent, so was Sam Kendrick, that was why he was with them, but agents were just suits that worked for you. Twenty percent and all out for their own glory. He knew what they were like—thought all the stars were scum to be bought and sold, but still labored under the delusion that they were stars themselves. He didn't trust any one of the bloodsucking assholes. It was just business, all the way down the line.

Megan was different.

Now he took a closer look at her, she was actually quite pretty. Soft brown hair that fell to her shoulders in gentle, natural curls, intelligent-looking chocolate eyes, and large breasts hidden away under her voluminous cotton sweater. OK, she had puppy fat, but she'd lost weight since that ridiculous flesh-pressing party. Anyway, the weight kind of suited her. Made her real.

Zach Mason wasn't used to real women, and he certainly wasn't used to intelligent ones. The groupies that made it through Dark Angel's military-style security were hardened cases, bleached-blond bitches ready to screw anything that had got within ten paces of *Rolling Stone* magazine, and to do half the crew on the way in for the privilege. Then there were the others, bored wives of record company execs, Hollywood starlets who wanted to double their chances of getting written about, models who wanted to "date" a rock star because that was fast becoming the tradition. In fact, Zach had more respect for the groupies. At least they were honest about what they were looking for. But all of them were dumb and starstruck and greedy, all of them were trading sex for fame.

And that could make you bitter. That could make you hate. Mason had seen normal guys turn into woman-hating pigs after six months on the road, the kind who'd fuck a groupie and then kick her out into a hotel corridor stark naked. The kind who insisted they put on a show for thirty members of the crew before they earned the privilege of giving a musician head. In public. And the sick thing was, the girls almost always agreed. He'd seen guys try to outdo each other in inventing new degradations for women, and yet there was always at least one of the bitches around for whom there was nothing, absolutely nothing, too gross. It could dehumanize you.

Zach hadn't let himself slide into hatred. He didn't *care* enough to hate. He just packed a gross of condoms and fucked his way around the world—pliant groupies, fame-hungry actresses, they all wanted that fake image. Zach Mason, lead singer of the world's biggest band, the prophet, the spokesman, the *superstar.* And he wanted sex. So every encounter was a trade; cold, insulated, lonely.

Zach didn't know how to talk to someone like Megan.

Her *Triple Feature* script had blown him away; it was beautiful and exciting and poignant and romantic. It was brilliant. It took his breath away. And then to find that the kid who wrote it was younger than he was . . .

Some of the words, Zach had had to look up in a dictionary. It made him feel small, in awe of the writer's learning. He himself had started Dark Angel at sixteen, got a deal at seventeen, and when his classmates graduated from high school he was out on the road. When they graduated from college he was out on the road. When they graduated from business, law, and medical school, he was out on the road. He had never had a proper education, and it bothered him.

Most of the time that was no great problem—the record industry wasn't exactly packed with university graduates. It wasn't William Morris, where you needed a college degree even to sort the mail. No, the music business was full of talents and gangsters and street-smart hustlers who paid armies of lawyers to do their thinking for them. But sometimes, just sometimes, he'd meet a real intellectual—Cliff Burnstein, say, Def Leppard's manager, Tom Silverman of Tommy Boy Records, or Rowena Krebs from Musica, and he wouldn't know what to say. He'd grunt monosyllables, and nobody even cared. What else would you expect, from a dumb-ass musician? And so what if all the magazines called him intelligent, profound, astute? They analyzed his lyrics as though he were Voltaire, and though those lyrics came right from his heart, Zach knew they would kiss his butt anyway. After all, if they didn't, Yolanda would just have denied them access to the band. And what music paper could sell copies without Dark Angel? So their opinions meant nothing. They were bought.

"Some of the stuff you have in there couldn't possibly happen," he said.

Megan shrugged. "OK. *You* tell me what's wrong and I'll change it."

Why did I ever think somebody would actually like my work?

Zach heard the reserve in her voice. "The warm-up scene with the other guys in the band," he said coldly. "It would never happen like that. If I'm playing Jason, the audience is still going to assume the picture is about me, and if this is *roman à clef*—"

Megan giggled.

"What the fuck are you laughing at?" Zach snapped.

"*Roman à clef.* It's French. You pronounce it 'clay,' not 'cleff'—the word means 'key,' not 'clef' like a treble clef," Megan explained, smiling.

Zach Mason went purple with rage and humiliation. Jesus Christ, the bitch was fucking *laughing* at him. "It's French." Like she was so fucking smart, and he was just an idiot with a guitar.

"Yeah? Well, you just *fix* it," he snarled.

"I'll do my best," Megan said, shrinking back in her chair.

"You'll fucking succeed. Or you're off this movie," Zach Mason told her, and stormed out of the room, slamming the door behind him.

chapter 14

"Come on, honey, you can do it."

David's voice was sweet and encouraging, urging her on. "Just ten more. Let's go."

Every nerve in her legs seemed to be screaming for mercy, but she obeyed him, her breath coming ragged and strained. Madonna was pumping from the stereo, but her tortured body had drowned out the music. All she was aware of was the floor and her elbows.

"Eight . . . nine . . ."

You have to. You have to.

Wearily she forced herself down and back up again.

"Ten! That's great, Megan. Just great. Now hit the showers," David said, throwing her a towel as she staggered to her feet. "I'll bet you feel great."

She caught sight of her face in the wall mirror—red as a beef tomato and shining with sweat, her hair plastered wetly to her forehead, her mouth open like a fish, gulping weakly for air.

"Yeah," she managed, trying for a smile. "I feel terrific."

"You *look* terrific," her agent said, as she stumbled toward her bathroom.

Megan peeled off her Lycra tights and T-shirt, both of which were clinging to her skin as if someone had thrown a bucket of water over them—*nice*—and chucked them in the laundry basket. Tentatively she climbed on the electronic scales David had brought for her last month: 131 pounds. Well, she was getting there. As she stepped gratefully into the shower and let the powerful jets of warm water hammer her aching shoulder muscles, Megan felt a small glow of achievement. She still hated seeing

herself naked, hated weighing herself, but every day the mirrors were a little less insulting, the electric tally a touch less traumatic. She could see the
changes in her body—the growing definition around her chin, the disappearance of the fat pockets above her knees. It *was* working. And she had
David to thank for it. As he kept telling her, if he didn't show up to supervise her workouts she'd never have had the willpower to keep them up.

He was more than an agent; he was her dietitian, nutritionist, stylist,
beauty adviser, and personal trainer. And as the work on *Triple Feature* got
harder and harder, David was there, always in her corner. She knew Zach
and Roxana both wanted her fired, as did Mr. Keller, but David was in
there arguing for her, defusing everybody's anger.

She owed him her house.

She owed him her job.

She owed him everything.

"Want some decaf?" David called from the kitchen.

"Yes, thanks," she yelled back.

Oh good, that meant he'd stay for a cup of coffee. Megan knew she
should tell him to skip it and get back to SKI—poor David was always so
overworked—but she was just too selfish to do that. Preproduction had
gone into overdrive, and thanks to David's efforts, she was still the sole
writer. But the Artemis team changed their mind about something every
single day, and it seemed that she was always working flat out to change
something, then scrubbing it all the next day and starting again. Megan
thought of herself as LA's Alice through the Looking-Glass, running her
heart out just to stay in the same place.

So she never got out. Who had the time?

Never—unless David took her out.

Those were the nights that made it all worthwhile, when Tauber would
show up in his cherry-red Lamborghini and tell her he was taking her to
dinner, and then she'd grab one of the outfits he'd told her to buy—oh yes,
she should add personal shopper to his list of roles in her life—and drive
her to Spago's or Morton's or Le Dome, where the maitre d' would invari-
ably greet David by name and show them to a good table, and they'd eat
something low-fat, and then later he'd take her along to the Roxbury or
the Viper Room, where the club doormen always ushered them past the
line and David would lead her directly into the VIP area. He was so powerful. And he knew *everyone.* "Hello, Brad." "Hi, Shannon." "How's it going,
Keanu?"

When Megan spent the evening with David Tauber, she seemed to
spend most of her time blushing and trying not to stare.

He was the perfect gentleman, too, always driving her home and seeing
her into her apartment building with a peck on the cheek, or kissing her
hand. Megan knew it was ridiculous to hope for anything more—hadn't

David done enough for her already? But she couldn't help herself. He was the proverbial knight on the white charger, rescuing her first from her mundane existence and then from herself. He had the power to open any door for her—he'd told her that often enough.

And he was so damn gorgeous. At least when he put her through this agonizing workout three times a week Megan knew that he practiced what he preached. His lean, mean body, muscles rock-hard and gleaming with health, was a testament to that. His thick hazel hair shone with a natural vitality only gained from the ideal diet. Even his perfectly shaped teeth were whiter than her own, whether Megan was using one of the expensive cosmetic pastes or not.

Since the second he'd turned up at Mr. Chicken with her contract, Megan had been daydreaming about him. But lately, those dreams had been getting more out of hand.

Megan remembered dumping Rory because she wanted something more.

Was David Tauber the one she'd been looking for?

Shaking her head to try and clear the familiar twitch between her legs, the warm flush of desire prickling across her nipples, Megan toweled herself off and got dressed, picking a flowing Indian-print skirt and tight black T-shirt top, pulled on over a 34C-cup Ultrabra.

"Coffee's ready," David called from the kitchen.

Her silhouette didn't look at all bad; the sweep of cotton forgave her hips a lot of their sins and in a push-up bra her breasts were impressive, even by Hollywood standards.

Megan pulled her top down tighter.

"Coming," she said.

·:::·

Roxana Felix was sobbing.

Her hands gripped the cool marble of the balustrade fence that surrounded her hilltop garden, manicured nails and tanned, slender fingers wrapped tightly around it like a drowning man clutching a raft. Her body was raised horizontally, parallel to the ground. In front of her she could see halfway to the ocean, the Hollywood Hills giving way to Los Angeles' busy grid, peaceful as ever from this height. The blazing sun sparkled off the tiny cars, logjammed on the freeway in the morning rush hour. All around her, birds were chirping and twittering, and the air was fragrant with roses and orchids and the honeysuckle wound into her tall, protecting hedges.

Her slender body bucked again as he crashed into her.

Her long, black hair, normally so sleekly coiffured, fell tousled about her shoulders and back, strands of it brushing against her pendant breasts. Her skin was hot and aroused, tight with wanting. Her nipples were almost painfully erect. She was close to orgasm.

"Had enough?" he asked, teasing her, deliberately slowing his rhythm.

Roxana squirmed against him, her knuckles white against the marble, urging him on. She could feel his large, strong hands under her thighs and belly, supporting her. She knew he could feel her heat, the blood warm under the skin, her stomach slick with sweat from her desire. His hands were on her. He was holding her.

The thought sent a spasm of lust right through her.

"Please," she said.

"Say it again." She could feel his cock leap inside her. This was turning him on, too. His voice was rough with sex.

"Please. Please. Don't stop. Just *do* it," she moaned, pushing the firm globes of her butt back against him, her vaginal muscles tightening around him and then relaxing again. He wasn't the only one who knew how to please, she thought, and hearing him groan, Roxana had a vague awareness of triumph through the hot mist of arousal that was consuming her.

He started to thrust, and thrust, and thrust, every time going a little deeper, every time a little harder, telling her how good she felt, telling her how hot she was, asking if she liked it, if she liked what he was doing, and Roxana sobbed yes, yes, and his rhythm was perfect, and suddenly there was a new sensation in her belly and she was climbing a great wall of ecstasy, she blocked out everything except his voice and his cock, all she could feel or know was herself impaled on his cock, moving with him, and he was getting more urgent and thicker inside her all the time, and deeper, and suddenly she could feel him right down inside her, hitting that exquisite, melting spot on her vaginal wall, Jesus Christ, the G-spot, and she felt the world go black and explode in blinding pleasure, breaking and shattering around her, her pussy and her stomach contracting into spasm after spasm as Roxana Felix rode the longest, strongest orgasm she had ever known.

For a second he stayed inside her, holding her in position, letting her regain her breath. Then he gently withdrew, still holding her, and scooped her up in his arms, naked and bathed with perspiration, and carried her back inside the house.

He set her down on the polished wood floor of the bathroom, carefully, as though she were made of the most delicate bone china.

"How was that?" he asked, grinning.

Roxana brushed past him, turning the taps on her bathtub. Showering was for people in a hurry; she preferred to soak. She reached out one toned arm and selected a small crystal bottle of lavender bath oil, especially blended for her by a chic Paris *parfumerie*.

"What, do you want a rating out of ten, Sam?" she asked coolly. "Eight and a half. You were very good. You get better all the time."

She emptied the entire bottle into the bath and the heady floral scent rose up in clouds of steam, overpowering any lingering trace of sweat or sex.

Kendrick reached for a bathrobe, not wanting her to see him limp.

"Oh, *you were very good,* she says, so matter-of-factly."

Roxana slipped into her bath, the perfumed oil making the water turn white. With her black hair and tanned skin she looked Egyptian. She glanced at him haughtily.

Cleopatra bathes in asses' milk, Sam thought. She was truly exquisite. And colder than ice.

"If you wanted hearts and flowers, Sam, you came to the wrong place. A great fuck is a great fuck. End of story."

She shrugged, sending tiny rivers of scented water trickling across the tops of her perfect breasts.

"It's just friction, at the end of the day."

"Just *friction?*" Kendrick repeated, disbelievingly. "Is that how you would describe what happened out there?"

This was the hottest, most sexual thing he had ever dreamed of, and Roxana could dismiss it as *just friction?* Shit, one moment he was screwing her in midair, feeling her buck underneath him, hearing her beg him not to stop, and the next . . . this? Wham, bam, thank you sir?

"Yes," Roxana said, beginning to wash herself briskly with a sponge. "Would you like a shower? There's a separate one in my bedroom."

Kendrick stood up and laughed curtly.

"I don't buy it, babe."

"Really." There was nothing in her tone, not even a pretense of interest.

"Yes, really. No woman thinks of making love that way. *Especially* not when it's as intense as that."

"I'm glad you were pleased," Roxana said, stepping out of the bath and reaching for a towel.

The sight of her wet, naked body, the smooth flesh shining from the water, her soft pubic hair flattened against the curve of her body, her berry nipples erect again in the cool bathroom air, crowning slick, damp breasts that tilted youthfully upward in natural perfection, did something to Sam Kendrick. Immediate hard-on. Despite the fact that he'd come less than five minutes ago.

Jesus, Sam thought. Is she for real?

He was forty-four years old, and Roxana Felix had him as horny as a teenager.

Roxana glanced at the bathroom clock. Nine-thirty A.M.

"If you wouldn't mind showering and dressing, Sam. I have a script meeting at Artemis at ten." She turned her back on him, heading for her walk-in closet, dismissing him.

"OK," Kendrick managed, astonished at her attitude.

"Thanks." She gave him one quick, dazzling smile. "Oh, and Sam, one more thing—*you* may have been making love, but *I* was having sex. That's all."

Openmouthed, Sam watched his new mistress walk away.

⁙

Declan Heath arrived unannounced in the middle of rewrites, banging on her door like a pizza delivery boy. When Megan angrily threw it open she jumped out of her skin, squealed, and gave him a crushing hug.

"Am I seeing things? What are you doing here?"

"You're not, baby, but I might be," Dec announced, stepping into her front room, mouth open. His eyebrows lifted. "I was too curious. I got on a bus."

"I'm so glad you're here," Megan exclaimed, almost tearfully. Dec was a throwback to another planet. The second she saw him she felt more secure, more grounded. "How long can you stay? I have a spare room, plenty of space . . ."

"So I see. I can't stay. Got to get back to the grind tonight. Besides, all this luxury would just make me bitter and twisted," he said. "My God, an office. A *fax*, you have your own fax machine? Megan!"

Declan prowled round her place, poking his tousled head into her cupboards and bedroom and kitchen. "It's a palace!"

"I only rent it."

"But you're rich. It's all true. Girl, I hate your guts," Declan said, flopping down on the couch. "Get me some coffee. Anything harder?" he asked hopefully. "Nobody's gonna believe it when I tell them. I should take some Polaroids."

She switched on the percolator. "No grass, no E. Sorry. David has me on a strict regimen and I feel great."

"Oooh, let's talk about that." Dec smiled beatifically. "You've got him bad."

He reached out to the dresser and picked up the framed agency black-and-white David had sent her. His fair hair and brilliant white smile beamed out over a smart Armani polo-neck.

"This is the guy?" He gave a long, low whistle. "*Girlfriend*. He's too cute to live. Oh, man." Dec took a deep breath, shook his head. "Oh, man," he said again.

Megan arrived with the coffee and Dec sipped approvingly. It was an expensive, import blend, nothing you'd get at Ground Zero. Casually he checked his best friend out. She looked terrific; puppy fat melted away, designer jeans, flattering blouse, suntan.

But she also looked stressed. Changed. The threads didn't look like stuff she'd pick herself. If Dec didn't know better, he'd say Megan was blue.

"Looking hot," he said.

"This?" Megan glanced at herself and blushed. "That's David's work. He made me throw out all my clothes and picked the new ones. And, uh, he made me lose weight."

"*He* did? You were unhappy about that anyway."

"Sure, but without David, I'd never have done it," Megan said earnestly.

"Bull*shit*. You always do what you say you will, girl. Look at the movie." Declan glanced back at the model looks of David Tauber. Strange, but he got bad vibes from the guy. "I don't want to rain on your magnificent parade. No one is happier for you than I am. But under all this sparkle you seemed a little blue—that's why I came down. Meg, now that I see you, I can see you're downright unhappy. And he made you throw out your wardrobe? That's obnoxious, Megan."

"Don't worry." She got all defensive. "He's protecting me, he wants me to fit in."

"So he won't take you out?"

"He takes me out. He just doesn't kiss me." Megan sighed. "I know I'm nuts. But it would have been so romantic . . ."

"The white knight whisking you off to the sunset," Dec snorted. "Well, at least you haven't completely changed." He pointed at the Dark Angel poster on the wall. "I see that hasn't come down."

"Dark Angel was more than Zach Mason."

"Like hell." Dec pulled on the coffee. "Your David's almost *too* perfect, y'know? How can you sit in a room with Zach Mason and not melt over his boots? I know I would."

"Because he's different." Megan thought of Zach Mason. Those feral, male good looks were devastating, sure. More sexual, more intense than David would ever be. And she'd once worshiped Zach like he was a god.

But not now.

Anyway, Zach obviously thought she was scum. Stars like him only looked at girls like Roxana Felix.

Mere mortals like Megan didn't even count.

-:::-

As her limo turned into the wrought-iron gates of Artemis Studios, Roxana Felix smiled to herself. She was wearing a Mark Eisen tailored suit in palest pink cashmere, her makeup a sweep of matching light rose tones: a breath of blusher on her perfect cheekbones, minimal highlights above her long black lashes, and her full mouth covered with the latest glamorous, wet-look lip gloss.

She was as sexy as hell.

And that was the idea.

A month in LA, and Roxana had learned a few things. The most surprising was that here, she was only a middling fish in a very large pond. Not everyone asked how high, ma'am, when she told them to jump. She didn't get her own way right away. And sometimes, as with Sam Kendrick at his wife's party, she even had to back down.

A lesser woman might have been disheartened. Might have shrugged it off and returned to modeling, where she ruled with a rod of hand-cured Italian leather. But not Roxana Felix. She had come to Hollywood to find true fame, to have the world fall at *her* feet, not the feet of her silent, frozen image. What had that artist done? Painted pictures of pipes and labeled them, *Ceci n'est pas une pipe.* This is not a pipe.

She had friends who'd never understood that. They'd stand there and laugh and say, "If it's not a pipe, what is it? Sure looks like a pipe to me."

But Roxana had understood right away.

It *looks* like a pipe, but it's not. It's a *picture* of a pipe.

Big difference.

So what if the world looked at her picture and adored? *Ceci n'est pas Roxana.* And she wanted them to adore Roxana. So *Triple Feature* was more than important, it was vital. She'd had to fight harder than she had in years to get into the goddamn picture, and now, it seemed, she was going to have to fight twice as hard to stay on top of it.

It was only preproduction, and already she was running into problems. Her part was way too small, and no matter how much she turned the screws on that dumpy, terrified mouse writing the script, the little bitch stuck firm. Morgan's part was just right. To increase it would be to tilt the movie too much toward the romantic subplot.

*Sub*plot? *She* wasn't sub anything.

But the trouble was that after the first, disastrous screenplay meeting, Eleanor Marshall had taken control. Nobody spoke to Megan Silver without her being present in the room. That way, it was always her fault and not Megan's—and most of the time, that bearded prick Florescu, who couldn't keep his eyes off Roxana's legs, agreed with her. And after Isabelle's party, Roxana had learned that she could threaten a writer, but the director and the president of the studio? No way. It was preproduction, and she could still be replaced. So she was smiling sweetly and biding her time.

But it wasn't in Roxana's nature to do nothing. She planned ahead. She'd learned that lesson the hard way.

Behind the tinted windows of the limo, a shadow of fear and pain crossed Roxana Felix's lovely face. She rarely let herself remember that far back. Pushing away these thoughts of her past that she had fought hard to keep at bay, she concentrated on the future.

Anyway, planning ahead. In less than a month, they would be on the set filming, and at that stage, she planned on throwing her weight around. She was going to make enemies. So what else was new? But she'd need allies. That much was clear. So she'd been quietly observing, surveying, calculating. Who had the power? David Tauber? No . . . it just looked that way. Megan Silver thought the sun shone out of his backside, and Zach Mason was happy with him, for now . . . but she was her own woman. She had no loyalty to agents. Bob Alton could tell you that. And David was too green, too cocky. He thought he was a lion, but he didn't realize that Eleanor and Tom and Sam were just letting him tag along. Sam had Fred, and this was Sam's movie. They were all Sam's movies. He really was a lion; David Tauber was just a jackal, feeding on the carcass his master had left and calling it a fresh kill. He was a good talent scout, but that was about it. And she suspected that if he ever deluded himself that he could cross swords with his boss and win, David Tauber would find that out.

Sam Kendrick, though, was truly powerful.

Sam had proved that to her.

Sam could be useful. *She* could use him. And when she had the bastard wrapped round her finger, when she'd eked out every bit of power he had and taken it for her own advantage, she was going to *break* him. Sweet, deadly revenge.

So what if he was good in bed? So much the better, if she could enjoy herself at the same time. It made no difference. Sam Kendrick thought he could insult Roxana Felix, and he had to realize that there was a price. He was going to pay her with everything he had.

But Sam was already falling for her. He'd be back for more, she knew it. It wasn't Sam she should be concentrating on this morning.

It was the man she'd decided she needed to be *publicly* involved with—the superstar romance that would help her with this movie, help her with its launch, help her with setting up her new career.

Her next lover.

Zach Mason.

chapter 15

"I have the results of your tests," Dr. Haydn said.

Eleanor felt like yelling at her, "Of *course* you have the results of my tests—you called me into your office, didn't you?" But she said nothing. She never did. The anticipatory fear was just too great. Her thrice-yearly checkup with the best fertility specialist in LA was something she both needed and dreaded; needed, so that she could be reassured that it wasn't too late for her, and dreaded, just in case this time it was, this time would prove to be the visit where Dr. Haydn would mutter something about conception being "unlikely." Not to mention the fact that actually walking into the Haydn Clinic was difficult, dragging to the surface her deepest conflicts and bitterest fears. With every day that passed, she knew she was heading closer to the line. She would have to choose. Commit to Paul, or leave him. Settle, or risk everything. Risk even her chance at a child. Because right now, she knew no other man that she could be with, and her time was running out.

Since *Triple Feature* went into preproduction, Tom Goldman had been cutting her dead. He saw her only in the company of others. Somehow, top-management issues always got discussed over the phone. And whenever Jake Keller issued a new protest about how Eleanor was directing the rewrite process, Tom went out of his way to have it formally minuted and documented. He had suddenly become the Studio Chairman again, the ultimate power, sitting in judgment, as impartial as King Solomon.

Eleanor was not surprised. He had come to his senses like she knew he would, and now he was retreating into his shell, embarrassed at whatever *might* have happened. She had thrown herself into her work, and there was more than enough work. She was solely responsible for this major, big-budget movie—a $95 million gamble.

But privately, secretly, she was mourning.

Something deep inside her had died.

"I'm glad to say everything seems to be fine." Dr. Haydn went on, and Eleanor felt a sharp crunch of relief in the pit of her stomach. She glanced around the elegant consulting rooms, a fantasy of maternal pastels in pink and eggshell blue, at the posters for breast cancer research and prenatal exercising, trying to avoid revealing her feelings. Dr. Haydn already thought she was weird. If she was so worried about her fertility, why wasn't she pregnant? She must be the only client on the specialist's highly expensive books who still regularly used her diaphragm. Somehow, as she sat the oak-paneled waiting room with the other patients—nervous, frightened women prepared to put themselves through drugs, calendars, artificial insemination, and God alone knew what else, women who Eleanor knew would have given anything for the news she had just heard—her actions seemed incomprehensible, even to her. She wondered what Dr. Haydn thought. Selfish? Thoughtless? Immoral, even?

Eleanor clasped her hands firmly in her lap. Who cared what the woman thought. She could test her own fertility if she felt like it and that *didn't* mean she was obliged to get pregnant. My body, my choice, she reminded herself.

"However, your fecundity levels have dropped somewhat," the consultant continued. Her voice was cold and clinical. "A woman's fertility naturally declines with age and that process is speeding up for you now."

Relief was replaced by a clammy fear.

"You said I could still conceive, though?" Eleanor pressed.

Dr. Haydn looked at her over the tops of her wire-rimmed glasses.

"At the moment? Absolutely. But *could* conceive and *will* conceive are two different matters." Her gaze was steady. "Ms. Marshall, you are entering the final years of your reproductive life. If you want to have a child, it is my duty to advise you that you should begin trying to get pregnant as soon as possible, and in any event, no later than six months from now."

Eleanor sat very still.

Liz Haydn reached across the desk with her wrinkled hand and patted Eleanor's smooth one.

"It's not too late, you know."

She made an effort and smiled.

"Thank you, Doctor."

It's not too late, Eleanor thought dizzily, but it soon will be.

❖

Megan said, "I want him to drink milk. It's deliberate. Morgan is sitting backstage and we've just seen her mixing a vodka orange—light on the orange, right? She's a bad girl, she scores drugs, she drinks. But Jason, he's supposedly the wild one, but he's not really. I want to highlight that by having him reach for a carton of milk. He's clean, she's not. It's the contrast."

The heat in the meeting room was incredible, even with all the windows open and the air-conditioning at full blast. Outside, blazing LA sun streamed onto the lot, beating down on the palm trees in the drive and the long stretch limos parked out front. Studio execs walked past with their shirtsleeves rolled up, or fanning themselves with scripts and treatments. The ice in their jug of iced water had melted in five minutes.

Nobody wanted to work. But they had to. There were just three weeks to go before shooting started.

The studio president sat quietly to one side, dressed in a cream suit, taking notes. Roxana Felix, her long hair plaited into two thick, glossy pigtails, lay on the black leather Eames sofa, propping up her head with one hand. Her exquisite face was delicately made up in soft tones of coral and apricot, and she wore a cut-off Mark Eisen T-shirt in peach silk teamed with tight white satin shorts by Adrienne Vittadini. No longer pale, Roxana's skin had tanned all over to a honey brown, no lighter, no darker, the tone controlled exactly by her choice of sunscreen. Acres of taut, slender, golden flesh appeared whenever she shifted position, and the stomach displayed by her schoolgirl-style outfit was as flat as a board. With the pigtails she looked as though she might have been some precocious sixteen-year-old, the budding breasts and subtle makeup designed to arouse. Only her shiny, wet lips with their kiss of tangerine gloss, and the two huge diamond studs that glittered in her ears, spoiled the picture. She looked breathtaking, rawly sexual. She was directly opposite Zach Mason, and every time he looked over at her, she moved a little, displaying herself for him.

Why does she bother? Megan Silver thought bitterly. It's like using a sledgehammer to crack a nut.

Never mind that she was a vain, selfish bitch. Never mind that her petty objections held up the script. Never mind that all she considered was her own part, and never the movie as a whole. Roxana Felix lived and breathed in the same air of fame and riches that he enjoyed. She was supermodel-cum-actress and apparently that was all that mattered to Zach Mason. Models and rock stars, a classic pairing. Like salt 'n' vinegar or sugar 'n' spice.

Whenever Zach cast an admiring, stripping glance over the superbitch, Megan felt a little dowdier, a little plainer.

She herself wore a loose shift dress in brushed cotton, sprigged with a pattern of roses, and the stacked sandals that were in fashion just now. Thanks to David Tauber's Professor Higgins routine, Megan now weighed

120 pounds. She was slimmer than she'd ever been in her life, her skin had a healthy glow, and she was nicely tanned. She'd have knocked the guys dead back in Frisco. But so what? Against Roxana Felix's awesome beauty, or even compared to your normal tall, blond, stacked California babe, she was a nothing. Invisible. The moth among butterflies . . .

Zach said dismissively, "A singer wouldn't drink milk before he performed."

"What's the matter? Milk lousy for your image? Does the guy *always* have to down half a bottle of Jack Daniel's before he faces his adoring public?"

Eleanor Marshall looked over at her, surprised, but said nothing.

Roxana Felix laughed. "Well! The mouse that roared."

Megan bit her tongue to stop the retort that wanted to fly out of her. Mason and she were sniping at each other constantly, but so far she'd always been polite. She'd always had to.

"That's got nothing to do with it," Zach said.

"Give me one good reason why Jason shouldn't drink milk before he sings," Megan pressed.

He looked at her levelly, liquid brown eyes meeting hers. God, he was gorgeous. It still got to her, sometimes.

"Because milk coats the back of your throat. You'd sing like shit."

Megan blushed, embarrassed.

"OK. Sorry."

Zach gave her a hint of a smile. "Maybe he could drink a diet soda."

"So, you don't know *everything*, Megan," Roxana Felix purred, stretching on the sofa. "Perhaps you could *listen* to Zach next time. You might learn something."

"Roxana," Eleanor Marshall warned her.

Roxana paid no attention. She wanted her pound of flesh. "Right, Megan?"

Megan gritted her teeth. "I guess."

"I *know*," Roxana said sweetly, and Megan saw her give Zach Mason the most dazzling smile. She lowered her head and crossed out "milk" in the stage directions, substituting "diet Coke." At least the bastard was right about that. A diet soda would serve the same purpose for her characters. *Focus on your work. Focus on your work.* All she had to do was write a great script and she was out of here; she could start another one that involved absolutely no fake-Messiah musicians and their bitch-goddess girlfriends.

After the session was over, Megan gathered up her notes and headed for the car, feeling a little happier. She was having lunch with David Tauber. He'd picked a new place specially, a Chinese where they had nothing but low-sodium vegetable dishes on the menu. Not normally her thing, but . . . he was teaching her how to look after herself. She should be grateful. She *was* grateful. After all, without David, she knew, she'd be lost.

Megan glanced at her watch. Twenty after twelve. She was meeting Tauber at half past one, so she spun her tiny BMW toward the apartment. She could do with freshening up.

❖

When she walked through the door Megan kicked off her shoes, reveling in the feel of the soft gray carpet against her bare feet, picked up her mail, and headed for the bathroom. Two bills to forward to the accountants David had found for her. A letter from Tina and Jeanne. Amazing how people got really friendly the second you picked up a little success. Well, maybe she would read it later. And a postcard from Dec. He was madly in love again.

Megan smiled. Some things never change.

She was about to hit the showers when she noticed the little red light flashing on her answer machine. That was weird. She'd only been at Artemis an hour, and she wasn't expecting any calls.

She hit play.

"Megan? This is Zach."

Megan froze. Oh, God. Had she gone too far? Was he going to tell her he was having her replaced?

"Electric City have asked me to jam with them on Friday night. I was wondering if you'd like to come along. For research. Anyway, call me."

Electric City. After Dark Angel, they were the second-biggest band in the alternative-rock revolution; though they'd never carried the social weight that Dark Angel had, they sold millions of records. She had two Electric City albums. Dec had all of them. The gig on Friday, a stadium show at the Coliseum, had been sold out for two months.

For a second Megan stood there, thrilled.

But he said research, and he meant research. Zach just wanted the movie to be the most realistic it could be, the perfect vehicle to show him off in all his glory.

He'd sounded different, though.

Forget it! Megan thought angrily, shaking her head. She'd seen the way he looked at Roxana Felix. And the bitch could have him. Those two were well suited.

She'd believed in Zach Mason once—before she'd met him.

Yeah, she would go to the show, Megan thought. Because it *was* good research. Zach could be as patronizing as he liked, but her only concern was for her script.

She turned on the shower. She couldn't keep David waiting.

❖

Roxana favored the gaggle of visiting executives with a slight smile as she strolled across the Artemis lot toward her waiting limousine. Tom Goldman escorting a bunch of Wall Street stiffs; young guys, analysts most likely, she guessed. It must be about time for the studio to announce its quarterly earnings—Roxana knew that some entertainment companies liked to put on a show for the bankers, take them around, show them some stars.

Well, these boys had got lucky. They'd got to see *her*. All eight balding heads had literally twisted around as she walked past, lean hips clicking and pumping under the white satin shorts. Once a model, always a model. She'd heard one of the businessmen mutter, "Jesus Christ!"

Roxana had sauntered past him, unimpressed. She always blew men away. She was used to it. If he got as rich and powerful and *useful* as that limp dick Howard Thorn, maybe she might give him a second look. As it was, though . . .

Seeing her approach, the chauffeur leapt forward to open the limo door, saluting. She didn't look at him, either. Zach Mason might drive himself around, but she was Roxana Felix and she wasn't into fraternizing with the help.

As the limo eased seamlessly out of Artemis's wrought-iron gates and headed toward Sunset Boulevard, Roxana bit her lip in frustration. Zach Mason. What the hell was *wrong* with the guy? Was he gay? Not unless every rumor she'd ever heard was a lie. Was he involved? All her contacts said no. And anyway, when had a man's being involved made a difference? She could make a twenty-year marriage fall apart with one flutter of her long, thick lashes. She *had*, more than once.

Roxana was under no illusions about men's morality. Sooner or later, every last one of them thought with his dick. And ever since she'd hit puberty, she had realized that her beauty was a potent weapon. If a guy was straight, she was a goddamn nuclear bomb. Nothing could withstand her. Never, not once in all her life, had she set out to seduce a man she wanted and been refused.

It just didn't happen.

It was incomprehensible.

And she was not about to permit Zach Mason to be the first to do it.

LA slipped by her, basting in the sun, palm trees waving gently in the faint breeze. The sky was a deep, cloudless blue.

Roxana noticed none of it. Her anger was consuming her. It wasn't like Zach didn't see her dressing up for him, didn't register it. On the contrary, he looked her over every time, as though rating her. Undressing her with his eyes. Sexually approving her. All tributes she received every day of her life, of course, but from Zach Mason they meant more—for the simple reason that he'd been linked with some of the most desirable women in

America. In the *world*. He was the ex–lead singer of Dark Angel, and as far as Roxana Felix was concerned, that made him a connoisseur.

So what was the fucking problem?

In script meetings, in public, no problem. He'd stare at her, flirt with her, whatever. The rock star and the supermodel. Great. And if they rehearsed a scene, there was incredible sexual heat there. Damn, she actually *wanted him*, in the way she'd wanted no other man for years, with the sole exception being Sam Kendrick—something she couldn't explain.

Desire for Mason was easier to understand. Even for a palate as jaded and cynical as hers, Zach Mason represented temptation at the deepest level. He was rangy and lean, but not in a wimpy way—more sinewy, well muscled, and dangerous-looking, like a wolf. Zach had wolf eyes. Long, black, unkempt hair, a chiseled face, and menacing, glinting wolf eyes. In a still photo, she knew, he might look angelic, Greek god beautiful, but to see him move, to watch him talk, that was something else.

Usually, Roxana was utterly uninterested in the career of anyone besides herself. And she was nobody's fan. But since she'd met Zach, she had ordered Tauber to send her up some videos of Dark Angel.

The music was dreadful, of course. Meaningless white noise. She had turned down the volume and merely watched Mason, watched him move across the lip of the stage, watched him cradle his rhythm guitar, watched him speaking to crowd after crowd that rose in a body to salute him.

For a few seconds she had been spellbound, unable to flick the television off. Just for a few seconds, of course. But nonetheless, Zach Mason was remarkable. She, Roxana Felix, had responded to him sexually. It wasn't just going to be great for her career to see him for a while, she thought; it was going to be great, period. And the next day, when she'd come on to him at the script meeting, he'd reacted perfectly; all raised eyebrows and long, slow, assessing looks—

And that was it!

He hadn't phoned. He hadn't called her over. He hadn't sent flowers.

The next day she'd worn a shorter dress and been more obvious.

He'd noticed, but—*nada. Rien.* Nothing doing.

Roxana invited him to lunch, in front of Megan and Eleanor. Zach accepted right away. And then he'd just discussed their characters, throughout the entire meal!

She had no idea what pathetic game Mason was playing. Hard to get? Did he want her to come right out and say it, was that what this was about? When she'd tried to grab him after the session this morning, he'd actually brushed her off!

Well, Roxana thought to herself, seething against the cool cream leather of her limo, if he thinks he's getting propositioned by me—he's gonna have a long wait.

But she had no idea how to break him down.

Roxana closed her immaculately made-up eyes and concentrated.

Zachary Mason is just a man like any other. There's a way round this. I just have to find it . . .

She reminded herself of her mantra.

I always get what I want.

Always . . .

chapter 16

The Manhattan skyline glittered below her, New York's concrete forest glinting in the thin winter sun. As the plane banked and veered, preparing for the descent into JFK, Roxana took another sip of her mineral water, swirling the ice and lime wedge around in her crystal glass. She felt refreshed and ready for action. After all her problems in LA, it was a nice break to come back to New York, a city she had conquered long before, and be treated like the queen she was. Among the pack of reporters waiting for her at Immigration there would be faces she knew. When they called the press conference at the Carlyle, the hotel management would already have prepared her favorite suite *exactly* as she liked it, right down to the number of kumquats in her fruit bowl. And when they set up the cover shoot for *Vogue*, Bob Alton would be there, and he wouldn't have any tiresome explanations as to why she couldn't do this or wasn't ready for that. He'd just be falling over his handmade English shoelaces to kiss her toned, tanned ass.

Exactly the way things ought to be.

The call from Unique had reached her via David Tauber on Monday night—Robert Alton wanted to speak with her urgently.

Roxana had checked her watch. Two A.M. Five in the morning on the East Coast. Well, it was time that fat, lazy asshole got up anyhow.

She dialed Alton at home.

"What?" answered a sleepy male voice.

Roxana tutted with impatience.

"Put Robert on the line. Right now."

A second's silence; then Alton answered angrily, "Do you know what fucking time it is?"

"Time you slept on the side nearest the phone, Bob," Roxana snapped. "I don't want to have to chat with your latest boyfriend when I need to speak to my agent. Is that clear?"

"Roxana? Oh yes, yes of course." He was stammering in his eagerness to please. "I'll do that. It's done. OK?"

"You called me," Roxana said icily. "I hope you had a good reason, Bobby. I *am* trying to make a movie here."

"Jackson Cosmetics," Alton blurted, wisely getting straight to the point.

Jackson was the hottest new European beauty firm. Their introductory range had sold out at Saks within twenty minutes when first introduced to the States two years ago. Now they were a major house, up there with Estée Lauder and Revlon, and they packed an extra-chic punch for being so new. Two unknown girls picked to model part of their skin-care range had become instant supermodels—Adelicia Louvaine and Catherine Braganza. Jackson was *the* house for younger women; innovative, stylish, and ultrahip.

"What about them?" Roxana demanded.

"They've offered you an exclusive contract. Five years. Thirty million dollars. And the exclusivity goes two ways—you can't model makeup for anyone else, but neither can they use another model. Like Isabella Rossellini did it at Lancôme."

"No makeup. Can I model clothes?"

"Absolutely. Of course. No problem."

"Other activities? Acting, for example?"

"Yes. You could do anything except model makeup," Robert wheedled persuasively.

Roxana's fist clenched by her side. Yes! Another triumph. Another laurel wreath. Another contract to end them all. And *thirty million dollars!*

"Tell them yes," she said.

Robert was gushing with gratitude. "You won't regret this, Roxana . . . I swear I—"

She cut him off in midflow.

"But Robert—the price is forty million. I made seven point five this year, and thirty million over five years works out at six million a year."

She knew he wanted to argue with her, tell her that this year was exceptional, the best she'd ever had, and there were no guarantees.

"Forty million, Robert. And I want an answer half an hour after business opens. Otherwise, no deal."

"Roxana—"

"Did you hear me, Bobby?"

"Yes. Of course." He fell over himself to back down. "Forty million. I'll tell them—"

"Get back to me," she said, hanging up.

He had got back to her. Forty million dollars it was. And she would take two days out of rehearsal to publicize the deal and pose for covers of English, French, and American *Vogue*.

"Can't you stay one more day?" Robert had pleaded, dreaming of all the juicy interviews he could arrange. *The Unique Agency Brokers Deal of Decade* . . . He'd be the talk of the town. And he'd get some snaps of the bitch to release over time, to hold her adoring public while she wasted everybody's time with this stupid movie stuff. "I mean, honey, forty million! The picture won't make you forty million . . ."

"Money isn't the point, Robert."

"Of course not, but—"

"If it was about money, I wouldn't be talking to Jackson. I've got enough money. Haven't I?"

"Oh, yes, sweetheart, but—"

"I fly back Friday morning. I have to attend something with Zach."

A beat.

"Are you . . . are you seeing Zach Mason?"

"Robert, whatever you think you know, you don't know," Roxana said coldly. "Keep it to yourself."

As she clicked her seat belt into place for landing, Roxana smiled in anticipation. Asking Bob Alton to keep a secret was better than an ad in the *New York Times*. She would have every reporter in the place creaming his pants, and then she'd fly back to LA and attend the Electric City show, where everybody would have heard the rumors . . . Zach was going to be there, and so would she, looking the hottest she could manage, with a megamillion-dollar contract and a new rush of desirable publicity under her size 6 belt.

What was it they said about self-fulfilling prophecies?

�„⋅⋅⋅„

"I have to express my concerns, Eleanor," Jake Keller said.

Tom Goldman's office was set up for the monthly senior-management meeting; cut-glass jugs of iced mineral water and plates of biscuits stood untouched next to a silver coffeepot. Eleanor was the only one drinking coffee, and she needed it.

"Certainly," she said, as calmly and coolly as she knew how.

Bill Jenkins, the young senior vice president of worldwide marketing, glanced at his notes. "Let's see. You list budget concerns, but I can't see anything in these figures that should worry us. For a Fred Florescu picture, this is looking pretty conservative."

"Nobody can call ninety-five million dollars *conservative*," Keller said, sarcastically.

"For an action movie, directed by Florescu, I think they could," Tom Goldman said, quietly.

Eleanor turned to look at her boss, surprised. Tom hadn't backed her up on a single issue since Isabelle's party. She was beginning to wonder if he ever would again . . . so what was this? A signal that normal service was being resumed?

"Possibly," Jake said, recovering quickly, "but his last three hits starred name actors. *Big* box office—Harrison, Keanu, and Tom. All three proven to open a movie. We have no such guarantees with *Triple Feature* . . . this project is turning into the Hollywood Unknowns Employment Center." He laughed loudly at his own joke. "And I must say that the romance part of the film is being totally overlooked. The Morgan character has nothing like enough lines."

"Jake." After the scene with Paul this morning, Eleanor had had enough. "First you object to my casting Roxana Felix. Then you want to triple her part. Which is it?"

"I objected to Ms. Felix for the part as it was written," Jake said smoothly. "I think she'd be perfect if the part were expanded. That would give her a chance to show off all the emotional virtuosity I just know she's capable of—"

"Bull*shit*," Eleanor snapped, oblivious of the stunned looks Bill and Tom were giving her. "You want to give her a chance to show off some world-class T and A. Don't think I haven't heard from Megan Silver what you told her to include: a rape scene, a gang-rape scene, two extra sex scenes with Jason, and a kick-boxing scene where she manages to get away, but half her costume is ripped off her."

There was a momentary pause; then Keller shrugged. "Sex sells," he said, somewhat defensively.

"Listen up, buddy." She was too furious to stay calm. "Rape is not sex. Rape is violence. And I do not make movies that glamorize rape. Now, if you speak to my screenwriter again without informing me first, I'm going to inform security that you are banned from all *Triple Feature* preproduction meetings."

"You can't do that," Keller said.

"Watch me," Eleanor said. "Oh, and Jake—you didn't object to Roxana being cast for the part as it was written, you objected to Roxana being cast at all." She imitated Keller's nasal whine. "'We didn't like Roxana's tests.' I think you'd better gather up all the objections you have—casting, script, budget, marketing proposals—and put them in a memo to Tom and copy me and Bill on it. That way you can't rewrite history whenever it suits you. And that way, I'll have something to frame and send back to you when *Triple Feature* clears costs in its first weekend."

"I don't think that's appropriate," Keller said waspishly, passing a hand through his thinning red hair.

"I don't know, Jake." Tom Goldman spoke up again. "I think it *is* appropriate. If you want any negative comments noted, maybe you should commit them to paper. Eleanor has a point."

Keller glanced from Goldman to Marshall, barely containing himself, but managed a nod.

"Very well, Tom. If you insist."

"I think I do," the studio chief said pleasantly.

"If that's everything, folks, I have an eleven o'clock," Bill Jenkins said, breaking the tension.

"Sure," Eleanor said.

Jake Keller gathered his notes stiffly and left the room without a backward glance, and Bill Jenkins followed him, checking his watch the entire time to avoid meeting anybody's eyes.

"Poor Bill," Eleanor said.

Tom Goldman smiled. "Yeah. Can't offend me, can't offend you, can't offend anybody . . ."

". . . because Jake Keller might be running the studio next year," Eleanor finished wearily. She sat back down in one of Goldman's cavernous leather armchairs, suddenly exhausted. Pressure. It had been crowding her from the moment she opened her eyes and saw Paul, standing in their bathroom doorway, examining her diaphragm. She'd asked him if he was planning to push a needle through it. The fight that followed had been one of their more memorable efforts. Then, arriving at her office, she'd found a bunch of anomalies in the *Triple Feature* budget figures; all things she was sure she had worked out last week, but she still had to fix them again. Three of their current movies had minor problems on set. A distribution chain was demanding a meeting. Then this happy little powwow, where her loyal deputy was trying to wreck her Artemis great white hope with his thousand-point objections plan.

It was too much. *And* her new Jimmy Choo heels in butterscotch calfskin were pinching her toes.

"Hey, Donald Duck might be running the studio next year." Tom shrugged. He looked remarkably *un*stressed; his black Hugo Boss suit picked out his eyes, his smile, and his tan. Eleanor thought to herself that black suits should be mandatory for all male executives. Nothing made a guy look so sexy, but nothing. Talk about power dressing. Paul didn't own a black suit.

"You can't let it worry you. The point is that you're running the studio *now.*"

"This a vote of confidence?" Eleanor asked wryly.

"You handled him great," Tom said.

"Thanks for the backup."

Her boss waved his hand. "It was nothing. You had a point. If he puts it on paper, it's fair both ways." He grinned. "Anyway, I asked them to make *you* president, not Keller."

"Maybe you should have done us all a favor and gone the other way," Eleanor said wearily.

"You don't mean that." Goldman looked over at her. "Bad day?"

"I've had better," Eleanor admitted, getting up to leave.

"You should feel better when you read these." He passed over a sheet of neatly typed figures. "Results for your first quarter as president; pretty good. The sale of the merchandising division and your rationalization program at international have made big inroads into the debt."

"We still need some hit movies, though."

Goldman nodded. "Indeed. The stock won't rise unless the bankers think Artemis is going to do a real convincing impression of Lazarus. Which is why I want you to come with me to New York next week."

Eleanor froze.

"You want me to come and present to the board?"

The quarterly results presentation to the board of directors, Artemis Studios' *real* bosses, was vital if the studio was to survive. Something Eleanor Marshall had learned fast was that true media power was something Hollywood rarely saw; the purse strings were clasped firmly in the hands of shadowy Wall Street financiers, media-shy moguls who gathered four times a year in some anonymous Manhattan skyscraper. The masters of puppets.

Tom Goldman had never let anyone but himself near the board since he'd been appointed chairman.

"You got it." He leaned forward. "And Eleanor—be convincing. This studio is in crisis. They need to believe that *Triple Feature* will be a hit and that more hits will follow."

She nodded. "All right, Tom. But what's the sudden crisis? You said yourself that the new quarterlies are good."

"They are, but that's not enough. You see—and this is absolutely confidential—the board has received an offer from Michiko Corporation."

"What?" Eleanor gasped.

"You heard me."

"But we're one of the last two studios still in American hands, Tom!"

"Yeah," Goldman said. "We are. For now."

⋯⋮⋯

She got in around ten o'clock, exhausted, and Paul was waiting for her. The dining room table was set for two; their best Delft china, a silver vase crammed with scarlet roses; champagne chilling in a heaped ice bucket; and Mozart, a lilting aria from *The Magic Flute*, floating softly from their CD player.

Eleanor felt a little of the tension lift from her shoulders.

"I didn't want you to dread coming home," Paul said, emerging from their bedroom to kiss her on the cheek. "I know you're having a rough time at work."

Eleanor smiled. That was the closest Paul would ever come to apologizing.

"This is lovely," she said.

"Have a seat." He wandered into the kitchen and brought out a steaming dish. "Vegetable lasagna with low-fat cheese. I made it myself."

Eleanor thought she might have preferred a rib steak or a pepperoni pizza, but still . . . at least he was making an effort. When was the last time either of them had bothered to cook a meal? They ate out or ordered in every night. *When* they managed to get home within two hours of each other.

"Sounds delicious, Paul," she said.

"Why don't you pour the champagne." He'd dressed up for her too, she noticed; he was wearing his loose Armani suit in navy-blue wool over a white T-shirt, his platinum Rolex, his gold cuff links. Obviously this was some kind of special celebration.

She tried not to compare him to Tom Goldman in his plain black suit.

Tom would never dream of wearing blue. Or using aftershave. He wouldn't give a damn about grooming; he'd think it was effeminate to preen in front of a mirror.

Eleanor tried not to think of it as effeminate.

"What's the occasion?" she asked brightly, helping herself to lasagna. "Are you working on a new deal?"

"No deal." He took a champagne flute from her. "This is just about us, Eleanor. This morning got me thinking. You're under pressure, I'm under pressure—"

She nodded.

"There's no need for us to fight all the time. We should try to spend more time together, see if we want to be with each other, see if we'd make good parents . . . figure out where this relationship is going." He pushed a small red velvet box across the table toward her. "Open it."

Eleanor gently unclasped it. There was an engagement ring nestling against a bed of cream silk: a vast dark green emerald surrounded by rubies and sapphires, mounted in white gold.

It was the most vulgar ring she had ever seen. It must have cost a fortune.

"Oh, Paul," she said. The ring winked at her like a set of jeweled traffic lights. "It's so . . . so . . . *colorful*," she finished faintly.

Halfin inclined his head modestly. "Everybody goes for diamonds. And don't worry, I know you're not ready to give me an answer right now. But I want you to take your time and think about this." His handsome face broke into a persuasive smile. "Eleanor, I think the time has come. We're both adults. We've both achieved a certain level of success in our lives. We make a great team, and the patter of tiny feet would complete the picture." He lifted his glass of bubbling wine. "Eleanor, it's time for you and me to consider a merger. We'd pay great dividends."

Eleanor smiled weakly.

"Now, I've got us tickets to the opera for next Wednesday and the ballet on Friday—"

"Paul, I can't go," Eleanor said.

"What?" His face darkened.

"I can't go. I have to be in New York all next week for a financial presentation with Tom."

"I see," he said stiffly. "Well, of course you must do what you have to. Another time, perhaps."

"Definitely," she said, feeling guilty. He'd gone to all this trouble to give her a perfect evening and the only thing she could do was cancel on him.

Anyway, he was right. They couldn't coast along forever. And with Dr. Haydn's latest pronouncement, she knew the time had come for her to make a decision. She just couldn't put it off any longer.

"Look, I really have to do this, Paul. But I'm truly sorry I can't come to the opera with you . . . it was a sweet thought. And I promise I'll think about everything you've said, and . . . I'll give you my answer by the end of this month."

There. It was done.

She had one month to decide.

Paul took a sip of his champagne.

"To us," he said confidently.

"To us," Eleanor Marshall repeated, smiling, and wondered why the only thing she could hear was the sound of gates clashing shut behind her.

chapter 17

T he limo drove right up to the backstage entrance before dropping Megan off. It was the only way the driver could guarantee
that she wouldn't get mobbed.

"Honey, if those kids see you walk past them with that thing,"
he said, nodding at the All-Access laminated pass that swung from
Megan's neck, "you are gonna get seriously jumped. Normally I'd
say just tuck it inside your shirt, but right now, I wouldn't take
any risks."

She nodded her agreement. Fans were crowding every available
inch of space on the route backstage; security was having a tough
time keeping them back behind the ropes, and every five seconds
some kid rushed up to the car and pounded on the windows before being dragged away, their face hysterical, contorted into a
weeping mask of adoration or frantic pleading. Megan had
thought it was merely another example of Zach Mason being ostentatious when a limousine with tinted windows, courtesy of the
promoters, arrived at her apartment to take her to the gig, but
now she wasn't so sure. Right now she was very glad that although
she could see this seething mob, they couldn't see her.

"Is it always like this?" Megan asked.

"Not for Electric City. But didn't you hear the rumors?"

"What rumors?"

"They say Zach Mason is gonna show here tonight. They say
he's gonna jam."

Megan glanced again at the packs of yelling, screaming fans.

"Are all these kids here for Zach Mason?"

"Every last one of 'em," the driver said.

⋅⋯⋅

David Tauber arrived five minutes before showtime. No point putting himself through any more of this garbage than he had to. Besides, twenty minutes before showtime he had been getting a highly skilled blow job from a very exclusive whore, and that wasn't an experience he cared to rush. You paid enough for it. He had made her perform a slow strip, then massage him, naked, and finally wrap up a very pleasant afternoon with some expert head.

Occasionally he liked to pay for it. That way you didn't have to talk to them. Something he'd appreciated as her warm, juicy mouth slid up and down his rearing cock, gradually increasing the pressure, her tongue swirling around the quivering head of his penis and then licking, hard, along the entire length of it. He fantasized she was Roxana Felix, on her back instead of on his, but that didn't really do it for him. Just thinking about Roxana could drop a fly into any ointment; she was the pushiest, most aggressive bitch of a woman he'd ever known. He preferred his women like Megan Silver—trusting and eager to please. She was no Roxana Felix, of course, but . . . she was pretty. Once he'd worked all that extra fat off her and put her in some decent clothes, yeah, she was quite pretty . . .

As his cock swelled even harder and he felt his orgasm build, David Tauber actually started to visualize Megan kneeling at his feet. He knew she'd love to do it. She'd love to do whatever he suggested . . .

On the short drive over to the Coliseum, Tauber thought about Megan some more. The vibe at Artemis was that she was extremely talented, but she'd made enemies of Roxana Felix and Zach Mason. But as far as David could see, *everybody* made an enemy of the bitch. It was the endless sniping with Zach that bothered him. If he could get Megan to swallow her pride and kiss up to Mason a little, her future would be very rosy. As Gloria had pointed out to him, the Michael Crichtons and John Grishams of this world were making five million bucks a script.

He wouldn't mind a piece of that action.

Maybe he would give little Megan Silver a thrill.

David strolled up to the box office and collected a stick-on VIP pass Zach had left for him.

He noticed that none of the kids packing the foyer and entrance hall were wearing anything decent. The scene was all leather and denim and Smashing Pumpkins T-shirts. Time to head backstage; if there was one thing David Tauber detested, it was hanging around the little people.

⋅⋯⋅

Roxana stepped out of her limo, All-Access laminate fastened conspicuously at the front of her belt. That way she could be sure it showed up in all the photos.

Zach had sent a stick-on pass, a little piece of nothing, over to her house. It was an insult, and if she hadn't been so determined to hook the bastard, she would not have shown up. As it was, she'd called Sam Kendrick.

"I need a laminate for the show tonight, Sam. Call the promoters and have one messengered over."

"Roxana, Zach is taking care of—"

"*Now*, Sam. Or you needn't come by this afternoon. Or ever again."

A pause.

"OK."

She had a second to relish the sense of power. So it was starting already. By the time they started shooting the goddamn picture, Sam Kendrick would be wrapped around her little finger. When he wasn't wrapped around the other parts of her.

A small spasm of desire rippled through her at the thought.

"Thank you, baby." She was pure sweetness. "Why don't you bring it with you when you come by."

"I want you," he said, quietly, urgently.

"It's mutual."

And it was. That was the strange thing. That was what threw her. The thought that she might enjoy fucking Sam Kendrick even if she had no other use for him at all.

"Did you really sign a deal for forty million dollars?"

"Yes, I did."

"So you don't need to be a movie star."

"I *want* to be a movie star," Roxana corrected him.

"Do you always get what you want?" Kendrick asked softly.

"Always," she told him, and hung up.

Roxana turned around and waved gracefully to the rabid crowd thronging the backstage entrance, trying not to let her momentary unease show. Dear God, what a pack of maniacs. Was this what music fans were like? Her own followers never, ever, exhibited passion like this.

As she turned and began to walk inside the stadium, a teenage girl leapt over the red crowd-control rope and lunged toward her, her face contorted with hatred. Roxana shrank back, a paralyzing fear knotted in the pit of her stomach. This was what every supermodel dreaded. The one crazed nut with the knife, the gun, the vial of acid . . .

Two security men rushed the girl and overpowered her before she got two feet past the barrier.

"Bitch! Bitch!" the girl shrieked. "It's you, isn't it? It's you! You've got him! You've got him! I love him!"

"Who?" Roxana managed, as the guards dragged her away.

"Zach! Zach Mason! You're his girlfriend! They said so on MTV!"

Stunned, Roxana managed a bright smile for the photographers waiting at the backstage door.

"Is that true, Roxana?" a reporter demanded. "Are you here to see your boyfriend?"

"Did Zach Mason send for you?"

"Who gave you the laminate, Roxana? Did Zach fix it up for you?"

"Is the movie going to be a love story off screen as well?"

"Were you guys a couple *before* you got cast?"

"Roxana! Roxana!"

Flinging her hair back, Roxana delicately removed her Ray-Bans.

"Zach Mason and I are working together on *Triple Feature*, people," she said, her voice honey-low, reserved and embarrassed. "That's the only thing I can say right now. I'm here to enjoy the show."

Immediately, cameras fired off around her, flashbulbs popping like machine guns.

"Roxana! Rox! This way, please! Just two seconds!"

She let them snap for a minute, then turned away. Always keep them wanting more . . .

"Roxana!" one of the journalists yelled after her. "When's the wedding?"

As she headed inside the stadium, Roxana Felix smiled to herself.

❖

The stadium headlights out front were switched on at full beam. From her viewpoint behind the stage scaffolding, Megan could see the roadies scrambling to put up last-minute adjustments to the rigging, technicians pulling at an amp here, moving a laser there. Electric City was renowned for its innovative stage set; the best thing since U2 brought the Zoo TV circus to town, it used giant holograms and computer morphing. Taped music was pumping out of the PA, loud as hell, punctuated by football whistles, screams, and cheers from the crowd.

Anticipation crackled through the air like static. The headliners would be on any second.

All-Access laminates at the Los Angeles Coliseum were outside her normal experience.

Being a guest of Zach Mason was outside her normal experience.

Where the hell is David? Megan thought, as she ducked out of the way of yet another roadie pushing a huge flight case across her path. *Why isn't he here yet? I need help! I don't know where the hell I'm supposed to be!*

She'd asked David to take her to the show, but he said he had to finish off some urgent work on his contracts that afternoon, and could he meet her there? Disappointed, Megan had agreed. She'd been hoping David might *want* to take her . . . but who was she kidding, right? Just because she'd lost a little weight, because he'd found her some half-decent clothes, that didn't mean she was suddenly good enough for David Tauber. David was a big agent, kicking ass on the fast track. He was sophisticated, he was elegant, he was superfit, and he was gorgeous. All things she would never be. No matter how many miles she ground out on the Stairmaster.

But she wished David was here now. She wished *somebody* was with her. It was terrifying, to be backstage at a stadium gig, no idea where to go or what to do, just wandering around the concrete labyrinth, trying to keep out of everybody's way. And thrilling. Totally thrilling, to know she could go anywhere she wanted to, talk to the band if she felt like it, watch a concert from the side of the stage instead of two miles away at the end of a sea of seats. Instead of straining to get a glimpse of five figures the size of matchsticks, she'd be standing behind the speaker stacks, close enough to reach out and touch the guitarist.

She would see the vast crowd stretched out before her. She would see what the band saw.

For any rock fan, this was a fantasy come true: that somebody would pluck you out of the crowd and set you down on the other side.

Megan wondered why Zach had done it for her.

"Hey."

She jumped round. God, she was pathetic; always under everybody's feet. Now they must have sent some official to tell her to get out of the way . . .

"Megan! Over here."

"Oh, hi, Zach," she said, embarrassed. "I was looking for you."

He walked over to her, amused.

"Dark Angel shirt," he said, reaching out to touch her T-shirt. "Were you a fan?"

Megan looked away. Somehow, when she was getting ready to come out, this had seemed like a really good idea; black 501s, heeled ankle boots, and her favorite Dark Angel T-shirt, the gold seraph logo on a black background. Dressing with a message. She would be a walking rebuke to the asshole.

As a scriptwriter, David had made clear, she was low girl on the totem pole. If she wanted to keep her job, if she wanted to write any more movies, she'd better shut up and smile; get along to go along. And a quarter of a million dollars was a lot of money. So she'd swallowed whatever insults Roxana Felix wanted to throw at her, and if she hadn't been able to control her tongue completely with Zach, she had tried her best. Minor retorts, sniping, that was about the extent of her comebacks to his constant goading. Since they'd started the rewrite process with that disastrous first meeting, Zach Mason had goaded her, teased her, called her writing unrealistic and naive. True, he'd got better as time went on, but still . . . and anyway, when Zach started being kinder to her, Roxana suddenly got ten times worse.

If Zach and she ever disagreed, Roxana would wade in behind her fellow star and pour acid all over Megan's point of view. Like last time. But that was to be expected; Roxana and Zach were obviously doing the wild thing, the way she posed for him in meetings and backed him up all the time. All the press and gossip columnists said they were an item.

It would be interesting to see if the bitch showed tonight. Megan doubted she gave a damn about rock 'n' roll, but this *was* a high-profile event, so she'd probably turn up. Megan couldn't wait. But she hadn't worn the Dark Angel shirt because of Zach and Roxana; the Beautiful People could do what they liked with each other. No, she'd wanted to say with her clothes the things she didn't have the guts to say with her mouth.

Like fuck you, Zach Mason.

You sold us out.

But then Zach sent round a limo and this incredible laminate, told her she could do whatever she liked, go wherever she wanted. Megan felt obliged and confused. Why was he doing this? What was his motive for this?

He hated her! It didn't make sense.

"Yes, I was," she muttered. "Everybody was."

Zach heard the criticism in her voice, but ignored it.

"Did you ever see us play?"

Megan looked him in the face. "Sixteen times. I saw you at the Omni in Oakland when you were just starting. I saw you at the Stone. And the last gig you guys played here"—she gestured around her—"two years ago, me and some friends from college saved up for a month so we could go."

Zach Mason nodded slowly.

Megan looked at him again. He was wearing jeans and boots too, all black, and a black see-through chiffon shirt, the latest cool thing in alternative-metal fashion. It revealed his torso; without fabric covering him, Megan could see that he was actually far more muscular than she'd imagined. With his long, dark hair and predator eyes, he possessed a feral, menacing quality.

She felt a hot shock of arousal, and hated herself for it.

"You look very pretty," Zach said. He reached out and touched her soft brown curls. "Too pretty to be so mad all the time."

Megan was completely thrown. He sounded like he meant it. The guy was dating the world's biggest supermodel, and he'd just called her pretty?

"Thanks," she muttered, and then remembering her manners, added, "And thanks for the pass."

He waved it away, still holding her gaze.

"*De nada*. Which record of ours did you like best?"

"Why do you care?" snapped Megan.

He was playing with her. He must be.

"I want to know. Indulge me," Zach said, smiling wolfishly at her.

As the crowd started to chant the name of the band, Megan felt her groin contract in a violent spasm of desire. Oh, God. She knew she should be stronger than this, but . . . he was so beautiful. Predatory and beautiful.

"*Auburn*," she snapped. "OK?"

"You don't sound much like a fan," he said.

"And you don't act much like a hero!" Megan bit back furiously.

He was silent.

Out front, the noise of the audience was deafening. Megan felt a wave of fear rush up inside her. Oh, God, what had she done? Zach was *the* star of this picture. If he chose to, he could make one call to David Tauber and she'd be off the project for good.

"You don't know anything about my life," Zach said softly. "Do you want to talk about why I split my band?"

She shook her head, mutely.

I know why you split the band, jerk. Money. T-shirt royalties. A manager who didn't kiss your toned ass hard enough. David told me.

"I had my reasons."

Yeah, about twenty million of them, Megan thought, but she said, "It's your life, Zach. Dark Angel was your band. Not mine. You can do what you like."

For a second he just stood there, staring at her, then looked away.

"Show's about to start," he said. "Come with me. I'll take you somewhere you can get a good view."

·:··:·

Roxana Felix was boiling with rage. She was sitting with Megan Silver and a few other women, wives and girlfriends of the band, in a tiny concealed VIP enclosure at the side of the stage. Lasers webbed the darkness; colored spotlights danced across the stage and illuminated hundreds of faces in the ocean of fans that stretched out in front of them. To her right, Electric City was blasting out its latest Top Ten smash. Roxana registered none of it.

She only knew that ten minutes ago, she'd been sitting in here when Zach Mason personally escorted Megan Silver, that dull little puppy, into the VIP booth, and *Megan*—a nobody, *a writer*, for God's sake!—had been wearing a laminate which she obviously hadn't had to pull strings for. Zach had sent the little tramp a laminate!

Zach preferred Megan!

And what made it worse was the look of surprise he'd shot her when he saw her pass—first surprise, and then a horrible knowing look, a sort of contemptuous stare. The mouse bimbo hadn't noticed it, of course. She was too busy gazing at the band and the crowd in some kind of pathetic wonder. Megan Silver actually cared about this stuff!

Roxana stared at the back of Megan's head. So, this was what Mason wanted, did he? A donkey instead of a unicorn. A sparrow instead of a peacock. And one who was so naive she probably didn't even realize it.

Well, the little mouse better not get in her way. Because if she did, she would pay for it!

chapter 18

Darkness had fallen over the massed ranks of the crowd. Just for a few minutes more, they would be kept waiting.

Her exchange with Zach Mason earlier had been *weird* . . . She'd been sure that when she came right out and condemned him, Zach would fly into a superstar tantrum, have her thrown out of the venue, have her fired. But he hadn't reacted like that, not at all. He'd been cool. Challenged her, but let her have her own opinion.

Megan didn't recognize the star she'd been sparring with.

She didn't recognize the prima donna David Tauber kept telling her about.

And here, in this stadium, she'd heard the Electric City fans scream his name all night long. When she ducked out of the viewing booth to use the bathroom, she'd heard near-hysterical reporters wondering aloud if it was true that Zach Mason was gonna sing. And walking through the hospitality area on her way back up to the stage, the vibe was just the same—Zach, Zach, Zach. It was Electric City's show, but all the anticipation, all the rumors, were centered on the guy she'd just been fighting with.

Two months ago, Megan knew, she would have been in precisely the same state of crazed excitement. To her generation, hearing that Zach Mason was going to play a surprise jam with another band was the same as somebody telling her mother that John Lennon's death was faked and the Beatles would play at Madison Square Garden this Christmas. Dark Angel was almost a religion, and Zach Mason was everybody's personal god.

In the heady, pumped-up atmosphere of the stadium tonight it was hard not to see it that way again. To see Zach through the adoring eyes of everyone else.

Working with him, Megan had come to think of him as a person more than a rock star. After all, he'd betrayed them . . . hadn't he?

She tried to get a grip, but she couldn't stop the butterflies squirming in her stomach. Zach would be onstage soon. Right next to her. And maybe, for a few minutes, she would see him again as the face she'd had tacked on her bedroom walls for the last five years.

Suddenly, there was a huge roar from the crowd, a howling wall of sound rising up into the warm night air. The hot rainbow of lights switched back on, bathing the crammed stadium in a pool of colors.

Electric City was back onstage for their encore. And striding out with them, one hand raised in salute, acknowledging the rabid adoration of the crowd, was Zach Mason, bathed in a single white spotlight, his hair fanning out around him like a black flame. She was close enough to see the tiny droplets of sweat beading on his chiseled face, close enough to see the intensity of his stare as he trained those wolf eyes on the crowd howling before him.

A raging desire gripped her, waves of lust starting in her belly and spreading out across her body, shooting little silver threads across her breasts and crotch. She felt her nipples harden under the T-shirt with his band's name blazoned across it. She felt her crotch grow warm and languid with blood, felt her pussy wetting up. Dear God, it was the most violent arousal she'd ever known in her life, and she wasn't even touching herself.

Dizzy, Megan gripped tightly onto the brass rail in front of her, leaning as close in toward Zach as she could manage.

Electric City's guitarist, Rick de Souza, lowered his fingers to the fretboard and bled out the opening chords to "Auburn," the title track from Dark Angel's second album. The record Megan had told Zach was her favorite.

As the crowd shrieked in ecstatic recognition, Electric City smiling and waving, the spotlight panned for a few seconds away from Zach and onto their own singer. And as he stood there, so close to Megan she could have touched him, Zach turned around in the darkness and smiled at her.

⋯

David Tauber sat on a wicker chair in the hospitality area, sipping a little champagne. He checked his watch. Fifteen minutes till the encores were over, and he saw no reason why he should have to stand out front, any closer to that unbelievable level of noise. From all the screaming, you'd imagine that somebody had turned a flamethrower on the audience. Which wouldn't be such a bad idea, judging from all the long hair and marijuana smoke. Thank God he had rescued Mason from this Nean-derthal crap.

Colleen McCallum concerts were never like this.

He might have shown his face in the hospitality booth on stage, but had been told by a grinning security chief that his pass wasn't good enough.

"But this is the same pass Zach sent Roxana Felix," Tauber insisted.

The guy shook his head.

"You don't get on that stage without a laminate. Roxana Felix has a laminate. Who gave it to her, I don't know."

"And Megan Silver?" Tauber demanded, glancing up to see the back of Megan's head on the stage above him. That Roxana Felix would have pulled somebody's strings didn't surprise him in the least, but Megan . . . she hardly had the clout.

"She has a laminate too. And Zach Mason saw to that personally."

"How do you know?" Tauber snapped, irritated.

"Because I set it up for him," the ape replied. "Now, you wanna keep inside your area, or you want me to throw you out?"

David had kept inside his area.

So, Zach Mason was setting up access for Megan Silver. Interesting. And Roxana was having to fight to keep up appearances . . .

As Tauber picked idly at a bunch of grapes laid out on the hospitality buffet, he started to think, fast.

Right now, he controlled three out of the four principles in the *Triple Feature* deal—the male lead, the female lead, and the scriptwriter. Sam Kendrick represented Fred Florescu personally, and that was a pity, but even David could hardly try to poach a client from his own boss. There were limits.

At the moment.

But anyway, as it stood, his fingerprints were all over the deal. If the movie was a smash, his name would be made. His salary would quintuple. He would switch from "up-and-coming" to "arrived." He would be a *player.*

There'd be a good shot at ousting Mike Campbell right away. Then he, David Ariel Tauber, would be head of Domestic Movies at a major agency, one of the youngest guys ever to do it. And before too long, he'd be able to walk away completely, set up shop on his own. David smiled pleasantly at the thought of it. So what if he was barely twenty-seven? He was kicking ass. And if Sam Kendrick wasn't exactly a clapped-out old lush like Kevin Scott, he was still getting old.

They were all old and weak and useless.

They could all learn from him. And if Sam Kendrick had to learn the hard way—so be it. That was the natural law of evolution; only the strong survive.

Well, he was surviving and thriving, but a lot of his power base was wrapped up in this movie, which was still only in preproduction. Right now, only Zach's position was absolutely secure. Megan could easily be fired, that happened all the time. Writers were plentiful, anonymous, and cheap. And Roxana—well, she had more security, since her tests with Zach had practically set fire to the screen, but ultimately, she was replaceable too. If Zach refused to work with her, for example, or if she tried playing the superstar with Fred Florescu. And it was important to him that neither of them be fired—David wanted as many fingerprints as possible on this picture.

That meant that all his little kids had to play nice together.

And something about this latest situation rang a lot of nasty bells.

Was it possible that Zach Mason actually wanted Megan Silver? *His* mousy, unassertive, bewildered little Megan? As far as the movie industry, Megan didn't know what the hell was going on, and she took everything David told her as gospel. Somewhat understandable, he guessed. Megan had come from the cool poverty of a slacker background in San Francisco, where she'd had a bunch of friends and been a clear part of a group, to Los Angeles where she knew nobody, got nowhere, and had wound up in a nothing job—even worse than the one she'd left behind her. Then by a fortunate coincidence he'd decided to annoy Kevin Scott right at the moment when Megan was begging for a chance in his office, and her brilliant, pacy, commercial screenplay had dropped into his lap like a ripe plum.

David smiled smugly to himself. He didn't believe in luck. You made your own.

But Megan wouldn't see it that way. Megan would only see a white knight in a red Lamborghini turning up at her chicken joint to rescue her. *She* had pulled his whole deal together, and she still thought *he* was doing her a favor. She'd had a very tough life, and she was still functioning in survival mode. It hadn't registered with her that since she'd impressed Eleanor Marshall, there was bound to be other work for her. In Megan's mind, *Triple Feature* was her only hope and David Tauber her only friend. And David liked the power it afforded him over her.

He had taken control of her finances. He had ordered her to change her eating habits. He'd even put her through a torturous training regime . . . It was amusing, the way she was putty in his hands. And let's be honest, it was pretty erotic, too. Lately, he'd started fantasizing about Megan. She was attractive, in a soft, non-LA kind of way.

But what if Zach Mason had started to think so too?

Impossible. Zach fucked models and porn stars and the best that the groupie sorority had to offer. His women had thirty-eight-inch breasts and matchstick legs and long blond hair. And Roxana Felix, currently rated the most attractive woman in the world—top supermodel, new forty-million-dollar deal—was throwing herself at him. David had seen the headlines from yesterday, the gossip running wild on MTV, the reporters outside this stadium yelling at him, asking him if he'd introduced "the couple of the century."

David lifted his champagne flute in the direction of the stage. He'd have to give it to the bitch, she was a smooth operator. Forget Charles and Diana or Richard and Cindy, a Zach-Roxana romance would mean banner headlines worldwide. It would *guarantee* huge box office.

But if Zach decided he wanted Megan instead—and if Tauber had learned one thing in this business it was that there was no accounting for taste—the whole thing could blow up in smoke. Roxana would insist Megan be fired. Zach might intervene, have *her* fired. One way or another David would lose out.

He listened to the manic uproar rising from the crowd out front. Zach Mason's voice was coming over the PA, but the kids were so loud they were almost drowning him out. And this insanity had been Megan's world. She *knew* this. She knew Zach.

If they could just stop squabbling, Zach Mason would really represent a dream come true for Megan. She might start to get ideas above her station.

David frowned to himself. This had to be stopped. Zach and Roxana should be together, and Megan should . . .

Think, David ordered himself. *There's always a way. But you better find it. Fast.*

⋅⋅⋅⋅

The last notes of "Black Rage," Electric City's biggest hit, faded into the darkness, lost against the waves of cheering beating up to the stage. Zach had only been doing backing vocals on this one, laying raw harmonies under Karl Olafsson, the headliners' lead singer, who now yelled into the mike, "You want some more?"

The affirmative roar was so loud even Megan took a step back. She was bathed in sweat from the heat of the spotlights and her own excitement.

"I guess we can do one more," Karl agreed, turning round theatrically to his bandmates.

Rick de Souza strummed the opening chords to "Fighting Fire." Dark Angel's signature song.

The crowd screamed fit to wake the dead.

"We'd like to introduce you to the guy singing lead on this little cover— our good friend, Zach Ma—"

The rest of the introduction was lost in the hysterical shrieks of the crowd. Zach walked forward to the front of the stage, bathed in three spotlights, arms extended to the audience.

"I want to thank Electric City for letting me jam with them tonight. They were fucking great," he said, nodding at Karl.

Massive cheers.

The band grinned.

"This is the last number I'm gonna do; something Dark Angel used to play."

He turned round and looked toward the concealed viewing booth.

"This is for Megan."

Electric City crashed into the classic, dark minor-key chords exploding around them, the lights flashed everywhere, the crowd began to chant, tens of thousands of voices taking up the chant.

Megan stood frozen to the spot, paralyzed with shock and delight.

"Were you pleased with that, honey?" a voice asked in her ear.

She turned round to see Roxana Felix, wearing a gold lamé minidress, smiling pleasantly at her.

"Yeah," she said. At this moment, not even Roxana could upset her. Zach Mason was singing "Fighting Fire" for *her.*

Roxana squeezed forward to the brass rail, so she was standing right next to Megan. She brushed her sweep of gorgeous, glossy black hair out of her eyes.

"I thought you would. It was my idea, you know. I suggested it to him last week; we thought maybe we'd been a little harsh on you."

For the first time, Megan noticed the laminate swinging from Roxana's belt. She felt herself crashing back down to earth, her stomach twisting in disappointment.

Of course Roxana had a laminate.

Roxana was Zach Mason's girlfriend.

How could she have let herself forget that? Did she *really* think a superstar like Zach would ever have anything more than a professional interest in her?

He'd said he was bringing her to this show for research, and that was exactly what he'd meant. If he'd decided to be a little more friendly to her, that was great. It would be good for the movie. But she was an idiot to think it was anything more than that.

She was standing in this booth, right next to the world's most celebrated supermodel, and she reckoned Zach Mason was gonna pick her? Yeah, right, Megan! Nice thinking!

"Thank you," she managed. "It was really kind of you."

Roxana smiled again, perfect, cherry-red lips blossoming across her face. Close up, Megan couldn't help noticing that Roxana's skin was absolutely smooth, tight, and unblemished, even without makeup. Like a searing knife, the recollection of Roxana's huge deal, announced on the news yesterday, with all the journalists bugging her about Zach, stabbed into her memory.

"And congratulations on your deal," she added bravely.

The supermodel shrugged. "I should congratulate *you*, dear," she said patronizingly. "Writing your first screenplay! I guess we're both career girls, huh?"

Both career girls . . . yeah. I'm worth two hundred fifty grand, less tax, less commission, less expenses, and you've just signed up to Jackson for forty million.

"Did you realize we're the same age?" Roxana asked sweetly.

"Are we?" said Megan, wondering if she'd ever felt less adequate in her life.

Onstage, Zach Mason was still holding the crowd in the palm of his hand. Megan thought he looked breathtaking; a hunter, a commander, young and beautiful but still very masculine, like the ancient sculptures of Alexander the Great. And Roxana was slim and exquisite, a delicate, sensual Aphrodite. They were made for each other.

Zach turned round again and smiled at Megan. But this time she looked away.

⋄

As soon as the lights went down, a security guard arrived to take them into the hospitality area, where the post-gig party was in full swing.

"I think I'll skip it," Megan said. "I have a lot of work to do." She glanced up at Roxana, every glossy black hair still in place. Maybe the bitch never sweated. "Zach, uh, Zach brought me along so I could get a better flavor of backstage life. I have a bunch of new ideas to—"

"Megan, no," Roxana insisted, threading one toned arm through hers. "You must come along. I insist. And I know Zach will be really disappointed if you're not there."

"Please, Roxana—"

"I *insist*," Roxana said, steel beneath the honey satin of her voice.

"OK," Megan agreed miserably. Like she had a choice. But she really, really did *not* want to see Zach entwined with Roxana Felix, not right now. Last week, she hadn't given a damn one way or the other. But to see Zach Mason play was to see him differently. And she was feeling like such a jerk . . .

The hospitality area was jam-packed; record company execs, loudmouthed radio-promo guys in Raiders shirts, bleached bimbos in dresses that looked like elongated T-shirts, and a few highly privileged reporters from *Rolling Stone* and other major magazines. The atmosphere crackled with excitement.

Still waiting for Zach, Megan thought, and wondered if he'd want to talk to these people. She hoped not. She wanted him to go to the backstage door and sign stuff for the fans.

"We probably won't stay long ourselves," Roxana confided, slipping her arm free from Megan's as a small clutch of photographers caught sight of her and ran toward them. "I want to get home." She struck a pose for the cameras. "Just a few, guys, please—I'm supposed to be having the night off."

Megan stepped out of the way.

"Roxana! Great to see you, glad you could make it," David said, swooping down on them. "Gentlemen, that will be all for now, OK? Ms. Felix is here to see Mr. Mason. Can we give her some space?"

Roxana shot Tauber the faintest hint of a smile as the media guys scattered.

"Congratulations on your Jackson contract," David added, hazel eyes sweeping across her glittering dress. "I think you were robbed."

She laughed. "David, you haven't said hi to Megan."

"No, I haven't," Tauber said, turning toward her. Megan tried not to let her jealousy show. Wasn't Zach Mason enough? Now she had David falling down her unimpressive cleavage. "I didn't see her there. Megan, honey, you look great."

"Thanks, David," Megan muttered.

She did not look great. She was wearing a T-shirt and jeans and her face was red with sweat. You couldn't jump up and down and slam against a railing for three hours and look great.

"Let me get you ladies some champagne," Tauber offered, turning toward a passing waiter.

A sudden hum of anticipation rippled through the glitzy crowd. Zach Mason, changed into an Electric City shirt and a new pair of jeans, had emerged with the band from their dressing room. Seeing Megan and Roxana, he immediately started to head toward them. David waved.

"Roxana," he said, passing her a champagne flute. "And Megan. That's for you."

Megan took the drink, grateful to have something to do. She didn't want to have to stand there like a jerk when Zach and Roxana stared pawing each other.

"Thanks, David." She smiled at him.

"You know, when I said you looked great, I meant it," David told her, moving closer. Megan breathed in the light scent of his aftershave. "You've lost so much weight."

"Thanks to you."

"You're a really pretty girl, do you know that?" David asked. Ignoring her look of stunned surprise, he put a muscular arm around her.

At that moment, Zach Mason pushed past the last knot of people, and stopped dead. There was Megan, pressed up against David Tauber, just like the first time he'd seen her. Only now the agent had his arm possessively around Megan's waist.

"Hi, Zach," Roxana Felix said, flashing him an incredibly sexy smile.

"You sounded terrific, Zach," David said pleasantly. His hand moved on Megan's hip, an unmistakably sexual caress.

"Hi," Zach said blankly.

Megan Silver looked at him, shyly.

"You were great," she said.

Mason looked from Megan to David and back again, not wanting to accept it. But it was true, of course. Why had he thought Megan would be any different? She wasn't the Blessed Virgin. She'd fallen for his competent, slick, rich Hollywood agent. She was exactly like all the others. And he'd dedicated a song to her in front of eighty thousand fans.

He felt like a jerk.

"Glad you enjoyed it," Zach said coldly. He turned to Roxana Felix, smiling brightly for the cameras that exploded around them, and took her exquisite head in his two hands, kissing her luxuriously on the mouth.

"Come on, sweetheart," David whispered in Megan's ear. "They don't need us hanging around. Let's go home."

chapter 19

Eleanor went through her notes on the way to the airport, knowing she'd have time to practice her speech on the plane. Tom had arranged for them to fly to New York on a private jet belonging to Howard Thorn, the billionaire financier, whose conglomerate, Condor Industries, had become the single largest shareholder in Artemis Studios last year. She would have to deliver her presentation to Thorn and the other six Wall Street moguls who comprised the Artemis board.

It was odd, she reflected, how the world had suddenly become so medieval in its structures. Real power no longer resided in presidents and prime ministers, but in the shadowy figures who controlled the flow of money; men with the power to devalue a currency or crash a stock market, who sent the world economy into growth or recession, and who could buy and sell the flow of ideas. George Soros. Bill Gates. Warren Buffett. Who was the most powerful man in the world? Probably Rupert Murdoch, Eleanor thought, the Australian who seemed to own half of all the papers on the planet as well as three major TV networks and a film studio.

These were the kind of men she'd be standing in front of. The modern-day equivalent of the Medici, the Italian merchant princes who had controlled Europe during the Renaissance. It was, she realized, going to be a baptism of fire. She had imagined that president of Artemis was one step away from the top of the power ladder, and she was now beginning to realize that in fact it was the very bottom rung.

She was nervous.

The car phone trilled against the cream leather of her seat.

"Eleanor Marshall."

"So, are you ready for this?" Tom's voice crackled across the line, and she could almost see the grin on his face.

"The question is, are they ready for me?" Eleanor told him.

Goldman laughed. "That's my girl. I'm sure we're gonna walk it. And besides, New York will be a vacation for you, the way things have been going back here."

"That's very true," she agreed. It would be pleasant not to have to think about Jake Keller's bitter little memos, or the *Triple Feature* budget problems, and especially her one-month deadline to give Paul his answer. "Where are we staying?"

"The Victrix," he said. "You're in the Presidential Suite."

"Ha, ha, very funny," Eleanor replied, but she was pleased. The Victrix was simply the most luxurious hotel in Manhattan, on a par with the Lanesborough in London or the Oriental in Bangkok. This trip was vital and nerve-racking, but at least Tom had made sure there would be certain fringe benefits.

"I'll see you in a while. Don't leave your briefcase on the back seat," Goldman teased her.

Eleanor blushed. "Tom! That was fifteen years ago."

He was reminding her of an incident that had happened when she'd just begun work at the studio as a reader. Tom Goldman, then senior marketing manager and her mentor, had asked Eleanor to bring over his notes on a merchandising deal for a kids' feature with Toys "R" Us. It had been an important presentation. Eleanor, then twenty-two, had left the wrong briefcase in her car and Goldman had had to speak extempore, pretending that the pile of rejected scripts in front of him was highly secret sales projections. He'd clinched the deal, but reamed Eleanor out. And hadn't stopped ribbing her about it for the rest of her career.

"Yeah, yeah, yeah. Once a flake, always a flake," Tom teased. "See you later."

"See you later," she agreed, hanging up.

As the Rolls-Royce glided smoothly and speedily down the freeway, deserted in the blue half-light of early morning, Eleanor Marshall felt her spirits lift a little. So, Tom was in a good mood. Whatever else happened today, at least she could be sure that the business-only, brusque awkwardness of their relationship since Isabelle's party was finished. Perhaps her performance with Jake Keller the other day had done the trick. Anyway, if Tom was joking around like this, things were back to normal. Eleanor checked out her face in her compact mirror. Light blusher, sugarplum lips with a neutral berry pencil, and equally subtle eyeshadow in pale pink and sand gold. She'd gone to bed early last night with a sleeping pill, so there was no redness in her eyes or sallowness in her skin from lack of sleep. In fact, her skin looked great, under its sheer mousse foundation; the fine lines around her mouth and eyes had become far less noticeable since she'd started with that alpha hydroxy moisturizer. Thank God, finally a beauty product that actually worked.

She could pass for thirty this morning. Sometimes life was good. Even under pressure.

-:·:-

When they pulled up on the runway twenty minutes later, Goldman was there and waiting for her.

"Got the briefcase? Good, let's go."

She thanked her chauffeur, took her case and overnight bag from him, and followed her boss up the steps.

"I thought you'd never get here," Goldman grumbled as they strapped themselves in for takeoff. "I was waiting out there in the freezing cold. Forever."

She checked her watch. "Tom, I'm five minutes early."

He waved that aside as they taxied down the runway. "Eleanor, I'm busy. Don't bother me with trivial details."

Once the plane had reached cruising altitude, Eleanor got up from her seat to take a look around. This was a Gulfstream IV, a serious jet, not your two-bit Astra or Lear that a mere multimillionaire might use. The only other man she knew who could afford a Gulfstream IV was David Geffen.

"Impressive, huh?"

Goldman walked up to stand beside her as she gazed at the decor. Howard Thorn had rigged his little toy up in dark blue leather with gold-leaf trim, the softest wall-to-wall carpeting, leather armchairs, a bathroom, a bedroom, and a kitchen.

"This baby costs twenty-five million bucks. And a hundred thousand a month to run," Tom said. "I know because I read it in *Vanity Fair.*"

Eleanor whistled.

"That's one hell of an expensive cab ride."

He nodded. "Sometimes I wonder if I got into the right game."

"I don't even see a company logo around here," Eleanor observed, glancing across at the young stewardesses in their smart navy uniforms. "I must say I'm surprised. I didn't imagine Howard Thorn to be the unostentatious type."

Goldman chuckled, clearly amused. "Are you kidding? This is Howard's *private* jet. Condor Industries has two more of these stacked down in Dallas, near their oil company. And in those you can't move for logos."

They sat down together on a cavernous sofa, and Tom laid out his projections on a glass-topped coffee table in front of them. They worked through the figures as Thorn's flight attendants served them breakfast: Earl

Grey tea from a Georgian silver service, tiny smoked salmon sandwiches, hot flaky croissants, and racks of toast with marmalade and strawberry jelly. Eleanor declined a second course of a Brie omelette, followed by hot pancakes with syrup.

"Tom, you're going to get fat," Eleanor warned him absently, her head buried in her speech.

"Nonsense." Goldman grabbed her hand and laid it against the thin cotton of his oxford shirt. "That's all muscle. Feel it."

He was right, Eleanor thought, her palm connecting with a rock-hard wall of flesh. It was solid muscle. Tauter even than Paul, despite his macrobiotic diets and rigorous exercising. She felt an instant stab of desire.

She snatched her hand away quickly, before things got any worse.

"Well, it won't stay that way, if you keep stuffing yourself with cholesterol," she said, hoping he wouldn't notice the slight blush.

Tom snorted, spearing a delicious-looking forkful of oozing cheese omelette.

"You sound just like Jordan when you talk that way," he said.

Clearly, not a compliment.

"Would you prefer some fresh strawberries and champagne, madam?" one of the stewardesses asked her, clearing away Eleanor's untouched plate. "We have Perrier-Jouet, Bollinger, Cristal . . ."

"No, thanks, I'm fine," Eleanor told her.

She took refuge in her speech for the rest of the flight.

⋅❖⋅

The Artemis board had convened at the studios' New York offices, an elegant couple of floors at 1 Madison Avenue, right in the heart of the Flatiron district in midtown.

Tom and Eleanor said little to each other on the way in. As they drew closer to the meeting, the mood subtly changed from humor to tension. Goldman was anxious, Eleanor could see that. He kept double-checking his statistics, like some nervous housewife who can never quite satisfy herself that she's *sure* she's got her passport with her, and needs to look in her purse every ten minutes.

What does *Tom* have to worry about? Eleanor wondered, looking out at the lunchtime traffic. He's a veteran at this, plus he knows all about the Japanese threat . . . but it's my first time at a board meeting, and I have no idea what they've been offered for the stock. I'm flying blind on this. And Tom gets to present figures—nice, clean, explicable figures our accountants have been working on for months. But I've got to wade in with my pep talk about *Triple Feature* and how it's gonna clean up with America's kids. Nothing provable, very touchy-feely. Very "feminine."

She began to wonder if there wasn't something sexist going on here.

"Who's going first?" she asked her boss.

"You are," he told her firmly.

"Oh, terrific," Eleanor muttered, as their limo pulled to a halt.

Tom held open the doors for her. "You're gonna be fine."

They announced themselves at reception and Tom led her to the far elevator.

"It's right at the top, but this is one of those express cars."

"Great," Eleanor replied, smoothing down the skirt of her pale pink Dior silk suit.

"You're nervous," Goldman said, looking at her.

"You're observant."

"Come on, Eleanor. You're the girl who was debating for Yale when she was twenty years old."

Eleanor shrugged. "Between twenty and thirty-eight, I think I may have got a little rusty on the public speaking front."

Twenty-seven, twenty-eight, twenty-nine . . . the floors slipped noiselessly by. They would be there any second. Suddenly, Goldman reached past her and pressed the halt button.

"Eleanor, look at me."

Surprised, she did. Tom was staring down at her, his brown eyes picked out by his dark Savile Row suit, tender and full of kindness.

"You remember when we first met?"

"Sure," she said, wondering where this was going. "In the corridor by the canteen. I was running down the hall and I cannoned into you and you spilled coffee all over yourself."

He nodded.

"You called me 'sir' when you apologized. Never showed me a second's respect since."

Eleanor recalled it vividly, just as Tom knew she would. Her first week at Artemis, when she was a lanky, nervous kid, barely out of college and desperate to make it in the all-male business world. And Tom Goldman, with a lot more hair and a lot less style, had been thirty and had been number two in the merchandising division, a senior executive as far as Eleanor was concerned. She'd been so terrified at spilling coffee down him she'd gone white with fear.

Tom had laughed and taken her to lunch, thinking she was cute. By the end of lunch, he thought he might have discovered a useful future lieutenant. Ideas, intelligence, and enthusiasm bubbled out of her every sentence. He became her mentor and friend practically right away.

"We were such kids," Eleanor said.

"We were." He leaned toward her. "Now, do you remember how we flew up here today? Do you remember the last time you called Mike Ovitz on his private line? Do you remember having Sam Kendrick sitting in front of you, begging you to green-light a Fred Florescu picture? We're not kids anymore, Eleanor. We've done absolutely fucking great. People fell aside, but we kept on going, and now we run the whole damn studio. And don't you forget it."

He released the hold button, and the elevator began to move again.

"You were a gangly college girl in jeans when I met you, Eleanor Marshall." The metal doors hissed open, and Tom followed her out into the studio's corporate headquarters. Eleanor felt his hand on his shoulder, and he leaned toward her.

"But today, you are the president of Artemis."

She had to blink back tears as she glanced up at him.

"We've come too far to give it up now," Tom Goldman said. "You go in there, Eleanor. And you kill them."

"Mr. Goldman? Ms. Marshall?"

A brisk, middle-aged English secretary in a tweed suit was walking toward them down the hushed corridor of the corporate suite. "If you'd care to step this way, the board are ready for you now."

They followed her past the polished mahogany tables, biscuit-colored walls, and discreet Impressionist paintings to a large set of double doors at the end of the hallway. Opening it, the woman discreetly ushered them into the Artemis boardroom.

Eleanor took the scene in at a glance. A long, square table polished until it reflected, like a mirror, the sober faces of the seven middle-aged men seated around it. Howard Thorn was the only director Eleanor had met in the flesh, but she recognized all the others from their glossy color pictures in the annual report: Harry Trasker, Kenneth Rich, Eli Leber, Kit Wilson, Conrad Miles, and Martin Birnbaum.

All of them serious Wall Street players.

All of them only interested in the stock.

Idly, she wondered if a woman had ever sat on the board.

"Tom, Eleanor, good to see you," Howard Thorn said expansively.

What a breathtakingly ugly man, Eleanor thought, smiling sweetly at him.

"I know you have a report for us. So why don't we just cut to the chase and get on with it?" He motioned to the empty chair at the head of the table. "Now, who's presenting first?"

Eleanor took one last look at the room. A porcelain coffee service. A mind-blowing view over central Manhattan, the city laid out behind and beneath them in a glittering panorama. And a bunch of financiers, completely uninterested in what she had to say—they were waiting for Tom's *real* numbers.

"I am," she said, clearly and confidently. She strode up to the head of the table, clicked open her briefcase, and unhurriedly hung her brightly colored demographic charts on the easel laid out behind her. Then she turned to face her multibillion-dollar audience, seven men who had the power to end her career with a stroke of the pen, and sell her studio out to the Japanese.

"Gentlemen," she said easily. "My name is Eleanor Marshall, and I am the president and chief operating officer of Artemis Studios."

chapter 20

They stumbled into the lobby of the Victrix together, laughing like teenagers. Goldman was still grinning at her when he checked them in, relaxed and loose in the aftermath of the victory high. It had been a great presentation; his numbers had been scrutinized and analyzed by the board and found to be impressive, but the real breakthrough had been Eleanor's speech. Goldman kept visualizing the surprised, attentive looks on the faces of the staid board members as she talked to them about the undefinable nature of the movie business, the difficulty in calculating future returns by past performance. With fluid gestures and easy words, she had demonstrated to them that just because Martin Webber had produced nothing but flops that did not mean she was going to. And finally, she had begun to talk about *Triple Feature*, driving home her point with such passionate enthusiasm that even bankers like Conrad Miles and Harry Trasker had begun to register what the project was all about, and how much money it could make for them. Howard Thorn had said nice things about Roxana Felix; well, Goldman expected that, after the arm twisting Thorn had done for her earlier. He wondered briefly if Roxana was screwing the fat jerk, but decided she wasn't. She was a forty-million-dollar supermodel. Surely it wouldn't be worth it to her, to fuck Howard Thorn just for help in getting cast. Thorn had only been able to guarantee her tests got seen, not to cast her, and *Triple Feature* would amount to a day's pay compared to what the woman was already earning as a supermodel. It just didn't make sense. But anyway, the clincher had come when Eleanor had pulled out a videotape from her briefcase, asked that a TV be brought into the boardroom, and then played the tests of Zach and Roxana together, drawing attention to the huge publicity angle in their relationship.

The suits had paid little attention to her words, though, Tom thought, smiling. They were too caught up in trying to control their erections. By the end of that five-minute tape, Eleanor Marshall had every one of the boys eating out of her manicured hand. As far as *Triple Feature* was concerned, they were believers.

Goldman wasn't out of the danger zone, he knew that. The Japanese would continue to circle overhead. But at least his president had managed to convince them that selling right now would be a mistake—*Triple Feature* would lift the stock price, help them to get more for the company later, if they still intended to sell. It wasn't rescue—it was reprieve. But they'd bought themselves a little time. And right now, that was as much as he could have hoped for.

"Here you are, sir. The Presidential Suite and the Emperor Suite," the receptionist said, handing him their keys. "Would you like a valet for your bags?"

Goldman hefted up his lightweight overnight case and shook his head. He picked up Eleanor's neat little Gucci case. "No, thanks, we'll be fine."

"Are you my porter now?" Eleanor inquired, amused.

Goldman bowed his head in her direction. "After the performance you just gave, I'm anything you want me to be, ma'am."

"Don't tempt me," she teased, as they headed toward the elevator.

The car hissed up the floors as smooth as silk.

"Not going to stop it this time?" Eleanor asked Tom. She was flirting with him, light-headed with victory. The relief of getting through their presentation was so enormous that it almost made her dizzy. And reckless. A little fun wouldn't kill them, not in New York, where even Isabelle Kendrick's bat ears couldn't pick up what she was saying.

"You can laugh—"

"Thanks," Eleanor said, smiling.

"—but you needed that pep talk. And if it got you results like those, I reserve the right to stop your elevator car whenever I feel like it."

"OK, coach. You got it. And how come I'm only in the Presidential Suite and you're in the Emperor Suite? Yours sounds way better."

"Age before beauty," Goldman said, airily. "And I *am* the emperor around here. Bear that in mind."

"Maybe it's about time we had an empress," Eleanor threatened him. "Maybe I'll do a Jake Keller on you."

They stepped out on the penthouse floor; their suites were right next to each other. Goldman opened up Eleanor's door for her.

"Look at that," she murmured, impressed.

The place was a Regency fantasy in white and gold; soft cream carpet was laid throughout with a delicate pattern of gold leaves, twisting in some unseen breeze, repeated on the walls and around the edge of the ceiling. Long, velvet drapes the color of burnished bronze hung from windows twelve feet high, offering a magnificent view down the Avenue of the Americas. On a white marble coffee table with gold detailing was a crystal vase filled with pure white lilies, stamens covered in thick yellow pollen that reflected the general color scheme. The bathroom, as large a room as the bedroom, was built around a centerpiece of a large Jacuzzi, with a sunken Japanese bath right next to it. But the third room was the thing Eleanor found truly luxurious: a perfect reproduction of an English country library, complete with mounted stag's head, leather-bound tomes, and a dark green leather armchair.

"Jesus," Goldman remarked. "Want to swap?"

Eleanor laughed. "You haven't seen yours yet. Look, why don't you go and get changed. I need to freshen up; then maybe we can go and have tea together."

"What, you mean cute little English sandwiches and scones with cream?"

"Exactly," Eleanor said.

"And you're gonna have a shower?" Goldman inquired. "Can I watch?"

She laughed lightly, but felt Tom's eyes hungry on the nape of her neck. Come on, now, Eleanor, you're imagining things, she told herself firmly.

"Nothing interesting to see," she said.

Tom took a step back from her, staring at her, his dark eyes taking everything in, from the elegant ash-blond hair fixed neatly in place, past the slight swell of her breasts visible under her jacket, to the soft curve of her calves, tapering down into Patrick Cox pumps that emphasized her slender ankles. Eleanor was beautiful and sensual and a pleasure to look at. He took his time, and she felt his gaze like a caress on her skin, a sudden lick of sexual heat following his eyes, as though he were actually stripping her, peeling away her clothes to examine her naked body.

"Somehow I doubt that," Tom said, eventually.

He saw her blush bright red, and the languid snake of lust curling in his belly stirred a little faster. He didn't know why he had done that, but it felt good. And it felt good that she seemed to know what he was thinking.

There was a long pause.

"I'll come and get you in twenty minutes," Eleanor managed, with an effort.

"OK," Tom Goldman said, and left the room.

⋅⋚⋅

Isabelle Kendrick didn't usually pay house calls. Either people came to her, at her convenience, or—more usually—she met with a favored few at the most highly visible restaurants in town. After all, what was the point of being a social lioness if one didn't shine in society? But on this occasion, she parked her Bentley at the front of the Goldmans' Beverly Hills mansion without even taking the time to gloat over how much more attractive her own gardens were.

Jordan had called this morning, and it was serious. *Extremely* serious. So serious, in fact, that for once Isabelle had absolutely no desire to discuss the matter in front of a crowded room. She had no wish to be seen to be discussing it with Jordan at all. And yet, as Isabelle stepped out of her car and walked quickly up to the Goldmans' pillared front porch, immaculate in her navy Bill Blass dress and Charles Jourdan heels, her heart actually began to beat faster, with the unusual sensation of excitement.

A uniformed maid answered the door.

"Won't you come in, Mrs. Kendrick," she said. "Mrs. Goldman's waiting for you in the drawing room."

Isabelle thanked her briskly and walked straight into the Goldmans' sub–Ralph Lauren reception room.

Just as she had expected, Jordan Cabot Goldman, overdressed in a glitzy Valentino pantsuit, was leaning tragically against the fireplace, weeping into a lace handkerchief.

"Isabelle, thank God you're here," she sobbed.

"My dear, I jumped in the car the second I hung up on you," Isabelle said, trying to feign compassion through the thrill of it all.

Forget about the parties. Here she had the opportunity for some *real* social engineering. And if she succeeded, not only would it be a strike against Eleanor Marshall, but it would mean that Jordan Goldman was indebted to her forever. Indirectly, she would control not only the Los Angeles Establishment society, but also the flavor-of-the-week PC crowd that Jordan had started to gather around herself. And Jordan would never be a threat to her position again.

Because Jordan would owe her. Huge.

"He's taken her to New York," Jordan sobbed, "and he didn't even *tell* me." Her voice rose to a little-girl wail. "I had to find out from Joanne."

His assistant. Isabelle's mind worked swiftly over the situation. The fact that Eleanor had accompanied Tom to New York was insignificant, just a professional feather in her cap. After all, she was president of the studio, Isabelle acknowledged with her usual mixture of envy and contempt. No, the significant thing was that Tom had tried to keep it from Jordan. And Jordan already knew her position was threatened, from the intelligence Isabelle had supplied to her from her party. That was why she had, on Isabelle's advice, thrown a fit of jealous rage and then wounded sorrow, demanding that Tom cease to socialize with Eleanor. He'd denied it, of course, but according to Isabelle's spies at Artemis he had been pretty clinical with Eleanor of late.

Evidently that time had come to an end, and so would Jordan's marriage, if she didn't move fast.

Tom had concealed Eleanor's presence on this trip from his wife. That was a major danger signal. Isabelle was relieved that at least the silly little tramp had had the good sense to call her about it.

"I know, dear," she said, calmly but firmly. "And you know what you have to do now, don't you?"

"But who knows how long that would take?" Jordan sobbed.

"Sometimes we have to anticipate problems, Jordan," said Isabelle with authority, "and sometimes we have to be *proactive* in solving them. Now, I shall tell you what to do, and I want no arguments."

"But it'll ruin my looks," Jordan wept.

"Not if you're careful," Isabelle told her. "And at any rate, dear, you may be out of options at this point." She crossed over to the mantelpiece and patted her protégé soothingly on the shoulder. "You have to do it, Jordan, and you have to do it now. Trust me. It's the only way."

⁘

Tom and Eleanor arrived back at the hotel around eleven. They had taken tea, gone for a walk, and then gone to see a movie.

"Are you kidding?" Eleanor asked, amazed, when Tom suggested it.

"No!" he said, grinning. "Don't you want to? I mean, when was the last time you paid to see a movie, in a theater, with popcorn, like everyone else?"

"Uh, 1978?" guessed Eleanor.

"Right! We should do this, it would be great market research." Tom warmed to the theme. "We can charge our tickets back to accounts as a business expense."

"I always liked the previews best." Eleanor adopted a heavy, mafioso tone. "And now, *Paramount Pictures* presents . . ."

"Exactly! Come on, let's go," Goldman urged, and they wound up in some little cinema off Broadway, watching a rerun of *Dazed and Confused* with a jumbo bucket of popcorn and two huge Coca-Colas.

"It was a great movie," Goldman said, as they finally walked into the Victrix's blue marble lobby. "Although you seemed to be enjoying it more than me."

Eleanor shrugged. "What can I tell you? I was sixteen in 1974. I lived all that stuff."

Tom looked at her. "You smoked dope?"

"Didn't everybody?"

Goldman shook his head, laughing.

Eleanor shrugged defensively. "I wasn't *born* like this, you know."

"Do you want a nightcap?" Goldman asked, and she was surprised to hear herself say yes. But she did want a drink with him, she realized. The pleasure of spending an afternoon with Tom Goldman, talking about everything and nothing, was too great just to be suddenly switched off with a stiff goodnight. They hadn't talked like this for years now, maybe even five or six years. The upper reaches of the greasy pole were too slippery and dangerous to do anything but climb.

They rode up to Tom's suite in companionable silence. It was similar to Eleanor's; decorated in silver and turquoise, it had shades of an Oriental harem, and instead of a library boasted a small private gym. His reception room was also fitted with a fully stocked bar.

"What are you drinking?" Goldman asked her.

Eleanor knew Paul would want her to say mineral water or a Virgin Mary.

"Bourbon on the rocks," she said. "Wild Turkey, if you've got it."

Tom raised an eyebrow, looking at her quizzically.

God, the guy is so handsome, Eleanor thought.

"Got a problem with that?" she asked menacingly.

He laughed. "No ma'am. I think I'm gonna have to bring you to New York more often. Dope, drink . . . this is a whole new side to you."

"I haven't done dope since I was twenty," Eleanor corrected.

Goldman mixed them both a whisky and they sat down together on his soft, vast blue sofa.

"To Artemis," Eleanor toasted him.

"To us," Tom corrected her, "because we got there, and today we made sure we're gonna stay there."

They touched their crystal tumblers together and drank.

"What did you mean earlier, when you said you weren't born like this?" Tom asked her softly. "What do you think you're like now?"

She leaned back, feeling the pleasant warmth of the alcohol spread through her. "Oh, you know. The Ice Queen. The Statue. All those things they say."

Tom looked her in the eyes.

"I never thought you were an ice queen."

Eleanor struggled to beat back the slow, heady wash of desire seeping through her. It was too much, sitting next to him like this, after the day they'd had, up here, on their own. She knew it was dangerous. And yet she made no move to get up.

"Why did you want to make movies?" he asked her.

"Why? I'm not sure." Eleanor considered it. "Because it seemed like a fun thing to do at the time. Maybe because I watched so many films as a girl. Because I liked the way they always had happy endings and the heroine always wound up with the true love of her life. Every woman's dream. In the movies, everything was passionate and larger than life and nobody ever compromised, and I wanted to believe my life was gonna be that way . . ."

Her voice trailed off into silence.

"And now you don't believe it's possible, for a woman to end up with the great love of her life."

"I believe it's possible." Eleanor toyed with the rim of her glass, then glanced over at Tom Goldman, sitting next to her, his brown eyes staring at her so intently, his large body so close she could hear his breathing, and his left hand, gripping his tumbler so tightly that the knuckles were white, decorated with a simple platinum wedding band. "I just don't believe it's possible for me."

"Look at me," Tom insisted. He put two fingers under her chin and turned her face toward him. "You are intelligent and talented and beautiful and brave. I knew you were special from the second I met you. You can have anything you want."

"No," she said, feeling her skin burning where his fingers had touched her. "Not quite anything."

For a few seconds, Goldman didn't reply. Then he began to look at her again the way he had done in her suite, infinitely slowly, admiring her sexually, his gaze seeming to lift away her clothing, until she felt herself juicing, felt her nipples stiffen in arousal.

"Don't," she managed.

"Why not?" Tom asked.

Eleanor tried to think straight, through the warm fog of her desire. Somewhere in the back of her brain, faint and far away, warning bells were ringing frantically. But the heady, liquid pulse of her blood drowned out all her normal caution. For once she didn't want to be sensible.

She wanted Tom. She had always wanted Tom.

"I want you," Goldman said, and Eleanor said, "Have me."

He leaned forward, very slowly, and brushed a lock of hair away from the side of her cheek, his rough palm cupping her soft skin, and then brought his left hand up to cradle the other side of her face, holding her head, letting her feel his strength. Then he bent down and touched his mouth to hers, a soft, dry kiss at first, then a more urgent one, and finally he ran his tongue across her lips and cheek, pushing it inside her mouth, desperate to taste her sweetness. His arm suddenly circled the small of her back and pulled her body tight against his, impatiently, insistently, creasing up her expensive silk suit.

Eleanor was overcome with desire. At the first touch of his skin on hers, fire shot through her, blossoming in her belly and breasts, everything animal and female in her in heat, her blood seeming to warm and melt. Naturally, she moved her legs apart, the center of them moist and ready for him. His caress was exactly as she had dreamed it would be for all these years; masculine and tender and gentle and dominant. His erection strained against her through the fabric of his pants, large and rock-hard with need.

"I always wanted you," he was murmuring, and Eleanor said, "Tom, my God . . ." and then his hands were fumbling with the buttons on her jacket, clumsily, and Eleanor twisted apart from him, stripping off her clothes, kicking off her shoes and peeling down her hose, as hungry as a teenager, until she was down to her bra and panties, tiny scraps of coffee-colored Italian lace, and then Goldman's hands closed over hers, stopping her, wanting to do that himself.

"You're so beautiful," he whispered, and then she groaned in arousal as his hands closed on the softness of her breasts, playing with her nipples through the lace, his finger and thumb rubbing them and stroking them until she was half mad with the pleasure, and just when she thought she couldn't stand it Tom's lips were closing over them, his tongue lapping and tugging, sucking them, the wet heat of his mouth making dark circles on the tips of her bra cups, the roughness of the lace contrasting with the smoothness of his slippery tongue until Eleanor was arching against him, thrusting her flanks against his.

"Do you like that? Huh?" Goldman was asking her, his voice hoarse with sex, and then his fingers were trailing down the front of her stomach, just the tips of his fingers brushing her skin, drawing a long, burning ribbon of fire across it. Eleanor sobbed with pleasure, unable to believe herself capable of such feelings, and then gasped out his name as Tom slid his hand into the soft, downy curls under her panties, covering her burning, damp mound with his hand, and then, infinitely gently, sliding two fingers inside her, rubbing lightly over the slick nub of her clitoris.

"Oh, Jesus! Jesus, Tom!" Eleanor gasped as she felt the jolting spasm, intense pleasure exploding all over her and fresh wetness flooding her between the legs as she came.

"That was nothing, sweetheart. That was just the start," Tom said, and she felt him unsnapping her bra and peeling off her panties, damp with her own juices as he rolled them down her supple thighs. When she was completely nude, he rolled her gently onto her back, stroking her lightly from her shoulders, along the curving sides of her body down to her buttocks, and before she could even twist in response Eleanor felt his warm breath on the nape of her neck, teasing her, making the tiny hairs there stand on end, and then he was kissing her, firm, circular butterfly kisses, licking and sucking at her skin, flicking it with just the tip of his tongue, taking his time, moving down her spine.

Eleanor felt conscious thought recede. She was only aware of Tom's mouth, and the heat of his body crowding hers, and his strong arms that held her relentlessly in place as she squirmed, maddened with desire, under the attentions of his tongue. Her entire body had become one huge erogenous zone; melting, pulsating streams of desire seemed to flow out of her spine, where his mouth was, and bathe her entire skin in ecstatic need. When he finally reached her coccyx, she was close to another climax.

"Tom, you're incredible," she sobbed, and Goldman said, "I want you so much, I've been thinking about this for months," and his hands were on her buttocks, gripping them, stroking them.

"You've got a great ass," he said. "I used to fantasize about doing this every time you walked down the corridor."

Eleanor tried to say something, but surprise and arousal strangled her voice and she could only twist under him, kissing at his forearm.

"Do you want me, Eleanor?" he was asking, and for answer she guided his hand to her pussy, open and more than ready for him, and begged, "Please, Tom, I can't wait anymore," and he murmured, "That's right, sugar, let it go," and he freed himself quickly, half ripping his clothes off, and Eleanor opened her arms to him, naked and hard and straining for her, his cock already dewed at the head, glistening with his arousal, and the two of them fell upon one another, kissing and biting, and he found her almost immediately and with one hard, impatient thrust sank himself deep inside her, all the way up to the hilt, and then all Eleanor knew, all she could think about, was Tom Goldman, above her, inside her, his swollen thickness drawing pleasures out of her she had never imagined existed, his intelligent, arrogant face now staring down at hers with an intense expression of desire and love, and she felt his cock, sunk deep inside her, hit some melting, blinding place, some sweet, secret trigger buried deep within her, and suddenly a new orgasm was gripping her, more powerful than the first, more powerful than any climax she had ever known, the sensations seeming to pour out of every inch of her body so she could feel the waves rock her from her forearms to her calves, her whole body convulsing in blinding ecstasy, and she cried out, "Tom, I love you," and somewhere very far away she felt him tense, coming inside her, and she heard him say, "I love you, Eleanor, I always did," and then the final, consuming, white wave of bliss broke across her body and swept everything away.

chapter 21

Eleanor woke slowly, her head swimming up toward consciousness very gradually and gently, her deep sleep pierced by soft
shafts of golden morning light. She glanced at the gold carriage
clock by her bedside. It was six-forty A.M.; in another five minutes
the alarm would have shrilled, waking her far less pleasantly.
Sleepily, she turned it off, stretching luxuriously as the memories
of the night before came flooding back. Despite the lack of sleep,
her whole body felt loose and relaxed, as though her very bones
had melted under Tom's mouth.

She twisted a little on the navy-blue satin Pratesi sheets. Tom
Goldman's large, solid back was turned toward her, moving
slightly as he slept. Eleanor admired him briefly for a second or
two, staring at the hard bulk of him, liking the masculinity of the
tiny dark hairs on his back, the scent of his body next to hers. She
debated whether or not to wake him now, so they could make
love again, but decided against it; they had a flight in two hours
and she wanted to dress and prepare herself, put her makeup on,
be as beautiful for him as she possibly could. Her hair was a
wreck, her face was a mess—well, she'd hardly had time for the
cleanse-tone-moisturize thing last night—and she needed to take a
shower.

Eleanor slipped noiselessly out of bed, careful not to wake him,
and gathered up her crumpled clothes from the sofa and the floor.
Then she tiptoed back to the bed, kissed Tom lightly at the top of
his spine, and crept out of his suite.

⋅⋅⋅❖⋅⋅⋅

Megan tried not to give herself time to think about what she was doing. If she paused for breath, she might back out of it. This was not something reversible. This was her chance to cast off her old way of life and plunge headfirst into a new one. It felt a little uncomfortable, but in Hollywood, perhaps this was the only way.

The Electric City concert had been the last straw.

Was she jealous of Roxana Felix? Megan asked herself. Roxana was an out-and-out bitch, a fashion princess on the receiving end of a lucky genetic accident which she obviously thought entitled her to be queen of all she surveyed. To know her was to loathe her. She was spoiled, pampered, unreasonable, and spiteful.

Was she jealous of Roxana Felix?

Absolutely.

Megan grabbed her favorite white cotton Gap shirt from her closet. A classic white shirt was the best choice for shopping—a plain background you couldn't go wrong with. She would be able to try out hundreds of different looks with this shirt. And a good white shirt, teamed with a pair of designer jeans and calf-length cowboy boots, could walk unembarrassed into the most exclusive store on Melrose or Rodeo Drive. And that was where she was headed.

Megan knew she'd never forget the image of Roxana, silken hair flowing around her alabaster shoulders, gold lamé minidress clinging to her curveless, ultraslim frame, leaning toward her in the viewing booth and cooing that she and Zach had discussed dedicating that song to Megan, that they felt they'd been a little hard on her . . .

Rage and disappointment had hit her with the force of a fist in the stomach. She had been so sure that Zach was finally talking to her, looking at her. He'd let her criticize him, he'd been kind and gracious, and when he got up on that stage and sang, Megan had felt he was interested in her, even though she wasn't a model, or a star, or a rich Beverly Hills babe like Jordan Goldman.

Well, Roxana had put her straight. And it wasn't merely the fact that Zach was with Roxana that infuriated Megan. The fact was that every single guy backstage had been mesmerized by her, paying homage as though the bitch was the Queen of Sheba. *Including* her David. And if that was to be expected, Megan also recalled that the other women—the blond bimbos, the groomed, polished trophy wives, the sexy female reporters in their elegant little Chanel numbers—had got their fair share of attention too, while she, the earnest, idealistic X-er in her T-shirt and jeans, with her loose brown hair and no makeup, had been completely ignored.

Zach had snubbed her. David hadn't even seen she was there, not at first. And none of the other guys in the place had so much as glanced in her direction.

Goddamnit! Megan thought, getting angry. I'll play the game too.
She knew what she was about to do was selling out, but that was too bad.
Megan Silver was just sick and tired of being invisible.

⋅⋙⋅

Jordan Cabot Goldman stepped carefully out of her limousine, trying
not to scuff her Versace mauve silk pumps on the New York sidewalk. She
shivered. God, she hated Manhattan. It was so bitterly cold in winter, so
unbearably hot in summer, and crammed full of people who seemed obsessed with work.

"May I carry your bags for you, madam?" a Victrix porter inquired, rushing forward from the lobby to assist her.

Jordan shook her head, girlish blond hair flying about in the early-
morning breeze.

"No, thank you," she said. "I'm not staying. I've come to collect my husband." She smiled brilliantly. "It's a surprise."

⋅⋙⋅

Megan hit the town with a vengeance. She had a gold American Express
card, a BMW with an empty trunk, and a ferocious hunger.

She was fed up with waiting for David to notice her. She'd lost weight,
toned her muscles, and learned to survive as a Hollywood screenwriter, but
she still couldn't get him to do anything more than flirt with her. That,
Megan told herself, was going to change. Today.

The first stop on her list was Fred Hayman. Then Frederick's of Hollywood, where she bought the most outrageous teddy in crimson lace, cut
high on the thigh and plunging at the neck, a sexy, sinful scrap of scarlet
that made her gasp when she saw it in the mirror. Then she headed to
Melrose and the boutiques, and shopped steadily for four hours, refusing
to look at the prices, just picking up the receipts to check later, after it was
too late to back out. She got a prêt-à-porter Chanel suit in bold purple
wool, with satin pumps to match; a minute Azzedine Alaia clinging dress
in black stretch Lycra; a vermilion satin-knit skirt and flowing tunic top by
Richard Tyler; an Anne Klein pantsuit in the softest butterscotch cashmere; ten different Ralph Lauren shirts; a halter-necked, bias-cut gown in
bronze satin by Isaac Mizrahi; and suits in pink, dark green, and turquoise
wool by Dior, Saint Laurent, and Anna Sui.

"Oh! Ma'am, you look *divine*," one of the salesgirls squealed when she
emerged from the changing alcove in the turquoise Anna Sui. "That cut is
so *you*. But wouldn't you rather try it in the red? Turquoise isn't the best
color for a brunette."

Megan shook her head, a little grandly.

"Turquoise will be fine," she said.

"Yes ma'am," the girl agreed, flustered, not wanting to upset a customer with so many glossy carrier bags.

After all, Megan added silently, *I'm not going to be a brunette for long.*

Once all her major outfits had been carefully packed away in the back of her car, Megan spent her lunch hour shopping for accessories. Court shoes from Kurt Geiger, two pairs of Manolo Blahnik heels, and trendy stacked sandals by Patrick Cox. A scarf from Hermès. A Gucci belt. A signature purse in cream silk from Chanel with matching kid gloves. And a bottle of Joy perfume to complete it all.

Megan tipped the girl who carried her new bags to the car twenty bucks and didn't thank her. If Beverly Hills bitch was what she had to be, Beverly Hills bitch it was. Rich, ostentatious, and don't talk to the help.

She had used David's name to get herself squeezed in at The Ivy for lunch. It was another glorious, sunny Los Angeles day. Megan admired the way the light sparkled on her water glass, and tried to calm her growling stomach with honeydew melon and a Caesar salad. For a second she longed wistfully for the char-grilled burgers she and Dec used to barbecue out in their yard on Haight, in the summer, when they had the guys over and everyone would drink cheap beer, and they'd put on a Green River CD and talk about God and sex and death and whatever else, or watch *Married, With Children* reruns. But she shoved that thought to one side. In San Francisco, she had been a nothing. In Los Angeles, she was going to be a someone, and surely, no self-respecting woman out here permitted so much as an ounce of spare fat on her cellulite-free thighs. Burgers and beer were out; salads and mineral water were in.

Megan made it to Le Printemps at two P.M. exactly. It had taken her a week to get an appointment with Jacques Roissy, the chief stylist, but she was certain it would be worth the wait; Le Printemps was the most exclusive, newest beauty salon in the city, boasting a range of antiage preparations and UV-filter products that had older women panting, and a team of hairdressers, overpaid refugees from Vidal Sassoon and John Frieda in London, that had taken the town by storm. In Hollywood, where beauty vies with fame as the local religion of choice, Jacques Roissy had already acquired his own cult, with all the worshipers drawn from the richest, most privileged echelons of West Coast females.

Megan knew she didn't need the antiwrinkle creams right now, but her hair could sure do with an overhaul, and she knew she had come to the right place. Face it—anything *this* expensive had to be good.

Le Printemps was tucked away on La Brea, behind discreet wrought-iron gates. Megan was greeted by a white-coated receptionist and her credit card details were taken while her car was driven away to be valet-parked. Moments later, when she had only just sat down with the latest Paris *Vogue* and a fat-free cappuccino, a short, plump man with slicked-back red hair and a huge diamond pinky ring burst into the lobby and swooped down on her, kissing noisily at the air on either side of her cheeks.

"*Mademoiselle Silver, n'est-ce pas? Mais qu'elle est belle! Comment ça va?*" he trilled.

"*Ça va très bien, merci,*" stammered Megan, hoping she wasn't going to have to rely on her eighth-grade French for the entire afternoon. "*Et vous?*"

"*Mon Dieu! Une Française!*" the apparition squealed, delighted. "*Mais il faut parler anglais ici, non?* We are enchanted to see you 'ere, mademoiselle. Already you are very pretty, yes? But not chic. We make you *très* chic. You will not recognize yourself." He paused to draw breath, and Megan stood up, wondering exactly what she'd let herself in for. A second white-robed flunky appeared with a blue cotton gown, and Megan tied it round herself as Jacques opened the door to the Printemps inner sanctum. She had a glimpse of a minimalist fantasy palace, the beauty salon decked out in Japanese prints, chrome, and dark wood. Expensive-smelling fragrances drifted toward her; jasmine, sandalwood, mimosa, attar of roses.

"*Ma chère,*" Jacques enthused, linking his plump arm through her slender one, "we are about to make you into a new woman."

Megan thought about Roxana Felix, sashaying into the backstage hospitality area with her shimmering dress, her glossy raven hair, and her million-dollar smile, and David and Zach just melting at her feet.

Firmly, she quashed her misgivings.

"That's what I'm here for," she said.

·:·

Eleanor checked herself out in the mirror again and tried not to worry. Maybe Tom was still asleep. Or maybe he was ordering breakfast for the two of them, something romantic, like strawberries and croissants and champagne. Just because he hadn't rung her room yet, hadn't knocked on her door, didn't mean anything was wrong.

Her reflection stared back at her, immaculate and charming in a new suit, a smart navy Jil Sander with a white trim around the collar and cuffs. She had packed black Stephane Kelian heels to go with it, and her makeup was a fresh mixture of apricot eyes and rose lips and cheeks. Earlier, when she was feeling lighthearted, almost dizzy with happiness, Eleanor had actually put on some jewelry—two discreet sapphire drop earrings, which now sparkled attractively under her neatly brushed hair. Her small Gucci overnight case was packed and ready to go.

She had been ready to go for twenty minutes.

Tom couldn't be regretting it, could he? Eleanor wondered, the thought clenching a tight fist of panic around her heart. He'd been so tender, so passionate . . . everything about last night had felt right, proper, good. She had loved Tom distantly for so long, fantasized hopelessly about him for so many years, and last night had been all she had dreamed of and more. He had taken her to a place she didn't know existed, he had changed her life forever, Eleanor knew that now. She felt more of a female, more of a woman, than she had ever felt before. And she would never see the sexual act the same way again—as a mildly pleasant activity for women, something the entire world overrated in one big conspiracy, pretending it was the best thing since sliced bread, when most girls she knew would prefer a good back rub, if they were honest. Last night with Tom had cured her of that idea forever. Eleanor could feel the echoes of that white-hot release inside her still, suddenly realized what the sexologists meant when they said that a woman reaches her sexual peak in her late thirties and early forties.

Maybe that was the difference between having sex and making love.

Last night was the first time that she had ever truly made love.

Tom *must* have felt it too, he must have. It was too intense to miss. Surely there was no way he wouldn't have been touched by what had happened between them, by what he had caused to happen between them . . .

Eleanor wondered what would happen now. She had tried to put off this question, but she couldn't hide it forever . . . Would Tom get a divorce? He must, surely, love her . . . didn't last night prove that? And as for herself, she had been trembling on the brink of commitment to Paul, trying to talk herself into conceiving a child by Paul, but that was over now. She had to be with Tom. She couldn't settle, not anymore.

The phone by her bedside purred.

Joyfully, Eleanor spun away from the mirror and sprinted into the bedroom, scolding herself—this was no way for a thirty-eight-year-old woman to behave—and dived on the receiver.

"Yes?" she said.

"Eleanor?"

It was Tom. Her heart flipped over in her chest.

"Hey," she said softly. "I thought you'd never ask."

There was a brief, uncomfortable pause.

"If you're ready, why don't you meet me in the lobby?" Goldman said stiffly. "I have a car waiting to take us to the airport."

The air seemed to freeze around her. Time pooled and stopped, and a terrible, clammy fear gripped her throat.

She knew Tom Goldman backward, knew his every subtle nuance of tone and gesture and expression. And this was Tom at his most businesslike, his most impersonal.

He thought last night was a mistake. He wanted her to pretend it never happened.

Tears of shock and disbelief prickled in Eleanor Marshall's eyes.

"Eleanor, are you there?" Goldman asked.

She took a deep breath, composing herself, and then replied, "Yes, Tom, of course. I'll be right down. If we're lucky, maybe we can catch the eight-thirty flight—that would give me a couple of extra hours with Megan Silver."

"OK," Tom said, and hung up.

Eleanor grabbed her case and her room key and walked straight out to the elevators, moving as fast as she could, trying not to give herself time to think. That was a luxury she could not afford. That would be fatal.

In the elevator car she counted each floor as it hissed smoothly downward, recited couplets from Shakespeare, anything to stop herself from thinking about Tom and what he'd done yesterday. She realized with a sick crunch of despair that she was never going to get in an elevator again without imagining Tom, and yesterday, and last night.

Mercifully quickly they reached the ground floor, and Eleanor crossed over to reception to check out. As soon as she had signed off on the form she turned left and walked into the lobby, looking for Tom.

She found him right away.

Goldman was standing by a huge black leather sofa, dressed in a nondescript gray suit, and looking awkward and guilty, and . . . happy? And with a start of absolute disbelief, Eleanor saw that Jordan was standing next to him, dressed in a fussy purple pantsuit, one hand firmly clasping her husband's.

Eleanor's mouth dropped open before she could pull herself together, but recovering at lightning speed, she walked up to them.

"Jordan! This is a surprise," she managed. "I thought you were back in LA."

"Oh I *was*," Jordan squeaked, her face a mask of childish delight, "but I caught a real late flight last night and got over here first thing in the morning. I wanted to meet Tom here and surprise him in person." She turned coquettishly to her husband. "Can we tell Eleanor, honey? I wanted you to be the first to hear it, but now . . ."

"Yeah," Goldman said, not meeting Eleanor's eyes. He looked away, subdued, embarrassed. "Go ahead."

"Eleanor, I just know you and Paul will be *sooo* happy for us," Jordan cooed, squeezing Tom's hand ostentatiously. "It's so fabulous! Isn't it, sweetheart? We're going to have a baby!"

chapter 22

Roxana Felix and David Tauber sat together at a corner table in the small, elegant dining room of Lutèce, eating lunch. Nothing about David Tauber's manner proclaimed him to be excited about this; he ordered comfortably, he ate slowly, and he never so much as glanced at another table. But inside, he was thrilled. The hum of discreet conversation all around him had the music of money rippling through it; this restaurant was where Wall Street mixed with Hollywood and flirted with the Social Register, and normally, he would have had to wait weeks for a table. Sam Kendrick might have been able to breeze in here, but not him. Not yet. But add a forty-million-dollar supermodel to the equation, and it was a different story.

Reservations had fallen over themselves to accommodate him. The maitre d' had rushed to seat them as prominently as possible. And David Tauber had the very pleasant sensation of knowing that here, in one of New York's most exalted meeting places, the great and powerful were ogling *his* table, and not the other way around.

Word of this lunch would leak out, he knew. It would send shockwaves of fear through the fat little fucks at Unique, Roxana's model agency. And it would be another feather in his personal cap—since he'd signed her, Roxana had been dealing more through Sam Kendrick than through him. For some reason. Well, obviously that was all about to change.

"Won't you have a little more champagne, Roxana?" he asked solicitously, extending the bottle of vintage Taittinger toward her.

"Not for me." Ms. Felix shook her lovely head. "I have to watch my figure."

Tauber laughed, and Roxana smiled encouragingly at him.

The two of us are so alike, he thought. She'll stop at nothing to get what she wants. She has already demonstrated that beyond doubt. My God, I remember when I didn't even think I could persuade Artemis to look at the bitch's tests. And she sees herself in me. She knows I can be useful to her. Face it, she didn't call me out here for the pleasure of my company.

"Your figure is beyond perfect, Roxana. Just like the rest of you," David purred. "And I bet your photographers out here are saying exactly the same thing." He shrugged boyishly. "We poor movie-business types have to hope the Jackson people will let you go in time for a few rehearsals."

"I'll go when I feel like it," Roxana said.

"Of course." He was all deference.

"And I didn't ask you here to discuss my figure."

David leaned forward. "You know your wish is my command, Roxana."

Roxana Felix regarded her agent through faintly narrowed lids. Hmm. He was good, no denying it. He'd dressed appropriately—Hugo Boss suit in dark charcoal wool, Turnbull & Asser paisley tie, no embarrassingly loose Angeleno style. And he hadn't so much as looked away from her once.

Triple Feature was about to go into rehearsals. One week of those, and they were on location in the Seychelles. That was when the fun would start.

Once she was on camera, she would be impossibly expensive to replace. She wouldn't have to take any more crap from that prissy bitch Eleanor Marshall and her mousy little screenwriter protégé.

It was going to be good. Establishing herself as a true star would be her first priority—but revenge would be number two on the list. Payback time. For every one of them that had insulted, snubbed, or thwarted her.

Zach Mason. Eleanor Marshall. Sam Kendrick. They all had it coming.

But Megan Silver, the dumpy little nothing, Megan Silver was going to pay the most dearly.

This was going to need delicate handling, though. And that was why she had summoned Tauber to New York. Because Roxana had some serious plans, and they went beyond just getting a few people fired.

She'd learned some valuable lessons during her time in LA. Dear God, she hadn't been screwing Howard Thorn for nothing. She was going to get more than real fame out of this movie; by the time she had finished, she was going to shift the goddamn power balance, at Artemis, at SKI, and socially.

Those pathetic sun-dried assholes had thought they could patronize her!

Roxana's fingers tightened imperceptibly around the stem of her champagne flute. Even David Tauber thought he was using her. Did he truly believe that she could be manipulated with some decent pecs and a cosmetically whitened smile?

"Have you seen a lot of Megan lately, David?" she asked sweetly. "Such a nice girl. I always hoped you two would get together."

David nodded. So that was it. His orders from the Electric City concert had been confirmed: Take Megan out of the picture, so I can concentrate on Zach.

"I haven't been over to Megan's since the concert," he said, "but I've been meaning to see a lot more of her."

"Good." His mistress was pleased. She shifted on her chair, displaying that magnificent body for him as it slithered luxuriously around under her amethyst silk Donna Karan slip dress.

"How *is* Zach?" David added. Let her know he was calling his marker. After all, like the old Mafia guy said—I don't do favors, I collect debts.

"Just wonderful," Roxana purred. "I'm sure he's as happy with you as I am, David. I'm sure he'll be boasting about being one of your discoveries in as many interviews as I shall. After all, Zach, Megan, me—*Triple Feature* is really *your* movie, isn't it?"

David Tauber felt the warmth wash right through his body, with a swift jolt of adrenaline following in its wake. Great. She was going to play with him. She would repay him. A few well-placed comments with the trades and his star would be shooting up faster than ever.

He'd have Kevin Scott fired.

He'd walk out of SKI.

With Roxana and Zach hitched to his wagon—there was no limit, Tauber realized. He suppressed an urge to clench his fists. *No limit at all.* He wouldn't have to try and impress Sam Kendrick anymore—he could *be* Sam Kendrick.

Forget about money. Forget about sex. *Power,* power was the only drug, and power was what Roxana Felix was offering him.

"It's good of you to say so," he replied.

"Oh, but I *do* say so." Roxana speared a forkful of lettuce. "And if you ask me, David darling, you should be exercising a little bit more control over it."

"More control?" Tauber looked blank. "How could I do that?"

The supermodel looked at her agent, a tiny half-smile playing across her blood-red lips.

"David, you don't really know Jake Keller, do you? He's the number two to Eleanor Marshall over at Artemis. He has some interesting ideas about this movie . . . I think you two would get on just fine. Perhaps I should arrange for you to play a little tennis?"

For a second Tauber sat there frozen, his mind racing at a million miles an hour. Jesus fucking Christ. What was the bitch proposing? A conspiracy? Was she out to get Eleanor Marshall? Who did she have in her pocket? And could he risk it? Because if you weren't with Roxana Felix, you were against her.

He was only treading water at SKI anyway . . .

"What a good idea," Tauber said smoothly. "I could do with some work on my backhand."

⋰⋰⋰

Flowers. They were everywhere she looked; huge, vulgar, ostentatious bunches of them, baskets stuffed full of them, wreaths and pot plants and every variety known to man. All the designer florists in Beverly Hills must be laughing their heads off, Eleanor thought bitterly. She couldn't walk into the Artemis executive offices without being overpowered by a wash of different fragrances, assaulted by an ice cream medley of colors: hyacinth, irises, jasmine, tiger lilies, snowdrops—where the hell had Isabelle Kendrick found *snowdrops*—and piles and piles of roses. Peonies and poppies were stacked next to orange blossom and orchids on every secretary's desk. Some of the arrangements were in cutesy shapes—a teddy bear of white chrysanthemums, a stork made entirely of cornflowers. Many of them were color-themed in pastel pinks and blues.

Jesus, but this town was tacky when you thought about it.

Eleanor tried to ignore the living gauntlet that she had to run on the way into her own office, the one space in the building mercifully free from greenery. On the second day after word of Jordan's pregnancy had leaked out, the overflow of blossoming tributes had gotten too much for Tom's secretary, who'd innocently inquired if Eleanor would care for some pale pink tulips or light blue roses, only to be told frostily that the president suffered from hay fever. A manifest lie, Eleanor knew, but what could they do about it? She wouldn't take any of Tom's goddamn flowers. She was still president here. That was one thing she could rely on.

Eleanor sat in the spartan, businesslike fortress of her office and bent her head, examining the latest projections for *Looking Good*, the Artemis comedy that had opened the week before. The figures were creditable, but Eleanor didn't see them. They swam before her eyes, meaningless, unimportant.

Oh, dear God. All she could feel was the pain. It occupied her thoughts one hundred percent of the time, drumming its agony deeper inside her with every pulse of her broken heart. Her skin was sallow from the lack of sleep. Her eyes had dark shadows under them, and she was losing weight rapidly as her appetite slowed and died. How she got through each day was a mystery to her. How she had managed the journey down from JFK to LAX, with Jordan sitting in the seat beside her, babbling excitedly on for the whole five hours, she could not even remember.

Eleanor knew she was still well dressed, even if she no longer bothered with makeup. After all, clothes were a form of armor. And she got through meetings with no perceptible loss of control; the words flowed smoothly enough.

But behind her cool gaze Eleanor Marshall was a zombie, going through the motions. Years of businesslike behavior had provided her with an automatic pilot, and she was just coasting along, utterly out of control.

The Panasonic on her desk buzzed.

"Yes, Mariah?"

"Mr. Keller on line one," her assistant chirped.

"Thank you," Eleanor said, hitting the button. "Jake."

Her deputy's voice was brisk and calm, no hostility to it at all. "Eleanor, I've got some more *Triple Feature* budget items for you to sign off on, and a few location ideas. Is it OK if I come over and run 'em by you?"

"Thanks, Jake," Eleanor said listlessly. "That would be great. Why don't you bring them across now?"

A week ago she would have told him to wait until she was through with what she was working on. But who cared? Now was as good a time as any. Jake was suddenly cooperative, and suddenly running off sheet after sheet of budget plans, production expenses, location arrangements. She'd thought all that stuff had been sorted out, but apparently it needed changing. Fine. Keller could change what he wanted . . . what did it matter? Minor alterations. Small adjustments. Whatever.

Two minutes later Jake Keller was in his immediate boss's office, clutching a revised set of forecasts and some new site decisions. The significant changes were buried in the middle of the third page, in a couple of clauses it had taken him all of last night to work out. They weren't hidden, though—they were clearly laid out, in language nobody could fail to understand. That was the way it had to be. If she signed these documents, the responsibility for them had to be hers—clearly, and without room for doubt.

Keller advanced toward Eleanor, holding the memos out to her. His heart was beating in a nervous samba, but he was sure it didn't show. And if it did, would Eleanor pick up on it? Would she notice *anything*?

Not in this state. He had to bet on that. She looked like shit, she looked really ill. Her cool blond head had been someplace else all this week, and Jake Keller was not a man to let an opportunity like that pass him by. He'd had the ultraintelligent Ms. Marshall signing off on proposals an intern would have objected to. Signing off on the presidency, he hoped. But these were the big two—two simple, irreparable errors that he was praying would get her approval, right on the dotted line.

"Sorry to keep bothering you with this stuff, but it's best we get it right,"

Keller said, watching the president's eyes skim over the first page of close print. Keep her talking, keep her involved, make her trust you. "Don't you think so?"

"Sure," Eleanor said blankly, turning to the second page.

Keller felt the roof of his mouth dry up. She *was* reading it. Was she taking it in? "Are you planning to go out on location yourself?"

"Maybe, I don't know."

She turned to the third page.

"I'm glad somebody's doing some work around here," Keller plowed on, desperately. "With all these delivery guys coming and going for Tom and Jordan, you'd think it was the first time anyone had ever conceived."

He was unprepared for the effect of his remark. Eleanor's face drained of blood as though someone had slapped her. She stopped examining the document, and reached for her pen.

With a dazzling burst of comprehension, Jake Keller suddenly realized what the hell was going on. Mentally, he kicked himself for not having sensed it before. Of *course!* All that jumping apart whenever he'd walked in on the two of them . . .

Oh, this was just great. His shark's nose had done more than scent blood in the water. Eleanor Marshall was badly wounded, a prey just waiting for a predator like himself to come along and restore the natural order. After all, this job should have been his in the first place, Keller thought. That Roxana Felix was a bright woman.

As he watched the Ice Queen sign her own death warrant, Jake Keller couldn't resist one final, delicious cruelty.

"Thanks," he said pleasantly as he took the papers from her. "That's great. You know, it's kind of sweet, about this baby stuff, don't you think?"

"Certainly," Eleanor managed, forcing herself to meet her vice president's eyes.

Jake Keller looked at her impassively.

"In all the time I've known him, I don't think I've ever seen Tom happier," he said.

Then he gave her a friendly smile, turned on his heels, and left.

⋅⁘⋅

Megan stepped smartly out of her BMW and tossed the keys to the parking lot attendant, usually a little smug and supercilious in his silver and gray Artemis uniform.

"Park it out back," she snapped. "And make sure it's near the exit. I'm leaving early today."

He gaped at her, did a double take, then a triple take. Megan could see the doubt forming in his eyes—could that *really* be Megan Silver?—and some of the icy nerves in the pit of her stomach thawed a little.

Today was the first day of rehearsals. There'd be one week of them in LA, involving just Zach, Roxana, and a few costars. Then the cast and crew would ship out to the Seychelles, to start the first part of filming on location. David told her she had to be available, to tinker with the script as and when it needed it. According to him, once they started shooting, that would be pretty much all the time.

This was the first day since the movie had been green-lighted that she wasn't actually supposed to work.

It would also be the first time she'd met most of the cast. Not to mention Fred Florescu, the most influential director of his generation and her new boss. The prospect thrilled and terrified her all at once. Megan loved all Florescu's movies; they were stylish and successful. People called the guy "the new Spielberg." *Light Falling*, his last picture, had made over $150 million—clean profit, since Florescu had shot it on a shoestring.

Triple Feature wouldn't have a shoestring budget—her exotic plot made sure of that—but Megan hoped Mr. Florescu would think that it had almost as good a script.

Recovering from his hesitation, the Artemis valet said, "Yes, ma'am," touching his cap as he did so, and opened her car door.

Oh yes, Megan thought dryly as she walked over to the soundstage where they were all supposed to meet up. Another first for the day. Everybody was going to get to see the new her.

She glanced down at herself as she walked. Well, it was certainly different. And from now on, she'd be packing an attitude to match. Maybe Megan couldn't compete with Roxana Felix, but she'd at least give the slut something to think about.

And will it give Zach something to think about?

Who cares? It's David I want, Megan told herself firmly. David. David.

⁘

You couldn't miss them. Even from a couple of hundred yards, Megan could hear the excited babble, see the studio production executives, low-level flunkies reporting to that scum Jake Keller, scurrying around like the sycophantic toadies they were. Her walk slowed as she got closer, giving her more time to take in the scene. There was David, beautifully groomed in some light brown Armani suit. He was standing next to a young guy with long black hair, jeans, and an Oasis T-shirt; it couldn't be Florescu? It *was*. Wow. And Zach, in a Metallica shirt and jeans, staring at Florescu with respect on his face.

Megan snorted. Check it out. Zach Mason respects *something!* Well, once he's got the measure of you like I did, it won't go two ways, you pathetic fake.

And Roxana. No more than normally exquisite today; some kind of demure pantsuit in ice-blue silk, navy pumps, and a pair of wraparound shades. Sitting next to Zach. Of course. But you're not gonna faze me, you bitch, not today.

There were the other cast members, and Megan couldn't suppress a slight blush. She'd never seen so many famous faces in one place together—Mary Holmes, Jack Richards, Robert Finn, Seth Weiss. But she pulled herself swiftly together. They were all here because *she'd* written them suitable parts. The old Megan might have been overwhelmed, she told herself intently, but the new one wasn't going to bat a professionally made-up eyelid.

Megan strode up to them, swinging her hips as she moved, working it all the way.

"Hi, guys," she said coolly. "Sorry I'm a little late. The freeway was solid for miles." Megan paused, drinking in the shock on the faces that already knew her. "David, why don't you introduce me? I hardly know *anyone*, and that can't be right."

"Megan?" Zach Mason asked.

"Megan?" David Tauber gasped.

"Who else?" She shrugged.

Tauber couldn't believe what he was seeing. Megan had disappeared— the old mousy, shy, invisible little Megan with her nondescript brown hair, T-shirts, and long skirts. In her place was a tall, slender woman, toned, tanned flesh bared to the world. Long, lean legs stretched up indecently from outrageous stacked heels, ending only in a thigh-high Azzedine Alaïa minidress of clinging black Lycra, a creation that left nothing whatsoever to the imagination—and certainly not the high, rounded cheeks of her ass nor the sizable proportions of her breasts, made to look even larger than normal in a balconette Ultrabra. It was as though she was flinging those curves in Roxana's face. And the surprises didn't stop there. Megan had a Gucci belt knotted loosely around her newly wasplike waist and a Piaget watch on her left wrist. The long, gentle brown curls had gone and in their place was a sleek, geometric Louise Brooks–style bob, except that Louise Brooks had never had hair so dazzlingly platinum-blond that she made Marilyn Monroe look like a brunette. And the usually naked face had been painstakingly made up, with an expensive-looking foundation, heavy bronze blusher, dark green eyeshadow melting into a dramatic plum shade swept under the brow, and full, shiny lips, lined and glossed into a wet scarlet bow.

She looked rawly sexual. Demanding attention, Megan had revealed her new, desirable body in a way that could only be called exhibitionist. And there was something more than the hair and the dowdiness that she had cast off. David had been prepared to start screwing Megan anyway—not a wholly disagreeable prospect—at Roxana Felix's orders.

But now it would be a definite pleasure. The new Megan Silver was something David recognized, something he could deal with. Like Gloria Ramirez, Megan Silver was tough. Like him. Like Roxana. Like that ambitious teenager he'd fucked last week.

Megan Silver was no longer the little idealist.

She was *hard*.

"Megan, you look terrific," David said, feeling the beginnings of an erection. "Don't you think so, Roxana?"

"Very dramatic, dear," Roxana Felix commented icily, in a backhanded compliment that delighted Megan. And as Tauber started to introduce her to Fred Florescu and the rest of the cast, Megan was aware of the unfamiliar sensation of being ogled, of men's eyes roaming across her body, of being an object of desire. Every guy in the group had to be staring at her!

Every guy but one. As she finished shaking hands with the last supporting star, Megan glanced furtively at Zach Mason.

He hadn't taken his eyes off her either, and as soon as she looked at him, Zach's gaze met hers.

It was filled with shock, disgust, and contempt.

Fuck you, Megan thought furiously, and turned back to David, whose eyes were roaming her with a new hunger, the hunger she'd longed to see there since the day she'd first met him. *It was always David I wanted, not you.*

Zach Mason meant less than nothing to her. Right? Right.

Megan slipped her hand firmly into David Tauber's, and smiled, as brilliantly as she knew how.

❖

She pulled up outside David's apartment, slipping the BMW sharply into his reserved parking space, making sure to show off acres of nut-brown thigh as she pressed down on the brake with her Manolo Blahnik shoes. Jesus, even driving was a production now.

But, obviously, it was working.

"Thanks for the ride," Tauber said, and Megan noticed both the hoarseness of his tone and the impressive bulge in his pants. She was triumphant. So it *had* turned him on!

"No problem," she replied, as casually as she could.

"I was, uh, wondering if you'd care to come up for a coffee?" David asked her, and Megan turned to see the glitter of lust in his eyes. Unmistakable desire, and it was all for her.

How would Roxana play this?

"If I come upstairs, I'll be wanting more than coffee," Megan said.

Tauber smiled at her, the smooth, practiced smile she had longed him to use on her for months now.

Why isn't it more fulfilling? Megan asked herself. She shifted against the leather. Unbidden, an image of Zach Mason flashed in front of her. Frowning his disapproval.

David Tauber unclipped his seat belt and leaned over toward her, his hands finding her breasts. Megan gasped. It was the first time a man had touched her in months. David was smooth, lightly rubbing across the tips of her nipples, his lips and tongue flickering across her mouth. She returned the kiss, moaning. Fire shot down from her breasts into her pussy. She was hot already, her hungry body responding to his skill. David felt her squirm and moved closer, covering her. Megan could feel his cock, rock-solid against the skimpy black Lycra of her dress. Desire rushed through her and she pushed herself hard against him, all her doubts receding in a hot burst of physical need.

chapter 23

Eleanor Marshall rushed into the women's executive bathroom and flung herself into the nearest stall, her fingers fumbling in her haste to bolt it shut. The lock rattled into place just in time as she knelt forward, gasping, gripping the seat with both hands, and threw up. Wave after wave of nausea racked through her, and she knelt there, shuddering and wretched, until it finally passed and she was left with a dry, raw throat and an empty stomach.

Eleanor flushed the vomit away and took a deep breath, trying futilely to calm herself. Then she reached into a concealed pocket in the lining of her smart beige jacket and took out the three essential items she'd taken to carrying around with her: a travel toothbrush and a tube of paste, and a trial-size flask of antiseptic mouthwash.

Male chief executives react to extreme pressure with stomach ulcers, Eleanor thought wearily. *Why can't I do that? It would be so much simpler . . .*

She scrubbed and rinsed out her mouth right there in the stall, thanking God that there was obviously nobody around to hear her. So far all her attacks had come in the early morning, when none of the secretaries were around, but she dreaded the day the sudden, terrible crunch in the pit of her stomach would hit in the middle of a meeting, or in the lunch hour, when this bathroom was always so full. Then it would be tough to hide, and the inevitable rumors would begin to fly around: *Eleanor Marshall can't take the heat. Eleanor's cracking up. Eleanor's throwing her guts up every day at work . . .*

Eleanor stood slowly, looking around her at the cool eggshell-blue walls with their pristine white accents, trying to compose herself before she walked back to her office. OK, that was better. She flushed again, unlocked the door, and surveyed her reflection in the wall mirrors opposite; pallid as hell, but otherwise acceptable. A Ralph Lauren pantsuit in caramel wool, a crisp white Donna Karan shirt, Walter Steiger black suede pumps.

Elegant and understated as normal. Perfect dressing for Eleanor Marshall, president of Artemis Studios and emotionless control freak.

She smiled without humor. Some joke. Well, her universe was crumbling around her, but at least she was wearing the appropriate clothes.

Jordan Cabot Goldman was pregnant with her husband's child. *Tom's* child. The child of the man she, Eleanor, loved, the man she had let herself hope for, with silent desperation, for some fifteen years, the man whom she had finally made love to, and spent the most blissful night of her life with. The man whom she could never have.

It wasn't as though she could avoid the agony of that, run from it, ignore it, block it out the way an ordinary mistress might have. No, she had to be with Tom every day, witness an endless stream of congratulations every day. The flowers had eventually dried up, but that wasn't an end to it; every producer or agent who met with them opened the meeting with good wishes, congratulations, or most often, father-to-father advice and jokes. Jordan herself had started to come by the office, and though Eleanor made an effort to be somewhere else when she arrived, she couldn't help but see her sometimes, her face so incredibly young and blooming with health, graciously accepting everybody's attentions, especially Tom's. That *really* hurt; watching Tom scramble to open doors for her, rush to get her a chair, refuse to allow her to lift anything heavier than a porcelain coffee cup. He treated his wife like she was the most precious thing in the world, and made of spun sugar, liable to break at any second.

And it wasn't merely the loss of Tom Goldman, rubbed in mercilessly every day like salt in an open wound. It was the idea of Jordan, twenty-four and pregnant with her first baby, a little Goldman son or daughter, with more to come. Eleanor had read somewhere that twenty-four was the average age for American women to marry, and twenty-five for the conception of their first child. So blond-haired, blue-eyed, all-American Barbie was doing it exactly right, perhaps a little ahead of schedule, while she, Eleanor, was almost forty, still single, and childless.

A year ago she hadn't given a damn about that, couldn't have cared less. But Jordan's pregnancy had changed things, dragged all her background regrets howling viciously into the foreground of her mind. Now Eleanor *did* care, very much.

Her own longing for a child was amplified to obsessional proportions. She thought about it all the time, but then again, how could she do anything else? It was Jordan this, Jordan that, all day every day. Eleanor kept recalling the story of Elizabeth I of England, how she had turned her face to the wall when told that Mary Queen of Scots had given birth to Prince James; on being asked what was the matter, she had replied, "The Queen of Scots is delivered of a fine son, and I am but barren stock."

Barren stock . . . that was exactly what Eleanor felt, every day. Barren. Empty. Lost.

It would be easier if she was one of those women, like Isabelle Kendrick, who only wanted to be married, to have children, to take a place in society's tight, inviolate ark of coupledom, that huge boat that only lets the animals in two by two. She knew she could have that, if she wanted it. Paul Halfin was right there, with his polished good looks and successful investment banking firm, holding out an engagement ring and a one-way ticket to permanent respectability. Eleanor smoothed down the soft lapels of her cashmere jacket, thinking how many other women would kill for that opportunity. She tried to be grateful. At least she had a ticket; do not pass go, do not collect two hundred dollars.

But she had never wanted to be married for the sake of it. She had wanted to marry for love, she'd wanted Tom Goldman. And she had wanted her child to be a bright, shining star, to meld her own genes with those of the best possible father, the brightest, funniest, most ambitious and intelligent and passionate man she'd ever known . . .

A month ago, perhaps she could have forgotten all that. Taken heed of Dr. Haydn's six-month warning and wrapped things up with Paul. After all, what hope had Tom ever given her? He'd married his baby *shiksa* princess and there was an end of it . . .

Until those hints in the office, the stolen moments at Isabelle's party, and that final, earth-shattering night in New York, when he had reached out to her, and his touch had awoken her body and exalted her soul.

She *could* have lived with settling. But Tom had taken that away from her. In those few, glorious hours he had opened life itself to her, revealed to her everything she was capable of feeling and being.

Son of a bitch, Eleanor thought, and struggled against the new tears forming in her eyes. *You made it ten times worse. You make it so incredibly painful.*

Shaking her head, Eleanor opened the bathroom door and walked quickly back to her own office. A plastic cup of thin coffee from the machine in the hall was cooling there, next to an untouched bagel she'd brought with her from home; she didn't have time to eat breakfast there these days, she'd been at the studio from half past six. It was necessary. Work was in crisis.

Funny, isn't it, Eleanor thought, the way you can get to be grateful for the weirdest things. She took a sip of the watery coffee and picked up her report on *Dog Days*, an Artemis comedy she had bought for half a million dollars that was now recommended for turnaround, a polite way of saying you didn't want to make it anymore. The director was fighting with the screenwriter, and three lead actors had pulled out at the last minute, leaving Eleanor with her fourth choice, if she wanted him, or the option to cancel. But Mary Truant, the director, had a pay-or-play clause in her contract which meant they would lose a further two million if Eleanor killed the picture. Yet a turkey of a movie could wind up costing a lot more than three million bucks.

Dog Days was only the latest crisis. There was that fiasco in marketing in Southeast Asia, the one where their advertising for *Heavy Artillery*, a minor Artemis hit of last summer and the kind of action-adventure that normally did well in Asia, had been designed to read "Rick Hammond Raises Hell," and had apparently wound up meaning "Rick Hammond Desecrates Graves." Not good, in a market where ancestor worship was all the rage. They'd been staying away from that in droves. Plus, the Miramax distribution deal had gone sour at the last minute—with the other side claiming Eleanor's figures were false and misleading. She had a team of lawyers battling desperately to stop a lawsuit.

That was the story of her life right now, Eleanor thought, trying to take in the words and figures that swam before her eyes. Fighting fires. The last month had been a succession of disasters; ever since that triumphant presentation to the board in New York, it had just been one crisis after another. She had no time to manage the studio, to give it the kind of planned leadership that Tom Goldman had been banking on when he chose her for the job. Every spare moment was taken up with brainstorming a solution to the latest problem.

It was cool in her air-conditioned office, the silent fans cycling artificially chill breezes around the room, providing her with constant protection against the blazing LA sun, already streaming over the lot outside, but the cool wasn't helping her concentrate. Eleanor had no idea how this had happened, and she felt helpless, as if her grip on her business had somehow slipped . . . but then it *had* slipped. Every new problem arose on matters she had already considered, budgets she had already approved, papers she'd already signed off on . . .

How could I have been so stupid? Eleanor asked herself, her forehead creasing in a frown. I'm usually so together. All this stuff is second nature to me.

She felt a renewed throb of anxiety. This was no time to be cracking up. If she wasn't careful, the shark pool would start to scent her weakness, and then it would only be a matter of time before she lost not only Tom but her job, too.

Eleanor began to make notes on *Dog Days*, her mouth set in a hard line.

Well, if they were waiting for her to give up they'd be waiting a long goddamn time. She might not be able to prevent Tom Goldman smashing her
heart, but then love was something that was out of your control. That was
why it was so dangerous. Artemis Studios was *in* her control, and she
wasn't about to let it slip away from her, no matter how many fires she
had to douse.

She had struggled all her life to get here. She wasn't about to give up now.

There was a knock on the door.

"Come in," Eleanor called absently. "Mariah, is that you? I need the Mary
Truant contracts, and the production executive's notes on the script meetings. And I'd kill for some real coffee."

"Would you go for just the coffee?" Tom Goldman asked gently.

Eleanor looked up, startled.

Tom walked toward her, carrying his normal paper bag. He was wearing
the same black suit he'd worn to their meeting in New York, a gold Cartier
watch, and a Yale tie. He looked great.

"No doughnuts," Goldman said, unpacking two polystyrene cups of filter
coffee and handing one to her carefully. He gestured toward the uneaten
bagel. "But then I see you're not hungry."

Eleanor took the coffee without comment and put it down on her desk.

"What can I do for you?" she asked coldly.

"Eleanor—"

She didn't want to hear it, didn't want to hear anything. "Tom, like I
said, what can I do for you? Because if it isn't business, it'll have to wait.
I'm busy."

Goldman looked at her for a long moment, his handsome brown eyes
soft with tenderness and compassion.

Eleanor felt sadness and weakness and longing well up inside her. Panicked, she felt a lump start to form at the back of her throat. Oh no,
please, not kindness. Not pity, she thought. I can handle anything but that.

Almost of its own accord, her right hand fumbled to open the small top
drawer at the side of her desk.

"We have to talk, Eleanor," Goldman said.

"We talk every day," Eleanor answered, "about this studio." Her fingers
closed around the small velvet box which she kept there, flicked open the
lid. "And other than that we have nothing to discuss."

"We can't pretend New York never happened," Goldman insisted.
"Eleanor, you must believe that it meant a great deal to me—I know
you're hurting, and I'm so sorry you—"

"Tom!" It ricocheted out of her. *How dare you pity me? How dare you offer me comfort?* "As far as I'm concerned, *nothing* happened in New York.
Certainly nothing that meant anything to me." She turned on him, her
eyes bright with fury. "We both had too much to drink, and as far as I'm

concerned it was an embarrassing indiscretion we'd both better forget."
Her tone was pure ice.

Tom shook his head. "I don't believe you."

"Believe me." Her fingers were working behind the desk, out of sight. "In
fact, I hope you will be able to offer me some congratulations this time."

He was confused. "Congratulate you? Why?"

Eleanor Marshall brought her left hand out from behind the desk and
held it up to him, defiantly. On the fourth finger Paul's ring sparkled brilliantly, rubies and emeralds glittering ostentatiously in the morning sun.

"Paul proposed to me this morning," Eleanor said, pronouncing every
word clearly and deliberately, "and I accepted." She looked hard at him,
her whole body brittle with the pure flame of her anger.

"I'm getting married, Tom," she said. "And you know something? I can't
wait."

·:⋮:·

David sauntered into the bedroom, spritzing Chanel's *L'Egoïste* under his
arms. He admired his magnificent body for a few seconds in Megan's wall
mirror, then picked up a white toweling bathrobe and belted it around
himself.

"Did you finish packing yet?" he asked.

"Not quite." Megan tried to drag her eyes from Tauber's chest. She had
to stop staring at him like that, and yet somehow she couldn't stop looking, couldn't stop checking to see if he was real. Naked, David was quite
simply superb, even more muscular than she had pictured him in her fantasies. Standing there at the door to her bedroom, the white toweling
throwing his golden-brown tan into sharp relief, he looked like some guy
off a schoolgirl's pinup calendar.

David was gorgeous. And didn't he know it, Megan thought, surprising
herself with the sharp stab of disapproval that ran through her at that idea.

Come on, now, she lectured herself. Women spend hours in front of the
mirror. Why shouldn't a man? You're operating the double standard.

"We leave tomorrow morning," David reminded her. "Nine A.M. flight."

Megan patted her tickets, laid out neatly along with her passport on the
bedside table. "Air Seychelles number 3156 to Victoria, Mahé. I'm not
planning on missing it, don't worry. I've got everything packed except a
couple of books."

Her cases were stacked by the front door, ready to go; no T-shirts, just
one pair of jeans, and all the designer outfits she'd bought, even the high
heels. The new Megan would wear those to dinner in the hotel, she
thought. Roxana Felix wouldn't leave her heels behind just because she
was heading to a tropical island, so neither would Megan. And if she
looked longingly at her Oasis T-shirt once or twice, she was just looking.

"Books? You're not gonna have time to *read*," David said scornfully. "Look, Megan, I told you, it's really unusual that you're the only writer on the project and really unusual that you've been allowed so much control—"

"I know, you've been a great agent, David," she said hastily. "I won't let you down, I know I'll be working most of the time—"

"You'll be working *all* the time when you're on the set. Little things always need redoing. And if you're not working that minute, you have to watch what's going on, be ready to offer suggestions . . . you've got to stay around to be in control. Otherwise you turn into Sam Kendrick." He laughed at his own joke.

Megan smiled dutifully back, but she didn't think that was so funny. David always seemed to be dissing Sam these days, except for when he dropped in on rehearsals himself, when David was always dutiful and respectful. Whenever Sam Kendrick had spoken to her, he'd always been helpful and kind, and Megan knew that Eleanor thought the world of Sam. And Sam had given David Tauber his first break. It wasn't pleasant to hear him getting at the guy the whole time.

Not to mention the way David was coming on strong to the costars. Mary Holmes and Robert Finn, both Sam Kendrick's personal clients and big celebrities. If David were with another agency, she'd have said he was trying to poach them.

There was something about it she didn't like. That, and the way David suddenly seemed to be in conference with Jake Keller the whole time. Eleanor Marshall hadn't been attending rehearsals, so maybe Jake was the logical exec to be hanging around . . . Still . . .

Megan shook her head, swatting those thoughts aside. She'd *longed* for David; now she had him. That was what was important.

Not one quick conversation backstage. Not her childhood illusions, a few hours at a gig, transported by music.

Not a weak fantasy that her lifelong hero might have noticed her. When he had a forty-million-dollar, satin-skinned, doe-eyed supermodel as an alternative.

Megan shook her head, pressing her small fists to her eyes.

So *why* did she keep thinking about Zach?

⁛

"I brought you something," Tauber was saying. "A going-away present."

He walked over to the wall where his coat was hanging, fished in the pockets and drew out a small package wrapped in tissue paper.

"What is it?" Megan asked, delighted.

David threw it across to her. "Open it and see."

She unwrapped it, drawing out a tiny gold pendant on a filigree chain, a delicate gold star with a cursive letter "D" set inside it.

"So you don't forget me," Tauber said, giving her a bone-melting smile.

"Oh, David, it's lovely," Megan said, breathlessly. Nobody had ever given her anything romantic. And from what she recalled of the guys back on Haight, none of them were real big on gold necklaces.

"Here, let me put it on you." Tauber was beside her, pushing her cardigan back from her shoulders. Megan bent her neck, feeling his large hands skillfully undoing the clasp, hanging it around her. The metal was cool against her skin, and she reached up with one hand, touching the slender little star.

"It's beautiful," she said.

"You're beautiful," Tauber murmured, passing a hand through her newly shorn, chic platinum bangs. "And you're wearing too many clothes."

Megan pressed up against him as he unbuttoned her cardigan and tailored slacks, slopping the fabric slowly and smoothly away from her skin, stroking her lightly where every piece of cloth had been, then undoing her bra in a swift, practiced movement, playing expertly with her breasts so that Megan was too aroused to wait for him to peel away her strawberry silk briefs and ripped them off herself, leaving her naked in his arms. David shrugged off the robe and pushed her back on the bed, bending his mouth to the newly flat surface of her belly, his dry lips and wet tongue trailing a line of fire across her skin.

Megan gasped with desire, feeling the blood in her nipples throbbing with a new intensity as his fingers started to tweak them, then caress them, rolling around in a firm circular motion, sometimes leaving off so his hand could grab her whole breast and squeeze it.

"Yeah, that's right," David said, his breath hot against the downy hairs of her belly. "Tell me how much you love it, Megan. Tell me how much you want me."

"Oh, God, you know I want you," she groaned, feeling his mouth poised right above her, and then he was doing it, his lips on hers in the most intimate caress, his tongue swirling around, knowing exactly what he was doing, and she felt every objection, every reservation, evaporate into nothingness under the blinding heat shooting through her . . .

chapter 24

"M agic," Fred Florescu said.

They were sitting together on the terrace of the Meridien Hotel, watching the sun set over the Indian Ocean. To the west, the sea past the Anse Polite beach was lapping gently at the shore, its heart illuminated down the center by a red carpet of light, constantly shattering and re-forming, as the waves reflected the dying light of the sun. On the fine powdery sand that would be picturebook white at daybreak, several bonfires were burning, throwing up sparks into the twilight, while around them the laughter of holidaymakers mixed with the shrieks of some Seychellois children, giggling and yelling to each other in the local Creole patois. To the east, the slopes of the mountains, covered in palm trees, wild cinnamon, and thick vegetation, stretched up into the darkening sky behind them. Megan saw a flock of shadowy shapes wing up from the edge of one of the slopes and veer to the left in a ragged flurry of movement; whether they were birds or bats she had no idea.

"I think so," she agreed.

"I hope you don't mind having a drink with me," the director said, reaching over to refill her glass with the local specialty of crushed ice and lime, frosted with salt. The tartness was delicious after the sweetness of her evening meal: octopus curried in coconut milk, slices of baked breadfruit, and a sorbet made of pawpaw and *jamalac*, a native pink-skinned fruit. David had insisted on grilled chicken and rice; as far as Megan could tell, his fitness regimen never wavered. But she had rebelled against his attempts to make her do the same; exotic travel might be commonplace to him, but Megan had never left the States before, and she refused to pretend she was still there.

"Of course not," she said.

She was delighted to be drinking with Mr. Florescu. Not that she'd have had a choice about it; his word was law on the set, and an invitation to drinks with him was like a command to tea with the Queen of England. You just didn't turn it down. But then who would want to? The guy was king of this movie now and one of the best directors in the world, and on the set everybody was clamoring for a piece of his time: Mary Holmes, Jack Richards, Robert Finn, Seth Weiss, and all the other actors; Tom Lilley, the Artemis production executive, a Jake Keller drone who slimed around the set taking notes all the time; David, whose most burning desire seemed to be to get close to him; Peter, Steven, and Rick, his three assistant directors or ADs, who were glorified flunkies who slavishly worshiped their master's every utterance; and most of all, Roxana Felix, who had started acting like the prima donna from hell the second the first camera rolled.

David had told her to keep away from Fred. She was just the screenwriter, which put her only a few rungs above the catering staff, he said. Until and unless she was needed, she wasn't to bother Mr. Florescu.

Megan resented his tone—she wasn't a child—but did as David said. After all, he was her agent, he knew what was best. And hanging around on the fringes of the set helped her to avoid Roxana Felix, who took every opportunity to insult and snub her, and Zach Mason, who basically gave her the odd contemptuous glance, and apart from that, ignored her.

"I wanted to get to know you better," Florescu said. "I never seem to see you around unless it's with David. Does he have to chaperone you everywhere you go?"

Megan blushed. She had been thinking the exact same thing, and now she felt horribly disloyal. After all, David was the reason she was here sipping iced lime on a tropical island, instead of serving greasy chicken wings to jerks. Right?

"He's been very good to me," she said defensively.

"He's very good to all his clients," Florescu snorted. "You wrote a great script, plus you look great. All it would have taken was for one agent to read your script, and you would have been signed. It was *his* lucky break that he got to read it first, not yours. I hope you realize that."

Covered in confusion, Megan managed, "He's my boyfriend."

"Sure he is," Fred said, sounding unconvinced, and then, seeing her flustered, added more kindly, "David's a smart guy. So long as you're happy."

"Oh. Yes, of course," Megan said.

The director nodded down the beach, toward the sealed-off area where they were filming. "We might need you there tomorrow. I'm gonna want some options for the scene where Morgan confronts the drug lords. In case Roxana tries any more dumb moves, and I want to shoot around her."

"OK, no problem," Megan agreed immediately, her mind running through the dialogue he was talking about. It would be tough to change it without unbalancing other scenes in the film, but she was glad to have something to do.

"Roxana Felix," Florescu commented absently, "has one major attitude problem. She's read too many magazines. She thinks that being a lead actress means being a major bitch and throwing tantrums all the time, and she really has no idea of the work an actor does."

Megan sipped her drink and said nothing, listening to the ocean crashing on the shore. She didn't dare say what she thought of the supermodel. Roxana was David's client, and if David found she'd been bad-mouthing her to the director, he'd kill her.

"Your David doesn't seem to be having much effect," Florescu went on. "I asked him to talk to her a few days ago, and he said he did his best, but . . ." He spread his hands in a frustrated gesture. "If it was anybody else I would fire her. I guess I still may."

Megan watched as his eyes glazed over, staring into space as though seeing something in his head.

"Why don't you?" she asked. "Because she's a supermodel?"

Fred laughed, and Megan found herself warming to him, liking his easy manner and his beard and his lack of pretentiousness.

"I could get another supermodel like *that*." He snapped his fingers. "Or even better, a pretty actress who'd know what to do on a set already. Or Andie MacDowell—a supermodel *and* an actress. Don't get caught up in thinking Roxana Felix is as special as she thinks she is, honey."

Megan warmed to him even more.

"It's the way she is with Zach." Florescu sighed, and Megan suddenly felt a chill from the cooling evening breezes. She didn't enjoy thinking about Zach, didn't like remembering the offhand way he was acting with her now, either treating her with contempt or ignoring her. So he obviously hated her new look, so what? He was dating Roxana Felix. He was an asshole. And she had David, after all.

She'd always wanted David, not Zach.

Megan told herself she didn't care.

"I've never seen a sexual chemistry like it on screen," Florescu went on. "The tests, and the love scene we've shot so far—it just blew me away. I know I could get a more professional actress, but if I can just get her to work a little, nobody else would be better for this movie."

"You'd do anything for the movie," Megan said slowly, understanding him. "Is that what you're saying? That if Roxana Felix is the best Morgan, you want her, no matter what?"

"Exactly." The young director leaned toward her. "Megan, this is *my* movie now. Every director feels that way, or they should. You wrote it and Zach's acting in it and Joe Friedman lights it, but the way it looks on the screen, the whole package together, the movie itself—that's mine. And it has to be as close to what I saw in my head when I read your script as I can get it."

"And Roxana will get you closest?"

Florescu nodded. "She and Zach. They set the screen on fire. People will walk out of the movie theater and go home and make love. And when you combine that with the rock 'n' roll backdrop and your CIA plot—it's going to blow everybody away. Believe me. I know what I'm talking about."

He gazed out at the beach for a long moment. "I don't like having to deal with Roxana, but if that's what it takes, I have to."

"Maybe you could call Sam," Megan suggested.

"What?"

"Sam Kendrick. When we were having script conferences, he used to come by. Roxana dealt more with Sam than with David, mostly, even though David was her agent."

"Really? Makes a change to have it that way around," Florescu said dryly. "OK, OK, he's your boyfriend, I know. Don't look like that, I was just kidding. So you think Sam might have an effect? Thanks, Megan, that's exactly the kind of break I've been praying for. I'll call him, get him out here."

"Don't tell David I suggested it," Megan said hastily. For some reason, she had a sudden premonition that her lover might be none too pleased to see his boss on the set.

"OK. Don't worry, I'll keep quiet. Maybe I just wanted to have *my* agent around for a change. But I'll owe you one." He grinned. "You reckon Sam might hurt the palace coup, huh? You could be right."

"What?" asked Megan, shrinking back.

"Oh, come on, don't play it so innocent," Florescu said sharply, picking up a sliver of sugared papaya from the dish in front of them. Megan Silver could see whoever she wanted, but he didn't like seeing her with a class A shark like David Tauber. "David tries to crawl up my ass every day, hands out all these little hints at how *he's* out on the set taking care of his clients, when Sam's back in LA, sunning himself—like Sam doesn't have an agency to run. I should ask him why he isn't in Texas with Colleen McCallum, but I guess McCallum's small fry when you have Zach Mason. And he's all over Seth and Mary and Jack and Robert—bends over so far backward for them he must be double-jointed."

"Don't talk about David like that," Megan said.

Fred stood up, smiling at her unrepentantly. "Hey, whatever. It's sweet that you're so loyal. None of my girls ever are—gotta stop screwing actresses, that's a director's major occupational hazard." He winked at her. "So I'll see you on the set tomorrow." He turned to go, then paused, and added, "Remember what I told you about the script—*anybody* would have bought it. I would have. And one other thing—do your boyfriend a favor and tell him to keep away from Zach Mason."

"But he's Zach's agent," Megan protested.

Florescu shrugged. "Zach doesn't like him. That's all I know," he told her, and then wandered back into the hotel.

Megan sat still for a few minutes, sipping her chilled lime juice and watching the beach, the fires now bright gold against the night, the last streaks of sunlight having sunk down beneath the ocean. Behind the blazes and the cries of the native children she could see the black silhouettes of the mountains, looming up into the sky. In the darkness they somehow seemed menacing; not travel-brochure playgrounds of palm trees and orchids, but a real jungle, alive, impenetrable, and dangerous.

❖

Megan arrived on the set the next morning at eight o'clock sharp, threading her way through the heavy cables of the lights, cameras, and reflector shields to where Fred Florescu was sitting, aviator shades and White Sox cap firmly in place, talking to Zach Mason. Roxana Felix stood a little apart from them, in costume, but evidently not about to step into a take. She was staring at the ground, her hair blowing softly around her face in the tropical breeze, her mouth set in a mutinous line.

Megan felt her heart sink. Just another great day at the office.

"Hey, Megan! Got a copy of the script? Great," Florescu called. "Come over here. We need to do something with this scene."

"Already?" Megan asked, trying not to look at Zach. The less she had to deal with him, the better. She wished that David hadn't been so determined to get through his push-ups before he followed her out here; he said he'd be right there, but she wanted him with her *now*. When she had to deal with Zach and Roxana.

She tried to call on the memories of David's body moving over hers. Her groin was still warm from it; they'd been in bed together less than twenty minutes ago, and her quick shower hadn't completely wiped the feeling away. Sex with David was always satisfying, always ended in at least one orgasm, which was more than she could say for Rory, back in Frisco, or indeed any other guy she'd been with. Not that there had been many. But . . . maybe she was just getting greedy, but it *still* felt like there was something missing. What exactly, Megan didn't know. Perhaps it was just too smooth—was there such a thing as being *too* good in bed? Megan wondered, and then shook her head. No way. Now she was getting seriously deranged.

Only it sometimes felt like her arousal was almost involuntary, just a physiological response to well-practiced moves. Of course she knew David *would* have practiced, he wasn't a virgin. But why did it feel, after the slipperiness and the heat had passed, as though she was just the latest in a long line . . . Why do *I* snap out of it so quickly? Megan wondered guiltily. I'm thinking about something else almost the second after I've come! Isn't that what men are supposed to do, the real jerks among them anyway, just climax and then roll over and go right to sleep? I should be thinking about David, not the script . . .

"I guess so." The director's voice snapped her out of her reverie. "Roxana doesn't want her character to appear weak."

"Weak?" Megan asked, bewildered. "How is she weak? This is the scene where a bunch of cocaine smugglers are threatening her with torture!"

"Oh, look. Our resident Shakespeare has finally shown up for work," Roxana Felix remarked acidly, sauntering across to Megan with a nasty smile. "What's the matter, honey, you missed an alarm? Or maybe college graduates need more sleep than the rest of us nonintellectuals." She glanced across at Zach Mason, but he refused to meet her eyes.

"I was here when I was supposed to be," Megan muttered, flushing a deep red.

"Don't talk back to me," Roxana said with casual insolence. "You're just the writer and don't you forget it."

"Lay off," Zach said, very quietly.

Roxana glared at him, but subsided.

"It would be nice if we could work at *all*," Fred Florescu sighed. "Now, Roxana, tell me why you think Morgan is shown as weak here."

"I don't think she would have been captured without a fight."

"Megan?" Fred asked.

She shrugged. They had been over this scene a thousand times back in LA and Roxana had never objected to it once.

"Morgan Meyer is a supermodel. This is toward the end of the movie, and she's just been taken hostage by fifty mercenary guerrillas armed with AK-47s. How is she going to put up a fight?"

"She could kick-box," Roxana suggested.

"Can you kick-box?" Zach Mason demanded. His tone was sharp.

"We could use a stuntwoman."

"I don't *have* a stuntwoman who kick-boxes," Florescu explained with exaggerated patience, "because the script doesn't call for one."

"So fly one in from LA." Roxana's almond-shaped eyes were narrow with the blind fury of somebody used to having her commands accepted without question.

"How would kick-boxing help her against fifty automatic weapons?" Megan asked reasonably. "It doesn't make sense."

Roxana turned on her, scarlet lips drawn back in an almost feral snarl.

"You know what?" said Fred Florescu, looking from Roxana to a mortified Megan seething with anger and humiliation. His tone was measured, but there was a line of steel underneath it none of them could mistake. "I don't think this is productive. We'll work something out for Morgan in that scene, but we'll do it later. The light's real good right now, too good to waste, so . . . we're gonna shoot something else. The first approach scene to the gangsters' base."

That was an action scene. It involved only Zach, Seth, and Robert.

"OK, sweetheart?" Fred asked easily. "I'll talk to Megan about that scene. You can relax for the morning."

Roxana stared at him for a long moment, then pirouetted on her heel and stalked off in the direction of her trailer.

"Jesus," the director said.

David strode up to the group.

"Hey, people," he said pleasantly.

Zach stiffened. Megan noticed it, surprised; so Fred was right about that. But why wouldn't Zach like David? He'd chosen David. Oh, they were all children, Megan thought angrily, struggling to contain the tears of frustration that rose in a lump in the back of her throat. She'd so wanted to tell Roxana to go to hell, but she *couldn't*, she had to sit there and swallow every insult the bitch threw at her.

Because Roxana was the star and she was just a writer. It was true. And when she'd sold this script for $250,000, Megan realized, she'd thrown in her self-respect as part of the deal.

She wondered if it was worth it.

"David, good to see you. Will you do something for me?" Florescu asked him.

"Name it," said Tauber, smiling engagingly.

"Go back to the hotel and call SKI. I've been thinking about what you said about Sam, and maybe you're right, he should be here. So call him and ask him if he'll come out."

"You want Sam Kendrick here?" David repeated, paling slightly.

"I really think I do," Florescu said amiably.

Megan stared at the ground.

For a split second Tauber hesitated; then he said, "Right. Great idea," and turned back to the hotel.

Florescu motioned to his lighting director, and the technicians scuffled around the sand, moving the heavy lights into place for the new scene.

Zach walked slowly over to Megan.

"Thanks for asking her to get off my back," she muttered.

Mason ignored her. "What if I tell you I want this scene rewritten, Megan? Would you do it? I bet you'd jump."

"If the director agreed with you," she replied, staring up into his breathtaking dark eyes, hating him for the derision she saw there. "I'm the screenwriter, I'm out here to fix problems as they arise."

"Nice speech." He reached out and touched the delicate gold star nestling in the hollow of her neck, fingering it. "*D*. What's that for?"

"David gave it to me," she said defiantly.

Mason raised an eyebrow, his gaze narrowing. "He gave you a pendant, and he put his *own* initial inside it? But I guess that figures. It's badge of ownership."

"Fuck you," said Megan, before she could stop herself.

Zach smiled into her eyes. "What's the matter, lost a little control there? Well, that's still more balls than David Tauber would ever display for you. Of course, I could have you fired for that. Unlike Roxana Felix, I *am* indispensable." He leaned forward. "And you know what would really be amusing? When David gets back here, I could tell him to give you the news. In public. And he'd do it, Megan."

"No he wouldn't," Megan said.

"Oh yes he would." Mason looked down at her intently. "And you know it."

She did know it, Megan realized with a sinking feeling. It was true, David would do that if Zach ordered him to. And he probably wouldn't even think twice about it.

Suddenly she felt very cold, despite the blazing sun; cold, and totally isolated.

"Am I fired?" she asked.

"No," Mason said. He shrugged. "I like the way you write."

"Zach, get over here!" Florescu roared. "Are we making a fucking movie, or what?"

"OK, I'm coming," Zach Mason said, and he strode off toward the klieg lights, leaving Megan Silver standing on the beach, watching them, alone.

chapter 25

"Everything's ready," Paul said.

Yes, Eleanor thought. I guess everything is.

The house alone was decorated to the tune of eight thousand dollars; wreaths of orange blossom trailing over every balustrade, white satin ribbons looped over all the doorways, turtledoves and nightingales in silver cages piping away merrily in every room. The reception room and the dining room had been cleared of all furniture that morning in order to make room for their guests, except for the various mahogany tables which the wedding designer had draped in ivory chiffon, before weighing them down with silver dishes of sweetmeats and savory tidbits and hundreds of champagne flutes in Baccarat crystal. Of course, the main luncheon would be served outside, on the wrought-iron tables they'd had shipped in for the event, each one covered in watered silk and bearing more vintage champagnes, a Taittinger rosé and a superlative Cristal, nestling in individual ice buckets beside the centerpieces of rare white and pink orchids. Huge oak trestle tables were lined up for the buffet, which was as sumptuous as the most expensive caterer in Beverly Hills could come up with: pheasant, grouse, wild boar, venison, pâté de foie gras; smoked salmon, caviar, oysters, rainbow trout; fresh truffles, wild strawberries, asparagus; anything and everything a jaded palate might possibly aspire to, with special sections for vegetarians, vegans, dieters, and anyone who might wish to keep it kosher. The desserts had a table to themselves, and they deserved it: apples formed out of delicate spun sugar; freshly made ice cream and sorbets in eighteen different flavors; hot pears in a mulled wine sauce; a warm pecan pie that had made Eleanor's stomach growl just looking at it; a chilled chocolate parfait rippled with the bitter, dark, milk, and white varieties; some light concoction made of honey and burnt almonds; an exotic fruit salad; a quivering raspberry Pavlova . . . there seemed to be no end to them. And next to the desserts, a bar, with everything from freshly pressed strawberry juice to a very English bowl of ready-mixed Pimms, complete with floating slices of apple and cucumber. After the meal, their guests would have their choice of ten different flavors of filter coffee, six different flavors of decaf, espresso, cappuccino, or herb tea, not to mention the twelve vintage liqueurs Paul's wine merchants had recommended. At this very moment there were forty waiters and waitresses hovering among the crowd, replenishing every empty glass, endlessly circulating with tray after tray of delicious hors d'oeuvres.

And that was merely a small part of it. The actual area set for the wedding was a masterpiece of floral design; each gold-backed chair for the guests had its legs and back wreathed in lilies, roped seamlessly to the wood with invisible threads; the canopy overhead was one solid sheet of flowers, a gorgeous, scented mass of pink dog roses and white orchids, irises, clematis, jasmine, and freesias, designed to permit just enough space for the sunlight to filter through in strategically positioned beams; and the arch under which Eleanor and Paul would stand was a single, contrasting blaze of color, a curving loop of eight hundred red roses. And as for the cake . . .

"Thanks, Paul," she said brightly. "Maybe you could ask everybody to take their places now? I'll be down in just a second."

"You got it," he agreed. In the mirror in front of her Eleanor could see him pause, look her up and down, that familiar, satisfied smile creeping across his face. It had been there a lot recently. No more fights; he couldn't agree fast enough to everything she wanted, he couldn't have been more solicitous or supportive.

I have to hand it to Paul, Eleanor told herself, he's a gracious winner.

"That dress is stunning," Paul said.

"Thank you, sweetheart. You look wonderful too," she replied, sounding as enthusiastic as she possibly could. And he *did* look handsome; all that toned muscle and distinguished salt-and-pepper hair packed neatly into a custom-made Savile Row suit of the finest dark wool. They would look great in all the trades and society magazines and gossip columns; the hotshot banker and the studio president, Los Angeles' latest power couple.

Oh, come on, Eleanor. This is your wedding, not your funeral. Remember?

"OK, I'll see you later. Give me about ten minutes."

"All right," Eleanor said.

If she had her time again, she would happily have given him ten years.

"It's so beautiful," Linda Orenstein sighed, fussing with her train. Linda was an old friend from Yale, and one of her matrons of honor. The other one was her cousin Philippa, a happily married Boston mother of two. Eleanor had seen neither of them for years, but that somehow seemed more appropriate. To any of the women producers or agents who were her real friends, her true feelings might have shown, and that was something she just couldn't risk. And anyway, she didn't have a single female friend close enough to have confided in about Tom. That was another problem; for many years now, Tom Goldman had been her closest friend. She had never bothered to maintain a tight network of girlfriends; maybe she'd let herself be put off by the social mountaineering of the Tennis Club trophy wives, all scrambling for position in the court of Queen Isabelle and her new protégé, Crown Princess Jordan.

Too late, Eleanor realized that had been a mistake.

"It *is* beautiful, Eleanor, really! And the bouquet is simply *divine*," Philippa gushed, adding enviously, "Oh, the whole thing is so *glamorous*. And Paul looks so handsome in that tux, doesn't he, Linda?"

"He does," Linda agreed, pulling the train straight. "There. You're perfect."

They all looked at their reflections; Linda and Philippa in subdued, grown-up gowns of dusty pink organza shot through with gold thread, falling down to their feet where matching heels in rose silk peeped from under the hem. Their bouquets were laid to one side, small bunches of the purest white roses and lilies, gathered round with a ribbon of snowy velvet.

Eleanor Marshall stood between them, gowned, veiled, and crowned like a queen. She knew she looked magnificent; the mirror told her so. There was the dress, full-skirted in a crinoline style, antique lace sweeping down over rich folds of ivory satin, her white silk slippers beneath them embroidered with silver thread. The bodice was a tight whalebone corset—which she had laced into easily enough—that pushed her breasts together and lifted them up, enhancing her already impressive cleavage and encasing it in creamy silk and lace, the front of the dress studded with seed pearls and opals that glinted in the midmorning sun. Her ice-blond hair was swept upward and backward in the Edwardian style, giving height to her forehead, and her veil of the sheerest white chiffon was pinned at the crown, ready to be thrown forward as they left the room. Behind that, fixed firmly but invisibly in place by her extremely expensive hairdresser, her train of white Prussian lace cascaded down, twelve magnificent feet of it. The whole headpiece was finished off with a startling coronet; not merely a wreath, her wedding designer had worked carefully in collaboration with the florist and the contents of Eleanor's jewel box to weave strands of pearls and diamonds in with the white roses, lilies, and orchids, so that she seemed to be wearing a blossoming, sparkling crown, the diamonds glittering among the petals, catching the light with her slightest movement.

The makeup artist had spent two hours on Eleanor's face, and now her blue eyes glistened, her lashes were long and full, her cheekbones protruded gracefully with a healthy, romantic-looking glow to the skin, and her lips, lined with a natural pencil and glossed over in the smoothest apricot, seemed full and soft. Of the pallor her client had shown earlier that morning, nothing remained.

Eleanor looked beautiful. No, more than that. Breathtaking.

"Shall we go?" she said.

⋯

Jake Keller, navy-blue morning suit contrasting rather unhappily with his ginger hair and sallow skin, sipped purposefully at a crystal flute of rosé champagne, his practiced eyes glancing backward and forward over the well-dressed throng. He wasn't totally pleased at what he saw. Every player in LA seemed to have turned out—there was Sherry Lansing, head of Paramount and the only woman in town with power equal to Eleanor's, elegant in a tailored Armani pantsuit, chatting amiably to Steven Spielberg; David Geffen was talking to Jeff Katzenberg and Barry Diller in a corner; there was Mike Ovitz and Nora Ephron; Dawn Steel with Jeff Berg . . . He sidestepped to avoid a curious white peacock, one of several wandering around the lawns. The place was like a goddamn Hollywood who's who. Well, at least there was *one* face missing, Keller comforted himself. Sam Kendrick couldn't make it—he had an appointment on the set of a $95 million movie, only two weeks into filming and already running into problems.

Jake smirked. He'd never liked that pushy little Florescu. It would be interesting watching his reaction to the events that would start to unfold in—what? A week or so from now? And once that all got going . . .

He hoped Eleanor Marshall took a long, hard look at her Hollywood A-list crowd, because it would be a long time before she saw them again.

"Jake, would you look at that?" Melinda whispered loudly. His short, dumpy blond wife dug him in the ribs, pointing to the wedding cake, standing six feet tall under an orange blossom canopy of its own, its myriad tiers adorned with every kind of delicacy and ornament. "Isn't that amazing?"

"Yeah, very nice," he said curtly. Melinda had been trying all day to work out what this wedding had cost. It was bugging him. All this conspicuous consumption . . . What, did Eleanor Marshall want her picture in the dictionary next to "traditional" now? He could have sworn she was depressed about Tom's baby. But this display of wealth and power—not exactly hiding her light under a bushel, was she?

Keller scanned the garden, looking for Tom Goldman. With any luck, he'd get to rub it in a little more about Roxana Felix. David Tauber's information was that things were still terrible, the arrival of Sam Kendrick notwithstanding. And Eleanor Marshall had been the one who insisted on casting the lovely lady . . .

"Jordan! Jordan, over here!" Melinda was simpering.

Jake turned around just in time to see Goldman and his gorgeous babe of a wife bearing down on them. His chairman was wearing a dark suit and looking pensive—maybe he was worrying about *Triple Feature*; he should be. Jordan Goldman, sorry, *Cabot* Goldman, Keller corrected himself sarcastically, was somewhat overdone in a skintight cream silk minidress with a plunging neckline, revealing acres of glorious, firm young breasts and miles of shapely calves, tapering down to the thinnest, sexiest Manolo Blahnik strappy heels in silver leather.

Not for the first time, Keller envied his boss. Jesus, it must be fun to be able to afford a cute toy like that.

"Hello, Melinda, hello, Jacob," Jordan twittered. "Melinda, what a lovely suit . . ."

"Tom, good to see you," Jake said enthusiastically.

Goldman nodded at him absently.

"Did you speak to Sam Kendrick this morning?" Keller pressed him.

"Should I have? It's Saturday."

Get with the program, buddy, Keller thought angrily. Listen to me, and stop staring off into the middle distance like a dope fiend.

"I thought he might be sending daily reports about the Roxana situation. It's getting worse, Tom. Thursday she disrupted an entire morning's filming and so far none of the rushes Florescu's sent me have featured her . . ."

"Maybe we can replace her," Goldman said vaguely.

Jake pounced. "Nearly a month into filming? I hardly think so. She's got a pay-or-play clause in that contract, Dave Tauber insisted on it. Smart kid, Tauber. Although we may have to anyway, the way things are going. Of course, that's Eleanor's call. After all, it was Eleanor who was so insistent on casting Roxana—I tried to dissuade her, but she wouldn't listen, and now—"

Dragging his gaze down to Jake's, Tom Goldman gave him a hard stare.

"Shut it, Keller," he said. "This is Eleanor Marshall's *wedding day* and you're here as her *guest*. If I hear another word from you this morning, so help me, I'll fucking fire you."

Keller flushed and threw up his hands.

"OK, OK," he said hastily. "Point taken. Incredible catering, huh? She's worked wonders with this garden."

Tom gave him a contemptuous glance and walked off.

"Tom, baby, wait!" Jordan squealed, running after him.

Jake Keller seethed with anger and humiliation.

⁘

"Eleanor, they've struck up the music!" Linda begged, her round face creased with anxiety. "We have to go! Can't you do that later?"

Philippa shrugged, and rearranged the shimmering folds of her skirts. Eleanor had always been weird, even as a child . . . if she wanted to read faxes ten minutes before her wedding ceremony, well, that wasn't totally surprising. She thanked the good Lord that her Aunt Berengaria had died before she could see the way her daughter was behaving . . .

Reluctantly, Eleanor put down the sheaf of papers Sam Kendrick had just sent through. She'd insisted on having her bedroom fax machine switched on all morning, and today, like every day, she'd been reading the reports on *Triple Feature*. It was in trouble. Roxana Felix was playing the world-class prima donna, but other things were going wrong too; lights were failing, individual scene locations had proved unworkable, the crew had unwittingly violated local government rules on working practice and shoots had been forced to shut down early—all minor problems, so far, but they were mounting up. And as the ranking executive on the project, Eleanor was responsible. Personally.

Still, she admitted to herself as she picked up her bouquet—a heavy, gorgeous mass of the palest pink roses entwined with trailing jasmine and honeysuckle, with a pair of golden tiger lilies threaded through its heart— there was nothing she could do today anyway. It was a Saturday. And she was getting married in a few moments' time. A psychiatrist would have a field day with her . . .

Working, right up until the last minute, Eleanor thought. As if that's gonna help, as if that's gonna buy me any more time . . .

This could not be delayed any longer. The strains of the string quartet were floating up to them from the packed garden, crammed full of movie-business royalty. They were all waiting for her, all waiting to see her finally adopt the correct LA social procedure: a husband, children. She'd be part of a couple, which was the only thing to be in the nineties, when monogamy ruled, and a baby was the chicest lifestyle accessory you could have. And chic or not chic, Eleanor had longed for a child for years, but . . .

At least she was doing it in style. That, nobody could deny. This would go down as the most lavish wedding party since her friend John had married Gina Christiansen in the medieval Greek Orthodox chapel that had been the traditional wedding site in his family for generations . . . which was nice but unspectacular, until you realized that the chapel was situated right next to Dracula's castle in the Transylvanian Alps. She and two hundred Angeleno guests had all flown out for five days of intense celebrations crowned with a reception in the ex-dictator Ceauçescu's summer palace. Probably not something she could have topped, but today they'd come close . . . Eleanor hoped Gina and John were having a good time out there.

Certainly from the windows it looked as though everybody else was. And that was the idea . . . grace under pressure! She, Eleanor Marshall, was not about to lie down and die like a beaten dog. If Tom was happy fathering children on his little bimbo, her heart might be ripped asunder, but not one of the circling vultures was going to realize it. That much she had sworn. And she would have her child, even if its father was not the one her body longed for. Once it arrived, once she held it in her arms, Eleanor knew she would love it, because even if Paul and not Tom had begotten it, *she* would be its mother. And once she got married, here, now, with enough pomp and circumstance for a European princess, she would never again have to endure Isabelle Kendrick's sly whispers, Jordan Goldman's public possessiveness, Jake Keller's subtle digs about Tom. Nobody would ever pity her in that way again. On the contrary, everybody who heard about this little shebang would assume that Eleanor was the happiest woman in the world, and that was exactly the way she wanted it.

A final glance in the mirror reassured her about her looks. Well, God knew she had paid enough to guarantee it. She wanted to be sure that Jordan Goldman looked at her today with envy, and not pity. She wanted to be sure that Tom Goldman was blown away; she wanted him to see what he had lost; she wanted him to think that she took Paul Halfin's ring with a joyful heart; she wanted him to *hurt*.

But it was kind of sick. She had spent sixty thousand dollars on this wedding, and not one cent of that had been used to impress her bridegroom. No, this was all about business; all about pride; and all about Tom.

"OK, ladies," Eleanor Marshall said. "Do you want to get the train? Let's go."

Her matrons of honor fussed happily around behind her, picked up the long, beautiful sweep of antique lace, and followed Eleanor down the stairs and out into the garden, emerging into the bright sunlight just as the musicians' melody segued into the first familiar notes of the wedding march.

The guests on their seats all turned round as one, and Eleanor, through the faint white haze of her chiffon veil, was rewarded with the sight of shocked faces and gasps at her beauty. Her gaze fastened on Tom Goldman's instantly; he was staring at her, looking directly into her eyes with an expression she couldn't read.

Immediately, coldly, Eleanor slid her eyes away and turned them to Paul Halfin, her fiancé, handsome, distinguished, powerful, waiting for her at the altar.

She'd made her choice, and now she would have to live with it.

chapter 26

Roxana Felix strolled barefoot along the shore, feeling the fine-grained sand sinking soft and dry between her toes, enjoying the cool breeze of the night air. In front of her, the inky-black sea crashed and subsided, crashed and subsided, its endless sighing providing her with the perfect sound track to her thoughts.

The beach was deserted, cast in the silvery light of a tropical moon hanging low and full on the horizon, and the stars were scattered like so many icy diamonds across the jet-black backdrop of the sky. She had not seen a sky like it since she was a child; the neon boards of Manhattan and blazing night lights of LA, Chicago, London, and Paris had not left much room for real stars.

Roxana glanced up at the arc of the heavens.

They're shining and beautiful and untouchable and distant, and they wheel in their orbit miles above everybody who looks up to them, she thought. I guess it's a good metaphor for everything I'm working for.

They're also cold and dead. Just like you.

She shook her head sharply, refusing to listen to the carping voice of her demons. She never listened to them. Never let them through. They could not be permitted so much as a second of her time, a moment of her thoughts, Roxana knew that. Because if she succumbed to her memories, they would break her.

No. It was far better to look up toward the clearing in the mountainside, where they were shooting, and think about *that*. They were two months into filming, and everything was going according to plan—according to *her* plan, that was. For everybody else it had been a disaster—the wrong equipment arriving from the studio; location shoots set up, and then having to be dismantled at the last minute because of Seychelles government regulations; her own disruptiveness, which had been imaginatively handled, Roxana congratulated herself, smiling—after the first week, she'd alternated between a superbitch and a remorseful, modest actress, pretending to listen to Sam Kendrick when he arrived. That had meant that she had not been fired; Roxana was a world-class expert in judging just how far she could push it. And as a result, they now had two months' worth of footage featuring Roxana Felix as Morgan—footage which it would be financially impossible to reshoot. She had made herself indispensable, and now the fun had really started.

Superbitch was back, and this time she had the whip hand.

Roxana smiled as she ticked off all the other problems on her long, manicured fingers. Union. Equipment. Location. Support cast—and that was too easy, reading a line oddly to throw off Mary, feeding a poorly timed cue to Jack, or simply shifting her body before Seth or Robert so they got aroused. Subtle tricks she'd employed a million times before with fellow models on shoots across the globe, in those long-gone days when Roxana had *done* shoots with other models. Throw in David's insidious sabotage of their creature comforts—Mary's contact lens solution, unobtainable on the islands, getting delayed for three weeks, or Sam Kendrick's soothing faxes full of logic and reason never reaching Jack, for example—and compound it with the daily battle to get anything right logistically, and the costars' performance had taken a dramatic dive. Fred had already had to reshoot three scenes with Mary Holmes, because when he reviewed the rushes he wasn't satisfied.

They were several weeks behind schedule. Already, the budget was looking hopelessly optimistic.

Triple Feature was in big trouble. And that meant so was Eleanor Marshall, and so was Sam Kendrick. Eleanor's studio-saving flick was turning into a creative and commercial disaster. And Sam Kendrick's big SKI package deal was less of a big deal every day.

Of course, that was the beauty of the thing, Roxana thought to herself, the way all the blame would fall exactly where she had intended it to. Eleanor Marshall and Sam Kendrick would learn the hard way not to mess with her; they had both insulted her, and now they were both clutching a one-way ticket out of their precious industry, at which she, Roxana, had apparently been such an insignificant novice. She smiled, her lips curving coolly. As far as she was concerned, there were certain lessons in life which you could apply anywhere. As Ms. Marshall and Mr. Kendrick would find out. And at the end of it all, she, Roxana Felix, would be established as a great movie star, a real powerhouse, famous for herself rather than her picture—accepted, and *loved*.

Triple Feature would see the end of all her enemies, but the movie itself was not dead. Just a little bit sick. And when the time was right to administer the medicine, her chosen acolytes, Jake Keller and David Tauber, would be right there to play doctor, rescue the picture, and put it smoothly back on track to smash success.

Roxana breathed in deeply, drawing the fragrant tropical air into her lungs. She might head back to the hotel now, see if Sam was around to offer her a little more physical release. There was something so amusing in watching him sink deeper and deeper under her spell, and after all, he did offer her body incredible pleasures. He was good enough even to drive out the memory of her unaccountable failure with Zach. And surely there was no danger of her starting to feel anything for him, was there?

The supermodel checked her feelings as she strode back across the deserted reaches of sand, watching herself, observing her own emotions as though an unbiased, outside witness. That was the only way to survive, that had always been her way; to keep the core of your soul distant and unwatchable, so that nothing could crack it, nothing could violate it. She had suffered once before, and she would never do so again.

Roxana knew that she despised men like Keller and Tauber—they were jackals, unprincipled, greedy scavengers with giant egos and a combination of cold ruthlessness and low cunning that had bought each of them every gain they had. Sam, her Sam, was not like that. He had principles. He was ambitious and tough, but not ruthless. And he was strong and bold, he played with a straight deck. You could trust him. She did not despise him. But she did dislike him, she did want revenge . . . he had insulted her in public, beaten a submission from her. Well, Roxana hoped he had enjoyed his momentary thrill of domination. Because it was going to cost Sam Kendrick very, very dear.

No, she reflected, as she walked into the orchid-scented gardens of the hotel. Her heart remained a fortress. Sam Kendrick would find no mercy there.

❖

"There's an explanation, Tom, there has to be."

"Not good enough!"

Goldman's fist pounded down on his desk, his angry face flushed red with fury. "You authorized those budget projections, Eleanor. You signed off on three location choices which have proved unworkable. And you had ultimate authority over casting choices which have gone badly wrong. We developed this project from scratch, and that means *you* took on the role as producer."

"Thank you for the recap," Eleanor Marshall replied coldly. She stood in front of her boss's desk, poised and immaculate as ever in a navy Georges

Rech pantsuit, a platinum wedding ring glinting on the fourth finger of her left hand.

"*Triple Feature* was going to be our comeback movie, and now it's going to hell in a handbasket! Our pitch to New York to save this goddamn studio was based on the movie—"

"*My* pitch."

"Oh, yeah. *Your* pitch, that's right. And your movie, your casting decisions, and your mistakes!"

"Casting Roxana Felix was not my decision, Tom, if you remember."

"I remember that your signature is at the bottom of the memo confirming her casting."

Eleanor took a step backward, her expression darkening.

"You would deny responsibility for that, Tom? Is that what you're saying?"

Goldman paused, took a deep breath.

"Look, Eleanor. The board knows about our problems on the set. Don't look at me like that, I *know* it's supposed to be top-level privileged. But Howard Thorn has heard about it and he's on my back . . ."

Eleanor felt a fresh tendril of fear coil its way around her heart. Holy Lord Jesus, why was it Howard Thorn, out of all of them? Thorn was the one who owned stock, a fifteen percent stake, to be precise. The director who would be most inclined to scream for blood if it all went wrong. And whose blood? Not Tom Goldman's, evidently. She had seen this kind of thing before. Greedy as he would have been to take the glory for a smash, Tom was pedaling away from a budgetary disaster just as fast as he could. And if that meant passing the buck on Roxana Felix, so be it.

The moment she had dreaded had come to pass. Tom Goldman would be responsible for firing her or sparing her, and his own job was probably on the line too.

Maybe all Hollywood friendships end this way, when you get right down to it, she thought. Torn apart in the scramble to survive. Was that what their fifteen years of companionship meant to Goldman? Kill or be killed?

"Are you saying," she repeated slowly, "that you would lie about the part you played in casting Roxana Felix?"

Tom Goldman stared hard at her.

"What I'm *saying*, lady, is that if you want to stay president of this studio you had better find a way to fix this mess, and you'd better do it fast."

Eleanor turned on her heel and walked out of his office without another word.

Tom Goldman watched her go. When she had disappeared into the corridor, he slumped back in his Eames leather armchair, despair racking him. He was being hard on Eleanor, as hard as he could.

It was the only way he stood a chance of disguising his feelings for her, and disguise them he must. Because she belonged to Paul Halfin. Because he had sired a child on a woman he now realized he didn't love, maybe didn't even *like*, but who would be the mother of a baby that *he* was responsible for.

It had taken that night in New York to show him what true love was, what real passion was. It was difficult even to get aroused with Jordan now. He pretended it was her pregnancy, but he wasn't sure she was buying that . . . and meanwhile the studio and his great white hope of a movie were falling apart.

It was all turning to dust, his whole life, crumbling into ashes in front of him. Made worse because for a few shining hours, he had seen it all clearly, he had had everything . . .

Too late, Tom. You're just too late.

⋰⋱

"Fire her." Fred Florescu's exasperated voice broke into Sam Kendrick's self-absorption. "You've got the seniority, Sam, for God's sake. Call Eleanor Marshall and have her *do* it."

"It would cost far too much money at this stage," Kendrick said, his eyes still fixed at the projection room screen. He had seen the rushes now, all of them, and he knew this movie was salvageable—just.

If nothing else went wrong.

If he could persuade Roxana to do her job.

If the support cast pulled themselves together.

A lot of ifs, Kendrick knew. But he just could not, would not accept the alternative. She was a drug, and he was becoming addicted.

"Maybe we should consider firing Mary or Seth, or both," the agent suggested. "I know they're my clients, but these are lousy performances. What you've got of Roxana is actually terrific."

"Yeah, what we've *got* of her," Florescu ranted, passing his hand across his forehead. "But that's not fucking enough! First I'm ready to replace the bitch, then she does a little work, and now, when we're getting too far in for changes, she starts screwing around again!"

"Mary and Seth are doing their best," Zach Mason chimed in quietly from a corner. "She's putting them off deliberately. Sabotaging their performances. I see it time and again on the set."

"*Sabotaging* them? Don't you think that's maybe a little molodramatic, kid?" Sam said. "This is a movie, not Kennedy in Dallas."

Mason shrugged. "That's what I see, Sam."

"I'll ask David to talk to her again," Kendrick said finally, standing up, "and I'll speak to Seth and Mary and Jake. They're all my clients, so maybe I can put the fear of God into them—do something about the personnel problem."

But even as he rolled out the soothing words, Kendrick winced inwardly at the lie. The personnel problem was sleeping with him, and he knew it.

·:·

Megan sat alone in the bedroom she shared with David Tauber, staring into space. Outside their balcony, the wine-dark sea crashed softly against the shore, and gray clouds scudded swiftly over the moon.

David was off somewhere, eating with Seth Weiss.

Megan found she wasn't sorry. It gave her a chance to call Dec.

She glanced down at her latest rewrite. It took her all day, and David hadn't even noticed. On the other hand, Zach Mason had scrawled, "Great stuff, Megan, you genius," right across the top.

"So, how are you getting on?"

Dec's enthusiasm crackled down the line. "Paradise found, with lover boy?"

"Not exactly," Megan admitted.

"Honey, will you go nuts if I say I hate the new look? It's all harsh . . . those photos weren't you."

"Zach Mason would agree with you." She sighed.

"Is it rough, being on set with him? You guys get on so badly."

"I know." Megan cradled the phone against her cheek. "But . . . it's weird. He gives me respect, he's supportive. At least about the script. Roxana's the nightmare. Nobody can believe how hard Zach works."

"And David's supportive?"

"Sure." It was a lie, and she knew it.

There was a moment's silence on the other end.

"That's good. Maybe you and Zach will patch it up," Dec suggested.

She wondered where Zach was. She had a vision of Roxana Felix sitting astride him, grinding her perfect body over that flat stomach. Of Zach smiling up at her, wolf eyes alight with pleasure.

"I don't think so," Megan said. And wondered why she felt so down.

·:·

Bewitched.

The word floated through his mind, settling on the surface level of his consciousness, above the deep levels of happiness and sensual nirvana that had practically hypnotized him. Sam Kendrick lay on top of the double bed in Roxana's hotel suite, feeling sexually sated in a way he had not in years. He had started to make love to her, slowly at first, getting more and more aroused by the way she would slide that silken skin against him, trail the feathery ends of her glossy, coal-black hair over his cock, rub her erect nipples across his dry, burning lips, cup his balls in her warm hands and massage them with the lightest, most exquisitely teasing touch, until he was massively erect, his cock aching and throbbing with need, and then she had slid away from him onto those slender knees and taken him in her mouth, perfect red lips sliding up and down him in a heavenly rhythm, then breaking off to lick him seconds before the pleasure got too acute, flicking her tongue across the sensitive, straining tip of his penis, then all the way down the length of him to the base, her fingers trailing lightly over his balls until he thought he might go mad, and finally, seeing her pretty face curving into a secret smile, he had roared with amused frustration, grabbed the little minx by her underarms and hauled her onto her stomach across the bed, sliding into her inch by inch, delighted at finding her soaking wet for him, and had started to tease her, his cock pounding into her, his fingers slipping into the slick down between her legs, brushing over her clitoris, bringing *her* up to the brink and back several times, until she was weeping, kissing weakly at his forearm, begging him to do it to her, begging for release, and with an incredible sense of masculine power pumping through his veins Kendrick had agreed and slammed himself deeper and deeper into her velvet body, taking them both across the final barrier into an immense orgasm, one that had torn from him as though he were a boy of seventeen, one that he had felt rock his lover's slim body as her belly convulsed in spasms beneath him. Now she was curled in his arms, naked and catlike, her small, incredibly perfect body resting against his, her head nestling in the crook of his elbow, and he was almost breathless from the adoration and protectiveness that gripped him every time he glanced at her.

"I think Isabelle must be the luckiest woman alive," Roxana murmured.

Sam laughed. "Isabelle and I haven't slept together for years."

"Oh, come on. You're just saying that to please me." She snuggled against him.

"I swear! You know she isn't interested in that kind of thing. Isabelle loves giving parties, she loves the social thing." Kendrick shrugged. "It works out OK; we just never confront anything. I think a lot of good marriages survive that way."

"It doesn't sound so good, Sam. It sounds lonely."

Her words were an icy dagger plunged right into the most vulnerable places of his heart. Until he had started to see Roxana, he hadn't cared—he hadn't *known* there was anything missing from his life. He'd been consumed with getting to the top and staying there, and there had been exclusive whores to provide the sex which Isabelle withheld, and Isabelle to provide the social backdrop which she did not withhold. And love? Well, he loved his kids, both in their teens and away at English boarding schools. The best, apparently, and Isabelle had insisted on it. The other kind of love, the feelings he had once had for Isabelle, that had died of malnutrition, and had wasted away so silently he neither realized when it died nor missed it when it was gone.

"Are you ever lonely?"

The words came out before he could stop himself. He didn't want her to know how strongly he had started to feel for her, didn't want to scare her off. How many men would a supermodel have cast off? How many lovers would this icy beauty have broken in two? Sam didn't want to think about it. But he also didn't want to let her go.

"I'm lonely all the time. I'm lonely on this movie," Roxana told him, her voice a whisper. "It's hard, Sam, it's really hard. They're all blaming me." Her words trailed away, filled with pain. "Don't bother to deny it, I know it's true . . . Seth and Mary and Jack, they're all acting so well, and I know my scenes probably aren't great on tape . . ."

"Your performance is fine, sweetheart."

She squeezed his arm gratefully. "You're too soft with me, baby. But they make up for it. Ever since I told Zach Mason I didn't want a relationship with him, he's just made it impossible . . . and Fred won't cut me any slack . . . but it's mostly Megan Silver."

"Megan?"

"She keeps rewriting all the scenes and changing my part! I *try* to act it, Sam, but sometimes I just can't . . . I've asked David to speak to her, as she's his client, but he's tried and I really don't know what the hell else to do—Fred just loves her."

"Why is she rewriting scenes now?" Sam asked, bewildered and angry. The hurt in Roxana's voice tore at his heartstrings.

"Oh, she has to, I guess. Because of all the set stuff that keeps going wrong, you know? It has to be changed for the new locations and stuff . . . but she's using it as an excuse to rip up my character, and nobody's stopping her . . ."

"She's history," Sam said bleakly.

"Oh, no, Sam. She was really sweet a couple of months ago, in LA. But she got that makeover and the bleached hair and the expensive clothes . . ."

"She did change," Sam said, recalling the last time he'd seen Megan Silver, when she seemed a good kid, maybe a little naive, kind of cute with her brown hair and her jeans. The stylish, sexy creature he'd encountered over here, writing furiously at all hours of the day, was someone else—a little brittle, very self-possessed. And, apparently, a new addition to the swollen ranks of backstabbing Hollywood bitches.

"She's history, Roxana. Forget about it. Just do the best you can," he repeated, kissing the top of her head.

"I will, Sam," Roxana promised. A small, secret smile curved across her ruby lips. "Don't you worry. I will."

chapter 27

"I want you to go to the doctor," Paul repeated.

Eleanor stared at him miserably. Her husband's lips were set in a tight gray line, his face white with anger and frustration.

"It's a bad time for me at work," she said, willing him to understand. He had to be supportive, to be there for her in her hour of need. Otherwise, what did they have together? A new respectability for the dinner parties she didn't have time to throw, a joint bank account, and rigid, monotonous sex, prescribed by Dr. Haydn, designed solely for the purpose of getting her pregnant. She was due for her first checkup at the fertility clinic in a month, and every night she prayed they'd find out she had conceived. Because what with the wall charts and stupid positions and thermometers, Eleanor wasn't sure she could take much more of it.

They had had the first major fight of their marriage on their wedding night. Eleanor, striving to beat back the sense of claustrophobia, the feeling of being trapped, had come to her bridegroom's bed in the sexiest piece of lingerie she possessed—a beautifully cut black satin teddy by Janet Reger—and without her diaphragm. Trying hard for a little humor and camaraderie, she had sliced it in two with a pair of kitchen scissors and placed the remains in a small cardboard box, wrapped up like a present in red ribbons, and placed it on Paul's pillow.

He'd opened it, laughed, and then handed her a small bottle of pills.

"Sorry I didn't wrap them in ribbons," he said.

"What's this?" Eleanor asked, smiling. "An aphrodisiac?"

"Not exactly," Paul told her, his handsome face suddenly serious.

"This is a new fertility drug, the latest thing. Only just cleared by the FDA. It won't work right away, but the quicker we get you on a course of treatment, the better."

"A fertility drug?" Eleanor repeated, stunned.

"That's right." Paul nodded proudly. "The best available."

Eleanor remembered that she'd had to take a second to compose herself, before managing to say, quite quietly, "And you don't think we should allow my body to try and conceive naturally first, before you unilaterally decide I need to be pumped full of hormones and chemicals?"

It hadn't been a good evening. And lately things had been getting worse.

In perfect harmony with the rest of my life, Eleanor told herself.

"It's a bad time for everybody at work," Paul replied, shrugging. "You're not the only one that has troubles in the office, you know. And it isn't fair to me to use that as an excuse to shirk your spousal duties."

"My *what*? My spousal duties?" Eleanor shot back. "And what are those, exactly, Paul? Being ready to have sex the second I get home, in case we miss the optimum daily window for conception? Accepting that you won't make love to me at any other time in case you waste a few precious sperm? I don't *have* 'troubles in the office,' Paul, I have a huge crisis that's threatening to consume my career! I'm about to lose everything I've worked for all my life! And you expect me to come home, *every night*, and be ready for sex, *every night*, whether I feel like it or not! I'm not your goddamned brood mare!"

"We can discuss that another time," Halfin said, his eyes cold. "Right now I want you to get this recurrent nausea seen to. If you've got some kind of allergy or virus, it could be affecting everything we're trying to do."

"OK, OK," Eleanor told him wearily.

His words seemed to have knocked all the fight right out of her. She should see a doctor for her sickness—not because a virus might be causing *her* harm, but because it might upset her darling husband's grand conception design!

He doesn't care about *me* at all. He cares about his wife, the soon-to-be mother of his children, Eleanor thought. No wonder he was so furious when I insisted on keeping my own name. It took a little luster off his carefully designed family picture. But Eleanor Halfin? Eleanor Marshall Halfin? Over my dead body . . .

She reached for her Hermès purse and slung it over the shoulder of her smart Rifat Ozbek suit in dark green cashmere, picking up her briefcase in the other. Suddenly she just didn't care anymore, all she wanted was to get into her office and spend another hellish day trying to save her job.

I *deserve* this, she told herself. Maybe Paul doesn't love me, but who said he had to? I hardly accepted him in a heady rush of romantic passion.

I wanted a husband to save me from everybody's pity. He wanted a wife to complete his New Model Lifestyle. We're alike—two cynical people in a partnership of convenience. Maybe, in the end, everything comes down to that; whether you're swapping wealth and power for youth and beauty, sexual skills for a green card, or social approval for an available womb in a suitable body, maybe all marriages are really just trades.

I was a fool to believe it could be any other way.

"I'm out of here. I'll have my assistant schedule me an appointment with Dr. Haydn this morning," she promised.

Her husband nodded curtly, pleased.

"Thank you." He spread his hands. "Who knows, maybe it's morning sickness. Maybe you're pregnant already, and we just didn't realize it."

"Who knows?" Eleanor agreed, walking out.

She pressed a button on her remote and unlocked the Lotus, sinking thankfully into the soft leather of the driver's seat, her mind already turning to *Triple Feature*, trying to figure out ways around the latest budgeting disaster.

After all, what was she going to tell her husband? That her sickness predated all their fertility contortions? As far as she was concerned, it hadn't been brought on by any allergy or virus. It had been caused by the stress of a broken heart.

⁘

Megan Silver leaned forward over the PowerBook Eleanor Marshall's office had sent out to her, typing away furiously. The scorching midday sun was beating down on the back of her neck, heat hitting her from all sides, reflected up against her face from the powdery white sand. Her skin felt sticky and uncomfortable from all the lotions and gels she was having to rub into it just to survive—factor 15 sun lotion, antiperspirant, deodorant, insect repellent, and coconut butter oil as an emergency moisturizer, and despite everything small beads of sweat kept dewing her forehead and legs. Her hands were getting cramps from overuse and her head throbbed with a crunching migraine.

Not the best way to concentrate.

Not the best way to write an inspirational script.

But that was what she had to do, or this movie was history. All the delays, equipment failures, location problems and reshooting of scenes had sent them over budget and behind schedule. The only things that held it patchily together were Florescu, who screamed at everybody, worked like a maniac, and shot and reshot until he had something he could use, and Megan herself, who found herself doing emergency rewrites all day, every day, as they were forced to change this scene or that one, bringing the mountain to Mohammed over and over again. Florescu had told her he was relying on her, and Megan, desperate to impress the one person on this goddamn movie she had any respect for, was trying hard to rise to the challenge.

The pressure was intense.

"Megan, do you think you could put something in about Peter?"

She looked up, shading her eyes with her hand, to see Seth Weiss standing in front of her. The actor was looking diffident; something she always liked about Seth, he was too secure a star, at forty-five, to have any kind of an ego. Roxana Felix could take a few lessons from Mr. Weiss, Megan thought sarcastically. Although even if she won three Oscars, like he had, it probably wouldn't be enough to calm the bitch down.

"Where, in the escape sequence?"

Weiss nodded, his handsome eyes unfocused, and she could see he was going over the scene in his head. Another plus for the guy. He actually cared about *acting*.

"He was wounded when we were going to shoot it in the forest, right? And he's still wounded, but now we're on a beach, and if the shot hit him in the foot, he'd get sand in there . . ."

"And sand is excruciatingly painful in an open wound," Megan finished for him. "Like salt. Of course, I should have thought of that before, Seth, I'm an idiot."

"You're a bona fide heroine, Megan," Weiss told her, grinning. "Saving this movie single-handedly. Or at least, that's what Fred keeps telling us all."

"Get out of here," Megan said, but she flushed with pleasure as she punched the code into her machine, looking for Seth's character, Peter Cavazzo.

"Seth, Megan, how's it going?" David Tauber asked amiably, striding over to them and giving Seth the benefit of a full-wattage smile.

"It's going," Megan said curtly.

Why did David only ever ask her that when Zach or one of the costars was in her vicinity? The way he sucked up to Sam's clients was truly disgusting, she thought. Kissing ass, telling them how wonderful their performances were, contradicting any honest advice Mr. Kendrick might have given them, pretending to apologize for little creature comforts SKI had failed to provide, when what he was really doing was drawing attention to it. And yet in private, he never bothered to compliment *her* work, never gave her a shred of encouragement for the effort she was making. On the contrary, he got pissed off if she wasn't always praising him, telling him how clever he was. And if she felt too exhausted for sex, forget about it! He was furious! What had he called her last night? Totally selfish, wasn't that it?

Megan felt resentment bubble up inside her. She was starting to suspect that she'd fallen for a class A jerk.

"We're putting in some new dialogue for Cavazzo," Seth explained.

"More agonized than sassy. Maybe I'll be able to play agonized better." He shook his head, a wry expression on his face. "Sam told me straight that the forest scene didn't work well anyway. Said I looked angry, instead of witty. I told him it's hard to be witty when the leading lady keeps blowing your cue on purpose."

Megan winked at him. Most people on the set had a strong dislike of Roxana Felix in common.

"Hey, I thought you were terrific," David said smoothly. "Maybe the scene needed work, but you were great."

"Thanks, man," the actor said, smiling as he walked away.

Megan glanced up at David.

"That's not what you said last night. You told me a cartoon would've been more convincing."

"Jesus, you want to keep it down?" Tauber hissed, glancing over his shoulder to check that Weiss was out of earshot. "He's talent, Megan. You only ever encourage talent."

"I don't notice you encouraging mine much lately," Megan said, pushing her blond hair out of her eyes.

"You're a writer, Megan. And you've got me all the time," David said impatiently, checking his Rolex. "I have to get back to the set."

"Can't miss a chance to kiss up to Mary, huh?" Megan asked, wondering where this was coming from. She'd never dared to criticize David since the day he rescued her from Mr. Chicken. Maybe the heat was getting to her . . . but somehow it didn't feel so terrifying, somehow it felt pretty good.

What if Fred was right? a little voice in her head was asking. *What if David didn't rescue you? What if* you *rescued you?*

"What?" David sputtered, glaring at her. What was this bullshit? Was *Megan* going to start up on him now? Who the hell did she think she was? Roxana?

"Mary and Seth are *Sam's* clients, David," Megan said stubbornly. Sam Kendrick had always treated her with respect, she thought, which was more than she could say for her own agent. "You're undermining him. I don't think it's right."

David Tauber leaned forward toward her, menacingly, his eyes narrowed.

"Listen up," he said softly. "It's none of your business. And if you repeat what you just said to anybody on this set—and I do mean *anybody*— you're going to regret it."

Megan gazed at him coolly.

"Are you threatening me, David?" she replied.

He straightened up. Didn't want to push the stupid kid too far—who knew what she might do in this mood? Megan with an attitude? That had to be nipped in the bud, and fast. Except that right now he didn't have the time.

"We'll talk about this tonight. In private," he said curtly.

Megan clicked off her computer and stood up, smoothing down her skirt.

"I don't think so, David," she said. "I'll be sleeping in another room tonight."

"You don't mean that," he said, unfazed, confident.

"Oh, yes, I do," she said. "I need a little time to myself."

"Right. *You* need time to yourself," Tauber sneered, and Megan found herself staring at his handsome, mocking mouth with dismay. She tried to remind herself that David Tauber was the guy she'd been longing for, but it didn't work. The polished veneer David assumed with everyone else slipped a little further every time he was alone with her, and right now, he seemed less like an infallible superagent and more like a spoiled brat every second. "It's always me, me, me with you. You're not the only one putting in time on this project, Megan. What about *my* needs? What am I supposed to do tonight? After everything I've done for you?"

Megan felt desperately tired and unhappy. She ran one sticky hand through the platinum-blond mop she'd been regretting ever since she had it done; yet again, she'd been twisting herself into something she wasn't in the hope of pleasing a guy, only to find it was all for nothing. That short-skirted, blond-haired, designer bitch thing was a million miles from the real Megan Silver, and suddenly she felt a sharp pang of remorse. As soon as she got home it was back to brown hair, comfy jeans, and Veruca Salt T-shirts. Because, as she now realized, David Tauber wasn't worth it.

She admitted to herself she didn't love him.

"David, please. I'm knocked out. I just need some sleep, a little time to breathe."

"No. No way, lady. You'll be in our room tonight as usual." David was bristling with anger. "You wanted to be with me so bad? Fine. But you play by my rules."

"It's over, David," Megan said wearily. And it was; yet another brilliant Megan Silver waste of energy, romantic dreams, and hope. Because David Tauber, no matter how hard she'd tried to kid herself, had never been any substitute for . . . for . . . .

She suppressed that idea as soon as it surfaced. Reality check, girl, he's way, way out of your league, and you know it. No amount of makeovers are gonna turn you into Roxana Felix.

"You're just hysterical!" Tauber's smooth features were purple with fury. *Megan* thought she could dump *him!* "You don't know what you're saying!"

Megan picked her laptop up.

"Well, David, that's where you're wrong," she said calmly, and then she turned on her heel and walked away, leaving him standing on the beach, spluttering with rage and disbelief.

⋅⋰⋅

Tom Goldman sat perfectly still in the air-conditioned comfort of his office, wondering if there was any way out of this situation. His normally resourceful mind would once have known exactly how to handle things; it would have presented him with several options, it would have offered him some kind of a get-out, some excuse not to do what Jake Keller was suggesting. The trouble was that right now he couldn't think of a single one.

Everything the vice president said made perfect sense. You couldn't argue with it; he had a $95 million movie that was already a month behind schedule, $9 million over budget, and by all accounts turning out to be a creative turkey.

Triple Feature had been his big rescue package for Artemis Studios. If it failed, Eleanor Marshall was history. And since he had pushed for her appointment, *he* would be history.

"Eleanor Marshall took over the production on this project," Keller was saying, his nasty weasel face looking smug. "You heard her, Tom. She threatened to have me barred from script meetings. And she forced me to draw up all my objections to the film in a long memo, sign it, and copy you on it."

He fished about in the document wallet he was carrying and placed a copy of the memo on Tom's desk.

"At the time I was somewhat offended." A beat, an unpleasant smile. "But on reflection—maybe the little lady was doing me a favor. Once I finished this, I submitted a copy to Mr. Thorn, too. After all, he is the chairman of the board. I felt I should have the courage of my convictions."

Keller leaned back in his chair, enjoying the effect his words were having. At the mention of Mr. Thorn, his boss had gone pale.

Thanks for the tip, Roxana, he thought.

"I see," Goldman said.

"Do you, Tom?" Keller packed sarcasm into the words. "I wonder. Eleanor has been responsible for buying a weak script, using unnamed actors in a terrible miscasting, and for a series of location and logistical errors that are sending costs spiraling out of control. This studio doesn't even know what's going on over there. As of last week, Florescu has stopped sending me the dailies. And without rushes, how are we supposed to know if there's something worth using coming out of this mess? You must admit that what we've seen so far isn't encouraging. And word is out in the industry, Tom."

"Already?" Goldman asked, his expression stricken.

"Well . . . rumors are starting up. I have the publicity department working flat out to counter them, but . . ." Keller shrugged. "You know how it is."

Yeah, Goldman thought. I know exactly how it is. If I don't give you what you want, you're gonna put word on the street yourself, and that could be fatal for us . . .

On the rumors of a smash with *Triple Feature*, Artemis stock had soared. They'd gone so long without a hit that it had been cruising along at the bottom of its price range, undervaluing the company when you considered its software library and real estate assets. The Mason/Florescu project had been seen as a surefire smash, and given Eleanor's reputation for accuracy and tight budgeting, nobody had figured it would do worse than break even. The stock price had responded accordingly. But if news of this fiasco got out . . .

My God, Goldman thought, experiencing a renewed burst of panic. How many shares have *I* got? Preferred stock options had been a big chunk of his salary package over the last twenty years . . .

He did a quick calculation and felt ill. Forget about losing his job. He could lose his *house*. Millions would be wiped off the value of his portfolio . . .

How would he explain *that* to Jordan? "Oh, gee, honey, I'm sorry, but you won't be able to throw that Save the Rainforest bash after all? And I think we should talk about selling one of the cars, to see the baby through college?" Jesus H. Christ, he could see her face now. And it wasn't exactly wearing a supportive, stand-by-your-man expression!

Eleanor would stand by me, Tom thought.

No! Screw Eleanor! She got us all into this mess!

"Jake, I hear what you're saying," Goldman told him, reluctantly. He didn't want to have to cooperate with the little prick, but Jake had been right all along and he and Eleanor conspicuously wrong. Who had a choice?

"Good." Jake Keller smiled thinly. He had Goldman by the balls, and they both knew it. "So it's settled, then. I'll bring my plan to save the movie and a revised budget along to the big production meeting next week. I intend to challenge Eleanor on every point in this memo." He tapped the document arrogantly. "That way, if she's got a defense or a better idea, she'll get a chance to counter. But if she doesn't—you put me in charge of the film, effective right away."

Goldman sighed. Such a move would be the same as firing her. No president could accept a demotion like that from the CEO; Eleanor would have to resign, right then and there, in front of the entire management team.

"Do we have to do it so publicly?"

Keller smiled again. "That's the only way I want to do it. Out in the open. You know how I hate sneaking around behind people's backs."

He stood up to leave.

"Do we have a deal, Tom?"

Goldman took the limp hand thrust toward him and shook it without enthusiasm.

"I guess so," he said.

·:·:·

"Jesus," Zach Mason muttered, looking around him.

"Impressive, don't you think?" Fred Florescu asked, pleased by his star's awestruck reaction. "I wanted you to take a look at this place tonight, get a feel for it before we start shooting tomorrow."

The two men were standing on the side of a dusty mountain road, at the entrance to a tourists' walking path, carved out of the vegetation by the Seychellois government. Photographs of the mist forest were what had made Florescu choose Mahé for his jungle, and now he was showing Zach Mason the real thing. As they climbed out of their battered four-wheel truck, the emerald slopes of Morne Blanc had looked pretty ordinary, just a dense, impenetrable tangle of trees. But two steps into the pool of green shadow, and Mason's mouth hung open in astonishment.

They were standing on the edge of a mountain ridge, the path dropping away downward and to their left. The woodland before them was a mass of open space, creepers and small green plants growing under the verdant canopy, shafts of bright sunlight piercing through here and there, illuminating the mist and the tropical palms. Gnarled *bwa rouz* trees dripping with damp, red moss crowded the sides of the path, orchids curling around some of them. There was a thick scent of wild cinnamon and albazia, vast ferns were everywhere, and *coco marron* palms sprouted across the slopes. Zach saw a small electric-blue bird swoop down from some perch and flit through a sun-dappled glade. The whole jungle was alive with movement and noise; insects humming, frogs piping . . .

"It looks like something out of *Raiders of the Lost Ark*," he said.

Florescu clapped him on the shoulder. "Exactly, amigo. Got it in one. This is the most atmospheric backdrop I ever saw, I swear. Which is why I refuse to give up on this thing, despite what David Tauber is telling me."

Zach glanced at him sharply. "What?"

The director shrugged. "He says that Artemis may be about to pull the plug on the project."

"Bullshit. Why would they do that?"

"According to your agent, because of the weather."

Zach looked up at the dazzling blue sky behind them, burning hot and without a single cloud. "The weather looks OK to me."

"We should have wrapped by now. Which would matter a lot less, except that the rainy season apparently starts up around about now." Florescu shrugged. "Tauber says Eleanor Marshall made a huge miscalculation in picking the Seychelles; she didn't take any delay into account, and the result is that the longer we stay here, the more likely we are to get caught by the rains. And I ain't talking about a little drizzle, either."

"You mean we'll be trying to film in a monsoon?"

"You ever seen a monsoon? We'd be packed up. It would break my equipment like matches."

Zach shook his head. "I don't like it, man."

"Me neither!" the director said, laughing. "My movie is turning into a fucking disaster area!"

"No. I mean I don't like all this stuff going wrong. I don't *buy* it. Eleanor Marshall seemed like an intelligent woman to me. Savvy. Not the type to authorize filming in a hurricane."

"If we were on schedule, that wouldn't have happened."

"She'd have factored in delays. All those corporate types do stuff like that; always covering their asses."

"Possibly."

"And I've been watching David. He's been way too calm."

"He's the smooth type," Florescu said, but he was watching his star closely, intently. He knew Zach Mason now, and he sensed a picture crystallizing. Mason was uneducated, but he had a keen intelligence buried under all that ferocious sexuality. That was what made the screen come alive; that was what ignited the footage they had managed to shoot, what made it such compulsive viewing. Zach Mason was a natural. He could sink so deep into his character that when Florescu called "Cut!" Zach would sometimes just stand there, a little dazed, taking a few seconds to snap back into the real world. Zach had been Florescu's hero, and after months of filming together the guy still overawed him; he had the soul of a poet and the aggression of a samurai, and those deep, savage eyes that mesmerized everybody he gazed at.

God, Florescu thought, I have to show that on screen, I *have* to be the one to do it. Nobody's blended beauty and masculinity like that since Marlon Brando.

"He's more than smooth, he's *calm*," Zach said. "*Triple Feature* was the big break for him, right? He has Roxana, Megan, and me. He should be totally panicked to see it slipping away, but he's not—he's just hanging around Mary and Seth and Jack, always providing little solutions for them."

"Jesus," Florescu said slowly. "You're right. He's acting like somebody who doesn't *need* to worry—"

"Because he knows everything is gonna be OK."

"Jesus!" exclaimed the director. "You think all this is deliberate?"

"Why would the studio cancel the project? They must have spent a ton of money already—"

"You got that right," Florescu agreed grimly.

"So they *have* to finish it. Maybe somewhere else, but they have to. We're nearly done filming, we've got under a month to go. They'll need something to show to set off their losses, right? They can't *afford* to kill us off now."

"How would Artemis know we're in trouble? I haven't sent them any rushes for months. Unless Roxana Felix is phoning in."

"Roxana's with David," Zach said. "He's the only guy on the set she never gives a hard time to."

"It has to be something to do with Jake Keller," Fred butted in, excited. "He hates Eleanor Marshall. He got passed over for her job."

"I've heard David call that guy from the production office a few times."

They stared at each other.

"Speculation," Florescu said finally. "We're just guessing. Pretty left-field stuff."

"But we're right," Zach countered. He brushed a strand of long black hair out of his eyes. "You know we are. You can feel it."

"So what do you want to do? Confront David? Confront Roxana? I don't see what good it would do. They won't admit jack, trust me."

"I'm gonna confront Megan," Zach said. "She's weaker than the other two. She'll talk."

The director did a double take. "Megan *Silver?* Now I know you've lost it, amigo. She's been working her butt off, rewriting the script every day. She does what I tell her and she does it fast. There's no way she wants this movie to fail. The kid works harder than anybody on the set."

Zach nodded. "And that's something I don't understand. But she's fucking David Tauber, she's been his girlfriend for months. She thinks the sun shines out of his ass. She must know what he's doing."

Florescu noticed that his tone was suddenly sharp with contempt.

"All right. When we climb up to the top of Morne Seychellois to shoot the hideout sequence—that's for just you, me, and Don with a high-eight camera—I'll ask Megan along. That's scheduled for tomorrow afternoon, you can talk to her then."

"Good." The singer stared into the tropical forest before him, his handsome face dark with anger. "She's gonna have some serious explaining to do, and then we should know what the fuck's going on. Because she's gonna tell me *everything*, Fred. Megan is the key."

chapter 28

"Where's Megan?" Zach Mason asked. "I want to talk to her."

The crew were scuttling around on the beach like tanned worker ants in a hurry, rushing to wheel cameras into position, focus klieg lights, and mike up sound recorders as quickly as possible. Eight A.M. and everybody was already in position; Florescu was standing in a corner, going over the next scene with the cast, huddled together for warmth against the early-morning breeze. They were behind schedule, and every minute of filmable light was precious.

"Dunno, man, haven't seen her," the cameraman replied. "Not like her to be late."

"Seen Megan?" he asked Seth Weissman. "She's always here on time."

Weissman shook his head. "You could ask David or Roxana," he said, pointing to the two of them, who were walking toward the set together, over the sands.

Zach shaded his eyes to see better. The two of them were walking arm in arm, which confirmed one suspicion. David Tauber seemed confident and self-possessed as ever, dressed for the heat in loose, unstructured Armani slacks and expensive-looking shades from Cutler and Gross. Roxana was in costume, a deliberately torn and dusty evening gown, slashed at the sides where her character had torn it in an escape from the gunrunners. Miles of lean, tanned legs were exposed, and there was another rip baring her left shoulder. Her long glossy hair whipped around her neck in the breeze.

What a beauty, he thought. And what a cold, selfish bitch. He'd always admired her stunning looks and never once wanted her; there had been too many beautiful girls for Zach to be impressed, and too many ice maidens melting underneath him for that trick to hold any novelty anymore. True, Roxana hadn't tried to play ice goddess with him. On the contrary, she had thrown herself at him, but even so . . .

Zach Mason knew Roxana Felix the way these others could not. He had walked under the blazing spotlight of fame for years, longer even than she had, and he could tell what was part of the image and what was real. And while most people were comfortable believing her bitchiness was part of the package, Zach was sure it was not. Roxana was damaged. There was a fist of cold wrapped tight around her heart, and when he looked at her, he saw somebody frozen to the core. She would reach out and slash violently at anybody who approached her. Her ruthlessness, her silken savagery with underlings, was no surprise to Zach. Like most wounded animals, she was dangerous.

"Zach," David Tauber said expansively. "Looks like it's gonna be another hot morning."

Yeah, you moron. Like it's gonna be twenty below in the Seychelles.

"Where's Megan, David?" he demanded.

Jesus, I can't stand this asshole, Mason thought fiercely. He's so fucking slick all the time, never gets a hair out of place. What the fuck was I on when I signed up with him? What does a girl like Megan Silver see in him? But I forgot, she's nothing special. Just another bleached LA blonde with a designer closet . . .

Even to himself, the words rang false. Megan *was* working flat out for this movie. She was clever. She'd written a dynamite script. And if she wanted to be with David Tauber instead of him, so what? She could choose who she liked.

Jesus, I'm turning into Roxana, Zach thought wryly. Like I got a divine right to any partner I should happen to favor . . .

"Megan won't be with us," David replied casually. "She's packing to go home."

"She's doing *what?*"

"I fired her," Roxana Felix said calmly.

"Excuse me, Roxana?" Zach repeated, stunned. "You did what? You can't fire Megan! What are you now, the director? Does Fred know about this?"

"Hey, Zach, calm down," David Tauber said soothingly. "In actual fact, Artemis Studios terminated her contract. They're the ones that are paying for her stay here, as well as authorizing her salary. Roxana felt she could no longer work harmoniously with Megan, and Sam Kendrick, who runs my agency—"

"I know who Sam Kendrick is."

"Of course. Well, Sam discussed the situation with Jake Keller over at Artemis, and it was felt that for the good of the picture, Megan should start working on some other project." David beamed at him reassuringly. "You don't need to worry about the script. I've told Kevin Scott to fly out Gordon Walker this morning—Gordon's been familiarizing himself with *Triple Feature* and he'll be able to carry out any further rewrites. You'll like him, Zach. He's very competent, he's worked on two Quentin Tarantino films."

"I see," Zach said, ominously quietly. "Isn't Megan Silver your girlfriend, David?"

The agent shrugged. "I can't let personal feelings get in the way of business. That would be unprofessional. And where *my* clients are concerned," he added, flashing a warm smile at Zach and Roxana, "I'm always professional. You can take that to the bank."

"And have you told Fred about the change of plan?"

"I was just about to," David said.

Roxana Felix gazed at him triumphantly, the light of victory shining in her eyes.

Mason took a deep breath. "You know what, Tauber? I wouldn't bother. I'd run along back to the hotel and tell Megan you just reinstated her. Then you can call Mr. Keller and tell him that *I* wouldn't be able to work harmoniously with any other screenwriter. OK?"

Paling, David Tauber took a step backward.

"But what about Roxana?" he protested. "Her creativity as an actress—"

"Roxana and I are going to have a little chat about that," Zach told him, his voice cold. He stared hard at the supermodel. "I'm sure that by the time you get back, I'll have persuaded her to see things from my point of view."

"David, stay where you are," Roxana snapped.

"David, get your ass back to the hotel *now*," Zach repeated. "Or you're fired as my agent."

"David!" Roxana insisted.

"It's a tough break, isn't it, Tauber?" Zach said menacingly. "Whatever you do now, you're either going to annoy Roxana or me. Because if you aren't gone in ten seconds, it's going to get ugly between us."

David Tauber hesitated, his eyes twitching from Zach to Roxana and back again.

"David, stay there," Roxana warned him, her mild voice suffused with fury.

"Ten," Zach Mason said softly. "Nine. Eight. Seven. Six—"

With a small, agonized cry, David Tauber turned on his heels and fled.

⬧⬦⬧

"It can't be true," Eleanor Marshall said blankly. "It can't be. You've made a mistake."

"No, my dear. No mistake, I assure you," Dr. Haydn replied cheerfully. She gave Eleanor a conspiratorial smile. "Tests these days are very accurate. Especially when you go to the best hospitals, as we do."

Eleanor clutched onto the armrest of her pale pink leather chair, feeling dizzy. Thank God she was sitting down, she thought. If she'd heard this news standing up she might have fainted.

"Eleanor, I swear you must be the *most* unobservant patient I've ever had," the old woman went on. "Even if you thought the nausea was related to something else, didn't you realize you'd skipped a period?"

She shook her head. "No, I . . . I didn't notice . . . It's been chaos at work, I haven't had time to think about much else. And to tell you the truth, I wouldn't have thought anything of it if I had. I skip periods occasionally, if I'm stressed."

"You work too hard altogether," Dr. Haydn said severely. "And you'll have to reduce as many stressful activities as you can."

I.e., do none whatsoever, Eleanor thought wryly.

"But the charts, doctor!" she said. "All that lovemaking in the right position and at the right time of day . . ."

"Evidently not needed," Dr. Haydn told her. "Quite amusing when you think about it, dear. You were pregnant the whole time anyway." She chuckled. "At least you didn't have to start with the fertility drugs."

"I'm *two* months pregnant."

"You are. And quite soon we'll be able to scan for the sex of your baby, if you like. Are you hoping for a boy or a girl?"

"I don't mind," Eleanor said blankly. Her head was spinning with all the implications of this, trying to accept it, trying to make some decisions.

Tom's baby! I'm pregnant with Tom Goldman's child!

"You must have taken my advice on your last visit, and started to make love to your fiancé without a diaphragm. And that was all it took!" the doctor said, with obvious satisfaction. She leaned across the desk toward her patient. "Your little one will arrive *eight* months after the wedding, Eleanor, but that's hardly something to be concerned about in this day and age. In *my* young day, it was very different. I had to tell everybody that my eldest son was premature!"

Eleanor smiled at the old lady as she laughed, warming to her. She'd misjudged Dr. Haydn; her joy in being able to pass on good news was infectious.

"You're going to have a baby, Eleanor!" the doctor exulted. "Isn't it wonderful?"

And suddenly, with that simple expression of delight, Eleanor felt all her confusion crystallize into one gigantic wave of happiness. Because come hell or high water, she *was* going to have the baby of the only man she had ever loved.

"Oh, Liz, it *is* wonderful," Eleanor Marshall said, her eyes suddenly full of tears. "It truly is."

⁘

Roxana Felix settled back against the dark blue leather sofa in Howard Thorn's private jet, making herself comfortable. She had called him that morning and told him to send it to Mahé immediately; if she was forced to leave the set for a while, she was damn well going to do it in style.

"Can I get you anything, Ms. Felix?" a stewardess inquired, her eyes roaming enviously over Roxana's stunning Chanel suit in white cashmere. "Champagne, wine, mineral water, fruit juice?"

"Bring me some fresh orange juice. Slice of lime. No ice," Roxana snapped.

"Yes ma'am." The girl scurried away hastily.

Roxana took several deep breaths and tried to control her temper. This situation was going to require careful handling, and disintegrating into white rage wouldn't help her.

But it was so hard!

Who the hell did Zach Mason think he *was*? Taking her aside like that after he'd crushed the fight out of David Tauber, that spineless little worm, and threatening her? The conversation ran through her mind, the words searing into her memory: "I want you to take a week off, Roxana. And back off Megan. She's the only reason Fred hasn't given up on this movie."

"And what if I don't?" Roxana had spat back at him, her chocolate eyes narrowed in venomous fury.

"Simple, babe," Zach replied—God, she could see it now, his gorgeous face set hard as rock against her, his thundercloud eyes so alive with menace that even she had shrunk from it. "If you don't, I'm going to walk off the film *today*. Right now. And I'm going to fly straight back to Los Angeles and call a press conference, where I'll tell the entire world what a class A bitch you are. In fact, I'll get Florescu to sit alongside me. We'll both tell them how you disrupted this movie, and if you say anything different, I'll get statements from a hundred different people agreeing with me." He gestured sharply toward the set. "Little people, Roxana. The ones you tread on every fucking day—the catering staff, the makeup girls, the lighting director. That'll look good on *Oprah*, don't you think? 'Working with the Beauty Queen Bitch from Hell.' A nice feature in *Vogue*, too. I could give them an exclusive. And I'll tell them that you tried to have the screenwriter fired because you were jealous of her relationship with me. I'll tell them that all that coy posturing at your cosmetic deal and the Electric

City show was bullshit. I'll say you flung yourself at me, but you're such a fucking snake that I'd rather fuck a leper."

"You wouldn't," she'd managed.

Zach Mason shook his head. "Don't let's play games here, lady. You know I would. I don't need this movie; whatever little web you're spinning, you can't trap me in it. I'd do all that in a heartbeat. And what would that do to your fat contract with Jackson Cosmetics?"

That son of a bitch! Roxana thought.

She'd been off the set, packed, and waiting at the airport in Victoria within the hour. What Mason had done to David Tauber she didn't know and couldn't care less about. The little prick had zero *cojones*, not that she'd expected better.

But it didn't matter. Nothing mattered. This was just a temporary annoyance; within days Jake Keller would present his new plan to Artemis, Eleanor Marshall would be fired, and the movie would be back on track. Then she could go back to the set, relocated to somewhere more suitable, and act her heart out. She'd be Meryl fucking Streep, as far as the cast was concerned. And she'd be so hardworking and so sweet to all the stupid little hired hands that Zach Mason's heart would melt.

Roxana picked up a copy of *Variety* laid out for her on the smoked-glass coffee table and idly flicked through it.

Maybe she *had* overdone the leading-lady routine a little, but so what? Everybody loves the return of the prodigal son . . . or daughter. Once Zach had been won over by the new-look, hardworking, polite, and considerate Roxana Felix—*that's* when she could have the little mouse bitch fired. Sam Kendrick was already eating out of her hands, and Eleanor Marshall was history. She could wait for Megan. It was no big deal.

"Your juice, ma'am," the flight attendant said, handing Roxana a Baccarat crystal flute full of freshly squeezed juice and topped with a slice of lime, exactly as she'd ordered it. The girl placed a mahogany tray laden with a plate full of lime wedges and a silver pitcher of juice in front of her. "May I get you some lunch? The chef suggests melon and prosciutto, followed by caviar with blinis, and then strawberry sorbet with a Cointreau sauce."

Roxana nodded. "That will be fine."

The familiar cocoon of respect and luxury was enveloping her again, and it felt good. She began to look forward to spending some time in LA. It would have definite fringe benefits . . . Sam Kendrick, for one. Her body pulsed at the thought of him, warm desire beginning to melt and pool in her belly. He gave her pleasures she had never dreamed of, and there was something comforting about his love, his protectiveness toward her—she was enjoying the process of enslaving this one, more so than any other man she'd yet encountered.

You're enjoying it too much, warned a little voice in her head. *You're falling for Kendrick. You think about him all the time.*

No! Roxana thought, angrily. Not true! Kendrick was just a puppet like the others. If she was amused by his body, what did that signify? Nothing and less than nothing!

I know what I'll do, she thought with a sudden flash of inspiration. I'll have lunch with that stupid bimbo Jordan Cabot and tell her all about it . . .

Yes! That would be stage one in the progressive destruction of Samuel Jacob Kendrick—putting word out around town that he screwed his clients. Not to mention having the pleasing side effect of snubbing that old witch Isabelle. After all, what was the point of having the great Sam Kendrick dangling on the end of her strings if she couldn't boast about it a little? And Jordan would make an admirable audience—married to Tom, so it would be all over Artemis and therefore the rest of town in five minutes.

Roxana Felix laughed aloud. Great! What were old school friends for?

"Can I help you, ma'am?" a steward asked, rushing over to see if she required anything.

"You know, I think you can," she said. "Get me a phone. I want to call Mrs. Goldman."

⋄⋄⋄

"Jesus Christ," Fred Florescu swore softly. He wiped a palm across his forehead, trying to clear away some of the beads of sweat that were dewing it. "How much longer?"

"Not far now, mon." Their guide smiled at them indulgently, pushing a huge tree fern out of the path. "We make the clearing very soon. Very beautiful view."

"I hope so," Zach said heavily. He plucked at the soaking cotton of his once-white shirt, now plastered transparently across his chest.

Megan, panting from the exertion, looked at him and thanked God she'd chosen black. Otherwise she'd have been the top entry in a one-woman wet T-shirt contest by the time they were ten minutes into this mountain climb.

"You guys got *no* problems," Keith, the Texan cameraman, butted in. He was stripped to the waist and red-faced with exertion. "You don't have to carry equipment."

"That's why I picked you and Jim," Florescu said, nodding at his soundman. "Southern boys. Real men. You're used to heat like this."

"Fuck you, Fred," Jim Dollar said amiably. "In Texas you *breathe* the air, you don't swim through it."

He had a point. The atmosphere in the jungle was not only swelteringly hot, it was humid, too, the air muggy and oppressive. Megan couldn't believe that Fred would insist on climbing halfway up Morne Seychellois in weather like this, just so he could shoot Zach's hideout scene with the perfect view. Or maybe she could. Florescu was an absolute perfectionist— over the course of two hideous months on location, that much had become clear. If something wasn't perfect, they shot it again. And again. And again, until it was absolutely right. It drove the cast and crew crazy, but nobody ever complained. That attitude was what made *Light Falling* into the artistic masterpiece and commercial smash it had been. That attitude won *Peter's Lieutenant* five Oscars. And that attitude was going to make *Triple Feature* one of the most shining, exciting love stories ever committed to celluloid—if the damn thing ever got finished.

But why did they need me to tag along? Megan wondered. *Is he really going to want a rewrite on a scene for one character?*

"*Vienz, sivouplé,*" said their guide, grinning and lapsing into Seychellois patois. "Come, please. We continue. Not much further."

She followed Mason up the thin path, kicking aside thorns and fungus that had crept across it here and there. This was little more than a track, a derelict trail into the heart of the mountains far from the tourist walkways, and accessible only with an experienced local guide. That was on account of the steep drops and sheer ridges that curved away from the edges of the track now and then, sheer plunging walls of granite and creepers that an unwary hiker might not have noticed.

Megan thought, *Christ, I know I'd have noticed.*

She kept her eyes firmly on the back of Zach Mason's legs. *One foot in front of the other, right? And don't look down.*

To take her mind off it, Megan went over that morning's events yet again, trying to make sense of them.

What the hell's going on here? she wondered. *First that little asshole David comes into my new room and tells me I'm fired. No arguing, just pack up and get out, and if you make a fuss it'll go worse for you in the future. And then runs back in thirty minutes later, says he made a mistake, I should get on the set, and clears clean out of my way before I even get to call him on it! And on the set, nobody's seen David, nobody knows where he is . . . Everybody's on drugs, I swear.*

"*On arrive,*" said their guide triumphantly. "We here."

Megan looked up and gasped. The clearing Florescu had been so set on was worth every second of the climb; forty feet wide, it was an outcrop of gray granite stone on the edge of a vast precipice, backed up by the green, palm-covered slope of Morne Seychellois and overlooking the rest of the mountain range, the whole national park spread out below it. From here you could watch the mist drifting across the jungle, look down on birds winging over the tops of the trees below, see all the chasms and peaks, the emerald valleys and lush flat plains of the undergrowth. She could hear the screech of monkeys mingling with the low calls of the bulbuls and the omnipresent hum of the insects. The sea in the distance was sapphire-blue, sparkling even under the patchy clouds that had begun to drift across the sky.

The scene was utterly deserted and primeval. She could not see a single man-made structure in the whole panorama.

"Oh, man," Jim Dollar breathed. "This is incredible."

"It's going to make the best long shot in history," Florescu said, almost beside himself. "All right, guys, set it up. I don't want to waste any of this light."

"*Non, sivouplé.* No. You go back now," the guide insisted, shaking his head. "Watch, then go back. Yes?" He waved down the mountainside, pointing at the trail they had just emerged from.

"No way, buddy," Keith said, grinning. "We just got here. And I didn't lug that camera halfway up Mount Everest just to take a couple of holiday snaps."

"*I* go back. You come with me." He shifted impatiently from foot to foot, glaring at the Americans. "Storm is coming. Very dangerous to stay."

"A storm?" Florescu asked.

The guide nodded. "Monsoon season. Winds, rain." He made a sweeping gesture with his arms. "Very dangerous. I go back. You come, or not?"

"No!" Florescu said. "You have to be out of your mind. There's not gonna be a storm, at least not today."

"Wait," said Megan uneasily. "Fred, I think we should listen to this guy. I mean, he's a native. How likely is he to be wrong?"

"Come on, Megan," Keith protested.

"Sweetheart, take a look at the sky," Florescu said gently. "I know it's the start of the rainy season, but just look at it! Practically clear blue. If there's a monsoon on the horizon, I sure can't see one."

Megan glanced up. He was right; apart from a couple of white, cotton-wool clouds, the sky stretched clear and blue out to the horizon.

Muttering angrily, their guide disappeared back into the undergrowth.

"That's what happens when you pay in advance," Florescu said, shrugging. "But we've done it once, we should be OK for the trek back down. We'll take it real slow."

"You got that right," said Jim, positioning the lights.

"Zach, are you ready?" the director asked.

Zach nodded.

"OK, people. Let's go."

❖

Two hours later, while Florescu and Keith set up the equipment for a few panoramic shots before the light failed, Zach Mason walked across to

Megan, who was sitting perched on a granite outcrop, scribbling ideas in the margin of her script.

"Can I join you?" he asked.

She glanced up at him, surprised. "Sure. Pull up a boulder, be my guest."

"I want to talk to you about David Tauber," Zach said, propping himself against a rock. He stretched out his long legs, hard and muscular under the costume calfskin pants. Megan tried not to stare at his bare chest, muscular and covered with a smattering of wiry black hair. That was how Florescu wanted to show Zach's character while on the run; animalistic and savage, the survival instinct taking over. It was supposed to set up a mood of sensuality before he was reunited with Morgan and they made love on the beach, at night, while their pursuers could be heard all around searching for them. And looking at Mason now, Megan was pretty sure it would work.

"Don't waste your breath," she said coldly. "I've got nothing to say about him."

"Yeah? Well, I do," Mason insisted. "You have to have been aware of—"

"Zach, we have to get out of here," Megan interrupted him. "Look at that!"

She pointed toward the western skyline. Zach could see it; a huge mass of dark, heavy clouds had gathered, and were moving quickly toward them. The winds were picking up, and the smaller white clouds in their part of the sky were scuttling across the sun, casting swift-moving shadows across the mist forest below them.

"We'll be gone in half an hour," Zach said impatiently. "Don't change the subject. It's—"

"No! We have to pack up *now*," Megan said. "It'll take us at least ten minutes to dismantle everything. We're going to get caught in a thunderstorm halfway up a mountain if we don't."

"You're being paranoid."

"Am I, Zach? Look how fast those clouds are moving!"

He glanced at the sky, uncertainly. The clouds *had* got quite a lot closer in the last few seconds, even if it didn't look like they were raining.

"Fred," he called. "Check out those clouds. Looks like our friend's little tempest might have arrived. I think we should pack up."

"Yeah, OK. Just give a minute," the director called. "They're making for great light over the jungle. I have to get this."

"Fred!" said Megan. "You—"

Her words were suddenly cut off by a violent gust of wind, slicing across the clearing and pushing her back against the boulder. The mikes swayed backward and forward on their stands.

"Shit!" Jim Dollar said. "Where the hell did that come from?"

"Come on, Fred. Let's go," Zach said, leaping to his feet and strolling across to the director.

"Ten minutes," Florescu said, not taking his eye off his shot. "That's all I ask. Then we'll have it in the can."

Another gust of wind blasted toward them from the west, and this time Megan found herself spattered with raindrops. Alarmed, she spun round to see the sound equipment toppling over. Her script was wrenched out of her loose grip and went flying toward the brink of the clearing. Keith lunged for it, but too late; the white papers went soaring off the edge of the cliff, snatched up by the wind like a dead leaf, papers tearing away from it as it disintegrated over the jungle.

"Man, we're going to be in trouble if we stay much longer," Keith told Florescu anxiously. "I don't like the look of this."

"All right. Let's get out of here," the director said reluctantly. "Shut it down, guys. Zach, can you give us a hand? We might as well leave as fast as—"

Suddenly they were plunged into gloom as a bank of black cloud swept across the sun. Almost simultaneously rain started to fall all around them, and as the technicians scurried to and fro, cursing and flicking off every switch in sight, there was a deafening thunderclap, and Megan shrieked as a dazzling flash of sheet lightning blitzed across the mountain behind them; she ran forward blindly, her feet slipping on the small pebbles and chips of stone lying loose on the outcrop of the granite. Zach Mason, his lean frame silhouetted against the light, reached out for her as the sky opened and the rain began hurling down, drenching everything in sight, the long lines of water waving through the tropical gale that was ripping through the forest, bending over young palm trees and sending sticks and bushes bowling across the ridge. As Megan reached Zach, Jim Dollar screamed in agony as his skin connected with a torn wire, and Florescu, half blinded by the rain, watched in horror as the thin blue light of an electric shock crackled around his soundman. He tried to take a step forward, pushing himself into the wind, but was flung back by a fresh blast that half lifted him from his feet, smacking him against a jutting outcrop of granite. Pain and horror surged through Florescu's body together, as he watched Zach and Megan, clutching each other, lose their footing in the hurricane and bowl backward, Megan screaming in terror, and tip over the edge of the chasm in front of them. On his hands and knees the director inched across the clearing, battling against the storm, until he reached the ledge and managed to peer over it, shouting their names, trying to see if he could see where they had fallen. There was no trace of them, just the thrashing jungle canopy, flailing in the wind and dark green from the driving downpour. It was the last thing he saw before he passed out.

chapter 29

They met at Chasen's for lunch. It was another blazing-hot day, but Isabelle Kendrick did not notice; she picked through her Caesar salad and sipped delicately at her chilled mineral water, exactly as usual, nodding graciously now and then at various courtiers who wandered up to their table to pay homage, but her heart wasn't in it. Under the tailored elegance of her ice-blue Bill Blass suit, the blood in Isabelle's aristocratic veins was running as cold as liquid nitrogen.

"Really? She said that, did she? Go on, dear. I'm simply fascinated to hear the rest of it," she said, leaning forward to encourage her companion.

It was true; every word pierced Isabelle's heart like a rapier wound, setting off screaming, jangled alarms of fear and fury, but she was nonetheless fascinated. The more she knew about her enemy, the greater her ammunition against her. It was as though Isabelle herself was detached; one part of her mind remained aloof from the storm of emotions boiling within her, and merely watched the scene calmly, a dispassionate observer, curious to know just how far, just how deeply, Roxana Felix had dug her own grave.

"Oh, Isabelle, I can't," Jordan replied hesitantly. "The rest of it was just more of the same. You know—what Sam used to say in bed, how he used to tell her he would protect her, if anybody tried to hurt her they were dead in this town. And she discussed, uh, his, uh . . . *technique* . . ."

"Indeed?" Isabelle inquired. "And did she say she found my husband satisfactory?"

"Oh, yeah," Jordan replied enthusiastically, caught off guard. "You should have heard her. She said he was the hottest thing on two legs—said she was coming so often she lost count. Rave reviews. According to Roxie, Sam's the hottest fuck on the planet. He . . ." Jordan's voice trailed away at the sight of the frozen expression that had settled across Isabelle's face. "He seemed to please her, anyway," she finished lamely, trying too late to recapture a little decorum.

There was a long pause.

"How embarrassing for you, my dear," Isabelle said eventually. She fixed Jordan with a gimlet eye. "To have been forced to sit there and listen to such a pack of lies, and from somebody you once knew at school too. But we must be charitable—perhaps the poor child is merely delusional, instead of being a pathological liar."

Jordan Cabot Goldman smoothed down the immaculate rose silk of her Calvin Klein on-the-knee dress and swallowed hard. This would have to be handled delicately. It wasn't often, OK, it wasn't *ever*, that you got to see Isabelle Kendrick humiliated, and once upon a time Jordan would have enjoyed every second of it—getting to play the loyal, sympathetic friend while inside she was doubled over with glee, and they both knew it. But things hadn't quite turned out that way.

She knew to avoid the gory details, using instead as dry a recounting of the facts as she could manage.

Isabelle was watching her like a hawk, and Jordan knew instinctively that if she showed the tiniest bit of satisfaction, she was a dead woman. That would mean the end of her spell as crown princess. That would mean social war on a massive scale.

Anyway, now she had received the official line, loud and clear. Roxana was lying. Isabelle was not prepared to admit, even for one second, even to her closest acolyte, that Sam had been unfaithful to her with somebody that mattered—a supermodel he was seeing regularly, as opposed to a faceless, and presumably discreet, whore. Like most of the Beverly Hills ladies who lunched, Isabelle paid no mind to *those*. On the contrary, Jordan thought, she probably relies on them to relieve her of certain "unpleasant duties." But Roxana was different. Roxana would mean a loss of face. And possibly, if Jordan believed everything she'd been told—which she did, implicitly—a loss of everything else, too. Jordan tossed her blond mane, slightly annoyed. This meant Isabelle was setting herself firmly above Jordan—after all, *she* had confessed her anxieties about Eleanor Marshall to the older woman. *She* had been prepared to expose herself, to admit weakness. Apparently it was not going to go two ways. Isabelle wished her to say that Roxana was lying, when the whole manner of Jordan's report up to now had strongly implied that she believed her.

"Or don't you think so?" Isabelle asked, calmly.

Jordan looked deep into her eyes and saw the steel behind them. It was a challenge. She had to make a decision—was she with La Kendrick, or against her? Evidently there was to be no middle ground.

"Oh, no, absolutely," she said hastily. "I expect she's horribly insecure. They say all these model types live in a fantasy world, don't they?"

Was it good enough? Jordan wondered. She'd have made a terrible mistake if she'd crossed Isabelle on this subject. She was in a *very* dangerous mood.

"I expect that's quite right, dear," Isabelle said, smiling softly at her.

Jordan felt herself almost sag in her chair with relief. She hurried to pin her colors even more firmly to her mentor's standard.

"That was why I came to you, Isabelle. When people like Roxana start convincing themselves of such ridiculous ideas, it's time to put a stop to things." She took a decisive sip of her mineral water. "I mean, she may be delusional, but we simply can't have her going around and spouting such rubbish, can we? We have to put a stop to it."

Isabelle settled back into her chair, satisfied.

"Indeed we do, dear. Indeed we do." She speared a few glistening green leaves with relish and popped them into her mouth, savoring the tiny croutons and Parmesan and warm hazelnut oil. Suddenly food tasted good again. Isabelle was limbering up for a fight, and she found the experience rather exciting.

It had been too easy for too long, Isabelle mused. Crushing the social pretensions of various would-be rival queen bees. Throwing *the* most glamorous and spectacular parties, year after year. Honing her guest lists to absolute perfection, until she could achieve such an incredible human potpourri at each dinner party that nobody ever turned her down—just enough glamour, nobility, and sheer beauty to amuse the power players, just enough power players to attract the more glittery crowd. For years, the whole town had known that more deals were done over cognac at the Kendricks' than breakfast at the Polo Lounge. Isabelle ruled LA's social set with a rod of designer wrought iron. She *had* no rivals. Life had become, perhaps, just a *little* dull.

Roxana Felix would change all that. She was a worthy rival. Isabelle acknowledged it without a qualm; she was utterly unafraid. Let the world's most famous supermodel compete with her for her husband.

Isabelle would crush her.

She would crush her so completely that she never recovered. She would *crucify* the pretty little snake. Skewer her through and through without mercy. Los Angeles would watch in amazement, because this was going to be a complete massacre. And then nobody would ever challenge her again.

"But it's so boring to discuss unpleasantness all day, don't you think?"

she continued smoothly. "Tell me about *your* life, Jordan. Your little problem is taken care of, I gather?"

Jordan nodded appreciatively.

"She's on her way out."

"That was my impression." Isabelle sighed compassionately. "Poor Eleanor. To have worked so hard for so many years, and in the end, for what? But at least she's now married." A pause. "To a banker," Isabelle concluded triumphantly.

Actually, it was rather annoying that Paul Halfin was so suitable. A successful investment banker was not the husband she would have picked for Eleanor—better a "resting" actor, or a minor artist, or something. But it would have to do. A major agent and a studio chairman far outranked any vanilla businessman.

"And what about you and Tom? Everything rosy?"

"Oh, of course," said Jordan, uncertainly.

Isabelle shook her head.

Without me, this girl's got no future, she thought despairingly. She's the worst poker player I ever saw.

"What's the matter now?" she asked patiently.

Jordan shifted uncomfortably. "Nothing," she lied. "Tom just seems a little—uncommunicative. He's very solicitous, but . . . he doesn't seem to, uh, that is, he's kind of . . . We don't make love as much as we used to," she finally blurted.

"I see. And is that because of the baby, dear?"

"He says so." She pouted. "But I've told him it's safe."

Isabelle waved a bejeweled hand, dismissing it. "Problems at work, dear. He's a little stressed, I expect. Now, more importantly, how *are* you progressing with the baby? Are you enceinte?" she inquired delicately.

"No. Not yet."

Isabelle frowned. "You're going to have to hurry up, dear."

"How can I?" Jordan demanded, losing her cool. "He doesn't hardly ever *want* it anymore, I don't know what's the matter with him. And *anyway*, Isabelle, I don't know that I *want* one . . . once Eleanor's gone, what do I need it for?" Jordan's voice rose to a petulant wail. "It'll *ruin* my figure—Joanna Lowell did that and she had *horrible* stretch marks and she put on *ten pounds* and her breasts! Ugh!" Jordan shuddered in horror. "They used to be so *firm!* And now Tom is saying he doesn't want to get a nanny—"

"Jordan. Jordan, dear." Isabelle's voice was firm. "It is the only way."

"But—"

"No, dear. If you want to consolidate your position it is the *only* way. You can always insist on a nanny. *I* did. Now, the fact that you haven't conceived is starting to get problematic." She paused, thinking. "Once Eleanor has resigned, you must have a miscarriage. We can discuss that later."

"But I'm not *pregnant* yet."

Isabelle sighed, exasperated. Really, sometimes the girl's stupidity was just too much.

"I know that, Jordan. You pretended to be pregnant, and now you will pretend to lose the baby."

"Oh."

"You'll be devastated, of course. Tom will go out of his way to comfort you. At that stage you can conceive for real." She signaled imperiously to the waiter. "Check please. My dear, you can call me later this week and we'll have a little chat about it."

"Thank you, Isabelle." Jordan bit back her protests—there would be another time. She smiled engagingly. "You've been most helpful."

"As have you, dear," said Isabelle, regarding her protégé thoughtfully. "As have you."

⋰⋱

Eleanor replaced the receiver on its cradle and sat bolt upright. Outside their long sash windows the sky was still pitch-dark; she glanced at the red, glowing numbers on her bedside clock radio. Four-thirty A.M.

"Who the hell was that?" Paul grunted sleepily. "Do they know what time it is?"

"It was an emergency," Eleanor told him. "Go back to sleep."

"Goddamn. Can't your office call during *business* hours with their little crises?" he demanded. "Your attitude to work is ridiculous. You—"

"It was a *real* emergency." Eleanor cut him off; she did't have time for Paul's whining now. "And it's only half an hour before our alarm is due anyway. Now go back to sleep. I have to deal with this."

Ignoring her husband's mumbling complaints, Eleanor stood up, reaching for her robe, and walked into the kitchen, flicking on the light switch. She blinked as her eyes adjusted to the dazzling glare, then turned on the coffee percolator. Although she would hardly need caffeine to wake her up. Despite the fear and anxiety, Eleanor Marshall had never felt more alert in her life. Adrenaline was racing through her veins. Forget business— this was a real crisis, a genuine catastrophe. Two young people might be dead, and if not, they were depending on Eleanor for their lives. And she was going to come through for them.

Four-thirty in LA. That was seven-thirty in New York. Eleanor picked up the kitchen extension, and, from memory, tapped in her personal attorney's home number. If everything that Fred had just told her was true, she was going to need his help. Because if she was going to fly out to the Seychelles to coordinate a rescue mission, she intended to have her job waiting for her when she came back.

Maybe it was Zach and Megan's plight. Maybe it was the sudden knowledge of Tom's baby. Or both together, she thought—the threat of death and the promise of life. But whatever the stimulus, as she sat in her kitchen holding the phone, Eleanor felt a veil tear from her eyes.

She saw Jake Keller's betrayal clearly. Almost from the second Fred had mentioned Jake's involvement with David Tauber, Eleanor understood exactly how she had been duped. She was angry with herself, but that wasn't important. That was the past. It was her actions now which would matter.

Eleanor's eyes focused on the wall chart which Paul had insisted on tacking to the freezer door, her most fertile dates ringed in thick red marker, the days her period was due canceled out with equally thick red lines. Well, I guess you won't have to worry about that anymore, she thought wryly. She was amazed to find there was no anger inside her anymore at the sight of it—just a mild wonderment at herself, for ever having let him bully her on this matter. She'd let them all bully her. Tom, who'd married a bimbo sex doll and then expected her either to sympathize or tread on eggshells around the subject, depending on how he felt about his wife that week. Paul, who demanded marriage and demanded children, not out of love but out of some pathological desire to conform to society's latest blueprint for the successful man. And Jake Keller, who had always hated her, and whose jealousy of her career had driven him to good old-fashioned sabotage, a sabotage which she had actually assisted. Yes, Eleanor realized, that was exactly what she had done. Keller had found her in sickness and torment, and he had taken advantage of her weakened state. And had laughed at her while he did it, like every other bully since time immemorial.

Well, they were going to be in for a surprise. Every damn one of them. Because now, as she found herself confronting a crisis situation, now, as she sensed the miracle of her child inside her, Eleanor knew she was no longer afraid. And that was going to make her strong.

The phone purred in Alex Rosen's apartment. Once, twice, and he picked up.

"Rosen."

Three thousand miles away, Eleanor thought, and he sounds like he's in the next room.

"Alex, it's Eleanor Marshall. Did I wake you?"

"Of course not, Eleanor. I've been at my desk for an hour already, you know me. But it must be somewhat early in LA, right?"

"That's right," Eleanor replied, smiling. Alex was more than a lawyer; they'd been to Yale together and squabbled bitterly over everything from feminism to Shakespeare for four years. And been close friends ever since. It was good to hear Alex's voice; gossipy, clever, confident, and at her disposal. And Alex Rosen was one of the most prominent corporate lawyers in the United States.

"Then I take it you have a little local trouble you'd like me to help out with. A minor problem at work, perhaps?"

"A major problem, Alex. A big, fat, hairy problem that's going to finish my career if I allow it to."

"Oh, *good*." Her friend's voice was a sigh of satisfaction. "Those are the kind I like the best."

⋯⋰⋯

Grant Booth leaned forward across the polished mahogany surface of his desk, barely containing himself. It was all he could do to keep from rubbing his hands with satisfaction, but he managed to restrain himself. Such an attitude of unholy glee would go right against the sophisticated, reliable image he was trying to project. And Booth, Warwick & Yablans were very big on sophistication and reliability. That was one reason their client was here.

Booth glanced round the air-conditioned comfort of his offices, admiring them. The dark oak paneling. The severe, masculine leather chairs in somber shades of burgundy. The antique carriage clock placed atop the equally antique bookcase. Yes, it was quiet, expensive decor, and the firm could afford it because of clients like this one.

"Let me get this straight, Mrs. Kendrick," he began, but she held up one hand, cutting him short.

"No, Mr. Booth. Allow me to repeat myself. I want you to be quite clear about my instructions."

It was a voice used to command, and Grant Booth obeyed it. He sat back in his chair, attention focused compliantly on Isabelle Kendrick.

"I wish to find out everything about Roxana Felix, the model," Isabelle said, calmly and clearly. "And I do mean everything. Her parents. Her childhood. Her teenage years. Whom she is sleeping with. Whom she has slept with. Any enemies that she might have made in her modeling career, and the manner in which she made them. In short—everything. You may use whatever methods you wish, as long as you do not break the law. You will keep these instructions, the fact that I am your client, and any and all communication between your firm and myself in absolute confidence. And you will give me a legally binding written promise to that effect before I leave this office. Money is no object."

Booth smiled unctuously. "I am happy to hear you say so, ma'am." He cleared his throat. "You are aware that our retainer is fifteen thousand dollars?"

Isabelle looked at him blandly.

"No, Mr. Booth," she said. "In my case your retainer will be fifty thousand dollars. Plus expenses. And if the investigation is concluded to my satisfaction, there will be a further hundred thousand to follow." She gave him a wintry smile. "*Everything*, Mr. Booth. I trust I am making myself clear?"

Grant Booth nodded eagerly. He had a very shrewd idea of what would constitute "satisfaction" to this lady. She wanted blood. And for $150,000, his firm would happily see that she got it.

"Oh, you are, madam," he said. "Very clear indeed."

chapter 30

It was the heat that woke Megan up. The burning, sweltering feeling on the back of her neck was too uncomfortable to let her lie unconscious, and she groaned and blinked, opening her eyes, unsure of exactly what had happened, where she was. The pain in her neck intensified and Megan realized she was lying slumped over a fallen tree trunk, her head rammed against a branch. All around her were ferns, uprooted bushes, and glistening dark green foliage, bracken, and scrub, which been drenched in the down-pour. Millions of insects buzzed and chirped through the under-growth, their low hum mingling with the constant bubbling calls of the tree frogs. Startled, Megan jerked away as a huge butterfly flew past her, brilliant scarlet wings fluttering jerkily.

She moaned in horror as it all came back to her.

The last thing she remembered was the blanket terror of her sheer fall, clutching onto Zach, then finally crashing through leaves and branches and blacking out. She glanced upward at the emerald canopy of the mist forest; there was a patch of clear blue sky visible directly above her, in the midst of the green tangle of palms and *bwa rouz* trees. The sun had been beating down on her through that hole.

That must be where we fell, Megan thought. Zach! Where's Zach?

She tried to jump to her feet and immediately fell backward with a piercing scream. Agony blazed through her, knives of pain lancing into her flesh. Megan glanced down and saw her left ankle, twisted and grotesquely swollen, the flesh puffed up and darkly bruised, like a purple plum.

"Megan! Megan, are you OK?"

She looked behind her to see Zach Mason, his shirt in shreds and his chest bloodied, standing in the shade of a towering palm tree. He looked shaken but otherwise all right. Megan burst into tears with relief.

"Oh, Jesus, sweetheart," Mason said, rushing over to her and clasping her in his arms. "You're in pain. You poor girl. Have you broken something?"

"No," she said, and then burst into tears. "I'm all right. I'm so glad to see you, I thought you might be dead."

He shook his head, stroking her hair with one hand. It was ridiculous, but she found the movement comforting; she wanted to nestle up against him and believe that this nightmare wasn't happening, that everything was going to be OK. She forced herself to control her tears and broke away from him.

Zach Mason is hardly my father, Megan reminded herself sternly. And anyway, my father wouldn't have wasted his time stroking my hair. So less of the weak-damsel bullshit—we're in trouble here, and I have to think clearly if I'm gonna get out of this alive.

"Neither of us is dead, thank God. Let's see if we can keep it that way," Zach said. He looked her over, and winced as he saw her ankle.

"Jesus, you poor kid. Is it broken?"

"I don't know. I think it's just sprained," Megan told him. "I can't stand on it."

Infinitely gently, Zach reached out and touched the bruised, violet flesh. "Does that hurt?"

She shook her head.

"Does that?" He gave it a soft push.

"No."

"Well, at least that's something," Zach said. "Probably means you haven't been infected yet." He examined the angle of her foot. "It looks real nasty, though. Do you think you might have dislocated it?"

"What am I, a nurse?" Megan snapped. "How the hell should I know?"

He glanced up at her. "Hey, I didn't mean—"

"Oh, look, I'm sorry. All right? I shouldn't have bit your head off, I know you're trying to help. It's just that I'm in pain here." She shrugged, and Zach tried not to look at her breasts, clearly outlined under the sodden black cloth of her wet T-shirt. "I don't think it's dislocated. I guess I'd be lying here screaming if it were. What about you, are you all right? What happened to your chest?"

He touched the dried blood on his skin, dismissing it. "Just a few scratches from the fall. Thorns, or something."

"My God," Megan said quietly, gazing around her. "It's a miracle we're alive."

Zach hooked his arms under her shoulders and lifted her up, slowly and carefully so that no weight pressed on her hurt ankle, and helped her sit upright on the trunk of the tree. Megan noticed that her 120 pounds was nothing to him; Zach's lean, hard body was evidently pure muscle. Just as well, she thought dryly. We're going to need all the muscle we can get.

Mason sat next to her, staring at their surroundings. The jungle was alive with sound and movement; they could see nameless small creatures scampering through the undergrowth ahead of them, birds flitting and swooping through the canopy. A brightly colored pigeon, its body electric-blue with a downy white chest and a crimson crest, plunged through the forest directly in front of them.

"*Pizon Olonde,*" Megan said. "The Dutch pigeon. They called it that because it used the colors of the Dutch flag."

"Yeah? Where did you learn that?" Zach asked her.

"The guidebook," Megan said. "I tried to get a little local color when I wasn't on the set."

"Did you read anything about the jungle?"

"Actually, yes," Megan said. "Three pages. So I can tell you some plants you better not touch. And insects to avoid."

"Great," Zach said, giving her a smile. "Finally, something useful from you."

"Get lost," Megan said, grinning.

"I got some news for you, babe." He waved at the green shadows of the forest, pierced here and there by long, dusty columns of light where shafts of sunlight had managed to break through the treetops. "We already are."

"Apparently so," Megan agreed, trying to keep her tone light.

"Three pages between us and certain death from poisonous berries," Zach said, pushing his long black hair out of his eyes. "Well, that's reassuring. You want to give me a run-through of those insects now?"

"Take your pick." Megan looked at him, and despite their joking, she felt the fear start to return. "Tarantulas, crazy ants, yellow wasps, wolf spiders, scorpions. And the jungles are home to some of the world's crack mosquito squadrons."

"What's the good news?" Mason asked her.

"*Good* news? Uh, the snakes aren't poisonous."

"Terrific," Zach said.

"Plus, I have some insect repellent," Megan added, brightening. She fished around in the sodden pockets of her jeans and produced a large tube. "I thought I might need it on the mountain."

"Now you're talking," Zach said. "Any food?"

"No." Megan fought to control the creeping sense of panic closing in on her. "Zach, what are we going to do? We're miles from anywhere. You can't even see the ledge where we fell from here. They'll have no idea if we're right beneath it, or crushed on the rocks, and even if they do, how the hell are they going to find us? There's no paths into here. We're totally stranded, and I can't walk—"

Her voice began to tremble, and she bit her lip to keep herself from crying.

I won't break down in front of Zach, Megan thought fiercely. That's just what he'd expect me to do. The damsel-in-distress routine. And I'm not about to give him the satisfaction.

"Hey. I'm not going anywhere without you," Mason said. "Who would tell me what flowers not to touch? I wouldn't dare."

"But you can't carry me."

"Sure I can. I've been weight-training for years, since before the first tour. You have to keep in shape, if you're gonna survive three years on the road. It's tough."

"*This* is tough," Megan said, staring into the dense forest.

"Agreed." He fell silent for a few moments, thinking. Then he said, "OK; the way I see it, we have two options. One is to stay here, hope that we fell somewhere directly beneath that ridge and that they'll know where to look for us. If we do that, we have to try and figure out ways of making it obvious where we are. It would be nice to light a fire, but"—he patted the sodden log they were sitting on—"all the wood is soaked through. Plus, I don't have a lighter or a magnifying glass and I skipped Boy Scout classes, the kind where they teach you that thing with the two dry sticks."

Megan laughed. "Me, too."

"Pity," Mason said, giving her a warm look.

For a second Megan found herself jealous of Roxana again. Zach's thundercloud eyes, his predatory, wolf eyes, were suddenly softened, and she couldn't help thinking how attractive he was.

Get over it, girl.

She looked away.

"So, the other option is to get out of here. We'd have to pick one direction and keep going in a straight line, until we hit a road or something."

"That doesn't sound too scientific."

"Look, the whole island is only five miles across. Seventeen north to south. And the jungle's just one small part of it. We'll get out soon enough."

"Will we? I guess that's the sixty-four-dollar question," Megan said, looking down at her twisted ankle.

"Come on, Megan. You're not giving up on me now, are you?" Zach asked. "Not after all that work on the script. Think of the delay this is going to cause to the shoot. We have to get back, remember? We're making a movie."

She laughed. "Oh, sure. Except that I'm replaceable."

"I'm not," Zach told her. He stood up and walked over to the nearest fallen branch, hefting it up and testing its weight.

"Don't be too sure. It's incredible what they can do with technology now," she told him, silently admiring his hard body as he moved, the muscles knotting in his back, the wet cloth of his calfskin pants molded to the rocklike thickness of his thighs. "Remember *The Crow*? Starred Brandon Lee, Bruce Lee's son. Except that he was accidentally shot dead halfway through filming."

"No shit?" Zach asked, throwing one branch onto the ground. He took a careful look at Megan, then stepped hard on the wood halfway down it, cracking it in two.

"True story. They finished it with computer morphing. Virtual acting," Megan told him. She laughed. "Maybe we could use that for Roxana's part."

"Good idea," Zach said grimly.

"You shouldn't trash your girlfriend," Megan teased him.

Zach shot her a sharp look. "She's not *my* girlfriend, honey."

"Yeah, right," Megan said, shrugging. She couldn't be bothered to argue with him.

"She's not. Anyway, *you* should talk. David Tauber's little puppy."

"Fuck you!" Megan spat, nettled. "I'm nobody's puppy. And certainly not David's. We split up."

"Oh, really?" Mason asked softly. He kicked the branch to one side and walked across to her, standing over her. Megan shrank back on the log, but Zach reached forward, toward the neckline of her T-shirt, and pulled on the fine gold chain glinting against her tanned skin, yanking it free of the soaking cotton, twisting the small gold star with its cursive "D" between his fingers. "You're still wearing his dogtag, I see."

"I just forgot to take it off," Megan snapped.

"Uh-huh."

"God, you're so infuriating," she said angrily, jerking the pendant out of his grasp. "You think you're so smart. You and Roxana, you're two of a kind. Just because you're famous, you think the rest of the world should be permanently on its knees in front of you. You deserve each other. And let's see how many wild animals in here are impressed because you used to sing in a rock band."

"*I* think I'm so smart? That's good, Megan, really. Coming from the college graduate who was picking me up on my French pronunciation the first time we ever met. Do you know how that made me feel? It was like being back in grade school, I felt three feet high. And then you were always so bitchy in rehearsals, always putting me down. I never expected anybody to kiss my ass, Megan, everybody does it naturally. You get so sick of it all the time. Or they're like you, putting me down because I didn't spend years in a fucking classroom. Nobody is natural with you, except other musicians, maybe. But whatever. Anytime you want to get on your knees in front of me, that's fine, sweetheart."

"In your dreams, you son of a bitch," she snarled.

Their eyes locked for a second in mutual hostility; then Mason moved away from her.

"This won't help us," he said finally, reaching for the branch he'd tossed aside. "Like it or not, we're stuck with each other until we get out of this jungle. Right?"

"Right," Megan agreed, although her face was still flushed red with fury.

"So let's have a truce. Temporarily. We can take up with the insults when we're back in the hotel."

Megan looked away, biting her lip again, and just nodded. His words stirred the dread that was constantly with her. Jesus, who knew if they would ever get back to the hotel? She wondered if anybody had ever longed to walk through that lobby the way she did now.

"Check this out, another one," Zach said, pleased, bending down to pick up a second branch with a forked tip. He flung it next to the first and cracked it at the base, smashing it cleanly with his foot.

"Zach, what are you doing?" Megan asked.

"We gotta get you mobile," Mason said, holding up his two branches triumphantly. He smiled. "Crutches, courtesy of Mother Nature."

"You are out of your mind," Megan told him, but she gave them a hard look, and added, "Probably."

"Try them. You can't walk on that ankle, and it's better if I carry you only when I have to—I can save my strength that way." He came over and helped her hook her arms over the forks in the wood, then lifted her gently to her feet.

"How are they?"

"I'd prefer to get around in a cab, but not bad," Megan said, testing her weight against the wood. It held fine. "You got my height exactly right," she told him, surprised.

"I should. I've watched you often enough," Mason said.

She glanced at him, but he'd turned aside.

"I think we should head southeast," Megan suggested. "I remember watching the forest from the ridge—it was thinnest to the southeast."

"Got a compass?"

"We could use the sun. Rises in the east, sets in the west."

"Right." Zach smacked his forehead. "Trust Dr. Livingstone here to forget something like that." He walked under the sunlit patch of ground, shading his eyes, and gazed up into the sky.

Megan tried not to stare too obviously at Zach Mason's sun-drenched body, the light lovingly accentuating every taut muscle, the tangled, attractive mane of black hair that fell halfway down his back, the distinct, promising bulge between his thighs . . . She dropped her gaze, blushing, before he could spot her lusting after him and give her some superior put-down.

And I'm not that interested anyway, Megan told herself. Maybe it's just because he looks like a savage in those calfskin leggings, with that hair.

"Hey, Hiawatha," she called. "Which way?"

"Over there, I guess." He pointed. "Why Hiawatha?"

"You look like an Indian in those pants," Megan said, grinning.

Zach glanced down and laughed. "I see what you mean. But you kind of startled me; I'm quarter Cherokee."

"No shit. Really?"

"My father's mother," Zach said, nodding.

Megan shivered. *That's where he gets those strange eyes. Wolf eyes, predator's eyes.*

"I never knew," she said.

"Never read about it, you mean. That was one of my few successes," Mason told her, walking over. "I tried to keep my family out of it as much as I could. Besides, with the Indian stuff they'd never let it go. I had as much 'New Jim Morrison' as I could take." He helped her over the log. "Are you ready to go?"

"As ready as I'll ever be," Megan said. She swung the crutches, moved her right foot, then swung her left foot after it.

"Aah," she muttered, wincing from the renewed stabs of pain.

"I'll carry you," Zach said immediately, leaping forward.

Megan waved him back. "No, it's OK. It's just a twinge. Nothing I can't handle." She tried again, and took a step forward, then another. "See? No problem. Give me ten minutes to practice, and I'll be sprinting." She smiled at him, making light of it, trying to distract him.

If Zach thinks I'm suffering, he'll insist on slinging me over his shoulder. And then it'll take us three days to get out of here, Megan thought. I can't let him know how much it hurts.

She wondered briefly what David Tauber would have done if she'd been stranded with him instead. And felt a chill run through her at the thought.

"You let me know if you need help, Megan," Zach insisted, watching her carefully.

"I'm fine, really. Let's go find a nice restaurant, about four miles due southeast."

"I mean it." He was hesitating.

"So do I," Megan said firmly. She gave him a bright smile and took three paces forward, walking slowly but surely in the direction he'd pointed out. "I was a big fan of yours once, if you can believe that."

"You have to be kidding," Zach said, but he followed her.

"No. And since I'm stuck with you, you're going to have to answer all my questions, Zach. Because I'm going to need more than the pretty scenery to distract me."

"Will you answer all *my* questions? It has to go two ways."

"Sure. It's a better deal for me."

"We'll see about that," Zach said, giving her a lazy smile. "But OK, Megan. You get the exclusive interview."

"It'll be the longest one you ever give."

"You know that's the truth," he agreed, and they set off together, slowly, walking into the green, uncharted depths of the jungle.

chapter 31

Tom Goldman walked into his office with a heavy heart. Not that anybody would have noticed; he was at his desk by half past-seven, as usual; he was smartly dressed, as usual, this morning in a custom-made black suit by Anderson & Sheppard of Savile Row, a Turnbull & Asser pinstripe shirt, and a sober navy-blue tie; and none of the security guards or secretaries noticed anything different about his manner, because Goldman had been acting depressed and low-key for months. It was going to be another blazing hot day on the Artemis lot. Business as usual.

Except not for me, Goldman thought wearily as he logged into his computer. The password had to be changed every week and he did it without thinking. This morning he found himself tapping in *Victrix Hotel* and smiled grimly. Pretty Freudian. There was no getting away from it; he just couldn't stop thinking about Eleanor Marshall, about the miraculous night he'd spent with her, and all the nights that they could have had, and the time he'd wasted and the dumb choices he'd made. Maybe to an outsider, Tom thought, the irony of his situation would seem amusing or elegant, but to him it was simply pain; bitter, crashing waves of regret, and longing, and the hopeless sense of certainty that it was now too late, and it would be too late forever. Jordan, the sensational little sex bomb that he had so foolishly married, thinking she would add a certain *shiksa*, Bostonian class to his life—what a joke—had turned into a dead weight around his neck. It was impossible to talk to her about his work, or art, or music, or sports, or politics—in short, any of the subjects he was interested in. The sole topic of conversation that interested his wife was social mountaineering, and her babble was conducted in an arcane language that he couldn't understand and didn't want to learn—"Cochairman of the Junior League," "Secretary to the Benefit's Social Subcommittee" "Vice President's Assistant for Membership."

It seemed that that was Jordan's world—throwing expensive, thousand-dollar-a-plate benefit dinners for causes she didn't give a damn about and fitting in with a bunch of overdressed, bejeweled, bored Beverly Hills housewives who all hated each other anyway.

"But sweetheart, this stuff is so petty, don't you think?" Tom had asked her last Friday, when Jordan was insisting on dragging him out to some fancy-dress ball in aid of saving the whales, or inner-city literacy, or whatever the hell it was that week. He was tired, and he really wanted to just stay home, climb in the hot tub and veg out, just stare at the stars for a while.

"I don't understand," Jordan had replied, giving that little-girl pout he'd come to dislike intensely.

Tom tried again. "It's not important, Jordan."

"How can you say that?" Jordan's face was a mask of horror. "Don't you know that Susie Metcalf is the chairman? She's *totally* important, Tom! John only married her last year and this her first big evening! Of *course* it's important, she expects me to be there!"

"And what happens if we skip it?"

"Skip it? Don't be silly, Tom!" Jordan stamped her Chanel pumps in frustration. "If we don't show, Susie and all the other Metropolis Studios girls might not take tables out for my drug-prevention slave auction!"

"Heaven forbid," Goldman said with heavy sarcasm, and went upstairs to change.

But it's my fault, Tom told himself. I married a doll, a pretty, blond toy I thought I could never get tired of. I thought I could get companionship from other friends—but it's too lonely at the top to have that many real friends, and too busy to spend much time with them. You need to be able to talk to your wife, because she's the only one who's there all the time. All Jordan and I ever had was sex, and now . . .

Something had taken the bloom off that rose, too. He had been trying not to admit it, but this morning his feelings simply could not be brushed under the carpet. It was that evening with Eleanor. No whips, no chains, no baby oil and blue movies—just two people moving together, and it had been the most incredible sexual experience of his life. Like something you read about, where the climax was more than mere physical relief, where he felt it crash around his heart and his mind, touch his very soul. It had moved him almost to tears. And when it was over, he'd had no desire to go straight to sleep, no sense of slight embarrassment at whatever scene he'd just acted out—he'd wanted to stay there, with Eleanor, holding her and caressing her and finally drifting to sleep in her arms. It was a feeling of the sweetest, purest happiness. It was total contentment.

It was love.

Goldman stood up abruptly and began to pace up and down his office, distressed.

Why do I have to dwell on it now? he thought bitterly. Why today, of all days? Today, when I have to see her, when I have to tell her she's fired?

·:·

The icy winds sliced through him, and Joey Duvall shivered as he turned into the lobby of the elegant brownstone on West 74th Street, clutching his camel-hair overcoat more tightly around him. Another freezing winter day in Manhattan, not ideal weather for trudging around the Upper West Side. But Joey wasn't complaining. So far, it had been a very profitable morning, and it was just about to get a lot better.

"Mr. Duvall?" the receptionist inquired. Joey nodded curtly. "Mrs. Fransen is expecting you, sir. If you'd like to take the elevator to the fourth floor, I'll ring up and let her know you've arrived."

Joey nodded again, picked up his burgundy leather briefcase, and stepped into one of the elevators. He pressed the button and took a casual look around as the car hissed smoothly upward. All polished brass and marble detailing; very nice. Mrs. David Fransen had certainly risen in the world, Joey thought. Like most of her old colleagues. One in particular.

The elevator stopped on the fourth floor and Duvall stepped out into a long corridor, carpeted in thick, expensive-looking navy wool, its eggshell-blue walls hung with various gloomy paintings of horses and foxhunting scenes. More English than Buckingham Palace. The Fransens' door was one of only two on that level, marked with a discreet brass nameplate for "Mr. and Mrs. David Fransen." Joey was amused. What would Babette Delors know from class? But apparently she had learned.

It was gonna be interesting to see how she handled this blast from the past, Joey thought.

He pushed the bell, listened to a few soft, musical notes chiming inside the apartment.

The door opened immediately. A young woman, the picture of a stylish New York wife, stood in front of him, dressed in a smart, dark green suit, with a thin string of emeralds looped across the creamy skin of her throat. She could not have been more than twenty-seven or twenty-eight, he guessed, and she was extremely attractive, thick red hair cut in a geometric, Vidal Sassoon–type bob, bright blue eyes, and long, slender legs. Everything about her screamed of money and privilege, from the soft fabric of the suit to the large, dark blue sapphire of her engagement ring. But she was looking at him with hatred, and the sense of fear emanating from her was so strong he could practically smell it.

"Mademoiselle Delors?" he inquired blandly.

"My name is Barbara Fransen," she hissed. "What do you want?"

Duvall hefted up his briefcase. "Information, Mrs. Fransen. Nothing else. May I come in?"

Wordlessly she held open the door for him, and Duvall walked into the lower reception room of a magnificent duplex. Furnished in soft cream and butterscotch tones, it had great views over the city, antique mahogany furniture, what looked like a Ming vase on the mantelpiece, and a top-of-the-range speaker system. His eye fell upon some Baccarat crystal tumblers, one of which would have cost him a month's wage a year or so back, when he was schlepping overtime for the NYPD. Things were different in private work, but then he'd fallen on his feet. He would always be aware of the value of things, of the difference money could make in a person's life. You have to be a self-made person to really appreciate wealth, that's what he reckoned. And to truly fear having it taken away from you.

That was why he was so good at his job. And that was why Mrs. David Fransen was about to open her beautifully made-up mouth and sing like a canary. Because there was no way on God's green earth, Duvall congratulated himself, that this lady was ready to swap the Baccarat for the back streets. She was standing in the center of her Persian rug, twisting her hands nervously, and not speaking.

"May I sit down, ma'am?" he asked, nodding toward the high-backed ebony chairs ranged around one of the ornate glass coffee tables.

"If you have to," she said ungraciously, and then added, "I don't know what you want. If it's money, I can't take too much out of David's account before he notices, and I only have a little of my own—"

"I'm sure," Duvall interjected smoothly, cutting her off. He didn't want the bitch getting hysterical and doing anything dumb. "Like I say, Mrs. Fransen, this is not about blackmail. We aren't interested in you, ma'am. Just what you can tell us."

He laid the briefcase flat on the shiny glass tabletop and clicked open the lid. Inside, neatly ranged in order of importance, were typed notes from every subject they'd interviewed around the world. A Parisian hostess. A sheik's favorite wife, safely ensconced in a luxury Cairo penthouse for over ten years—a modern take on the harem, he guessed. An impoverished policeman from Kansas City who wasn't quite so impoverished anymore. A retired social worker, ditto. A court stenographer. Several ex-models, all of them current wives of wealthy, powerful men. It was a bizarre collection, but a useful one—like the oddly shaped pieces of a jig-saw puzzle, they made a very clear picture when you slotted them all to-gether. Joey Duvall had been the operative responsible for finding three of those pieces, more than any other agent. And Mlle. Delors was going to make four.

He grinned as he fished out the clear black photographs, chose the rele-vant pictures, and handed them across to her. This was going to mean more than a pat on the back for him. If he read the excitement at head-quarters correctly, the bonus on this baby would be the biggest payday of his career.

"Do you recognize that woman?"

She glanced at him, then nodded. "Yes."

"And did you have dealings with her in Paris, eight years ago?"

The answer was so low he could barely hear it.

"Yes." The woman was biting her lip, tears forming in the corners of her eyes.

"Don't upset yourself, Mrs. Fransen, my firm is *extremely* discreet," Du-vall told her softly. "I'm just gonna ask you for a few details, and then I'm gonna get out of your life and you'll never see or hear from me again. Right?"

"Right," she said, nervously, gratefully.

Duvall pulled out a silk handkerchief from his jacket pocket and handed it to her, smiling.

"Everything's gonna be just fine, Mrs. Fransen. *Ne vous inquietez pas.*"

❖

Eight A.M. Tom Goldman spun in his chair, gripped with misery and self-doubt.

Should I go in to her? he wondered. Normally, that's what I do in the morning. But for something like this, is that wise? I should get her in here. But it's not formal . . . it's a warning . . .

Despairingly, he passed a hand through his hair.

I do *not* want to do this, Goldman thought desperately. But he had to. It was now or later, and later would be worse. He just could not allow her to walk into the production meeting unprepared, to face Jake Keller's point-by-point demolition of her work on *Triple Feature* in front of everyone else. Eleanor had to be allowed time to write a good exit speech, something that would let her leave with dignity. Keller would hate him for doing it, but he could go screw himself.

I'm going to warn her, Goldman decided. I owe her that much.

Reluctantly, he lifted his handset and punched in Eleanor Marshall's extension.

Eleanor hit her office by six A.M., adrenaline still racing through her veins. She caught a glimpse of her reflection in the glass door of her secretary's office—despite the lack of sleep, she looked better than she had in years, her hair newly dry and full-bodied, her makeup bold and confident—God, when was the last time I bothered with mascara, she wondered—and her eyes were bright, lively, and alert.

After the conversation I just had with Alex, they should be, Eleanor told herself. She logged into her computer, pulled up a word-processing package, and started to type the list of points Rosen had dictated to her. Then she turned on the printer, accessed her private backup files for the *Triple Feature* memos, and began to run off labeled, dated copies.

Her fingers were flying over the keyboard, racing to get everything done in time. Eleanor didn't bother with coffee, she was already totally wired. Next up, e-mail, she told herself, punching in another set of codes and commands. A list of memos and letters, scanned by date and subject, appeared on the screen. Silently, Eleanor blessed Bill Burton, Artemis's resident systems maven, for forcing her to take the computing proficiency course last year. She'd wanted to refuse—who had the time?—but Bill had sternly told her that it was senior management's duty to set an example to the other staff. So she'd allowed him to lock her away for two days and show her the basics. "There you go, Princess, you'll never have to rely on your assistant again," Bill had told her proudly. Eleanor had shaken her head—the techno kids lived in a world of their own—but he'd insisted, "You'll be kissing my ass for this one day, Marshall, I'm telling you."

God. I have to send that boy a tube of lipstick, she thought gratefully, as she punched in Jake Keller's codes and told his machine to search for, and print out, discrepancies it found against her own original memoranda.

I've got Keller's codes, but he doesn't have mine, Eleanor exulted. Privilege of office! Read *this* and weep, you son of a bitch. I'm still the president here. And whatever you may have thought, it's gonna stay that way.

The phone on her desk shrilled. Eleanor picked it up with her left hand, her right hand continuing to speed across the keyboard, her eyes fixed on the screen. Jesus, this was unbelievable. Except for the fact that Jake Keller was behind it . . . except for the fact that the proof was unfolding before her eyes and shooting out of her color printer at four pages a minute. Eleanor's lips tightened. Maybe they should invent a new proverb—Hell hath no fury like a male executive scorned. Especially if it's in favor of a woman.

"Marshall," she said.

"Eleanor, this is Tom."

"Hey, Tom. Can it wait? I'm in the middle of something here."

"No. I have to see you now."

There was an urgent note in his voice that Eleanor did not miss. "OK. I'll be there in five minutes," she told him, and hung up. Then she took her small gold powder compact out of her purse and checked her makeup, reapplying a dab of lipstick as the printer spat out the last of her files. Once it was finished, she picked everything up and shoved it in her brief-case, locking it shut. She grabbed the neatly typed list of Alex Rosen's con-tractual points, spritzed a little scent across her neck—Chanel No. 5, Eleanor was in a classical mood this morning—and set off briskly for Tom Goldman's office.

Isn't it ridiculous, Eleanor thought. I'm fighting for my career and in a couple of hours I'll need to be on a plane to the Seychelles. I ought to be worried sick, but I'm not. Face it! I'm feeling terrific!

As she careered into Goldman's office, Eleanor felt a minor twitch of guilt at the exhilaration surging through her. After all, she was about to hang Jake Keller out to dry. His career was over, once she did this, not just at Artemis but anywhere else. And if Tom didn't like it, too bad. She had him by the balls, and she knew it. Was it unfeminine to feel such a thrill at the prospect of revenge? Eleanor wondered. But screw that. It had never stopped Queen Boadicea.

"Eleanor, come in," Tom Goldman said, rising to meet her. He shifted uneasily from foot to foot, obviously uncomfortable. "How's Paul?"

"Asleep," she replied irreverently, wondering what the hell had got into her. And what was with the personal small talk? Tom had never wasted time on polite preliminaries before.

"You look great," Goldman said truthfully, gesturing at her crimson Donna Karan suit and bright red lipstick. "Married life must be agreeing with you."

Eleanor strolled over to Goldman's desk and took the chair in front of it, confident and relaxed.

"Not so far," she said levelly. "But you can cut the banter, Tom. You said you had to see me. What do you want to discuss?"

He sat down heavily. "I don't *want* to discuss this, Eleanor, believe me. But I have to. We—we've been working together for a long time, long enough for me to owe you a warning." Goldman sighed heavily, hating what he was forced to say next. "Jake Keller is going to bring up all the dis-astrous production decisions that you made about locations, casting, unions, or whatever on *Triple Feature*, and contrast them with the objec-tions he lodged in that memo you made him write. We're facing a bath on this movie, Eleanor, and if word gets out, it could affect the stock. That would be the end of the studio." He glanced at her, then looked away again. "Keller says he has a detailed plan for completing this film at a mini-mal further cost, but the price he's demanded for giving it to me is that he replace you as the executive in charge of the project, and that I announce it publicly. He wants me to do it at the meeting this afternoon."

Goldman paused, took a breath. Why had he put it like that? He'd meant to say, *I'm going to do it at the meeting this afternoon. I'm sorry . . . I have no choice.* He'd meant to sit here and break it to Eleanor Marshall as gently as he could; he was sacking her.

It was his duty as CEO.

There was no other way.

It would be nothing personal. Right?

She gazed back at him, those sparkling eyes calm and unfazed. Tom felt his heart contract with respect and love. Eleanor was as brave now as she'd been when he first met her fifteen years ago. He flashed back to those eyes, warm and brilliant, looking up at him in bed in New York, filled with sweet love and hot desire.

Now he had to look into those same eyes, look at this woman who'd been his friend and partner for fifteen years, and tell her she was fired.

"And are you going to, Tom?" Eleanor asked quietly.

For a second she held her breath. So this was it. He was about to break faith with her, for the sake of business, for the sake of his job. And even though she knew that Alex Rosen could save her position, there would be no saving her love for Tom Goldman, not after this.

Once he said the words, it was all over.

❖

"I was wondering," Zach Mason started.

Megan hefted her lame foot carefully over a fallen log. Jungle stretched around them as far as the eye could see, green and gold. The heat was stifling. She knew how badly she had slowed them down.

"What?" she asked nervously.

This was it, then. Zach would suggest going off for help.

I won't stop him, she swore fiercely. I won't kill us both.

"Well . . . I guess I've been wondering why a girl like you would date David Tauber. I know he's good-looking and successful and all that, but . . . ." Zach kicked a boulder out of her path with surprising force, and Megan licked dry lips, watching the strong muscles knot in his back. "You seemed real different."

"I bet. A real hick," Megan said bitterly.

Zach glanced back at her, smiling, and Megan felt her stomach dissolve. *Oh, get a grip. It's not gonna happen.*

"No. I meant you were smart."

"Oh." Megan blushed, pleased despite her raging thirst. "He was handsome, successful, powerful . . . but it was more than that. He rescued me, or I thought he did. And I think I came out here looking for that."

"For glamour?"

"No." She laughed. "For passion, for love. My big adventure. I wanted David to be something he wasn't. My best friend always called me a hopeless romantic."

Zach threaded through a clump of towering *bwa rouz*.

"So you weren't interested in me?"

"Are you kidding?" Megan said sadly. "You were always out of my league."

⋅⊰⊱⋅

Tom Goldman looked at Eleanor Marshall, and suddenly, irrationally, felt a great weight lifting off his chest. He couldn't do it. It was that simple.

"No," he said. "No, I'm not. I can't do it to you, kiddo. Not that it'll help you any; the Artemis board will have you out in a heartbeat. But I'm not gonna point you at the exit sign. I'll resign first." He shrugged. "What the hell; we came in together, we'll go out together."

Eleanor stared at him, a thrill of exultant love rushing through her.

My God, she thought. If I'd waited one more day to do this, it would have been too late.

Goldman misinterpreted her silence, and felt a surge of pain and compassion.

"Look, I do know how hard this must be for you. If there's anything I can do, anything at all, just name it."

Eleanor shook her head, smiling. "Tom, I'm sorry. I was thinking of something else." She cleared her throat, held up Alex Rosen's list in front of her, and said coolly, "Now, let me tell you what's actually going to happen. My lawyer is taking the first plane out of New York, and he should be here by lunchtime, so he can go over it with you then. But I thought I'd give you a little rundown first. Number one, my contract as president of Artemis states that nobody can be hired above me or below me without my approval, unless the company is sold. I would regard Artemis placing Jake Keller in charge of production on my movie as placing him above me. And so would a court. They'd be in breach of contract, Tom, and I'll file a suit against the studio this afternoon. And I'll announce it at a press conference."

"Eleanor—"

She held up a hand. "I'm not done. Furthermore, I cannot be dismissed without three written warnings, none of which I have received, and a review with the board in New York. Again, if Artemis violates these conditions, I will sue. And I have the guaranteed right to see my first green-lighted project through to completion and release." She smiled gently. "If you recall, Tom, you advised me to have that clause inserted in the deal, so they couldn't do to me what they tried to do to Martin Webber.

And Alex Rosen, my lawyer, is very hot on this issue. He says if Artemis tries to get out of it, we'll sue for millions. Moreover, this binds any future owners of the studio. So Howard and his buddies can't just ship me off to the Japs and let them fire me either."

Eleanor tapped her long, elegant fingernails on top of Rosen's list.

"We've got three major breaches, right there, Tom. And it will be a splashy trial. I'll turn it into a feminist cause célèbre, and the nation can turn a spotlight on how Hollywood treats women—*all* women, not just the handful of us who make it to senior executive level. Remember when Dawn Steel was president of production at Paramount, and they ousted her while she was in labor with her little girl? Nice, huh? Well, they can *forget* about trying that with me. Or I'm going to make every Artemis stockholder rue the day they were born."

Tom Goldman sat back, gazing at her in total shock. He opened his mouth to say something, but no words came out.

"What about Jake's plan for *Triple Feature?*" he managed eventually. "We have to rescue that picture, Eleanor. We're looking at a hundred-thirty-million-dollar loss! We can't survive it!"

"We couldn't survive a loss that size, true. But we aren't going to take a loss. I spoke to Fred Florescu this morning, and he tells me that they'll be all done in a month, and what they finally have down is awesome. Now, let's talk about Mr. Keller." She reached for her briefcase, unlocking it, drew out the sheaves of memos and e-mail messages, and passed them across the desk to her boss.

"What are these?" Goldman asked, mystified.

"These are copies of my original memos, laying out all the location sites and production details we had decided on, after I took reports from my location scouts." Tom nodded. "And these are copies from Jake Keller's computer, showing where he altered them. The discrepancies are highlighted in bold type. You'll see that most of the changes are minor—one beach versus another, that kind of thing, although the changes resulted in lost hours and costly reshoots. Keller was switching locations to nature reserves, protected or dangerous areas, or beaches where the tide would come in too fast and cause a shoot to be abandoned."

"But how could this have happened, without you noticing?"

She nodded. "You're right. And that was my fault; it won't happen again. I was too trusting, it never occurred to me that a senior executive at this studio would actually stoop to sabotage. But Jake asked me to sign off on some 'minor changes,' as he put it. The big one I missed was the warning about the weather in the Seychelles. I advised the crew to switch to Hawaii if filming hadn't wrapped by a certain date, to avoid the rainy season. And Jake deleted that from my instructions."

"I don't believe it," Tom said, dumbfounded.

"Nor did I, but there's your proof. If you access his computer now, before he arrives, you'll see the same thing yourself. And there is one other matter—casting. Jake's condemnation of me for picking Roxana, and then his desire to enlarge her part."

"We did have major trouble with Roxana, Eleanor. We still do," Goldman said, feeling he should make some kind of a rally on the studio's behalf. The documents he was holding seemed to smoke in his hands. Jesus Christ. How come *I* never thought to investigate either? he asked himself, utterly dismayed.

"Yes. And perhaps these will explain some of that," Eleanor told him, passing across one final pile of papers. "I pulled them out of Jake Keller's private e-mail file. They're faxes sent to David Tauber at the Meridien Hotel, Anse Polite, Seychelles, discussing Roxana Felix's deliberate disruption of the shoot, and when it would be best for her to start working properly—after I had been fired."

Tom Goldman took them and glanced through them, his face darkening.

"Cancel the production meeting, Tom. You can reschedule it a week from now, that'll give you time to discuss Keller with our lawyers."

"Very well," he said quietly. "What excuse should I give?"

"Unfortunately, you don't have to give them an excuse," Eleanor told him. "The main reason Florescu rang me this morning is that Zach Mason and Megan Silver are missing." She gave him a brief description of her phone call. "You can tell them that I had to fly out to Mahé this morning to supervise a rescue effort. In my absence, you'll be taking over my responsibilities. Right?"

"Right." Goldman paused, leaned toward her. "Eleanor, I—"

"Save it." She gave him a quick smile. "We can talk when I get back."

chapter 32

"I hope you can appreciate, Mrs. Kendrick, that we have only been conducting the investigation for a matter of days," Grant Booth said nervously, as he watched Isabelle sort through the foolscap document wallet, occasionally holding up a photograph to the light, her face expressionless. "I realize that there is a certain lack of witnesses to the findings we have come up with so far. We normally obtain at least ten witnesses per incident or fact that we allege took place."

"Can you get me more witnesses to this?" Isabelle inquired.

Booth nodded hastily, flicking a finger across the navy-blue sleeve of his suit, a masterpiece of immaculate tailoring by John Lobb of St. James's in London, as if removing an imaginary piece of lint. It was so important to impress Mrs. Kendrick. Not only was she paying them more than handsomely, she was a social power in the city. Her recommendation to the wives and ex-wives of Hollywood moguls could double the firm's revenue in a year. He would bend over backward to please her. Indeed, he would contort himself into any position the lady required.

"Certainly, madam, certainly. And we have various employees doing just that as we speak. But since the story that was emerging was so, uh, so *surprising,* we felt you would want to have the basic skeleton of the matter right away. An interim report, if you like."

Isabelle closed the lid of the document wallet.

"Can I keep these?" she asked.

"Please, be my guest." Booth nodded reassuringly. "We have several copies of everything."

Isabelle nodded, pushed back her chair, and stood up to leave.

"Is—is everything satisfactory so far, Mrs. Kendrick?" he asked her anxiously.

For the first time that morning, Isabelle Kendrick favored him with a slight smile.

"I look forward to receiving your full report, Mr. Booth, but I must say your work so far has been excellent." She glanced coolly down at the document wallet, placed neatly inside her soft leather Gucci tote bag. "Absolutely excellent."

Grant Booth's pudgy face beamed with relief as he sprang forward to hold open his office door for her.

⋅⋅⋅⋅

Megan bit her lip to stop herself from screaming.

The shadows in the mist forest were drawing in. She'd misjudged the distance over that rock and slammed her ankle against it. Fiery loops of pain squeezed around the purple, swollen flesh of her foot. Then, as she gulped the air, dizzy with agony, a black, hairy tarantula, the size of a kitten, ran out from the stone and crawled onto her foot.

Zach saw her freeze and dived over, reaching down, brushing the spider off with his bare hands. It scuttled away into the undergrowth.

Megan couldn't help herself. She crumpled into his arms.

"It's OK," Zach murmured, kissing her forehead. She was bathed in sweat and he could hear her heart hammering against her chest. She was terrified, but she still didn't cry.

He wanted her so much it hurt.

"You're a trouper, Megan."

Zach could hardly look at her. He wanted to kiss her so badly. And she was right here in his arms.

"We're going to die," Megan said flatly.

"Sure we are." Zach set her straight. "But not just yet."

⋅⋅⋅⋅

Isabelle parked her Bentley in front of the house, trying to contain herself. It wouldn't do to let Sam see her in this state. She was bubbling over with happiness, her manicured fingers tapping out old Sinatra tunes on the steering wheel. A long time ago, when she'd been interested in things like music, Sinatra and Tony Bennett had been her favorites. Kind of appropriate, really, Isabelle thought, restraining an unseemly grin. She was about to do it Her Way. But Sam mustn't know until it was too late; according to these reports, Sam had actually developed *feelings* for the little slut. A blast of cold anger sliced through her elation, but she suppressed it. Never mind what her husband chose to do with his empty little heart. She had lost that years ago. And it was hardly important. It was *Sam* who was important—the man himself, and the status that his thick platinum band on her left hand represented. Isabelle had not come all this way to lose it to some twenty-four-year-old mannequin now.

But peace, peace, Isabelle soothed herself as she stepped out of the car, smoothing her peach Bill Blass suit as she did so. That was all taken care of—Mr. Booth and his cohorts had seen to that. Now, the only thing that remained was for her to pick a reporter to give this story to. She would choose carefully, for it was the show business scoop of the decade, and whomever she handed that foolscap binder to would owe Isabelle huge forever. She had to select somebody with appropriate clout, somebody worth having in her designer pocket. There was no point in rushing things, Isabelle thought. She had to keep one eye on her future. Unlike Ms. Felix, who after today didn't *have* a future.

Isabelle practically bounded up the steps of the terrace, nodded curtly at the maid who admitted her, and walked through to her study right away. First things first. Because she wanted so desperately to believe what Booth, Warwick & Yablans were telling her, that didn't mean it was true. For her own peace of mind, she wanted to check up on a couple of details. She dialed Jordan Goldman's number and waited, one foot tapping impatiently on her antique Chinese rug.

"Goldman residence."

"Isabelle Kendrick for Mrs. Goldman," Isabelle said impatiently. She wished dear Jordan wouldn't insist on having the servants always answer the phone. Really, so affected.

"Isabelle! I'm so glad you *called*." Jordan was gushing. "I've been wanting to speak to you about my slave auction next month. Do you think I should make togas mandatory?"

"Oh, definitely not, dear," Isabelle said, shuddering at the thought of all that wrinkled male flesh exposed. "But we can talk about that in a second. I want to ask you a few questions about Roxana Felix."

"Anything, Isabelle," Jordan said obediently.

"You always said Roxana had been a school friend of yours, dear, but how long was she actually at the Sacred Heart?"

"Only one year. She was enrolled in senior year," Jordan said, surprised at the question. "She was eighteen when she arrived."

Isabelle gave a sharp intake of breath. So it was all true.

"Are you OK, Isabelle?"

"I'm fine. Tell me, did you ever see her mother or her father at the school? Did they ever come to pick her up, or attend graduation?"

"No. As a matter of fact, they didn't come to graduation," Jordan mused thoughtfully, remembering it. "We all thought that was weird, but Roxie said they were in Europe on business and couldn't be there. But they never came to pick her up, either; at breaks, she always left for the airport in a cab."

"Thank you, dear. That's very useful," Isabelle said, one hand balling into a fist of triumph at her side. "I have to go now. I've got a few calls to make."

"But what about my togas?" Jordan whined.

"I'll call you back," Isabelle said firmly, hanging up.

She stood there for a few seconds, racing through the possibilities, and finally settled on the ideal person. Marissa Matthews, the most widely read gossip columnist in New York—an old acquaintance, and syndicated all over Los Angeles. Marissa would kill for a story like this, Isabelle congratulated herself. And Marissa would be the perfect ally for an entrée into New York society. After all, she had already conquered Los Angeles, and one had to expand one's horizons.

Smiling, she lifted the phone and punched in the number.

"Marissa? Darling, it's Isabelle Kendrick. I have a scoop for you. Rather a big one, in fact. Do you have a decent fax up there? . . . Oh, it can take photographs, too, can it? Splendid . . ."

<hr />

Eleanor leaned back in the air-conditioned comfort of the hotel's sedan, sent to collect her from the Seychelles airport, and gazed out of the windows. Physical fatigue was beginning to hit her, but she forced herself to stay awake. This was going to have been a big day for her, but it wasn't over yet. Not by a long shot. First, she'd managed to save her job, and that had been fun; Tom, looking gorgeous in that somber black suit, and sitting there with his mouth hanging open in astonishment, was a sight she would never forget. Blown away by the new, tough, improved Eleanor Marshall. But that was the easy part; she just prayed she could be tough enough for Megan and Zach. *If* there was any Megan and Zach left to rescue. But somehow, Eleanor was sure they had survived. She could feel it in her bones. They were alive, and stranded somewhere in that emerald-green jungle that she'd stared at from the windows of her plane.

Fred Florescu, looking pale and anxious, was waiting for her in the lobby when she arrived.

"Thanks for getting here so quickly," he said. "It's the second day they've been missing. I've notified all the authorities, and they've got a search under way . . ." The young director shook his head. "I don't know what else we can do. There's been no news."

"OK. Here's what I've been thinking," Eleanor said. "First up, I'm going to hire every private helicopter available on this island to fly over the national park, with spotlights, backward and forward, all night."

"That'll cost you," Florescu said.

"That's my problem, Fred. I'm authorized to draw on Artemis funds for this search. Next, I'm hiring locals to go into the jungle and look for them."

"The mist forest they're lost in is eleven miles square," Florescu told her, despairingly. "You'd need hundreds of people to make any impact."

"And I'm prepared to hire hundreds. Thousands, if necessary. We'll pay them five hundred dollars each to look for Zach and Megan, and give the guy that finds them a five-thousand-dollar reward."

Florescu looked at her with a new respect.

"Jesus, Eleanor. Studio execs are supposed to be tightwad assholes. Where did you come from?"

She laughed. "Hey, we *are* tightwad assholes. This is just an investment, as far as I'm concerned. A dead Zach Mason means a big loss for Artemis Studios, and Megan Silver will make a lot of money for us, down the line. I've got a lot of personal capital in *Triple Feature*, Fred. I want to see this movie released."

"And you know what? You're going to be sitting on one hell of a god-damned smash when it is," Florescu told her.

"Good. Now, you get the rest of the cast together and start shooting."

"Do *what?*"

"Start shooting," Eleanor repeated. "Film some scenes without Zach or Roxana in them. There have to be a few left, right?"

"There are, but—"

"Forget *but*, Fred. You're no use to Zach and Megan sitting here moping. None of you know the forest, and I'm not risking any more of my people in there." She gave him a soft smile. "I intend to get those kids out alive and well. I want them to have a picture to go back to. Now, are we making a movie here, or not?"

"Yes ma'am!" Fred Florescu replied, smiling broadly.

-:::-

"It's getting dark," Megan said.

She tried to keep the fear out of her voice. They might have already spent one night in the undergrowth, but she'd been unconscious, knocked cold by the fall. This evening would be different. Megan doubted if she'd sleep at all, despite her exhaustion, every muscle shrieking in protest as she took another step forward with her right foot, balanced her weight on the makeshift crutches, and swung her useless left foot forward to join it. She had gone as fast as she could all day, refusing to stop for a rest despite Zach's urging; Megan knew that if she'd sat down, she'd never have been able to get back up. Twice she'd stumbled and fallen, screaming with pain as her swollen ankle jarred against some hidden rock or branch, and Mason had insisted on carrying her until her kicks and scratches finally persuaded him to put her down. Megan refused to wear Zach out; deep inside, although she was too scared to face the possibility right now, was the feeling that maybe Zach was their only hope; maybe he'd have to leave her in the jungle and run on ahead, gambling that he could get out of the forest and that help would arrive quick enough to save her. Although somehow she doubted that they'd find her again; one patch of jungle looked much like another.

Well, Megan thought, gripped with gallows humor, at least this is a pretty spot for a grave.

Beautiful but deadly. That summed up the mist forest; gnarled northea and screw pine palms covered with damp moss and creepers, bright sunlight penetrating into the green gloom of the woodlands, primeval giant ferns rearing up everywhere under the jade canopy overhead. Brightly colored birds swooped and plunged through the trees. The scent of wild cinnamon, vanilla orchids, and passion flowers hung in the air, underlying everything, along with the buzz of insects and the calls of the tree frogs and the geckos. Never in her wildest dreams had Megan imagined anyplace so strange and lovely. But it was terrifying with it: twice Mason had scooped her into his arms, trembling and frozen with fear, and carried her several yards away from a scorpion; they had passed three huge, hanging nests of yellow wasps, a savage genus of the species that could paralyze if they attacked in numbers; a thick Seychelles wolf snake had slithered out of some leaves and writhed right through Megan's crutches; and although she knew they were harmless, she had trouble suppressing her natural dread of the giant palm spiders, each one the size of a human hand, that hung from every other tree in thick, white cobwebs. She was frightened of nightfall, she couldn't help it. She kept thinking about tarantulas, and the jungle would be swarming with bats. What she could cope with in the green and gold of daylight would become horrible, unbearable, in the dark, the blackness crawling and slithering with nameless terrors.

Thank God she wasn't alone. Zach had been with her when she woke up and he had been by her side every step of the way, carrying her, comforting her, protecting her. Megan felt suffused with gratitude for the way the guy had behaved; picking her up when she needed help, joking around to distract her, forcing her to talk about herself incessantly, so that she could get through the day. He'd never once complained over the way she was slowing them down; he would wait for her, with total patience, for as long as it took. And Megan knew she had slowed them down. Despite all the agonies she'd put herself through, they couldn't have traveled more than two miles in the whole day.

Mason looked up at the patches of sky visible through the treetops. Sunset was definitely falling, streaks of red and gold blazing across the darkening blue heavens like so many banners.

"Looks like it. We'd better stop," he said, leading her across to an overgrown, mossy stump. "You sit there while I build a shelter. I'll do it right away, before the light fails." He gave her a warm smile. "Relax, you get to rest now. You did great."

"Can I help?" Megan asked, watching him cracking branches and stacking them against the bark of the nearest large tree.

"No. This won't take me five minutes," Zach told her, jumping up to rip off a few large leaves for thatching. He moved confidently, quickly, the muscles in his back sliding around under his tanned skin, his back covered in a thin sheen of sweat, the tattered shirt long since discarded in the heat and tied around his waist. Megan couldn't help noticing how firm his thighs looked under the calfskin leggings, molded around his body like a second skin. And his biceps were pretty impressive too, large and rockhard, as though sculptured by a master craftsman.

David would kill to look like that, Megan thought, and was suddenly overwhelmed with embarrassment at her own stupidity. How could I ever have looked up to that guy? she wondered, blushing a deep red. He's such a weasel, such a peacock, such an ass-kisser! And I acted like putty in his hands! I thought *he* was the talented one, even when somebody like Fred Florescu told me different. I let David dictate to me what I ate, what I wore—I let him stand over me while I worked out! How pathetic can you get? And just because I lost a little weight, I convinced myself that I should put my life in his hands. But I was unhappy with how I looked anyway—I would have slimmed down of my own accord, with him or without him . . .

"There you go," Zach said, standing back. He had finished a small wigwam-style hut of branches, palm fronds, and leaves, backed up against the tree for security. "Not exactly the Ritz-Carlton, but it'll have to do."

"It's wonderful," Megan told him.

Zach glanced at her. "You're blushing."

"I was thinking about David," Megan said truthfully.

He turned away and started threading a few more leaves into the thatch.

She took a deep breath. "I was thinking what an idiot I was to see anything in that guy. You were right, you know. He's a complete jerk. We were fighting before we finally split up—I told him I was moving out of the hotel suite—and the next morning he came up to my room and told me to pack, because I was fired. Then he came running back twenty minutes later to tell me I wasn't fired. But I did realize he was an asshole before. Now, I just don't understand why I ever thought any different."

"Now?" Zach asked, his wolf eyes watching her steadily.

"Now I'm here with you," Megan said, unthinkingly.

Mason gave her a slow smile.

Megan felt the blush deepen to a rich crimson. "I didn't mean it how it sounded. It's just that you—I meant, you've been so good to me today, you've been really manly about it. David would have left me . . ." Her voice trailed off in confusion.

"Me Tarzan, you Jane," Zach said, but his gaze was traveling slowly up and down her body, and Megan wasn't completely sure he was joking.

"Why did you go with David? I knew you were hanging out together, but I never saw you with him until the Electric City show."

Megan shrugged. "He decided to make a move on me then, though nothing much happened that night. Actually, I was grateful—I was kind of embarrassed, standing there while you and Roxana were getting close."

Zach glanced at her. "I only did that because I saw you with Tauber. After we'd been talking. I was jealous, I guess."

"You were jealous? I don't understand," Megan said, feeling a warm wash of desire flood through her groin. Could he be saying what it sounded like he was saying? "You were with Roxana Felix. She told me so, in that little booth on the stage, remember that? She was wearing the laminate *you* got her." She tried to take the accusing note out of her voice and failed. "When you dedicated that song to me—this is going to sound really stupid, I know—I was so pleased. It meant a lot to me." Now she was really abashed, blushing harder than ever.

"Why would you think that sounds stupid?"

"Because I sound like a fan."

"Do you think I despise my fans?" Zach asked. "I'm glad it meant something to you. That was the point. We didn't write those songs so we could play them to ourselves in Nate's garage. Even if we never expected what happened, we wanted to be heard."

"She told me that she and you had discussed it together. That you thought the two of you had been a little harsh on me, so you'd do that onstage to make me feel better. And then I felt like a moron, because it wasn't your idea. It was Roxana's."

Zach Mason stared at her for a long moment, and finally shook his head, laughing.

"What?"

"Megan. It *was* my idea, of course it was. Roxana had nothing to do with it. The pass she was wearing Sam Kendrick got for her. Roxana Felix was never, ever my girlfriend! She was sleeping with Sam. She still is. God, you must be the only person on the set who never realized that . . . She wanted to get together with me, but only for the publicity, or so she could use me. I told her I was interested in somebody else."

"Oh," Megan said blankly.

Somebody *else?* Did I miss something here? Who? I haven't seen anyone else around . . . he can't mean Mary, surely, she's way too old . . .

"I told her I was interested in you," Zach said.

Megan sat very still on the log, trying not to breathe.

"But you hate my hair. You were always so rude to me." she stammered.

"I preferred you the way you were before, that's true. But I figured you were doing that for David."

"I was doing it to get some attention," Megan muttered.

Zach smiled at her, his eyes now full of desire. She felt her nipples stiffening in response.

I don't care if this is happening because we're stranded together. I don't care if this is all lies, Megan thought fiercely. I want him. I must have him.

Long-submerged waves of longing were beating up in her, making the blood warm under her skin, need pulling at her crotch.

"You always had my attention."

"I was frightened of you, because of who you were," Megan admitted.

He nodded, dark hair cascading around his shoulders. "And I was kind of frightened of you. Because you were so smart, so well educated, and I never even finished high school."

She stood up, and walked carefully over to the hut.

"Let me take those for you." Zach supported her as she let go of her crutches, one arm carefully encircling her waist, then lowered her down on the ground.

"You are one of the most intelligent men I've ever met," Megan told him, her brown eyes fixed on his. She could feel the warmth of his body, the tight, naked skin next to her face, and fought back the urge to press her lips against it. This had to be taken slow. "You must be crazy. Don't you understand that you were the voice, *you* were the focus, for our whole generation? What did you think made them respond like that?"

"It was just lyrics," he said, sitting next to her.

"Yeah? And who wrote them, Zach? Who wrote all those songs? You did! And you said what we all believed. You spoke for us. That's something you should be proud of, Zach. You have a genius with music and lyricism thousands of kids would do anything for, *and* you've proved to be an incredible actor. You don't need a little paper certificate to tell you you're smart. And deep down inside, you know that." She paused. "Why did you split the band?"

"You really want to know?"

She nodded, and he settled next to her, pressing his body up against hers. The touch of his skin on hers was electrifying.

Zach closed his eyes briefly. "I had always written everything. And last Christmas, Nate came to me with two songs he'd laid down, on his own, when there was a break from touring. I told him I couldn't use them. He said he wanted to talk to the other guys. And I freaked; I said I was always going to write all the songs." He tapped one rough hand on his knee. "Dark Angel was my baby, Megan. It was my vision, it had been from the beginning, from before our first guitarist left and Nate joined. Maybe I was feeling threatened. I don't know."

"So what happened?" she asked gently.

"We had a fight." He shrugged. "A lot of shit got said that couldn't be taken back. And then Yolanda Henry, our manager, came in on Nate's side. She said they were good songs, and we should use them. I was bitter, I was really incensed. I fired Yolanda and split the band. And within days, there was David, pouring oil all over my wounded ego, pushing the right buttons. He asked me if I'd like to try acting, and it sounded good—a chance to show the other guys that *I* had talent, I could make it without Dark Angel. And that's it. Not very noble."

"But you believed his songs would hurt your vision of the band," Megan said.

"You know what? I wish I could tell you that was true. I wish I could say that I acted with integrity. But it's not, and I didn't." Mason glanced at Megan. "They were great songs. Really beautiful. And I got jealous, I got protective . . . I thought I was so cool, but when it came right down to it I was just another big shot with an ego. Yolanda wouldn't bullshit me when I wanted her to. *She* had integrity. So, I fired her."

He fell silent.

"Go easy on yourself, Zach."

"I can't. I split my band, for nothing."

Megan grinned. "So what? When we get out of here, you fire David, call Nate Suter up, apologize, put the band back together, reinstate Yolanda Henry and apologize to her, too."

"Just like that, huh."

"Yeah. Just like that. What's stopping you?"

"Are you serious?" Mason asked, turning to her. His thundercloud eyes stared right into hers, and Megan felt her crotch tighten.

"I'm totally serious. Why not? I'm sure they're feeling just as bad about it as you are." Feeling hot, flustered at his gaze, she reached into her pocket and drew out the tube of insect repellent. "Let me put some of this stuff on you. At dusk, we're going to need it."

Zach said, "Take off your top."

"What?"

"Take off your top." He patted the damp ground beneath them and reached to his waist, untying his shirt. "We have to get some kind of solid covering underneath us, so nothing crawls out of the leaves while we're asleep. The gel should keep the bugs away from our upper bodies."

Megan did as he said, spreading her shirt next to his on the ground, trying to act naturally. This is a survival situation, she told herself firmly. Right? Just like going to the doctor. He won't think anything of it.

"My God, you're beautiful," Zach exclaimed softly. He reached out and stroked the soft, creamy flesh of her left breast with one finger, and Megan felt a liquid rush of renewed wanting surge through her like molten lava, his touch burning against her skin. Her nipples stiffened with pleasure, and they both saw it, the swollen buds pressing through the thin chocolate lace of her bra. Half hypnotized, Megan glanced down at Zach's crotch. He was already erect, the hard outline of his cock, large and thick, clearly visible as it strained inside the calfskin. Instantly, a burst of wetness exploded inside Megan's pussy in response, making her rub her thighs against each other with impatient desire. She moaned.

"I want to make love to you," Zach said urgently, his voice thick with desire, and Megan reached out to caress his chest, saying, "Oh yes, Zach, please, *now*," and then his hands were on her breasts, not softly this time, grabbing them, cupping them, his thumbs brushing her taut nipples, sending little shocks of sex through them, and Megan leaned forward, her fingers shaking, and unknotted the laces at the top of his crotch, pulling them halfway down his thighs, so that he sprang free, and Megan took his thickness in her hands and began to play with him, her fingertips lightly brushing against the warm skin of his balls, her fingers wrapping themselves around the stem of his cock, until Zach groaned with desire and broke away from her, ripping off his clothes as if he couldn't undress fast enough. Megan, her heart hammering against her chest, snapped open the buttons on her 501s and started to yank them down, then stopped, dismayed.

"What's the matter?" Zach asked her, seeing her sudden distress.

Megan pointed to her injured ankle, bloated and discolored above the leather of her shoe. "I can't take my jeans off. I'll never get them over that," she said, almost choking on her disappointment.

Mason took her head in his two hands and kissed her, a long, luxurious kiss, his tongue meeting hers, teasing the inside of her mouth, flicking under her top lip; then taking her bottom lip in between his teeth and sucking it. Desire bathed her entire body and she pressed against him, her breasts swelling with need, her nipples now sharp as a razor blade against his chest.

"You don't need to take them all the way down. They go far enough," Zach said, giving her a slow smile. Megan gasped as his left hand snaked around behind her, cupping the back of her neck, supporting her weight, and his right hand plunged between her thighs, covering her mound, his palm first barely touching the damp, silken down, then pressing harder, sending a blaze of pleasure through her crotch. Automatically she bucked underneath him, trying to move her thighs, to twist away from the caress, but she couldn't. Her jeans held her locked securely in place, her crotch exposed to him. Zach looked into her eyes and laughed, a low, throaty laugh, full of delight and desire. "No way, baby. You're not going anywhere," he said, and then his fingers were inside her, two of them, stroking her gently, probing her heat and her wetness, and he began to caress her, intimately, fingertips sliding over the smooth nub of her clitoris. Megan cried out, her back arching involuntarily under him, and waves of pleasure began to beat up in her, the ecstasy overtaking her, and she came in a blind rush, spasms of bliss rippling across her belly.

"We're just warming up," Zach Mason said, and he laid her down on their flattened clothes with infinite gentleness, taking care not to jar her ankle, and then Megan's fingers tightened in his dark mane as he lowered his head to her skin, his tongue flicking the erect buds of her nipples, so that she moaned again, feeling a new warmth between her thighs, and then shuddered with longing as he sucked her breasts, licked down past her navel, holding her body firmly in place with his hands as she moved under him, and then finally, wonderfully, he reached her pussy and his mouth was on her, licking her, sucking her, playing with her, and Megan was transported into a new place, a new kind of passion, her universe contracting and shrinking until she was aware of nothing except her own crotch, and Zach's head, and her breath, coming in ragged gasps, and the pleasure was so intense, it was so hot and unbearable and incredible that she thought she might pass out, and then, just as she was sure she was going to explode, Zach took his mouth away and moved across her and she felt him enter her, his cock thick and hard as stone, throbbing, pulsing with need for her, and he was inside her, making love to her, fucking her, deep and slow and rhythmic, the strokes coming harder, then faster, pushing into her, driving her further up, so she couldn't breathe, couldn't think, had never imagined sex could be like this, and then she heard herself cry out, as though far away, and suddenly the pleasure exploded around her, dizzying her so that she couldn't see, her whole world dissolving around her, her bones liquefying, her body melting into a sea of bliss, absolute, complete nirvana, the spasms seeming to contract her every muscle, groin, calves, forearms, back, and she sensed his climax rushing up to meet her, and finally the waves of rapture slowly receded, and Megan was left, sweating and shaking, gazing into Zach's wolflike eyes, and locked tight in her lover's embraces.

chapter 33

Roxana Felix was under siege. Literally. The reporters were everywhere: massing the road outside the front of the house, sneaking through the neighboring gardens, even flying past in helicopters to get a few aerial snaps of her gardens. The discreet seclusion of her coffee and white Moroccan villa was no match for the tabloids' rat pack, every one of them desperate for a photo or a comment, or better still, a snippet of footage. Her tall, private hedges rustled with unauthorized movements every few minutes, and all the available viewpoints on nearby tall trees or mountain outcrops were being bitterly fought over. She no longer dared even to sneak into a bedroom to take a look outside, because the slightest twitch of the curtains would set off a flurry of flashbulbs. Roxana Felix had graduated into the hottest type of celebrity around—the fallen angel, the Madonna exposed as a whore. It was a perfect piece of white-trash culture—the story of the supermodel everybody adored, America's sweetheart, the bashful, modest heroine of a million magazine puff pieces, uncovered as a teenage prostitute and brothelkeeper. America and the world licked sleaze-hungry lips. Who didn't relish a story like this? Marissa Matthews had been first with her scoop, announcing the grisly details to New York society over breakfast—a special edition of "Friday's People" released on a Wednesday—and the rest of the pack had followed enviously in her wake an hour later. Orders were dispatched and shuttles jumped on in London, Paris, Madrid, Adelaide. Bribes were offered wholesale to anybody who would talk—old clients, old hookers, old school friends, anybody—and suddenly acquaintances were pouring out of the woodwork faster than the TV shows could line them up. Her hairdresser. Her New York chauffeur. A secretary to her booker at Unique. And with every passing minute, another news crew or free-lance hack arrived at the "secluded" villa tucked away in the Hollywood Hills, now about as secluded as Times Square on New Year's Eve.

Roxana sat on a chair she'd dragged into her bathroom with her head in her hands, listening to the phone ring. She had chosen the bathroom because it was the only room in the house without windows, the only room where she could be sure that she was not seen. She would not disconnect the phones or the fax machines; that was what they would expect, but she would not do it. She was no coward.

So it had finally happened, Roxana thought. After all these years, after everything, they had found her. They knew almost everything. And the fame, the conquest, the safety, the adoration—her iron castle, the fortress she had built up, over eleven long years, inch by painstaking inch—in a matter of hours it had melted away, vanished like dew in the morning sun.

The demons had come for her. She had always known that someday they would.

Roxana sat on the chair and rocked herself backward and forward, singing gently, as though lulling a little child.

⋅⋮⋅

"Mr. Goldman, I think you should see this."

"Not now, Marcia. I have to call New York."

Tom Goldman did not conceal his impatience. It was one thing after another; first, Zach and Megan's disappearance; next, deciding on the best way to handle Keller; and now, the second he got into his office, he found piles of pink-slip telephone messages from various members of the board. Jesus, Tom thought as he sank into his black leather Eames chair, those sons of bitches better not be selling the company. Not now. Because when what's happened to Zach Mason gets out, the press'll be all over *Triple Feature*—and then it's all over for the stock. Right now, if those pencil pushers decide to sell, they'll find Artemis Studios trading for thirty cents and a can of Coke.

"Yes sir, I know," his secretary said, apologetically. "But you should really see this before you make any calls."

Tom glanced at his assistant, cradling the morning papers to her chest. Oh, God. "Is this something to do with Zach Mason, Marcia? I'd better have a look."

"Not exactly, Mr. Goldman," she said cautiously, handing them across to him.

Goldman felt his jaw slacken in blank astonishment.

The *New York Post* had two pictures of Roxana Felix—smiling, poised, and confident as the forty-million-dollar face of Jackson Cosmetics, and wafer-thin, overly made up, and dressed in a miniskirt, spike heels, and sequined top, leaning against a wall in Paris, a teenage hooker in an unmistakable pose. In bold black type the headline screamed: "MODEL MADAM!" And underneath, "The sensational story of Roxana Felix—from streetwalker to supermodel! How a teenage tart turned from brothel-keeper to America's Sweetheart!"

Aghast, Goldman pulled out the *New York Times:* "WHY THE LADY IS A TRAMP." The *Washington Post:* "FASHION PRINCESS WAS FRENCH PIMP." The *Los Angeles Times:* "REAL ROXANA REVEALED." They were all the same.

"Those are the late editions, sir," Marcia said, adding weakly, "They couldn't fit it in the earlier ones."

"Is this all over the radio and TV, too?" he asked, although he knew the answer.

"Yes sir. I thought you might have heard it on your car radio."

Dazed, Goldman shook his head. He'd driven in silence this morning, radio off, car phone switched off, so he could have a little time with his thoughts.

Just as well, Tom thought grimly. *Because that's the last peace and quiet I'll be getting for a while.*

"No calls for ten minutes, Marcia, OK? I have to read this story through. Tell them I'm on my way into the office." She nodded, but Goldman was suddenly struck with a dreadful, clammy fear. *The directors had been calling. The board was worried . . .*

"Wait! Marcia, get me Joel Spellman on the phone, right away."

"OK."

Goldman spun his chair around, his fingers drumming nervously on his mahogany desk. Spellman was on the phone in seconds.

"Joel, it's Tom."

His broker's voice was a screech of agony.

"Goldman, where the fuck have you been? I don't have power of attorney! You've been unreachable for the last hour, and I can't sell jack for you without an instruction! You *know* that!"

Tom nodded, pain crunching through his temples. The car phone. It had been the first time he'd switched it off for months. Christ, why today? Why had this happened today?

"Yeah, I know that. What's the damage?"

"The stock's going *south*, Tom. Nobody can dump it fast enough! I'm telling you, it's in fucking free fall!"

"What did we lose?"

Spellman snorted with disgust. "On paper? Your holdings have lost about eighty percent of their value. But it might be more by the time I get to lose whatever I can. Even the bottom-fishers don't want to touch it."

Eighty percent. The words echoed in Goldman's brain, sending new shock waves through his system. Eighty percent, possibly more, wiped off the value of his Artemis holdings. Holy Lord God, Tom thought, I'm ruined.

"So? *Talk* to me, Tom, goddamnit!" Spellman howled. "Give me a sell order, for God's sake! Let's salvage *something* from this mess!"

"No," Goldman said.

"*No?* What the fuck do you mean, *no?* We have to move *now!*"

"No, Joel. Don't sell anything," Tom said. "This studio is in trouble. I'm the chief executive, and I'm not going to dump my stock in my company during a crisis."

"Are you out of your *fucking mind?*" Spellman screamed.

"When you think the stock has hit bottom, buy ten thousand units."

"Do *what?*"

"You heard me. You're my broker, right?"

"Yeah, but—"

"No buts, Joel. Carry out my order," Tom said, and hung up.

He stared at the pink slips on his desk. Every one of them had called in: Conrad Miles, Howard Thorn, all of them.

Marcia buzzed him. "Mr. Goldman, should I get Mr. Thorn for you now?"

"In a minute, Marcia," Tom said calmly. It was strange; he knew his world had just blown up in his face, the studio, his personal fortune, all of it, and yet he suddenly felt as clearheaded as he ever had in his life. Joel Spellman and everybody else would probably think he was insane, but Tom Goldman had a responsibility to this studio and he was going to carry it out. "I'll call everybody back in a minute. But first, I want you to call the Meridien Hotel on Mahé in the Seychelles. I need to speak to Ms. Marshall."

⋅⋰⋅

Isabelle Kendrick sat in a soft, oyster-white armchair in her drawing room, composed and relaxed, and faced her husband. On a small Regency table, by her side, the late editions of the day's papers were neatly stacked. Next to them rested Isabelle's half-drunk cup of cinnamon coffee in a blue Sevres cup, her normal morning refreshment. She had not eaten a breakfast for the last ten years, and as far as Isabelle was concerned, this morning was just the same as any other. Possibly a little more enjoyable. Isabelle seemed just as collected and unruffled as ever; she was wearing an elegant, caramel Georges Rech pantsuit, her hair was neatly coiffed, and a subtle seed pearl necklace gleamed against the slack skin of her throat. Totally unperturbed, Isabelle glanced up at her husband as he paced back and forth, passing his hand through his hair repeatedly, his black eyes burning with rage and pain.

"You never said anything. You never asked me," he said, glaring at her. "How could you do it, Isabelle? *Why* would you do it? You're a monster, do you know that?"

"Don't be melodramatic, Samuel." His wife's voice was ice-cold, absolutely emotionless. "I only told you it was me as a courtesy. And so that you wouldn't indulge in any similar foolishness in the future."

Kendrick stopped moving and looked Isabelle directly in the face.

"What are you saying to me? That you were jealous?"

She shook her head, as if finding the suggestion distasteful.

"Of course not. We don't have that kind of marriage."

"The real kind, you mean," Kendrick said bitterly.

"Our marriage works very well, Sam." Isabelle felt the adrenaline start to flow again as she spoke, saying aloud the things that had been taboo between them for so long. This was her moment of victory; she was going to flex her muscles, lay it out for him. He was not the only power in this house, Isabelle thought viciously. He owed her. Let him see what she was capable of if he forgot that fact. She would fry Roxana and any other little toy that he got too public with. Nobody threatened her position, not Roxana, not Sam, not anybody. "You know I've never objected to your various liaisons, but this was different. This was public. And you may do as you please, as long as it does not reflect on me."

"You don't care if I screw prostitutes?"

Isabelle waved one bejewelled hand. "Not at all, dear."

"You don't care if I see other women? If I love another woman?"

"Not as long as you're discreet." Isabelle took a delicate sip of her coffee. "Good gracious, Sam, did you think I didn't know about your other girls? How many have there been? Eight or nine is it? Aside from the hookers. I simply hoped that you had the good sense to take precautions—all these nasty diseases going around. And of course there's always pregnancy to consider. That can get messy. But beforehand, none of the girls came from our world."

"You knew, and you said nothing," Kendrick whispered.

The woman sitting in front of him was a stranger, a machine. He couldn't believe that the change in Isabelle ran so deep. She looked the same, but the blond elegance covered stone, pure rock. It was true they hadn't been close for years, but somehow he hadn't realized, not completely, that the woman he lived with was such an automaton. It terrified him.

"Why should I care, dear? We're a highly successful couple."

He stared at her. She meant it.

"What about love, Isabelle?" Sam said quietly. "We loved each other once."

She gazed levelly at him.

"That was a long time ago."

He made one last effort.

"You can't mean that, Isabelle. You can't. There has to be more to your life than giving parties and ruling all the wives. You can't be that shallow. Tell me you hate me, or you were jealous of her, or you want all the affairs to stop. Tell me you feel something."

Deliberately, Isabelle reached into her bag and drew out her silver Chanel compact. She snapped it open, regarded herself in the mirror, and dabbed a little powder onto the end of her nose. When she had finished, she snapped it shut, and finally turned to her husband.

"Why should I say that, Sam? It would be a lie." She nodded at the pile of papers next to her. "Roxana boasted about you to Jordan Goldman. I can't have that. I won't be humiliated. So, if you keep your indiscretions quiet, I won't have to do this again."

Kendrick shook his head. Then he turned on his heel and walked toward the door.

"Where do you think you're going?" Isabelle demanded angrily.

"I'm going to see Roxana Felix," Sam told her.

"You can't do that!" she whispered, enraged.

He turned toward his wife, a certain sadness clouding his eyes.

"Yes, I can, Isabelle. I love her. I didn't realize how much until this moment, but now I do. And when I find her, I'm going to ask her to marry me."

Isabelle Kendrick paled in shock.

"I can't live this charade anymore," Sam said quietly. "Whether Roxana accepts my proposal or not, I want a divorce."

And he walked out.

⋯⋄⋯

"Wake up."

Megan stirred fitfully, restlessly, dragged out of an exhausted sleep by Zach Mason's warm, large hands gently shaking her shoulders. As her senses struggled toward consciousness, she felt overwhelmed by the sudden rush of feeling, her mind and her body mingling pain and pleasure in an extraordinary way. The wretched ache in her muscles, the sharp pain of her left foot, the hunger now raging in her empty stomach, were all balanced by the recollection of last night. Just remembering it brought a new softness to her groin, a joyful light-headedness that had nothing to do with being half starved. Megan's first conscious thought, embarrassingly enough, was that she hoped she looked OK for Zach.

How's *that* for shallow, she chided herself, as she opened her eyes to look up at him.

"Hey, sweetheart," Mason said gently. "Sorry to do this to you, but we really have to get going now."

She groaned. "I can't have had more than an hour's sleep."

Barely ten minutes after they'd finished making love, the noisy roar of a helicopter, spotlight blazing through the towering trees, had swept past their area of the forest and continued to make passes throughout the night. Zach had left the makeshift hut to try and attract attention, waving clothing, whatever, but he just couldn't get seen. The thick jade canopy of branches and leaves above them prevented any real chance of the searchlight finding them. About three Zach gave up and came back to take Megan in his arms, holding her and kissing her until she blacked into unconsciousness just before dawn.

Mason hadn't slept. One good thing about being a rock star, he'd had plenty of practice at that. Once he was sure Megan was finally out, he slipped away from her, checking out their immediate surroundings and looking for food. He reckoned they would need some fuel if they were ever going to make it out of here; that broken ankle was looking bad. He wouldn't let her continue to drag it around. Zach thought Megan was in more pain than she was letting on.

He'd looked at her tenderly when he got back, curled up where he'd left her, blond fringe curling incongruously over that cute forehead with its thick, dark brows, her soft lips half open in sleep, her muscled arm flung awkwardly over the heavy, beautiful breasts that had responded so superbly to him last night. Zach felt such a surge of protectiveness he was short of breath. He marveled at himself. He, Zach Mason, the rock icon who'd fucked a million groupies and turned down ten million more, who'd had his pick of starlets and models for the last five years, he'd finally fallen. Poleaxed by this embarrassed, clever, gauche, determined, idealistic little bunch of contradictions. Pretty, but no more than that. Feisty. Naive. Brave. His Megan.

Great time to pick out your true love, Mason, he told himself. Starving and stranded in the middle of the fucking jungle.

"You had at least an hour and a quarter," he teased her. "Stop whining and get your ass in gear. I reckon we'll be out of here by sundown."

Megan lifted a cynical eyebrow. "Right!"

"At least we know they're looking for us."

"That's true." She levered herself up, reaching for her shirt where they'd left it on the floor of the hut. "What do you have there?"

"Room service," Mason said cheerfully, tipping his findings onto a palm leaf in front of her. He'd managed to find one wild pineapple, growing in a crack in the granite glacis boulders that thrust through the forest floor all around them, a couple of leaves that his nose told him were cinnamon, and an armful of small pinkish-white fruits, the size of apples, that covered a grove of bushes to their left.

They looked at this harvest doubtfully.

"Call yourself a hunter-gatherer? Pathetic." Megan grinned.

"I blame women's rights. I've been robbed of my natural instincts," Zach said, carefully peeling the pineapple. He handed Megan a white sphere. "So is this poisonous?"

"Only one way to find out," she said, and before Zach could stop her, took a large bite. The flesh tasted like damp cotton wool. She devoured it.

"Coco plum," Megan told him. "Tasteless but harmless."

They ate in silence for a few minutes, Megan trying to slip most of her share toward Zach and Zach refusing to allow it. The fruit sugars weren't much, but on their empty stomachs they provided a surge of energy, and as soon as Mason had swallowed the last fragment of coco plum core he lifted Megan to her feet and ducked under her legs.

"What the hell are you doing?" Megan shrieked, clutching his shoulders. "I've got my crutches, Zach! Put me down!"

"No," Mason told her firmly, getting a restraining grip on her calves. "I'm not letting you walk. Shut *up*, this is nonnegotiable, OK?"

"But I'll slow you down," Megan protested. She tried to be nonchalant, but her eyes were brimming up with tears. She dashed a hand quickly across her face. "I'm serious. Only one of us has to . . . I mean, it'd be better if you went for help and left me, came back for me . . ."

"Get this straight," Zach said, taking a deep breath and walking forward, squaring his shoulders under her weight. "I'm not leaving you. Not ever. We're in this together, live or die, for better, for worse. All that stuff. Anyway, you're as light as a feather. Consider it an extended piggyback ride. You can navigate."

"I love you," Megan whispered.

His hands tightened on her legs.

"Let's get out of here, OK? You can go all mushy on me later," Zach said firmly, but as he strode carefully forward, his heart was singing.

It took Sam over an hour to make it to Roxana's front door, plowing the Maserati first through the rabid pack of journalists, camera crews, photographers, and gawking sightseers that crowded the road leading up to her villa, and then past the LAPD roadblocks that by this time lay seven layers thick. Eventually he managed to convince the sergeant in charge that he *was* Sam Kendrick of SKI by calling up Troy Savage, the guy's favorite soap star and an SKI client, on his car phone, and having him verify it. Thank

God for starstruck cops, Sam thought, as he swung the silver car into Roxana's drive, got out, and locked it. He glanced up at the villa. Every shutter was lowered, every curtain closed. Yeah, well. That didn't surprise him.

Kendrick felt compassion overwhelm him as he walked past the uniformed men on the door and pressed the buzzer on her entry phone. His poor baby. What she must be feeling today, he could only begin to guess at. He'd seen clients go through scandals, but never anything as bad as this. Only Jackson and Madonna had it as bad as this. And neither of *them* had been exposed as a teenage madam, running the most exclusive call girl service in Paris at the age of sixteen. He still couldn't believe it. There were so many pieces of the puzzle that didn't make sense: An American girl, hooking in France at fourteen, graduates to brothelkeeper at sixteen, makes enough money by eighteen to buy herself a whole new identity and a new life—enrolls at a Catholic convent school in San Francisco. Hits the model agencies the day she graduates, and the rest is history. But why France? How had she done this? And why? His Roxana, his shy and fragile girl? Was it possible? But it had happened. He'd seen the pictures, watched the news. He knew it was true.

I didn't know Isabelle and I didn't know Roxana, either, Sam thought, bewildered, as he stood there. All the time I was such a mogul, such a player, and I thought I read everybody like a book. But the people closest to me were the ones I couldn't see. And Florescu tells me David Tauber was working behind my back all the time . . . *Tauber*, who I thought was so smart, such a killer. I guess I was right. He'd have killed me, if he could.

The anger rose in him, thick and blood-red, and it was almost a relief. At least one emotion was clear. Once the little prick got back to LA Sam was going to smash him.

It was my own fault for not noticing, Sam berated himself. But I'd have seen it eventually. On the set I was distracted, couldn't think about anything except Roxana . . .

"Who is it?"

Her voice on the speaker was cautious and muted.

"Roxana, baby. Let me in. It's Sam," he said.

There was a long pause. He could hear the crackle of static through the metal grille.

"It's Sam Kendrick, sweetheart. Let me in," he repeated.

Finally, he heard a click as she released the lock. Sam pushed the door open and walked into the house, shutting it carefully behind him.

"Roxana?" he called.

She was nowhere to be seen. He could hear the constant sound of phones ringing and the babble of different voices, angry voices, as four separate answering machines took messages. Through the door to the home office Kendrick saw the lights on her fax machines glowing red, as sheets of paper inched slowly out of the tops of the machines and crashed onto the floor.

"I'm in the bathroom," Roxana called. Her voice was flat and strained, hoarse, as if she'd been crying. Sam raced upstairs to the bathroom, that sanctuary of polished wood and brass and cool marble, a place where he'd made love to her so many times he'd lost count. She was sitting on the floor, wrapped in a voluminous white toweling robe, her legs crossed, her eyes glazed, seemingly staring into space.

"Roxana," he murmured, and then she looked up at him, her liquid brown eyes narrowed with such vicious hatred that he took a step backward.

"You took everything," she said bleakly. "Everything. Bob Alton was so pleased to be able to tell me I was fired. Unique won't represent me. Elite and Ford and Models One wouldn't take my call. Jackson Cosmetics canceled the contract—forty million dollars, Sam. And no other house will use me. I can't work. My *Vogue* cover for next month is going to Christy now." She took a breath, and continued: "Jordan won't talk to me. She wouldn't accept a call. Neither would Susie Metcalf or any of those society bitches. I'm dead, Sam. You took everything."

"It wasn't me, sweetheart," he said, inwardly recoiling at the poison in her gaze. "It was Isabelle. And I told her I wanted a divorce, I wanted to marry you."

"It was *your wife*. It was because of *you*," Roxana hissed, her gaze still filled with venom. "*She* did this, she led them to me. But you don't know what it was like, none of you! *None of you!*"

Her voice rose to a banshee wail, and she started to weep, hot, blinding tears coursing down her cheeks. Sam took a step toward her but Roxana lashed out at him, wildly, like a madwoman, her long fingernails slicing through the cloth of his pants.

"Get the fuck away from me! Don't touch me!" she screamed, and then, as he watched in horror, she started to tear at her hair, ripping strands of it from her head, rocking backward and forward in a violent fit of grief. Kendrick lunged forward and caught her wrists, trapping them, forcing her to be still.

"Roxana! Roxana!" he said, and was shocked to hear the tears choking his own voice, he was so distressed at the sight of her anguish. "Whatever it is, you can tell me. You can trust me. I love you, whatever you did. I don't *care* what you did. I love you, don't you understand that?"

She froze, staring at him, her eyes suddenly calmer, flatter. It was as if the hatred had vanished, to be replaced by . . . what? What is she feeling? Sam wondered uneasily. He didn't understand the strange look on her face. She seemed to be . . . *laughing at him* . . .

"You are so fucking dumb, you know that?" Roxana said, her voice suddenly subdued, filled with scorn, mocking him. "I was using you, Sam. For the picture, so that you wouldn't stop me wrecking the shoot. So that you would help me fire Megan Silver. For whatever you could do for me. And because of the way you spoke to me at Isabelle's party, I was going to break your heart as soon as it was over. Why do you think I told Jordan? I *wanted* her to tell everybody else. I wanted to show the world the great Sam Kendrick was just another puppet dancing on my strings."

Dazed, Sam released her wrists, stumbling backward, numb from the malice of her tone.

"Your wife did this. You mean nothing to me. *Nothing.*" Roxana's brown eyes held nothing but contempt. "I despise you, Sam. Get the fuck out of my house."

Sam turned blindly around and walked down the stairs, his heart so full of pain it felt like a thick stone in his chest. He said nothing to the policemen standing around his car, who looked at him curiously as he came out. He couldn't speak. For the first time since he was a boy, Sam Kendrick was fighting back tears.

chapter 34

Eleanor Marshall walked quickly up the sunlit steps of Victoria Hospital, followed by Fred Florescu, her agitation betraying her nerves. Zach Mason and Megan Silver had been found alive, shortly after sunrise, by a guide trekking through the Anse Jasmin estate in the northernmost part of the jungle. He had fetched help and had the two Americans taken to the nearest village, where somebody called an ambulance. Beyond that she knew very little.

"Ms. Marshall and Mr. Florescu," Eleanor said to the thickset woman staffing the reception desk. "We've come to see the two people that were found in the mist forest this morning. Are they OK?"

The receptionist checked the names on a printed sheet in front of her and nodded, giving them a warm smile. "You want rooms twelve an' thirteen, jus' down the corridor there." She pointed straight ahead of her. "The gentleman told us to call Mr. Florescu here. You with him?"

"Yes. Thanks," Eleanor replied, striding down the corridor the woman had shown them.

"Jesus, do you think they're all right?" Florescu asked, his face clouded.

"We know they're alive," Eleanor said, checking the door numbers.

"Yeah. But it was a long way to fall," the director said.

They looked at each other, neither wanting to say it. What if either of the kids had cracked their head open, or broken their neck? What if they were paralyzed? Or if they'd cut themselves open and the wounds had become gangrenous?

"Twelve," Eleanor said, coming to a stop outside a closed blue door. There was no sound from inside the room. She hesitated.

"We have to see them," Fred Florescu told her softly.

Eleanor nodded, her heart crashing against her chest.

What if they *are* paralyzed? she thought miserably. It was my fault that they were filming in a monsoon. I didn't double-check my own location reports because I was so wrapped up in Jordan Goldman's baby. If I'd have been doing my job, Jake Keller would never have got away with it. And this would never have happened.

Florescu glanced at Eleanor Marshall, standing there twisting her hands, her face white as chalk. He was frightened too; Zach and Megan were such talented kids, both of them, and so young, and who knew what the hell had happened to them out there . . .

He slowly twisted the handle and opened the door.

Zach Mason was sitting up in bed, an empty cereal bowl stacked on the table behind him, sipping from a long, tall glass of milk, fresh dressings wrapped around his bare chest. Megan Silver, in a pair of green hospital pajamas and a dressing gown, was lounging in a spartan easy chair beside him, eating a delicious-smelling croissant, and looking at a copy of the *Herald Tribune*, her right foot in a tartan slipper and her left foot bandaged up in a splint. Both of them looked up, smiling, as Fred and Eleanor walked into the room.

"Hey, guys, it's good to see you," Zach Mason said.

"Are you OK?" Florescu asked, hardly daring to believe his eyes.

"We were a little hungry, but we're fine now," Zach told him, adding, "I sure as hell hope those scenery shots were worth it."

Eleanor felt weak-kneed with relief.

"Eleanor! What are you doing here?" Megan asked her.

"Looking for you," the older woman said.

"Oh yeah? We wondered if all those helicopters last night were something to do with us," Megan said. She held up the paper she was reading. "So what's the story with Roxana Felix?"

❖

By the time the cab drew up to her house Eleanor was feeling jet-lagged and exhausted. She tipped the guy a twenty and carried her small Louis Vuitton case into the porch, reaching into her purse for the keys. Her fingers fumbled around for a minute before she found them and managed to let herself in; she was so tired she tried to unlock the front entrance with the back-door key.

I'll take a nap for a couple of hours before I head back to the studio, Eleanor told herself. I'm no use to Tom or anyone else in this state.

It had been a sleepless night, all coffee and doughnuts in a suite at the Meridien, supervising the air searches and taking phone call after phone call of reports—somebody had found a strip of cloth from Mason's shirt, another man saying he'd seen footprints—but nothing of substance, and despite her best efforts, Eleanor had slumped into unconsciousness toward dawn. When the phone shrilled by her bedside to say they'd been found, she'd been asleep for barely three hours. The relief at knowing Zach and Megan were alive and almost completely unharmed had carried her through the rest of the morning, as she paid off the Seychellois involved in the search, packed her handful of clothes, and booked herself on the first flight off the islands. But that euphoria couldn't last forever, and when the jet had taxied off the runway and soared into the clear blue skies above the Indian Ocean, Eleanor Marshall had had to face the rest of her problems.

Tom Goldman's call had come through at eight P.M. the night before— eight A.M. in Los Angeles. Roxana Felix was the newest front-runner in the worldwide bad-girl stakes—a prostitution scandal that had completely buried her career in a matter of hours. And he wasn't exaggerating; a flick of the remote control and CNN confirmed everything to her, right there and then in her hotel room.

"The markets think this will kill the movie," Goldman had told her, his voice terse and pressured. "They know it was a costly flick. They know we're in desperate need of a hit."

"What's happening to the stock?"

Goldman laughed caustically. "Are you kidding? What stock? It's going downhill faster than an avalanche! At this rate the SEC's gonna suspend trading, before it hits zero."

"Christ," Eleanor muttered. "I've got about two million dollars' worth of stock!"

"Well, now you have about forty thousand dollars' worth. If it's any consolation, I've got a lot more than that. Do you want me to call your broker and give him your number there? Perhaps you could still off-load some of it."

"No. No, thanks," she replied. *Two million dollars, up in smoke!* "I'm the president, I don't want to be seen to be dumping stock in my own company."

On the other side of the world, Tom Goldman smiled, feeling a strong rush of affection for her.

"You know, I said exactly the same thing."

"Great minds think alike," Eleanor told him.

"And fools seldom differ."

She chuckled. "You've got me. Look, just hold on, OK? The second I know what's happened to Zach and Megan I'll be on my way home. We'll figure something out."

"Will we?" Tom sounded skeptical. "I called so you'd know what was happening, Eleanor. I don't think I'll be here when you get back. I have sixteen messages in front of me from assorted board members, and I don't think they want to chat to me about the weather."

"No way, Tom. You're not going anywhere. They can't fire you for something Roxana Felix did, and if they try, you just pull the same number on them I pulled on you before. Call your personal lawyer and check your contract. Tell them you'll sue. I'm sure they won't want any more scandal right now."

A pause, then: "You could be right."

"You *know* I'm right. And you'd have thought of that yourself given time," Eleanor said. "Tell them all to hold on to their stock. If it's plunged that low, there's no point in selling now anyway, right?"

"That's true. Maybe we should look on the bright side—we've got nowhere to go at this point except up."

"That's my boy," Eleanor said. She glanced down and noticed that she had her hands on her stomach, covering her womb. Somehow, without having even consciously considered it, she knew she was going to tell Tom the truth about this child when she got home. What would he say? And should she tell Paul? What would be best for her baby? All the anxieties pressed around her, crowding her, crushing her. Eleanor felt as if she were being swept along in the most fearsome current, swimming with all her might against the flow, fighting not to give in, not to be felled by each fresh disaster. It was her baby that gave her the strength, the deep, new knowledge of what was really important. They could take away her reputation, her wealth, and her job, but they couldn't take that. And she was going to fight like hell before they took *anything*.

"And there's another silver lining you haven't thought of," she added. "Now that the stock's dropped through the floor, Jake Keller has nothing left to threaten you with. So you might as well sack him this morning."

"Don't you want to wait until you get home?"

"No," Eleanor told him. "Sam Kendrick's already recalled David Tauber. I think you should just sack him now—no reference, no compensation. Make it as public as you can. Humiliate the son of a bitch."

"You got it," Goldman told her, hanging up.

So now she was back, Eleanor thought wearily. Back to a company in crisis, a media frenzy, an exposed leading lady, and . . .

"Where the hell have you been?"

Paul stood in the doorway of their bedroom, his arms folded, glaring at her. He was wearing a dark blue suit and smelled of too much aftershave. He had a brightly patterned tie on, and his hair was meticulously parted. She hated this side of him; the peacock, the dandy. It seemed too vain, almost effeminate. Tom Goldman wouldn't be seen dead in that outfit, Eleanor told herself.

"You know where I've been, Paul. I called and left messages here and at your office."

"You went halfway around the world to supervise some pathetic little rescue attempt," he said angrily. "Who do you think you are? Rambo?"

"Don't be stupid, Paul. Two of our people were missing and in danger."

"So you had to go out there, I suppose."

She was too tired for this.

"That's right, I did. Because it wasn't the kind of job I like to delegate. Now if you'll excuse me, I'm worn out and I need to get some sleep."

Paul didn't move.

"Do you realize you missed days thirteen, fourteen, and fifteen of your menstrual cycle, Eleanor?" he demanded furiously. "You *owed* it to me to be here."

She bit her lip to stop herself from screaming out the truth. If he had to know, it wasn't going to be like this, not blurted out in the middle of a quarrel.

"Well, I owed it to Zach and Megan to try and save their lives," she said, as calmly as she could. "Let's talk later, OK? This isn't a good time. I'm really tired."

"*I'm* tired!" Paul snapped petulantly. "Tired of how lightly you take this marriage! Have you *heard* about Roxana Felix?"

"Yes, I—"

He wasn't listening. "Do you realize how much crap I had to take in the office? All the analysts sniggering behind their desks. People going quiet when I walked past them. Don't you do *checks* on people before you hire them?"

"She wasn't an employee. She was an actress," Eleanor said, trying to keep her temper in check. "And Artemis is a motion picture studio, not the federal government. We don't tend to call in the FBI."

"Artemis *was* a motion picture studio, I think you mean." There was a curious note of satisfaction in her husband's voice. "The stock's plunged. It almost hit the one-day floor for losses, Eleanor. You've lost millions."

Eleanor took note of the "you."

"Well, at least I still have you to put bread on the table," she said sarcastically.

"This is no time for jokes!" Paul Halfin almost screamed. He was puce with indignation. "While you were playing around in some goddamn tropical island, your studio was crumbling! And your stock became worthless! I'll bet you didn't even manage to lose it in time! Don't you understand what this does to our reputation?"

"You mean, now I'm no longer the respectable studio president you married?" Eleanor asked him very quietly.

"Yes!" Paul said. It was a screech.

"Do you love me, Paul?"

He took a breath, backed down. "Of course I love you. But this behavior can't continue."

Eleanor nodded.

"You're right. I want a divorce."

"You can't be serious." He looked at her with disbelief. "*You* want to divorce *me*? Don't you understand that you're history in this town? You've lost your job and you've lost your money! What else do you have?"

"My pride," Eleanor told him simply.

Then, as Paul stared after her in blank astonishment, she picked up her case, walked into the guest bedroom, and bolted the door behind her.

⋰⋱

Tom Goldman had looked better. His skin was sallow from a lack of sleep, his eyes had dark circles under them, and he hadn't had time to shave. He'd been under pressure before in his life, but never had it been anything like this. The phone was ringing off the hook: distributors angrily demanding to know if the studio was bankrupt; directors, producers, and actors all frantic about their Artemis projects; media hacks clever enough to fool his assistants and get through; agents hysterically claiming that their clients had "senior debt" if the company went under; and distraught stockholders who screamed abuse. His neck was aching from the number of calls he had taken, and they never seemed to stop, six, seven callers holding at a time. Marcia had brought him in a pizza at lunchtime but he hadn't been able to stop talking long enough to eat it, and by four P.M. it was still sitting on his desk.

Eleanor stood in the doorway to Goldman's office, watching her boss pronounce soothing reassurances into his handset, his neck lolling at an exhausted angle against the headrest of his chair, his eyes closed as if in pain.

"I couldn't buzz him to tell him you were here, Ms. Marshall," Marcia Hearn said tearfully. "I couldn't get through. All his lines have calls holding on them."

"That's fine, Marcia. Forget it," Eleanor said gently. The secretary looked completely stressed out and shaken up; she was twisting her hands compulsively and she looked as though she might be about to burst out crying any second. On her desk, behind them, four different phone lines were ringing insistently and the fax machine was pouring out letters, old faxes spilling slowly over the edge of the containment tray and cascading onto the floor, mingling with a white and gray pool of paper. Marcia was a fanatically neat woman, and Eleanor realized with a start that she hadn't even had time to pick up the faxes.

"OK. Here's what we're going to do," she told her. "You switch all incoming calls to Mr. Goldman's answering machine. As of now, he's in a meeting and can't be disturbed."

Marcia looked doubtfully toward Tom, sitting at his desk with his eyes closed. "But—"

"He's in a meeting with *me*," Eleanor said firmly. "Senior management only. And you take the rest of the day off, Marcia. That's an order."

"Yes, Ms. Marshall," she said gratefully, and scurried back to her desk.

Eleanor closed Tom's door quietly, then tiptoed up to his desk, grabbed the receiver out of his hands, said, "He'll call you back," and hung up.

"Eleanor!" Goldman said, not believing his eyes. "What are you doing here? I didn't expect you until tomorrow!"

"Gee, everybody seems so pleased to see me," Eleanor said dryly.

"I am pleased to see you. You have no idea how much," Goldman said, giving her a weak smile.

"Has it been bad?"

He raised an eyebrow. "I'm not even going to bother replying to that."

"I told Marcia to take the phones off the hook," Eleanor told him. "We need to talk."

"Want some cold, greasy pizza?" Tom asked her, ripping off an unappetizing slice and stuffing it in his mouth.

"You tempt me, but no. Did you speak to the board?"

Goldman nodded. "Yeah. Told them what you said. They hated it, but they played ball. Present management stays in place for the time being, and they'll do what they can with the banks to shore up the stock. I guess they didn't have a choice; it was that or lose their whole investment."

Eleanor paced around the room, thinking fast. "Good. Have you spoken to Roxana Felix?"

"Left a message. No reply. No surprises there," Goldman said, thinking how good Eleanor looked. Even in the midst of complete and total disaster, she managed to appear poised, calm, and elegant. She was wearing the scarlet Donna Karan suit she'd had on for her confrontation with him a few days ago; bold, confident color and meticulous tailoring, it accentuated her slim figure and it looked terrific.

She's got such style. Such grace under pressure, Goldman thought, and tried not to dwell on the image of his wife last night—weeping uncontrollably, shrieking with fury that he wouldn't sell his stock, mascara running down her heavily made up face, throwing a tantrum like a spoiled brat. *How could you do this to me?* As if he had ruined himself and destroyed his career purposefully to spite her. And all she could think about was her stupid slave auction, screaming at him that now nobody would come.

"What about Sam?"

"Sam called to say SKI didn't represent her anymore."

"That's not like Sam, to run out on a client."

"He wouldn't discuss it with me. He sounded pretty upset, actually," Tom said. "But maybe that's because he's getting a divorce."

"Sam, too?"

"What?"

She shook her head. "I'll tell you later. First, I want to tell you what I want to do."

Goldman leaned back, smiling. "Go ahead. You're the only person around here with any fight left in you, Eleanor, I swear. I don't know what happened to you last week, but I sure as hell wish it would happen to me."

"I want to speak to Roxana Felix and persuade her to come back and finish the movie."

"You are certifiably insane," Goldman said amiably.

"Hear me out, Tom. Zach and Megan are in good health and the doctors told me he could be back on the set in a day or so. I had Fred continually shooting while we were looking for them. I've seen some of the rough cuts, Tom. *Triple Feature* is an incredible movie and production is almost complete. They'd only need Roxana for a week or so to finish up, and you know Florescu edits fast." She held up a hand. "No, let me finish, please. I know what you're going to say; Roxana won't do it, and even if she does, nobody will want to distribute."

"Right."

"Wrong. I'm sure I can persuade Roxana to come back to the set. She has nothing to lose, and precisely because she *was* such a class A bitch, she won't want the world to see her running away with her tail between her legs. I want to drive over there and speak with her tonight. And as for the distributors—once everybody's calmed down, people will go *crazy* to book this film. We're getting a billion dollars' worth of free publicity right now."

"Even if you're right about Roxana, I'm telling you, Eleanor, the chains don't want to do business with a bankrupt company. And if the stock crashes—"

She made an impatient movement with her hands. "The stock won't crash. In a day or two people will realize that we have a certain bottom-line value for our library and our real estate."

"True."

"And the only way they can write us off is if *we* write off *Triple Feature*. But I won't do that." Eleanor walked toward her old friend, her eyes bright with passion, and put her hands on the front of his desk, leaning toward him. "Tom, look. *We have nothing to lose.* Everything has already gone up in smoke—our careers, our bank balances, everything. But I want *something* to come out of the time I was president of a studio. I want to be able to point to this film and say I helped do that. I got into this business fifteen years ago to make pictures, Tom. And *Triple Feature* is a truly wonderful picture.

I believed in it when I first got the script, and I still do. If it's a success, we win. If it isn't—we have nothing left to lose. But I have to finish it. This is my movie."

Tom Goldman looked at Eleanor. There were tears in her eyes.

"Go talk to Roxana," he said softly. "I'll call my lawyers again. We'll make your movie before we quit."

"Thank you." It was all she could say. "Thank you, Tom."

Goldman reached forward, closing his hand over hers.

"We started together, and I guess we're gonna end together. I'm just sorry it had to be this way."

"Me, too," Eleanor whispered, briefly closing her eyes.

She had to say it now, she knew that. Tom had a right to know, and she had to tell him. If she waited for the right moment, she'd wait forever. There was no good time. She pulled her hands away. "I have to tell you something else, Tom. I'm getting a divorce. And I'm pregnant."

He gazed at her, puzzled. "You are? I don't understand. What does Paul say about it?"

"I don't know how to tell you this," she said. "But I always used a diaphragm with Paul. We didn't make love without protection until after the wedding. And I'm two and a half months pregnant."

"What are you saying?" Goldman whispered.

Eleanor gazed at him steadily.

"It's your baby, Tom," she said.

chapter 35

Roxana Felix opened the door to Eleanor Marshall and stared at her defiantly. It was six A.M., early enough for Eleanor's forest-green Lotus to crawl through the police roadblocks without attracting too much attention, and Eleanor had begged her for a meeting, leaving thirty-two messages in succession on the answer machine in Roxana's bedroom, until she'd finally picked up. There were no recriminations in Eleanor's voice, but Roxana wasn't fooled; the bitch had come to rave and shout and threaten. As if she cared. She had hit bottom, and there was no further to fall.

"Roxana. Thank you for seeing me," Eleanor said gently. "May I come in?"

She stood aside. "Be my guest. Come in, say what you want to, and leave. I just want to get this over with."

"Don't you disconnect any of the phones?" Eleanor asked, listening to the constant jangling echoing through the house. Roxana was dressed in a tailored Ralph Lauren pantsuit in royal-blue cotton, her long hair was swept into a chignon, and she was fully made up, a soft berry gloss on her beautiful lips and a sweep of damson blusher accentuating her razor-sharp cheekbones. She had even clipped on a small pair of gold earrings. She was wearing a subtle, sensuous perfume. She looked every inch as stunning as the last time Eleanor had seen her, as if she had just stepped blithely off another runway.

I was right about her, Eleanor thought. Roxana won't show me any weakness, she'd die first. She wants me to tell the world that she couldn't care less. She has her pride.

Yesterday's scene with Paul flashed back into her mind. Maybe, in the end, pride was all any woman had to cling to.

"What for? I'm taking messages," Roxana said. "People can say whatever they like. I'm not running from them."

"That's what I hoped you would say." Eleanor walked into the kitchen. "Can I make us some coffee? I have a proposal for you."

"If you must," Roxana said ungraciously. "I hope this isn't going to take long, Eleanor. If it's about your stock—too bad. There's nothing I can do. I didn't plan this. And if you want me to sign some statement saying that you had no knowledge of my past when you cast me, have it messengered over. I have no problem with that. I just want you to leave me alone. And if you came here for more information"—her lips tightened—"you should ask Isabelle Kendrick. She was the one who did this. You can blame your company collapse on her."

"None of the above," Eleanor said, spooning French Vanilla ground into the percolator. *Isabelle Kendrick!* Because Roxana had been sleeping . . . with *Sam*? "Did you know Sam Kendrick is getting divorced?" she asked casually.

Roxana shook her head.

"I think you'll find he decided to stay with his wife."

"No. I spoke to Sam earlier this morning," Eleanor said. "He's moved into the Bel-Air. He seems really upset."

"Yeah? There's a lot of that going around," Roxana replied, but Eleanor thought she detected a touch of confusion beneath the flippancy.

"Roxana. Listen to me," Eleanor Marshall began. Her heart was thumping against her chest; she *had* to convince this girl, she just had to. It would require a huge act of courage on Roxana's part, even a little selflessness, not qualities most people would associate with her right now. But Eleanor had to back her instincts, she knew that. She had given everything she had fighting for this movie. She wasn't about to give up now. "I didn't come over here today to shout at you, or demand informnation, or to get you to sign something. What happened to our stock was not your fault. Nobody said you had to confess your sins to us before you got to act in our movie. But I am here to ask for your help."

Roxana leaned back against the door, watching her with narrowed eyes. She's learned to trust nobody, Eleanor thought. Why? What happened to her, all those years ago?

"What do you want?" Roxana asked warily.

"I want you to go back out to Mahé and shoot the end of *Triple Feature.*"

She held her breath. There, it was out. This was the moment of truth; if Roxana wanted to shriek, or yell, or order her out of the house, it was all over.

There was a moment's silence.

"Why?" Roxana asked, looking at her steadily.

"Because if we get this thing finished, it's going to be an incredible movie. Fred Florescu showed me some of the footage. When you were actually acting, Roxana, and not trying to screw up everybody else's performance, you were brilliant. Really talented. And in the love scenes with Zach, you just set the screen on fire. I think if we ever get this film out to the theaters, and people can see it, the world will agree with me."

"And why should I do this?"

"Do it for yourself," Eleanor said. "I could tell you to do it for me, or Zach, or Fred, but I won't. You should understand that I know about your cooperation with David Tauber and Jake Keller, and I really don't care. That's all in the past. The only thing that matters to me is this movie, getting it completed and released, and for that I know I need you. But what you get out of this is some self-respect. You told me when I arrived that you weren't going to run from anybody. So don't! Make this movie! You wanted the world to see you as an actress, you came to LA, you forced us to cast you—God knows what you did, but you end up cast—"

Roxana gave her the briefest flicker of a smile.

"—and you made most of a great movie. They all expect you to crawl away and die, Roxana. Now, I'm not going to stand here and tell you that what you did was OK. It wasn't. And if that's what you have to hear, I'll get out of your house right now, because I won't say it. But I *will* tell you that I know we don't know the whole story. You were a fourteen-year-old American girl, so why were you in Paris? And how does a teenage hooker get to run an upmarket brothel in two years? It doesn't make sense. But what I do get from your story is a fierce need for independence—you came back to the States, you took your final year of high school privately, you got a new identity and a new career, and then you climbed higher in that field than anybody had done before. I'm not asking you to tell me anything, Roxana. I don't judge you, because I don't know you. But what I am asking you is to show them a little of that independence now. You couldn't be broken before; don't let this break you now."

Roxana Felix burst into tears.

"Hey," Eleanor moved forward and took the sobbing girl in her arms, stroking her hair, cradling her as she wept. "It's all right now, honey. It's going to be all right."

❖

It was night over Mahé by the time they arrived, the stars glittering above the Anse Polite beach, dancing around a huge harvest moon, hanging low and orange in the clear sky. The taxi drove straight past the hotel and pulled up two miles further along the shore, at an anonymous-looking oceanside diner which seemed to be closed. Eleanor paid the driver and helped Roxana out of the cab, checking the café for a single light in the downstairs window. It was on; that meant Florescu was waiting inside with Zach, Megan, Seth, Mary, Robert, Jack, and the rest of the cast.

"Are you sure you want to do this?" she asked. "You know you don't have to tell them anything. I can go up there and simply announce that you have returned to complete the film. Nobody will harass you. I can talk to Fred and make sure of that."

Roxana shook her head, her long black hair shining in the moonlight.

"No. I don't want to hide this anymore. If I can speak to those guys, maybe they'll understand the way you did, and they'll forgive me for the way I was before."

"You're a very brave woman," Eleanor told her.

"So are you," Roxana said simply.

Eleanor offered her her arm, and the two of them walked into the tiny shack together. The wooden door opened into a warm, sweet-smelling room, lit by three oil lamps. Fred and the others were arranged around a long trestle table, eating something that smelled like spiced lobster, and drinking long glasses of the local *bacca* sugarcane liquor. The conversation was loud and raucous, but as soon as they walked into the room, it went totally quiet. Eleanor felt Roxana stiffen a little beside her; thirty pairs of eyes were staring at her in complete shock.

"Ladies and gentlemen," Eleanor said. "I asked Fred to book this place for your meal tonight because I wanted someplace private for Roxana to speak to you. I realize this may come as a surprise, but Roxana has decided that she wants to come back out here and finish off this movie. You will have read the recent stories about her in the press. They are true, but Roxana has something to add to them. It took great strength for her to decide to tell you the things she is about to say. I want you to listen to her."

She squeezed Roxana's hand, and then walked across to the table and sat down next to Fred Florescu.

Roxana took a deep breath as she stood there in the soft light of the lamps, looking at the actors she'd been screwing over, as they sat in front of her, watching her curiously. There was no sympathy in their faces, just a neutral interest.

But I'm not asking them for sympathy, she told herself. Just understanding.

"My name *is* Roxana Felix," she said. "Legally. I had it changed by deed poll when I was nineteen years old. But I was born Heather Piper in Kansas City, twenty-four years ago. My father worked in construction and my mother had a part-time job working in the local supermarket checkout. We were poor, but I don't remember much about it. I was four when they were killed in a car crash. They didn't leave much, so I wound up in an orphanage, because my mama had no relatives, and my father's brother didn't want me." Her voice was dry, emotionless. "I stayed in that home until I was eleven. Then I was adopted, by a retired judge named Eli Woods and his wife. It's unusual for kids to get adopted that late, you understand. Most couples want babies. But I was real pretty by the time I was eleven, and I soon realized why the judge had chosen me. Two days before my twelfth birthday, Eli came into the bathroom when I was drying myself. That night he came into my bedroom and raped me." She paused, swallowed hard, and then continued. "He raped me for two years, and he told me all the things they all say—nobody will believe you, you led me on, it's your fault. I told his wife, and she slapped me around the face and called me a good-for-nothing welfare slut and a dirty little liar. A year later, when I was thirteen, I walked into town and spoke to a police officer. He said he would file a complaint. But that evening, Eli came to room and he beat me until he drew blood. Then he broke my little finger." The tears were coming now, she couldn't stop them; they rolled out and trickled down her cheeks, and she couldn't even see the faces of her small audience, staring at her, horrified. She plowed on. "As soon as it was healed, I stole his credit cards and his wallet and his wife's jewels, pawned them, took the money, and skipped town. I took my passport and booked a one-way ticket to Paris; told them Judge Woods was sending me on an educational trip. I don't know why I picked Paris. It just seemed so far away, and I was very good at French. He didn't speak French. Maybe I thought he'd have trouble tracking me down. So, I got there, and I started hooking. I hated myself, and I was good at sex, and it seemed like the fastest way to make a lot of money. Eli had power back home because of his money. And I didn't trust anybody, I wanted enough cash of my own. I guess I was better-looking, more promiscuous than the other girls, because I made a lot of money very fast. I was off the streets in two months, graduated to a call girl serving rich businessmen, discreetly, at fancy hotels. That's where I met a couple of other girls doing the same thing. One of them wanted to leave her pimp, because he'd been hitting her. I told her she should come and work for me, because I'd never hit her. I was only fifteen, but I looked older. I was already cold, hard, ruthless—the person you're used to. By the time I was sixteen, I'd rented my own small house for my girls on the Champs Élysées. We were successful; a lot of the call girls working for me became models, got new names, married out of the life. I thought I could do that; I was eighteen years old, and I had nearly a million dollars in savings and deposit bonds. A real entrepreneur." She stifled a sob. "So, I got a new passport, moved to California, picked the most conservative private school I could find—a Catholic convent—and contacted the model agencies. A scout had already tried to sign me in France, but I wanted to start fresh, back home, where nobody knew me. I wanted to be the biggest, richest, most famous woman in the whole world. I was determined I'd never love anyone and never trust anyone, because nobody had ever loved me. And you know the rest. So, I've been a bitch to you, and I realize it. I'm not asking you guys for anything, I just want you to understand why, so we can finish this film. Because Eleanor persuaded me to do something with my life, so at least, when all this is over, I can walk away with my head held up."

Roxana sank onto the nearest chair and dashed her hand across her eyes, trying to brush a few of the tears away.

For a moment or two there was a stunned silence, the only noise in the dim room Roxana's soft weeping and the breaking waves on the beach outside. Finally Fred Florescu cleared his throat.

"Roxana, I can't pretend that we know what you went through. I don't think anybody who hasn't undergone the kind of horrors you endured could ever begin to imagine what that must have been like. But I know I speak for everybody in this room when I say that I totally admire your courage in being able to tell us what happened to you. However you behaved doesn't matter in the least. So you were a little cold, so what?—I think you had every right to be mistrustful. But I hope you'll trust me now, when I tell you that you are a truly fine actress, and you're somebody I'm proud to be making this movie with," he said gently, and the whole cast began to applaud.

⁘

The sun was sinking over Beverly Hills when Tom Goldman arrived home. He parked his car in the garage and sat slumped in the front seat, his eyes staring into space, wondering how in God's name he was going to explain this to Jordan. The loss of most of his fortune would be the first blow; he realized his wife had expensive tastes, and he was about to tell her that they had to cut back drastically. Sell this house, for example, her favorite toy. But Lisa Weintraub, his accountant, had been totally clear; he could no longer afford to service the four-million-dollar mortgage on his five-million-dollar house. So, goodbye Beverly Hills, hello Laurel Canyon. He could live with that, but the question was, could Jordan? And there would be no more of those goddamned stupid parties she seemed to live for, either. With his new net worth of a million and a half, which had to cover a new house and a new baby, there was no way he could go for the caviar dinners and the Chanel suits anymore. It was only after sitting down with Lisa and going through the household accounts that Tom realized just how much money Jordan had been spending on clothes. An original Chanel couture suit cost twenty thousand dollars a pop. *Twenty thousand dollars!* And Jordan owned *five!*

Now he was going to have to go in there and tell her it had to stop. Not only were the big spending days over forever, she was going to have to sell most of her jewelry. He'd spent over three quarters of a million on rocks for her since their marriage, and they needed the money. She was going to hate that. She was going to hate everything about this conversation.

Oh well, Goldman thought wearily. She has her baby on the way. Once it arrives, maybe she won't be interested in the social scene anymore—because we sure as hell aren't gonna be hiring a nanny now.

The baby. Body blow number two. He had to confess to his wife that he'd cheated on her, and that he was having another child by another woman.

Tom rubbed his fingers across his temple, feeling every second of his forty-five years. How in God's name had he screwed up his life this badly? he wondered helplessly. As long as he lived, he would never forget the torrent of emotions that had raged through him when Eleanor dropped her bombshell. Astonishment. Exhilaration, for a fraction of a second. And finally, the searing, overwhelming, hopeless waves of regret.

Seeing Eleanor so decisive, so calm, so controlled under pressure, had underscored a truth he now realized he had always known—he was in love with Eleanor Marshall, and he probably always had been, from the moment that bright, gawky graduate crashed into him outside the studio cafeteria fifteen years ago right up to that moment when she told him she was carrying his child. If he was honest, the appalling jealousy that had racked him at her wedding was the first real signal he was in trouble—Christ, had she ever looked so radiantly lovely as she did that day? Or was it before that? In New York, when he had found such total release in her arms, when he had sired the child that she had carried ever since? Too late, Goldman understood everything; the flame that Eleanor had borne for him in silence for so long, and the pain she must have gone through when Jordan turned up in the lobby of the Victrix; even at the time, he had been embarrassed that Eleanor had to hear it like that, but only now did he understand the full depths of what she had gone through. It explained her weakness, her loss of control at work when she returned to LA—weakness that Jake Keller had exploited.

The same weakness that Goldman was feeling right now.

What a tragedy that he had never seen what was right under his eyes, all the time. She had been his best friend, his protégé, his most trusted lieutenant. She had been the first person he would run to with a new idea, his sounding board, his best critic. He had tried to spend as much time as he could with her in and out of the office. He'd never confronted the root feelings behind his strong dislike of Paul Halfin, not until yesterday, not until it was too late.

Three months ago, he could simply have asked Jordan for a divorce. But not now. His wife was an adult—of sorts—and though he might have hurt her, it would have been better that way than trying to inch through a sham of a marriage. But all that had changed in the lobby of the Victrix. Because the child Jordan was bearing had to come first, whatever he wanted to do. He had conceived that baby in wedlock, and Tom Goldman knew he had a duty to this child. He had to stay with the baby's mother until such time as the child was old enough to understand—at fifteen or sixteen, say. He'd support Eleanor's baby, but he could only have one family. And he had married Jordan first.

Goldman got slowly out of his car and walked toward the house, thinking about his mother. Hannah Goldman had been dead now for seven years, but he knew she would tell him that this was the only choice. He had to stay until he had seen this child's bar or bat mitzvah.

But dear God, it was a terrible price to pay for his mistake.

He let himself in through the back door, punching their security code into the entry system. A flashing red light above the panel told him that Jordan was already home.

So what were you hoping for? Tom asked himself wryly. That she was out shopping on Rodeo? You're gonna have to do this eventually, so it might as well be now.

"Jordan!" Goldman called. "I'm home!"

"Oh, *really.*" His wife's Bostonian tones were dripping with acid. "Well, I'm in the drawing room. I hope you don't expect me to come to *you*, Thomas."

Here we go, Tom thought, walking through to their lavish reception room. It was an ornate fantasy of William Morris wallpaper and English Regency antiques; the decorator had charged him a small fortune for them, Goldman recalled. Well, possibly he'd get another quarter million from an auction of every goddamn antique in the place. Nothing but functional, twentieth-century American for the Goldmans now.

Jordan was sitting bolt upright on one of their chintz armchairs, her long blond hair clipped behind her head in a severe ponytail, wearing her pink Chanel suit and her long diamond drop earrings. He noticed that she had also put on her pearl and sapphire choker and the diamond and ruby Eternity ring he'd bought her to celebrate her pregnancy. She was obviously making a point. And from the way she was scowling at him, she was pretty mad already, before he'd even started.

"I hope you're about to tell me that you've changed your mind about that *horrid* stock," Jordan snapped petulantly. "It was *hell* at the health club this morning, you know. Everybody whispering and pointing." She pulled a small lace handkerchief out of her sleeve and dabbed at some nonexistent tears. "I can't take much more of this, Tom. How could you do this to me?"

"I met with Lisa Weintraub today," Goldman began. The quicker he came out with it, the better. "She told me that we've lost a lot of our money. Almost eight million dollars."

"*What?*" Jordan shrieked.

"We're going to have to sell the house, most of your jewelry, and auction off a lot of our effects. Lisa knows a good real estate broker who'll get us a discount on a new place; we can get something compact in Laurel Canyon or Pasadena for about half a million. That'll leave us a million in disposable capital, so we should be able to get by until I find another job."

"It's not true," Jordan whispered, shaking her head. "You're making this up to scare me."

"Jesus, Jordan. Don't be so childish. This is tough, but we'll pull through it. We're a family; we've got each other."

The words rang hollow in his ears.

"I'm going to stay at my job until our current movie is released; then I'll resign. And I won't easily be able to get another job in the industry, certainly not at the level I was at before, so I'm afraid all the socializing is going to have to go. We don't have the money for expensive parties, anyway—we're going to have to economize, honey. I'll need to cancel most of your credit cards and arrange a small allowance for you. And you realize that we certainly won't be able to hire a nanny now; so it'll just be you, me, and the baby," Tom concluded, trying to give her a smile.

"No! I won't do it!" Jordan shrieked. "You can't do this to me, Tom! I won't live like that!"

"We don't have a choice," Goldman answered, suppressing his anger. She was reacting like a spoiled teenager, even now, in the midst of this catastrophe, at the one time a husband might look to his wife for support.

But I don't have the right to be angry with her, Tom reminded himself, considering what I have to tell her next.

"Jordan, listen to me. There's something worse."

"Something *worse?*" Her angelic young face was pink with fury. "*Something worse?* You son of a bitch, what the hell could be worse than that? Don't you understand that you've *ruined my life?*"

"You remember when you flew up to the Victrix, in New York, to tell me about the baby? Jordan, I have something to confess to you." He swallowed. "I slept with Eleanor Marshall the night before—it was the first and only time—and yesterday she told me that she conceived that night. She has decided to have the baby."

Silently, he waited for the storm. Over this, she had every right.

"Is that it?" Jordan asked.

"Isn't that *enough?*"

"I thought you were going to tell me we were being investigated by the IRS," Jordan sniffed. "You slept with *Eleanor Marshall?* Tom, how could you? She's so old!"

Tom Goldman stared at his wife, but the words wouldn't come. He wondered if he was hearing things. Jordan went into utter hysterics at the thought of lowering her lifestyle, but to his admission that another woman was also bearing his child, she acted as if it was a minor lapse of taste? Could she really be that petty? Could anybody?

Maybe she'd misunderstood him.

"Jordan, I just told you that Eleanor is also pregnant. By me. Don't you have anything to say?"

"Yes! Yes I do!" she screamed. Suddenly all the fury was back, and it was almost a relief. But then she continued, "How dare you humiliate *me* like that! Don't you realize how everybody will laugh at me? They'll say you preferred that *wrinkled old woman* to me!"

"Eleanor's thirty-eight—"

"And I'm *twenty-four!* And *don't* think *everyone* won't point that out! She doesn't even *work out*. She's just a bluestocking! How could you?"

He couldn't hide his disgust. "Jordan, that's the most—"

"*I want a divorce!*" She was yelling at him, the veins on her slender neck standing out like whipcords. "*I want a divorce right now!*"

"But our baby," Tom managed.

"What baby? I'm not pregnant, you stupid fool! There never was any baby! Isabelle told me to say there was, so you'd leave that old bitch alone!" She laughed hysterically. "Do you think I'd get pregnant with the baby of a stupid *asshole* like you? You just *wanted* me to *ruin* my figure! To stay home all day with some *screaming brat* when I'm young! You're just jealous of me because *I* know how to have *fun!*"

Goldman's head was reeling. "There's no baby?"

"No! Don't you understand English? I was going to tell you I'd had a miscarriage. If I *was* pregnant you'd have *made* me have a miscarriage!" Jordan was sobbing with rage. "*You* can live in Pasadena! *I won't do it!* I want a divorce! And I came to this marriage with two million dollars of my own in savings, and you're not having *any* of it!"

"You never told me that," Tom said quietly.

"You're not having any of it! It's *mine!*"

"I wouldn't touch a cent of your money," Tom told her with contempt. "You're welcome to walk away with everything you brought to this marriage. I'll have my lawyers get in touch tomorrow."

"I'm keeping the diamonds!" Jordan screamed after his retreating back.

Tom Goldman walked out of his house and out of his marriage. And by the time he hit the back door, he was smiling.

chapter 36

"All right. OK," Goldman said resignedly, looking across at Eleanor and shaking his head. "Two weeks. If that's the best you can do . . . Yeah, I know. Thanks, Janice."

He hung up.

"What did we get in Seattle? Two weeks?" Eleanor asked, disappointed. "I was hoping for a little more time than that. It's supposed to be the Generation X capital of the universe. You'd think that Zach and Florescu alone would be enough to guarantee some box office down there."

Tom shrugged. "What can I tell you? Everybody's fighting shy of the Roxana thing, I guess."

"No, it's not that. A scandal like that is just free publicity. My guess is that it's Jake Keller and David Tauber."

Tom Goldman and Eleanor Marshall were sitting together in Tom's office at Artemis Studios, surrounded by phones, piles of notes, and the remains of a tray of coffee and bagels. It was seven P.M., and the sun was just starting to sink in the rosy sky outside Goldman's huge windows, the pollution in the atmosphere hanging over LA distorting the light into wild streaks of scarlet and copper. That was one thing you could say for the smog; it made for great sunsets. But today neither of them had had much time to notice the beauty of nature. They had spent the entire day trying to persuade distributors to book *Triple Feature;* this morning it had looked as though the picture would get shown in two art-house theaters in Minnesota and one multiplex in Tucson and then die an ignominious, straight-to-video death. Nobody wanted to touch it with a disinfected ten-foot pole. Word was out there that *Triple*

Feature was going to be Fred Florescu's *Last Action Hero;* even Steven Spielberg had bombed with *1941,* and now it was about to be Florescu's turn. The Artemis marketing team had got the same message over and over: This movie is a total failure, absolutely unreleasable, how can you even ask us to book a flick which is practically forcing your studio into bankruptcy? It had taken Tom and Eleanor all day to salvage a minimal opening distribution for the movie. They'd exhausted a lot of stored good-will and personal credit in the process, cashing in fifteen years of favors owed, and even then the two of them had only been able to get a skeleton release. But that was the most they could squeeze out of the market. People just did not want to know.

"Tauber and Keller? I guess it's possible," Tom mused.

"You know I'm right. After Sam Kendrick finished trashing David Tauber around this city, no other agencies would pick him up, and he wound up working for some fly-by-night schmuck with one phone line and a PO box number, down in West Hollywood, casting pet food commercials." Tom grinned. "And as for Keller, when you put the word out, he was all washed up too, so he's—"

"—fulfilling his boyhood dream of becoming an indie producer," Goldman finished off, laughing.

"Exactly. So I think we can take it as read that neither one is wishing this movie the best of luck. David Tauber was out there on the set, and Jake Keller has a lot of memos detailing stuff that went wrong. All they had to do was plant a few whispers—you know, Florescu wouldn't let anybody see the rushes, Artemis was in despair over a creative and commercial disaster, Roxana Felix couldn't act her way out of a paper bag . . . It's very simple to do, and those two assholes want revenge."

Tom nodded slowly. "You have a point. Plus, we have to remember that the industry knows we only get to stay in our jobs for the release of *Triple Feature* because we have good lawyers. As soon as this movie is out—we're out. Howard and Co. are making that pretty clear. So nobody cares if they offend us by blanking this picture. Why should they? We're as good as gone."

Eleanor gave Tom a soft smile, nodding at his T-shirt and jeans. "At least you don't have to dress up for work anymore."

"If it's good enough for David Geffen, it's good enough for me," Goldman said unrepentantly. "I should have done this years ago." He reached across the desk and took Eleanor's hand, stroking it softly. "I should have done a lot of things years ago."

Eleanor looked at him, his dark eyes fixed so intently upon her, and felt the familiar warmth of desire blossom across her skin. But it was too soon. She had to be sure he wasn't on the rebound from Jordan, that he meant what he was telling her, that he wouldn't wait another couple of months and then trade her in for the latest trophy wife du jour. The pain of losing him was too recent; she just couldn't risk her heart again. Because if he smashed it this time, Eleanor Marshall knew in her deepest soul that it would be broken forever.

She pulled her hand free, gently but firmly.

"Maybe it'll be a huge hit. Maybe we'll rescue the studio with this picture. Fox was in trouble when they put out *Star Wars*, and nobody was expecting that movie to do anything either."

Tom Goldman swallowed his disappointment. Eleanor needed time to trust him, he realized that. But it was so hard, to be near her, to know she was carrying their child, and not to be able to hold her and caress her.

"Eleanor, you have to understand something here. We've done what you said; we beat all the odds in forcing the board to let us stay and finish the movie, persuading Roxana to go back to the set, and getting some kind of basic release going. But this was a hundred-and-thirty-five-million-dollar movie! Do you realize the kind of distribution, marketing, or whatever that we'd need to earn our money back? *Star Wars* cost *seven* million dollars. You've done the right thing, creatively, for your project, but you have to face facts. We're going to bomb, and we're going to bomb *huge*."

"It's possible that we could have a word-of-mouth hit."

"A hundred-and-thirty-five-million-dollar word-of-mouth hit? You're asking for a miracle."

Eleanor Marshall thought of Tom's baby, growing inside her womb.

"I believe in miracles," she said.

Tom shook his head. "You just don't know when to quit, Eleanor, do you?"

"Absolutely not," she agreed. "So are you coming out to the wrap party on Saturday? I'm going to book my ticket tonight."

"Are you kidding?" Goldman replied. "After everything we've been through to see this goddamn movie finished, I wouldn't miss it for twenty monsoons."

⋄

Triple Feature held its wrap party on the beach, under the stars. Tom and Eleanor arrived to a hotel already in chaos, as hundreds of crew technicians lugged packed suitcases down the main stairs or hogged the elevator, stacking all their stuff in the hotel lobby in great colorful piles of leather and plastic, ready to be ferried out to the Seychelles airport the next morning. The party atmosphere was in evidence even before they got out to the beach, the lighting director staggering past Tom with his hair covered in sticky coconut milk and the chief grip passing out thick, prerolled joints to everybody in sight. Relief was hanging so thick in the air you could almost smell it. And once the two of them stepped outside onto the soft, powdery sand, it was insane.

"Is this a wrap party, or Mardi Gras?" Tom asked Eleanor, gazing at the scene on the shore. Four huge bonfires were stacked along the beach, throwing up towers of flame against the inky black sky, silhouetting the dancing figures jumping crazily around them to the strains of some extra-loud rap music that was pumping from a beat-box somewhere. Florescu had organized a trestle table piled with food they could smell two hundred yards away: Creole lobster, octopus curry, shark meat with ginger sauce, parrot fish soup . . . As soon as they walked over, somebody from the catering crew shoved a tall glass of something tall and colorful into their hands.

"What's this?" Goldman asked warily, putting an arm round Eleanor's waist.

"*La purée,*" the girl said, laughing. "Local specialty. Try it!"

Tom took a gulp and gasped for air, the crushed-fruit brew searing the back of his throat. "Jesus Christ! What *is* this?"

"Fermented fruit alcohol. It's pretty strong," she said.

"No kidding," Tom said, putting it down on the table.

"You have anything nonalcoholic?" Eleanor asked. "I'm pregnant."

"Sure." She handed her a plastic beaker of *citronelle,* the light Seychellois brew of mineral water, honey, and crushed lemon.

"I'll take one of those," Tom said.

"Hey, you guys! You're late," Fred Florescu said, walking up to Tom and slapping him on the shoulder.

"It's good to see you, too, Fred," Tom said, smiling.

"Plane was delayed at Singapore," Eleanor explained. "How are you?"

"Pretty fucking pleased with this movie," the director told her. "I gotta thank you guys for fighting so hard to let us finish it. We've made an incredible film. It's gonna win the Palme d'Or at Cannes next year, *and* it's gonna break box office records."

"Really?" said Eleanor.

"Sure," said Tom.

Florescu glared at him with mock severity. "O ye of little faith. You care to place a bet on that? A hundred dollars says you make at least thirty million dollars profit on this thing."

"Sold," Goldman said, clasping the younger man's hand. "God knows I could use the money."

"We're out of a job after *Triple Feature* is released," Eleanor told him.

"No you're not. You can come and work for me," Sam Kendrick said, emerging from behind a crackling bonfire. "Artemis may be history, but we're not. Since the divorce I've thrown myself into work. We wrapped a fat deal for Troy Savage at Universal just this morning. I'm snowed under, I could do with some help. You gamekeepers should turn poachers. It'd make you more well-rounded human beings."

"By becoming an *agent?* You're on drugs, Sam," Florescu teased him. "Kendrick's just a moneymaking machine with a greedy, ruthless, one-track mind. Which is precisely why I signed to him."

"All directors are just kids whose bullying instinct never found enough expression beating up small children in grade school," Sam rejoined amiably.

"What are you doing here, Sam? I thought you didn't represent Roxana Felix anymore," Eleanor said, curiously.

Kendrick's face darkened, and he looked away.

"I don't," he said. "But Fred, Zach, and Megan are still my clients, and so are all the costars. I was never about to miss this."

"Where is Roxana?" Eleanor asked. "I'd like to see her."

"You will. Real soon," Florescu said. "Zach and Roxana are both about to make speeches. Have a seat."

He waved them to a place at the trestle table, and they sat down, aware of figures beginning to gather around and sit cross-legged on the sand, crowding the benches. Suddenly they exploded into cheers and wolf whistles as Roxana Felix, looking stunning in a sheer white silk dress, her long hair braided in a sophisticated French pleat, climbed nimbly on top of a pile of crates which somebody had erected specially for the occasion.

"Wow, they really love her," Tom Goldman muttered.

"Yeah, well, she turned from bitch queen of the universe into Mother Teresa," Florescu whispered back loudly. "Turned up early every morning, made coffee for the wardrobe girls, asked if she could help packing up the equipment—you name it, Roxana was in there giving a hand. Everybody on the crew was shell-shocked. Now they worship the ground she walks on."

Eleanor cast a sideways glance at Sam Kendrick, but he had lowered his eyes, refusing to look at Roxana as she started her speech.

"On behalf of the cast, I want to thank everybody in the crew who worked so hard to make this movie," Roxana said, to loud applause from the supporting actors, who banged the tables and whooped. "It was you guys versus spoiled models, Murphy's Law, studio politics, and the forces of nature—so naturally, there was no contest." There was a lot of raucous laughter. "I should also give a special thanks to Megan Silver, for writing us out of more dead ends than anybody can count"—huge applause and whistles—"and Zach Mason, for kindly getting his ass back here alive, so I didn't have to do love scenes with a cadaver. Although on second thoughts, maybe that might have been preferable . . . And lastly, let me say that I have always dreamed of working with the most talented young director in America." A beat. "So when I get home, I'm going to call Quentin Tarantino right away and ask him to give me a test."

The party exploded into laughter and cheering, and Roxana bowed and sat down, blowing a kiss toward Florescu.

"Bitch," he yelled, grinning.

Roxana's place was taken by the tall, muscular figure of Zach Mason, his long black hair blowing against his bare shoulders, his broad chest silhouetted in the firelight.

"Jesus, he looks terrific," Eleanor said.

"The guy's been pumping iron like a madman ever since he got out of the hospital," Fred explained. "He says he's going to get back on the road and he needs to be in shape. It's either that or it's love. He's been inseparable from Megan Silver since the moment they were found in the jungle."

"Ahhh, how romantic," Eleanor murmured, and Tom tightened his grip around her waist, squeezing her softly. She hesitated a moment, then settled back in against him. It felt good to be out here with Tom, in the darkness, Eleanor thought. If this was their final bow, it was right that they were doing it together.

I won't pull back from him, Eleanor told herself. At least, not this evening.

"They say a thing of beauty is a joy forever," Zach Mason began, "although in Roxana's case, I think I speak for everybody when I say that for most of the time, a thing of beauty was a pain in the ass."

"Amen," Florescu yelled, to more cheers.

"Seriously," Mason went on, holding up a hand for silence, "I have to thank Roxie, Seth, Mary, Jack, Robert, Fred, and the whole cast and crew for letting me see what it's like to make a movie. And when I next want to do something a little less stressful, I'm going skydiving over the Grand Canyon without a parachute." He waited for the laughter to die down, and then held out his hand. "Megan, get up here."

Eleanor watched quietly as Megan Silver, chic and slender in a short Donna Karan dress and loose sandals, climbed up next to Zach and nestled against him, her small hand clasped in his. She looked gorgeous, confident, and radiant with happiness.

"Is that Megan?" Tom whispered to Eleanor, staring at her disbelievingly. "What happened to that dumpy little mouse I met six months ago?"

"She made this movie," Eleanor replied, finding that she had tears in her eyes. "It changed all of us."

"I've got a couple of announcements to make," Zach said. "The first is that I'm really glad to have had the opportunity of seeing what it was like to act, particularly in such a great film as this turned out to be, because I won't be doing it again. I've talked to the guys in Dark Angel, and we're getting back together. Movies are fun, but music is my life."

There was deafening applause.

"Thanks," Zach said. "And talking of my life, the second thing I've got to tell you guys, saving the best for last"—he looked tenderly down at Megan, smiling into her eyes—"is that this morning I asked Megan Silver if she'd agree to marry me, and she said yes."

Anything else he might have wanted to add was lost in pandemonium, as the cast and crew burst into congratulations, everybody yelling and whistling and stamping their feet, and Megan and Zach were pulled down off the crates by people crowding around to shake their hands. Eleanor saw Roxana hugging Megan, and then Zach.

"Are you going to say something?" Tom asked Florescu.

"After that? Are you kidding? It would be the anticlimax of the century," Florescu said dryly. "No. I spoke to the crew when we did the final take of the final scene. That'll have to do." He swung his legs over the bench and stood up. "Excuse me for a second, OK? I have to go congratulate them."

"Me, too," Sam Kendrick added, following his client. "I'll see you two later."

"Come on, Tom," Eleanor said. "Let's go."

"In a second." He moved closer to her on the bench and grabbed her two hands, holding them tightly in the shadows, looking at Eleanor in the flickering light of the bonfires as people rushed past them toward Zach and Megan, the party raging around them, ignoring them, leaving the two of them alone at the end of the table.

"Not now," Eleanor whispered. There was something about the way Goldman was looking at her that made her nervous. His liquid dark eyes were fixed on her, scanning her face as though he wanted to memorize it, as though he would never take his gaze off her.

"Yes, now," Tom insisted. "Now. I have to say it, Eleanor. I can't wait any longer."

She was silent.

Tom reached out one hand and cupped her cheek, softly, gently, rubbing his rough palm across the softness of her skin.

"I love you," he said. "I've loved you since the day I met you. Maybe you felt the same way, maybe it happened to you a little later, but I *know* you feel something for me. New York proved that to both of us." He took a breath, struggling to find the right words. "I guess we were both too timid, or too comfortable, or too shy, but neither one of us said anything until it proved to be too late. I hadn't been with Jordan long when I realized what an idiot I'd been. I thought about you every second of the day. I thought about you when I was with her. I tried not to, but I couldn't help it. And the night we had together was the most perfect communion I ever had with another human being in my life."

Eleanor Marshall sat listening to him, tears forming in her eyes and rolling softly down her cheeks.

"The next day, when I thought Jordan was pregnant . . . I was trapped. It was too late. And I realized the full depths of what that meant when I saw you marrying Paul. So help me, Eleanor, I wanted to kill him. I wanted to rush up there and carry you away by force. And I couldn't do a thing about it." He touched his finger to one of the tears rolling down her face, and brushed it away. "Eleanor, I know I hurt you. I know you're frightened now. But I swear, I love you with all my heart." His voice was hoarse with the intensity of what he was saying. "Look at me. You *know* I mean what I say. I love you and I love our child with all of my heart. God gave us both a second chance, Eleanor. Don't let's waste this half of our lives."

"Oh, Tom," she whispered.

He slipped from the bench and sank to his knees in front of her, on the sand, holding her hands in his.

"I love you more than life," he said. "So help me, I don't want to live without you. Eleanor, will you marry me?"

She gazed at him for a long moment. Then she bent her head and kissed him softly, passionately.

"I thought you'd never ask," she said.

⋅⋅⋅

In the darkness, Roxana Felix hung back from the crowd, watching them all swarm around Megan and Zach, shouting congratulations and cracking jokes. She was truly pleased for both of them. Since the night she had spoken to the cast, neither of them could have been more compassionate or friendly toward her. Zach in particular had gone out of his way to be kind; Roxana knew that he realized, more than any of the others ever could, what it was like living in the center of the spotlight, where nobody could be themselves with you, and everybody already had an opinion the first time they met you. He'd told her last night that she'd gone from the most lonely kid in the world to the most sought-after woman alive, and added, "Maybe now you'll get a chance to be normal, Roxie. I really hope so."

God, I hope so too, Roxana thought fearfully, her eyes fixed on one figure breaking away from the crowd.

Sam Kendrick.

He had arrived yesterday, and refused to see her, refused to speak to her, and hung up on her when she'd called his hotel room. She'd sent a note, asking for five minutes of his time, and received no reply. Sam didn't want to know, and he was making it painfully obvious.

Roxana felt her heart crashing against her rib cage. She was so nervous, she half expected to look down and see herself bathed in a cold sweat. But she had to do this; she had to speak to him.

Sam Kendrick was the only man who had ever been able to reach her, whose caresses had actually aroused her, the only man whose touch she had ever truly desired. Oh, she might have kidded herself that she wanted

Zach, but Zach Mason, to her, had always been just another link in the master plan. She had set out wanting to use Sam Kendrick, to be revenged on him for some minor insult, and then . . .

. . . and then she had fallen in love with him.

Sure, she'd tried to deny it to herself. The more she thought about him, the more she told herself that she loathed the guy, the more ferociously she tried to break him. As though she were proving something to herself.

And when that terrible phone call had woken her up, Isabelle's mocking voice bringing her ice fortress crashing down all around her, Sam had been the only one to come and see her, the only one not to condemn her, the only one who would stand by her side and tell her he loved her. And then, terrified by the feelings he was evoking in her, seeing them as pure weakness, in her desperation she had turned on him like a wounded beast, snarling, and wounded him as desperately and as deeply as she knew how.

Only when Eleanor had arrived, later, offering her a second chance, had Roxana managed to let everything go. Weeping in her arms, too tired to fight the world any longer, she had discovered that at least one other person gave a damn about her. Then the cast had accepted her back among themselves, with complete forgiveness and acceptance, and working her butt off to finish *Triple Feature* had provided her with her own small redemption: a chance to work with other people, and to be considered, for once, just as an actress, just as herself. After Florescu had yelled "Cut! And *print!*" to the cheers of the crew, he'd come across to Roxana and told her he'd like to work with her again. Not such a big deal to most people, maybe, but at that moment, it seemed better than the most flowery compliment she'd ever been paid.

And finishing the movie had given her a little space to confront her feelings about Sam Kendrick; to acknowledge that she'd fallen in love, to look at Megan Silver as she walked around the set hand in hand with Zach, and know that she wanted that for herself, that simple, profound affection, that bond, the love that Sam had offered her. He was angry, and he had every right to be. She knew that. But she also knew, as she stood there and watched Kendrick walking back toward the hotel, alone on the beach, that she had to try and reach him. At least *try.* Or he'd be out of her life forever.

This was her only chance.

Roxana moved out of the shadows, running across the beach, down to the water's edge, and touched Sam Kendrick on the shoulder.

He spun around, smiling, but the smile died and froze on his face when he saw who it was.

"What the hell do you want?" Kendrick demanded, his tone sharp. "Can't you just leave it alone, Roxana? What more do you want from me?"

"Sam, please," she said. "Give me a chance. I just want to tell you I'm sorry. I truly am."

His eyes were cold.

Roxana tried again. "I've changed, Sam. I truly have. Can't we make a fresh start?"

Kendrick stood there, watching her for a second, and slowly shook his head.

"I don't think so, Roxana. I'll accept your apology, OK? Let's leave it at that."

She took a step backward in the damp sand. The finality in his voice was terrible.

"I know it's too late," Roxana whispered. "But for what it's worth—I love you."

For a moment she thought she saw a light flare in his eyes, but then Kendrick looked away, and the moment passed.

"You're right," he said. "It is too late."

And as Roxana Felix stood there, watching him, Sam Kendrick turned his back on her and walked away.

⋯⋇⋯

The crew flew back home the next morning, together with Sam Kendrick and most of the supporting cast. Tom had arranged for Zach, Megan, Fred, and Roxana to take Howard Thorn's private jet in the afternoon, along with himself and Eleanor.

"Privileges of office," he explained as they soared into the dizzy blue skies above the Indian Ocean. "And since this is the last time we're ever gonna get to enjoy them, we might as well make the most of it."

"So do you think you guys will take up Sam's offer?" Florescu asked Eleanor, as she sat on comfortable leather sofa, curled up against Tom.

"And become an agent? No way," Goldman said

"Speak for yourself. I might give it a try," Eleanor replied, digging Tom in the ribs.

He caught her hand and kissed it. "Eleanor Marshall Goldman. What do you think?"

"Sounds terrific. Apart from the 'Goldman' part," Eleanor told him, laughing.

"You guys, too?" Florescu asked in mock horror, glancing at Zach and Megan. "Jesus. I hope it isn't catching."

Zach laughed. "Fred, you're too macho to be infected."

"You got that right," the director told him, winking at Roxana. "So where are you going to be when the movie opens?"

"At the Bel-Air. We're renting a suite while we look for a new house," Eleanor told him. "In fact, everybody should give me a contact number, so I can let you all know how we're doing."

"Roxana, Paramount wants me to do a remake of *Breakfast at Tiffany's*," Florescu told her. "You interested?"

She nodded, delighted, "Are you serious?"

"Absolutely. You're a great actress," Florescu said, adding mischievously, "not to mention a world-class babe, which never hurts."

She threw a cushion at him.

Obsequious stewardesses bustled around them, handling out crystal glasses of champagne.

"I think we should toast the movie," Florescu said, raising his glass. "Because after this, nothing is ever gonna seem difficult again."

The plane was filled with laughter as they raised their glasses.

-:::-

On Saturday afternoon, Zach Mason and Megan Silver were lying in bed together, wrapped in each other's arms.

"Stop looking at the phone," Zach teased her.

"I am not looking at the phone."

"Yes you are. You've been waiting for the phone to ring all day. When Yolanda called this morning, you jumped three feet in the air."

"I did not," Megan said indignantly, then gave him a sheepish smile. "It was only two feet."

Mason laughed, cupping her breasts in his hands and kissing the tips of her nipples.

"You have a one-track mind. Will you cut it out? We've done nothing but make love all day."

"You have a better idea?"

"Maybe not," she said, reaching down between his legs.

They kissed softly.

"Declan was totally blown away when you called," Megan said. "He thinks I'm Cinderella, running off to fairyland and winding up with the handsome Prince."

"Well, you are," Zach told her, stroking the back of her neck.

"Are you kidding? I wound up with the frog," she giggled, squirming away from him. "I can't believe I'm going to spend the rest of my life in a tour bus."

"Writing novels. Your choice, babe," Zach reminded her.

"Stop changing the subject," Megan teased.

The phone rang.

They both jumped out of their skin.

"You get it," Megan said breathlessly. "It's probably for you."

He shook his head. "No way, sugar. *You* wrote the fucking movie. You get it."

"Get the phone."

"You get it."

"Get the goddamn phone, Zach!" Megan squealed.

He snatched the receiver off its cradle.

"Zach Mason. Oh, hi, Tom. Yeah, she's here too . . ."

-:⁝:-

Roxana Felix sat alone in her chic Century City apartment, curled up on her favorite easy chair, reading Florescu's latest script, and trying not to think about the movie. Since she'd given her press conference on her return to the States, life had gotten a whole lot easier. She had forgotten nothing, but she'd also discovered one fundamental truth: that demons turn to stone when exposed to the light. The cosmetics people had all come crawling back to her, even pathetic little Bob Alton had tried to reingratiate himself, but she just didn't want to know. There was more to being a woman than physical beauty, a lucky combination of genes, and something that had a sell-by date imprinted in every atom of her DNA. Eleanor Marshall and Fred Florescu had shown her that she had something worth nurturing, real talent that would grow with her, that would blossom with her age and experience, instead of fading away. That was something she could truly be proud of. And she was trying to concentrate on that, and not keep obsessing over *Triple Feature* and a phone that obstinately sat there, not ringing. She was more mature than that.

The phone rang.

Roxana leapt out of her armchair and pounced on it before it had a chance to ring twice.

"Eleanor?" she asked.

"I'm afraid not," came a low voice at the other end.

Her heart stopped.

"This is Sam Kendrick."

"Hi," Roxana managed.

"I'm sorry. I forgot, you'd be getting the opening figures for the movie today. I should have thought."

"Fuck the movie," Roxana said elegantly. She could hardly breathe.

Sam laughed. "I was going to ask if you had a date for the European premiere."

"Oh, Sam," Roxana said.

"I saw your press conference," he said, and paused. "I nearly didn't call, because I figured you'd hang up on me. I'm sorry I was so blind, Roxana."

"That's OK," she said, feeling her heart starting to pound against her rib cage. Oh God, was there another chance for her? Could there be?

She struggled to sound calm. "I know I gave you every reason to hate me."

"You know, Isabelle and I, we're still getting divorced."

"Yes. I heard, I'm sorry," she lied politely.

"I'm not," Kendrick said grimly.

There was a long pause. Roxana found she was literally holding her breath.

"Uh, look. I was wondering if we could have coffee, get to know each other . . ."

"Start again?" Roxana whispered.

"Something like that," Sam admitted. She imagined his smile as he cradled the receiver. "We'll take it slow, just see what happens."

"Good idea," she agreed coolly, then lost it, and added in a rush, "Are you free now? I have a great coffee cake in the oven."

"I'm on my way." Sam said, and hung up.

Roxana kissed the phone before she put it down on its cradle, and danced around the room, skipping like a ten-year-old.

The phone rang again, and she snatched it up.

"I love you, I love you, I love you!" Roxana sang.

"Roxana? Are you OK?" Eleanor Marshall asked her.

⋅⋰⋅

Tom Goldman had been sitting in his hotel suite reading a novel when the call came in from Artemis, with Eleanor lying on the couch, eating a bowl of strawberries. She sat bolt upright, watching him as he nodded expressionlessly, scratching some figures on a piece of paper, saying, "Yeah, OK," and then, "I see."

He put the phone back on its hook.

"Well? Jesus, Tom, don't play poker-face games with me now," Eleanor said, twisting her fingers around. "Say something, for Christ's sake! Or I'm going to have a major coronary!"

He let her hang for a second longer, then gave her a slow smile.

"Well," Goldman said. "It looks like I owe that Florescu kid a hundred dollars."

She sank back onto the couch, holding her breath.

"There are lines around the block in every theater that's booked it," Tom said. "Box office is totally sold out. There were riots in New York when the tickets sold out. They had to call the police."

Eleanor Marshall stared at him, tears forming in her eyes.

"The studio's been inundated with requests to show this movie," Goldman went on, coming across to her. "They're telling me some theater owners are going to court to get another chance at it. CBS is going to run a news segment tonight on the kids in Seattle who've taken sleeping bags to camp out on the pavement so they get a chance to see it tomorrow . . .

Howard Thorn is desperate to get hold of us, apparently. It would appear that they want to offer us our jobs back . . . the stock is going through the roof . . ."

"It's our miracle," Eleanor whispered.

Tom Goldman shook his head.

"What miracle? I knew this would happen the second I read the script. I always had complete and total faith," he said.

"Faith in me?" Eleanor asked, kissing him.

"In the movie," Tom replied, and they melted into each other's arms, laughing.